Praise

"Hallee writes wi................... detail that I felt the sweat drip off my brow, heard the buzz of the African jungle, and ran for dear life with Cynthia and Rick. A rich story of courage and seeing the world with new eyes. Riveting, this book will get under your skin and into your heart. Absolutely fantastic."

Susan May Warren, *USA Today* bestselling author, on *Honor Bound*

"What a fabulous story with perfectly crafted characters who grab your heart from the opening page. I loved everything about it—from the witty dialogue to the breath-stopping suspense to the tender romance. Once I started, I couldn't put it down. I highly recommend this book and can't wait for the next one."

Lynette Eason, award-winning, bestselling author of the Extreme Measures series, on *Honor Bound*

"Hallee Bridgeman weaves a military suspense with romance for a fast-paced adventure. *Word of Honor* kept me turning pages all night long."

DiAnn Mills, author of *Concrete Evidence*, on *Word of Honor*

"This book has something for everyone—action, adventure, romance, and true-to-life sadness and grief. Hallee crafts a complex story infused with spiritual truth, wrapped around intriguing lead characters with complicated personalities and backgrounds. Phil and Melissa will have you rooting for them the whole way through."

Janice Cantore, retired police officer and author of *Breach of Honor*, on *Honor's Refuge*

WORD OF HONOR

LOVE ★ HONOR
BOOK 2

WORD OF HONOR

HALLEE BRIDGEMAN

Revell

a division of Baker Publishing Group
Grand Rapids, Michigan

Published by Revell
a division of Baker Publishing Group
PO Box 6287, Grand Rapids, MI 49516-6287
www.revellbooks.com

Printed in the United States of America

Library of Congress Cataloging-in-Publication Data
Names: Bridgeman, Hallee, author.
Title: Word of honor / Hallee Bridgeman.
Description: Grand Rapids, Michigan : Revell, a division of Baker Publishing
    Group, [2022] | Series: Love and honor ; 2
Identifiers: LCCN 2022003557 | ISBN 9780800740214 (paperback) | ISBN
    9780800742294 (casebound) | ISBN 9781493438914 (ebook)
Subjects: LCGFT: Novels.
Classification: LCC PS3602.R531375 W67 2022 | DDC 813/.6—dc23
LC record available at https://lccn.loc.gov/2022003557

Baker Publishing Group publications use paper produced from sustainable forestry practices and post-consumer waste whenever possible.

22 23 24 25 26 27 28   7 6 5 4 3 2 1

Glossary of Military Terms and Acronyms

BAU: Behavior Analysis Unit (FBI)
CASH: combat support hospital
CHU: containerized housing unit (a small, climate-controlled trailer)
DHS: Department of Homeland Security
DOD: Department of Defense
EPX: a type of high-performance plastic explosive
HQ: headquarters
HRT: hostage rescue tactics
MIKE: minute
MRE: meal ready to eat
NATO: The North Atlantic Treaty Organization
NSA: National Security Agency
ODA: Operational Detachment Alpha (aka "A-Team")
PT: physical training
RDX: the explosive agent in some plastic explosives and C-4
RECON: reconnaissance

ROGER: understood and acknowledged

RP: recovery point

SF: Special Forces

WILCO: will comply

CHAPTER

ONE

Even in the late-spring night with the hint of light still in the sky, the headlights did little to cut through the fog. Lynda Culter used a penlight to try to read the paper map, something she hadn't had to do since field-training exercises at Quantico. The mobile signal had disappeared about two miles back, so the GPS offered no help.

"You turned the wrong way back there," she said.

"Nope. Turned right like you said," her partner, Jack, said.

"No, I said turn left. You asked left, and I confirmed."

"With the word 'right'!" Jack pulled over to the side of the mountain road. "Give me that," he said as he snatched the map out of her hands.

Frustrated, she tossed the penlight at him. It hit the steering wheel and bounced, dinging him above his right eye.

She slapped her hand over her mouth. "Jack!" she said on a breath. "I'm so sorry."

He hit the overhead light, then rubbed his eyebrow and turned to glare at her. Soon, though, the glare turned to mirth, and he beckoned her with the crook of his finger. "Come here," he said.

She slipped her seat belt off and shifted her body.

"Kiss it better."

"Jack!" she said again, laughing, then pressed her lips to his eyebrow. She breathed in the familiar scent of his aftershave and then sat back, running her fingers through his soft brown hair. "All better?"

"For now." He reached down and retrieved the penlight from the floorboard, then held it out to her. "I should keep this. Spoils of war and all."

With a grin, she took it from him. She admired his profile as he studied the map. He had a thin face with a long nose, and his sharp cheekbones were offset with a thin beard. His features had helped him blend in during the five years he worked in deep cover with the Russian mafia. He came to her FBI branch in Anchorage just months after finishing his assignment. It didn't take her long to fall head over heels for the charismatic, charming man from Philadelphia. So far, they'd kept their relationship quiet. Neither one of them wanted to be separated. Jack had convinced her to wait until after this weekend to make it official.

She glanced at her phone. She'd just put the picture on her lock screen of the two of them in a café that afternoon. In a clearly intimate pose, they leaned against each other, heads touching. Her dark auburn hair caught the lights of the restaurant, highlighting her lighter red streaks, making her brown eyes shine. His smile brought the dimples out in his cheeks. They looked happy.

"Too bad that warrant came through," she said, thinking of the Memorial Day weekend in front of them. "Who knew a judge would sign a warrant tonight?"

She worked as an analyst, so serving warrants didn't typically fall under her purview. However, she and Jack had been nearby, about to check in to a mountain retreat. Waiting for another agent to come from Anchorage would have taken a couple more hours out of their weekend.

"I told you to wait until Tuesday to submit it." He set the map on the seat between them. "I'm going back," he said, putting the car in reverse.

"Probably wise," she replied, giving a sweet smile. "Since you made a wrong turn."

He turned the light off, but not before she saw the clench of his jaw a split second before he smiled. After backtracking to the intersection, he made the correct turn and they continued forward about four miles before they saw the marker that indicated the turn onto the dirt road.

As Jack slowly navigated the terrain to avoid kicking up dust, she said, "I wonder if we should have arranged for backup. No signal out here."

"These people aren't killers," he said. "They're just protesting the oil pipeline. The threat they made isn't even proven."

"Allegedly." She glanced at her phone again as if willing the signal to give her just one bar, enough to complete a call.

Jack slowed the car down and turned off the headlights. They came around a corner and saw the shadow of a house through the fog. Light glowed from two windows. An all-terrain vehicle sat parked next to two pickup trucks. Jack slowly came to a stop, then killed the engine. Lynda glanced at her watch. It was already ten thirty. They didn't have a lot of daylight left.

They got out of the car and met at the trunk. The temperature had dropped into the midforties. It felt good to put on their FBI ballistic vests and jackets. Jack slipped on his cap and held hers out. She shook her head, then pulled her hair back into a ponytail. She hated anything on her head. Jack tossed it back into the trunk, then quietly closed it. Lynda made sure her 9mm pistol had a full magazine. She bent and secured her knife in her ankle sheath.

As they walked toward the house, Lynda mentally prepared herself for a long night ahead. After they apprehended the leader of this organization, they would have to question him. Once he was in custody, they had only twenty-four hours before they had to bring formal charges. So much for the romantic weekend. Of course, even after twenty-four hours, they could still get a day or two at the spa.

"I probably should call for backup," Jack said, pulling out his phone.

"Wise." She didn't add "like I said," because he wouldn't find that funny. She bit her lip to stop herself from smiling.

Stepping carefully, they walked up onto the wooden porch. Lynda ducked under the window to the other side, and they both peeked through the window. She could make out two men sitting at a table—a blond man and a black-haired man. She held up two fingers, and Jack nodded. He stayed where he could see them while she knocked on the door. He lifted his chin in her direction, communicating that someone inside was approaching the door. She stepped back slightly.

The door opened, and the tall blond man who had sat at the head of the table asked, "May I help you?"

Lynda pulled her leather wallet out and flashed her gold badge and ID. "FBI. We're looking for Damien Cisco."

His face relaxed, and he smiled. "Ah, I figured you must be lost. This is not exactly the place where we normally have people come to the door." He came out onto the porch, and she moved back to keep an arm's distance away from him. "Damien lives on down the road about a quarter mile." He took a step and lifted his arm northward. Lynda took another step back and looked in the direction he pointed. "His driveway is hard to see."

Before she could reply, pain exploded in her left ear. Her vision closed down to a pinpoint of light, then nothing at all.

Lynda's head pounded. Nausea rolled in her stomach. Why did she feel so terrible? She tried to roll over, to get more comfortable, but couldn't move her arms. What in the world? Some of the fog lifted, and she realized she wasn't in her bed. Instead, she sat on a hard chair.

In little flashes, she started to remember. Driving up to the house. Asking the man who answered the door about Damien Cisco. The flash of pain. Then . . . nothing. Her heart beat faster. Sweat beaded on her upper lip. With a rush of adrenaline, she pushed the grogginess to the background and every sense heightened. What to do now?

She kept her eyes closed and tried to assess anything that she could in her environment. The smell of damp earth in the cold air assaulted her nostrils. Something sharp and un-yielding cut into the delicate skin of her wrists, keeping her hands clasped behind her. Maybe a zip tie? Her shoulders ached from the position of her arms. Shuffling noises came from her left, the click of a switch a split second before a flood of heat. Behind her eyelids, she could see a bright light.

Footsteps. Low voices coming from her right.

Movement behind her, against her.

Her arms were tied to someone else. Jack? It must be Jack. Relief almost made her cry out. She wasn't alone. Praying desperately for courage and wisdom, she tried to listen to the low voices, tried to make out words. Jack started struggling, making her bindings dig deeper into her wrists. She fought back the discomfort and worked against the tight restraints to turn her hand, pressing her palm against his. He stilled at her touch.

Digging into her reserves for courage she didn't know for certain she possessed, she finally lifted her head and opened her eyes. It looked like they sat in the middle of a barn. She could see bales of hay in a loft, wooden beams, a concrete floor. The doors stood slightly open to the dark night out-side. How long had she been out?

"Well, that took a while. I was starting to get bored."

The man who had opened the house door sat in front of her. He smiled. "I wonder how many training procedures you ignored tonight. No backup, turning your back on the men in my house. Tsk, tsk, tsk. It seems like the Federal Bureau of Investigation should train their agents better than that."

"You're wrong about the backup," she said. "We called them." She could hear movement behind her but kept her eyes on him. "Damien Cisco, I presume?"

He raised an eyebrow. "So you know my name. You get the prize." He gestured at the tall black-haired man who had come into her line of sight and carried a camera on a tripod. She had seen him inside the house. "You're going to read a statement from Green War." He walked over to the wall and picked up a foam board leaning against it. Words were written on it in black marker, but from this distance she couldn't tell what they said.

Jack's muscles bunched behind her. He must have just come awake. He gave a small moan, and then his body stiffened.

Cisco walked around to face him. "Well, Agent Haynes. Good to see you. I wondered if maybe Antoine had hit you too hard."

"This is a mistake," Jack said, his voice hoarse. "You need to let us go right now."

He chuckled. "I love how the fascist agent of our government just hands down orders to private citizens as if they're going to be obeyed." The humor left his voice. "Right now, you do what I say. I don't do what you say. You might do well to remember that."

"We have backup on the way. I called them before you attacked us."

"Yeah. There's no signal out here and you know it." Cisco walked back into Lynda's line of sight. She tilted her head to look up at him. "You're going to read this statement on behalf of Green War."

"We are federal agents. You need to let us go." She tried to keep the fear out of her voice. "This will only end badly for you."

He leaned down and put his nose close enough to hers

that she could feel his breath. "You really need to quit worrying about my well-being and start worrying about you."

Terror flowed through her limbs. She could barely breathe. Nausea swirled in her stomach. Her wrists hurt and her shoulders ached, and to her humiliation, her eyes filled with tears. She looked down, hoping Cisco wouldn't see her distress.

"Leave her alone!" The chair rocked as Jack struggled against his restraints.

She wanted to cry out to him to stop moving because of the pain. To her relief, Cisco moved out of her sight and said to Jack, "Fine. Let's focus on you, Special Agent Jackson Haynes of the Fascist Bureau of Investigation."

A man with wire-framed glasses that shone against his dark skin came from behind her. She didn't recognize him from the house. He picked up the light stand next to her and moved it. Suddenly, the light no longer blinded her, the heat no longer made her feel like she couldn't breathe. She closed her eyes, a hated tear slipping down her cheek, and tried to figure out what to do next.

"Now, I have a statement here that you're going to read," Cisco said to Jack. "Only, don't call yourself Lynda Culter, because that would be embarrassing. Just replace that with Jackson where appropriate."

"Jack," she said. "Don't—"

He leaned back as if communicating with her, telling her he could handle it. "Fine. I'll read your statement."

"Jack!" she said again.

"Shut up, Lynda."

"Yeah, Lynda, shut up or I'll shut you up," Cisco said.

She looked all around, desperately searching for . . . what?

She sat with her hands tied behind her. So far, she'd identified three men in this room besides Jack. What did she think she could possibly do?

The light when cast onto Jack created a strange contorted shadow of the two of them tied to the chairs. "I am Jack Haynes, an agent of the United States government. I'm here under that authority, and you can all bite my—"

The sound of a hard hit and cracking bones came a split second before Jack's howl of pain. Lynda sobbed, wishing she could see what was happening.

"You really shouldn't improvise," Cisco said. "Shall we go again? You have another kneecap."

Lynda thought she had felt fear before, but it didn't compare to what she felt now. When Jack responded with an expletive and they hit him again, little white dots appeared in front of her eyes and her mouth went completely dry. Then she heard a splash, smelled the undeniable odor of gasoline. Some of it landed against the back of her hand. When she realized they'd doused Jack with gasoline, she started struggling against the restraints, ignoring the cutting pain in her wrists.

"Read the statement. Word for word."

Another expletive from Jack brought a scuffle behind her.

"No! Not in here," Cisco said.

Something cold and metal bit against her skin seconds before her hands fell free. With relief, she brought them forward, rubbing her wrists one at a time. The other two men dragged Jack past her line of sight.

He looked at her as they went by. "Don't give in, Lynda!" he yelled.

They went through a door into another room. Cisco

followed. He paused near the doorway and picked up the shotgun leaning against the wall. The men who carried Jack threw him to the ground. He tried to get up but fell again, likely from his busted kneecap.

Cisco stood in front of the open door and lifted his gun. "You're going to read a statement on behalf of Green War."

"Make me."

Lynda struggled, but they had secured her ankles to the chair. Sobbing, she bent over, fumbling to access the knife sheathed against her ankle. She could barely feel her numb fingers, and she couldn't lift her pants leg because of the zip tie securing it. "Jack!"

Cisco chambered a round in the shotgun. Somehow, she could hear the sound through the roaring in her ears. "Last chance. You will read a statement on behalf of Green War."

"Here's my statement, you dirty—"

The room exploded with the sound of the shotgun blast. Lynda froze, unable to believe what had just happened. Cisco turned back toward her. Jack lay just outside the door, unmoving. She could see only his legs and feet. One of the other men lit a match, fired up a hand-rolled cigarette, and tossed the match on Jack. His body went up in flames.

A sound came from Lynda—a scream, a yell, a guttural moan.

Cisco strode across the room toward her, aiming the shotgun at her face. He stopped close enough that she could see the wild look in his eyes. "Now, Agent Culter. Let's have a conversation."

Red-and-white lights strobed from her right. Through the open barn door, she spotted police cars coming their way. A sob of relief had her close her eyes and bow her head. She

18

didn't know if the man would kill her before help arrived, but at least she and Jack wouldn't die out here where no one would know what had happened to them.

A sharp whistle from the black-haired man made everyone scramble. A thick, bound stack of papers landed at her feet.

"That's our manifesto," Cisco said. "Goodbye for now, Agent Lynda Culter. We'll meet again."

As two police cars pulled into the yard, a door slammed behind her. Sobs tore through her, feeling like they'd rip her body in half. The smell of gasoline-laced smoke filled her nose, burned her eyes, became all she could taste.

"Jack!" she screamed.

CHAPTER

★

TWO

FORT CAMPBELL, KENTUCKY
NOVEMBER 23

Bill Sanders initiated a video call to his professor. As he waited for it to go through, he picked up the orders again and read them. He had to leave next week for an unnamed mission. That didn't sound very promising. As one of the weapons specialists of a US Army Special Forces Operational Detachment Alpha, or A-Team, by the time he boarded an airplane, he and his team usually knew where they were headed, if not why.

The call connected, and Doctor Mike Herowitz's face filled the screen. He raised his eyebrows. "Mr. Sanders. Don't usually see you so dressed up."

Bill looked down at his Army uniform, then around at the ready room. "Doc. I wanted to let you know I just got orders."

The professor rubbed his eyebrow. "When do you leave?"

"A week from tomorrow. Thursday."

"You have three weeks left in the semester."

Bill sighed. "Yeah. There's nothing I can do about it. I'll have to try again next semester."

"Listen," Doctor Herowitz said, shifting his phone to his other hand. "Where are you in your thesis?"

Bill shrugged. "It's done. Just needs editing. I finished it last week and set it aside."

Doctor Herowitz cleared his throat. "I wouldn't do this for just anyone, but my daughter edits for income. If you send it to her, she'll edit it and turn it in to me on time."

Bill didn't think his paper was anywhere close to a standard for editing, but did he have much of a choice?

"Do you have time over the Thanksgiving weekend to take the final?" Doctor Herowitz asked.

Bill barked a laugh. "Sure. If I want to fail. I haven't studied for the final, and like you said, there are still three weeks left in the semester."

"You know the material. You just need to pass, and then your master's degree is in your hands. I'll open it up until midnight Tuesday. If you can afford the time to take it, it can't hurt, right? If you fail, you'll need to retake the class. If you don't take the final, you'll need to retake the class. Get where this is going?"

A burst of elation spread from Bill's chest to his fingertips, but he kept his face neutral. "Deal. I'll try."

"And send me the paper. I'll get it to my daughter."

"Fair enough." He smiled. "Thanks. And, uh, have a good Thanksgiving."

Bill hung up, sat back in the leather chair, and started to create a mental checklist of the things he needed to do before he left. He had to read his thesis tonight. That would take hours. But if he could finish up the semester, he would have his master's degree in psychology, something he'd worked toward for twelve years.

His commander, Rick Norton, came into the room but stopped short when he saw Bill. He had released their team for the Thanksgiving holiday an hour ago.

Bill and Rick had been friends since they met in Ranger school eight years ago. Despite Rick's rank as a commissioned officer and Bill's as an enlisted non-commissioned officer, they'd connected in a deep way. Since then, their career paths had constantly intersected until Rick led Bill as the commander of their Special Forces ODA. Out of uniform, they were brothers in Christ, lifting each other up, supporting each other through the many trials of life that came with their vocation.

"What's up, brother?" Bill asked.

Rick sat down across from Bill. "I'm going to ask Cynthia to marry me tonight."

Bill's eyes widened. Rick and Cynthia had met on a mission in Katangela, Africa. She had run a medical clinic there for a mission organization. During a firefight with a local warlord, Bill and their medic, Phil Osbourne, had taken bullets. Cynthia had saved their lives, then traveled with them through the jungle to the American embassy in the capital city.

"Well, many happy returns."

Rick smiled. "I know you don't approve."

Bill sighed. "It's not a lack of approval. It's just concern about what that means for you. Nothing more."

"What it means is that I get to have the woman I love by my side, as the other half of my one, for the rest of my life.

I think I can live with that." Rick stared at him, his green eyes unwavering. "I hope one day you can say the same."

Bill believed that men in their profession shouldn't get married. A wife provided a distraction, affected decisions, and influenced career choices. He had decided to go the route of the apostle Paul. Yes, the Bible said it wasn't good for man to be alone, but he felt like he had a bigger mission than to have a wife and family. He needed to have all of his focus on the mission and to have the power of acting and reacting without considering how his actions might affect the future of another human being. He would tolerate occasional moments of loneliness and be a better soldier for it.

"Well," he drawled, "you're assuming she'll say yes."

Rick laughed. "Exactly." He reached over and slapped Bill's knee. "Either way, I'd like you to be at the wedding. Friday."

"Like day after tomorrow?"

"Yep. In Charula. Assuming she says yes, her parents plan to meet us there for the holiday, and we'll get married the day after."

"You haven't even asked her yet."

Rick's face grew serious. "I don't want to go on a mission without securing that part of our relationship. I want to marry her before I go. Or else I need to know we never will be."

Bill already had plans to go with Rick to his parents' home for Thanksgiving. Even though he had a final to study for and a thesis to finish, Rick took priority.

Bill winked and stood. "Guess I better go polish my boots."

"You better." Rick stood with him. "Did you get ahold of your professor?"

"Yeah. He's going to let me try to take the final."

With a grin lighting up his face, Rick said, "That's great."

Bill shrugged. "We'll see. It's a lot of missed lectures to try to pass."

"That's baloney. You could teach that class." They started out of the empty room. "What will that mean for your future? Have you decided to reenlist?"

"Not yet." He thought about the reenlistment packet waiting for his completion. He had to turn it in by January 10. "I'm praying about it, though. I'm just not sure what God wants from me yet."

"I guess wait and see how the final goes."

"I guess." Bill shrugged.

Outside, they slipped on their green berets, lining up the crossed arrow-and-dagger crests above their left eyes, and walked toward the parking lot. Clouds obscured the sun, but the air was still moderately warm.

"I'll be praying for you," Bill said. "And I guess I'll see you in Charula tomorrow?" For the last several months, they had been stationed just three hours from Rick's hometown. His family had taken Bill in as one of their own years ago.

"Yeah. Mom said dinner's at four eastern. Make sure you account for the time zone change."

That would give him the whole morning to study. He wouldn't have to leave until noon. "See you then."

ANCHORAGE, ALASKA
NOVEMBER 30

Lynda looked at the aerial view of the devastation. Domestic terrorists had blown up an oil pipeline in northeastern

Alaska. The resulting explosions caused a fire to surround a nearby town, killing twenty-seven people, including six children. She pinned the photo to the board above the report of a similar attack in South Dakota in October. Thankfully, no one had been killed or injured in that attack.

As she turned back to the stack of papers, the door opened and her director, Perry Blake, marched into the room. He had dark-brown skin, salt-and-pepper hair he kept cut short, and a bulbous nose. Lynda had worked under him for three years and couldn't imagine a better supervisor.

Three people Lynda did not recognize came into the briefing room behind Perry. "Agent Lynda Culter," he said, "this is Agent Natalie Lewis, a senior analyst with the CIA. Agent Mason Cartridge, cyber on loan from the NSA. Last but not least, Agent Neil Smith, Homeland Security. They have been working on this case in their individual capacities. After what happened in May, it's time we all did this in the same room."

Lynda studied each one as they were introduced. Agent Lewis had light-brown hair worn in loose curls to her shoulders. She stood about five six, with light-brown skin, honey-colored eyes, and red-framed glasses. She wore a blue pantsuit with the jacket open and shoes with no heel.

Agent Cartridge had curly brown hair, red freckles splashed across his face, and headphones draped around his neck. He wore a pair of olive-green cargo pants and an open button-down shirt over a black T-shirt depicting a scene from the arcade game *Centipede*. He did not meet Lynda's eyes when he shook her hand and wiped his hand off on his pants afterward.

Agent Smith stood at her height, about five nine, with a U-shaped black hairline. His scalp reflected the fluorescent lights above. He had green eyes and a thin mouth. He wore a gray suit with a gray-and-white-striped tie and had a wide wedding band on his finger.

Lynda had communicated with each of them in different capacities during her investigation. "It's good to meet you all in person," she said as they all took seats at the table.

Perry's deep voice resonated around the room. "Gary Owens died this morning." He walked to the board and tapped the face of the Oregon State sophomore they had found collapsed from crush injuries caused by the explosion near the Alaskan pipeline. "Mason, please share your report of your team's findings on Owens's computer."

The cyber specialist swiped on his tablet until he got to a particular screen. "Yeah, uh, yes. We found emails with detailed instructions for perpetrating the attack and making the explosives." He hugged the tablet to his chest and looked at Perry for the first time. "He'd deleted them, of course, but not efficiently."

Lynda tapped a photograph of a symbol spray-painted in fluorescent green on the side of Owens's car. "Dot-dash-dash. The Morse code for *W*," she said. "Green War's signature." She looked at Agent Cartridge. "So, he was emailed instructions?"

"That would appear to be the case."

After a moment, Perry said, "And?"

"We were able to trace the origin of the emails," Agent Cartridge said. "They'd gone through some proxy servers and onion routers to obfuscate, but I found them."

He didn't elaborate, so Lynda asked, "Found what?"

"The origin. They're in Istanbul."

She frowned. "Why are they in Istanbul?"

Perry gestured toward Agent Lewis. She stood up. "Four months ago, there was an attack on an oil field in Kuwait." She tapped on her tablet, and the smartboard on the wall came to life. "Last night, I was looking through the images from the bombing site the Kuwaiti government finally provided and spotted this." A picture of the back of a street sign showed green spray paint and the Morse code for W. "And there was another one on a pipeline in Colombia six months ago." She added another picture to the smartboard. On this one, someone had painted the symbol on the side of a large rock, barely seen through the brush. "The authorities in these locations didn't know to look for this tag. They also didn't think to look beyond their own borders for the perpetrators."

Frustration bubbled up in Lynda's chest. "So it's global, not just domestic." She shut the file folder as Agent Lewis sat back down. "How can we go after a group in Istanbul?"

"We're all smart people in this room." Perry smiled as if he knew the punch line to a joke. "You're going to find a way."

Lynda looked around the table and back at him. "Me?"

"You're the only one we know of who's seen any of them in person."

Immediately, she mentally flew back to the barn. Unwillingly, her nose filled with the smell of gasoline and burnt flesh. The fear she'd felt that day suddenly rose up again, threatening to suffocate her.

Clearly oblivious to her internal struggle, Perry continued. "We've established a joint task force with DHS, the State Department, and Interpol with support from US DOD since they have bases there. We're going to go into Turkey and find them."

Sweat beaded on her upper lip. Somehow she knew what he was about to say. "Go into Turkey?"

"Yes. You. With Agent Smith. There's a Special Forces ODA that DOD assigned to take part in this mission since they are trained in HRT and have a lot of experience in that theater of operations. You'll liaise with them in Kuwait and then travel into Turkey."

She shook her head. "DOD doesn't do police actions, and the FBI doesn't go into Turkey. Their focus is combat, and our focus is domestic crime."

Agent Smith spoke up. "On paper, that's all true. At the end of the day, this is our mission. All you're doing is acting as eyes for us. You do what they say and go where they go. Your job will be to observe and report. We'll handle the rest."

"I'm glad you all have this figured out."

A scattered chuckle moved around the room. She stood and picked up her file folder. Despite her vocal objections and the nerves painfully stabbing her stomach, it felt good to have a plan after weeks of information gathering. Energy hummed in the background of her brain.

"Where do I need to go?" she asked.

Perry slid a packet toward her. "You'll meet with Agent Smith at a private airfield outside of Anchorage this evening. You'll get where you need to be midmorning Friday."

She could manage only a closed-lip smile as she scooped up the packet. "Great. I'll go pack."

Perry nodded, and Agent Lewis stood again. "Actually, you're going to need some special clothes. If you'll come with me."

On her way out of the room, Lynda paused beside Perry.

"Why does it feel like I'm the only one who didn't know about this?"

"Everyone has known about their individual parts as the plans came together. Because this is unprecedented, it all required approval by officials at echelons above mine." He put a hand on her shoulder. "I didn't want to get your hopes up if the task force fell through."

She nodded and followed Agent Lewis, who led the way to an empty office. Several brightly colored dresses hung on a clothing rack.

"What's this?" Lynda asked.

"You're going to be undercover as a woman of Muslim faith. You'll be going into a mosque every day while you're in Turkey. Our intelligence suggests Damien Cisco is somehow affiliated with that mosque."

She drew her eyebrows together in a frown. "With a mosque? None of the men I saw were Arabic, and none of the language in their manifesto suggests radical Islamic ideology."

"Nevertheless, all of the emails came from a cell phone using the mosque's Wi-Fi. It's the best lead we have." Agent Lewis ran her finger over a sleeve the color of rich coral. "You can wear Western clothing, but you'll need to have your head covered. It's also important to have one or two dresses like this in case you're invited to a more formal event."

Lynda looked down at her white blouse and black slacks. "Western clothing like this?"

Agent Lewis shrugged and nodded in a single movement. "Almost. You'd need long sleeves." She helped Lynda pick out dresses and hijabs, then showed her how to put them on. "You can hide weapons here or here," she said, showing pockets on the sides of skirts and pants. "These outfits should accomplish two things. First, they should adequately obscure the fact that you're armed, and second, they should give you ready access to your weapons. But you will need to practice."

"Got it," Lynda said, mentally rehearsing how she would reach her pistol or knife if needed. The scarf made her head feel hot and caused her scalp to itch, but she'd cope. She would do whatever she needed to do to put a stop to the men who ran this organization—to the men who had murdered Jack.

"You'll have a contact on the ground there who will tell you what to wear when," Agent Lewis said. "You'll need to wear the hijab anytime you're outside or in public."

"They know what I look like."

"Trust me. With your head covered and heavy eye makeup on, they'll never even see you."

Anxiety that hadn't existed before May welled up in her chest, threatening to make her heart beat right out of her rib cage. "I don't know anything about being in a mosque."

"Like I said, we have someone on the ground who will go in with you."

Lynda folded the dresses and scarves she'd chosen. "I'll go pack."

"Make sure your shirts are long-sleeved. Pants are fine, skirts need to go all the way to the ground." Agent Lewis handed her a pamphlet explaining how to dress. "A car will be at your house at nineteen hundred."

Twenty minutes later, she stood in her living room and looked at the tree outside her apartment window. Beyond it, she could almost see the water of the Knik inlet. On the mantel sat a photo of her and Jack taken just over six months earlier. A picture of her with her parents at her graduation from the Academy sat beside it. On impulse, she pulled her phone out of her pocket and hit her mother's number.

Her mom answered on the second ring. "Well, I'll be," she said in her smooth Southern voice. "A call on a Wednesday."

"Hi, Mama. How are things?"

"Just fine, darlin'. Just got in from Christmas shopping. You still making it home?"

Lynda had a flash of a memory of Christmas morning with homemade doughnuts and spicy apple cider. "I will definitely be there."

"Do you know your travel dates yet? I'm hoping you'll make it for the Christmas program at church. Your daddy's playing the innkeeper again."

Nostalgia tightened her chest and filled her with unexpected emotion. "Let me know the date and I'll try to plan around it."

She took a breath to speak again, but her mom interrupted. "Aunt Finola finally got her house sold, so she's moving into the nursing home next week. But I know that's not why you're calling."

She wanted to ask questions about the nursing home and Christmas plans and just hang on the phone a little longer. Instead, she said, "I have to go out of town on a work trip."

"You're already in Alaska, dear. It's not like we're next-door neighbors."

"I know. I just don't know if you'll be able to get in touch with me if you need me."

"You let us know as soon as you get back. Ya hear?"

Lynda could detect a hint of worry in her mom's voice but knew she'd never ask specific questions. "Yes, ma'am."

"And pack an extra jacket. You never know what you'll need."

"Yes, ma'am." After a heartbeat she said, "I love you, Mama. Tell Daddy I love him too."

"Will do, dear."

After she hung up, she walked over to her mantel and looked at the picture of Jack. "We'll get them. I promise," she whispered.

KUWAIT
DECEMBER 2

As the runway rose up to meet the plane, Bill looked straight at Lieutenant Jorge Peña sitting across from him, not really seeing him. He hated landing in airplanes. He didn't mind taking off, and he never minded the altitude. In fact, he had experienced several hundred more takeoffs than landings in aircraft. In his mind, every single landing inside an airplane amounted to a controlled crash in which he was a helpless participant. He'd much rather jump out and parachute to the ground and control his own destiny than trust that the giant metal tube weighing several tons would come to a safe and proper stop.

"Yo, Drumstick. Looking a little green around the gills," Chief Hanson said with a laugh. Bill's affliction had become the source of mirth every single time they had to land somewhere.

Bill blew a kiss in Hanson's direction. Every member of

his team had a nickname. Because of his last name of Sanders, "Drumstick" made perfect sense. He preferred it to Hanson's, derived from the nineties boy band. "Keep laughing, MMMBop."

He ran his fingers through his thickening beard. In preparation for the upcoming deployment, he hadn't shaved in a week. They all wore beards to protect themselves and their families in case of facial recognition. His grew thick and black, allowing him to fairly effortlessly blend in with the locals in many different areas of the world.

As soon as the Air Force C-17 jet rolled to a stop, they stood to gather their gear. The interior lighting changed to all red, and the rear ramp opened. He shifted his weapon so he could grab his pack. He followed Gerald "Jerry Maguire" McBride, Daniel "Pot Pie" Swanson, and Travis "Trout" Fisher down the ramp and into the early morning sunlight. It felt good to move after so many hours in the air.

Bill looked all around him at the flat desert landscape. "Ahh, Kuwait. How I've missed that particular color of tan."

Rick met them as they came down the ramp. As the team leader, he was nicknamed "Daddy." He slapped Bill on the back as he walked by. He'd arrived two days before them as part of the advance party. "At least here we have a sea breeze," he said in an accentuated Kentucky drawl. "Good to see you guys finally made it."

"Good thing I brought my suntan lotion," Sergeant Timothy Waller said.

"You'll need it with that lily-white skin," Swanson said, taking in Waller's blond hair and light-blue eyes. His own dark skin gleamed in the bright sunshine. "Where's your family from anyway, Bourbon? Iceland? Greenland?"

"Germany." Waller grinned. "Could you not tell?"

For the next hour, they unloaded gear and set up their ready room. As soon as they stored and locked up the last box of ammo and met back in the room, Rick said, "Go grab some chow. They started serving breakfast twenty minutes ago. Then meet back here. Forty mikes. We have a situation."

"We always have a situation, sir," Lieutenant Jorge Peña "Colada" said.

Rick chuckled. "Speaking of, Selah's here. Go find your wife and give her a kiss. That's all you have time for."

Peña grinned. "I can work with that, sir."

"No doubt." Rick gestured behind him. "She should be over at HQ. Let her know I want her in on this briefing if she can break free."

"Roger, sir. Wilco," Peña said, then disappeared at a trot.

Bill waited until the rest of the team had left before approaching Rick. "How was the honeymoon?" He couldn't believe only a week had gone by since Rick and Cynthia's hastily planned wedding.

"My honeymoon consisted of briefings, packing, and Cynthia driving me to Delaware to catch a C-5," Rick said, his eyes crinkling as he smiled. "We had five marvelous days, though. I told her I owe her a real honeymoon when I get back."

"You both deserve an actual vacation," Bill said. He gestured to the door. "You eating?"

"Yeah. Give me just a sec to set this up for the colonel." He pulled cords out of a computer backpack and connected them to the laptop on the podium. "How was the flight?"

"Nothing to write home about. It's a long way to be stuck in a tin can that could have killed me at any moment."

"At least you didn't have to lay over anywhere. I got off Space-A and flew commercial from Germany. Got stuck there for six hours."

"That's not enough time to leave the airport and make the layover worthwhile."

"I know. I just found a corner and slept."

With everything connected, Rick picked up a remote control and turned on the overhead projector. Once he confirmed that the projector talked to the computer, he turned it off again.

"What's the scoop, brother?" Bill asked. "Why are we back here?"

Before Rick could answer, the door at the far end of the room opened and Colonel Jenkins came through. "Ah, Captain Norton, there you are. I need you with me. The rest of the detail just arrived."

Rick gestured over his shoulder. "I'm on my way to chow right now, sir. Can you give me ten mikes?"

The colonel checked his watch. "No need. I have food waiting."

"Yes, sir."

When they went outside, Bill slipped sunglasses on to battle the unforgiving light of the sun. "Only seventy degrees," he said. "Way better than the last time we were here. Remember? July two years ago. It was a hundred and fifteen in the shade. How is that legal?"

"Well, the weather isn't always fair, but it makes its own rules," Rick said. He slapped Bill on the back and went into the tent next door.

Bill continued down the street toward the larger mess hall in a circus-sized tent. Kuwait allowed the United States to have a military presence here, but they did not allow them to build any permanent structures. Consequently, the military had composed the entire base of tents and rectangular structures called CHUs, pronounced "chews." They used the versatile CHUs for everything from sleeping to restrooms, showers, and even fast-food restaurants and improvised movie theaters.

Nothing had changed much at this particular base. Even though Bill hadn't been here for over two years, he still knew what road to turn down, which way the good shower tents were, and where to go.

Inside the mess tent, he picked up a tray and moved through the line. When he had a tray piled with scrambled eggs and toast, he stopped and filled his cup with cola, then found his team. "Mmm, runny eggs and burnt toast. Just like my meemaw used to make."

Emma "Selah" Peña speared a slice of pineapple with her fork. "Stick with fruit and veggies like me."

He glanced her way. "That might work when you're five two and ninety pounds. I'm afraid I have a bit more bulk to feed."

Peña ran a light hand across his wife's back. He'd had a permanent grin on his face since seeing her. Bill shifted his eyes away from the couple who had too few days a month together.

Born and raised in Mazar-e-Sharif, Afghanistan, until she was almost ten, Selah often blended in with the locals during the times Bill's unit utilized her services. She was a contractor with the Department of Defense and the State Department and worked as a translator who also had interrogation training. She had filled both roles for their team in the past. She and Peña had met on duty during a Middle East deployment a couple of years ago.

Bill remembered their rocky relationship that had nearly torn Peña in half. He was glad his friend had finally found happiness, even though he worried that the married men on the team wouldn't always make the right decisions in the field. A spouse added a layer of complexity to the psyche and didn't belong in the mind of a team soldier.

Not that anyone ever asked his opinion on the matter.

He looked at Jared "Honest Abe" Ibrahim. His slight build, dark beard and eyes, and olive skin made him look very much like a local. His family came from Jordan. He and Bill served as the team's weapons specialists.

"We need to do sensitive item inventory after the briefing," Bill said to Ibrahim. "You good with it?"

"Yeah, I'm good," Ibrahim said. "The jet lag never hits me until I go back to the States. It's weird. This direction, I can hit the ground running. Going back kicks my tail."

"Same." Bill tried not to flinch as he drank the cola. Whoever had mixed the fountain drinks clearly had never done it before. However, bad food and horrible locations came with the job. He'd eaten worse in his life.

Hanson stopped at their table. "I know y'all are worn out from the trip and it's after eleven at night back at Fort Campbell, but I need you bright-eyed and bushy-tailed. The cooks just put on fresh coffee for you. It's going to be a long day." He glanced at Bill and pointed at Ibrahim as he turned to go. "You two square?"

"Yes, Chief," Bill replied. "Abe and I are knocking it out right after the briefing."

Ibrahim pushed his plate away. "I'm ready anytime. Not hungry right now."

Hanson nodded. "It needs to be done before lights out.

I don't know what our exact timetable will be, but I expect we'll be moving tomorrow."

"The air of mystery is killing us, Chief," Dave "Mr. Miyagi" Morita said. He had straight black hair and a close black beard. He and Fisher served as the communications experts, and he could probably make a radio out of a copper wire and a potato.

"It will all be revealed," Hanson said with a smile. He spun on his heel and left the tent.

Anticipation coursed through Bill's bloodstream. He looked at Fisher. "This seems bigger than normal."

"It does." Fisher glanced at Hanson's retreating form. "My interest is piqued."

CHAPTER

★

THREE

From the air above Kuwait City, the turquoise waters of the Persian Gulf met the gray concrete of the city. The plane continued past the hubbub of life and on into the desert, where Lynda could see only shades of tan sand and brown. Brown landscape, brown buildings, brown vehicles—quite the opposite of the Alaskan landscape. The dichotomy intrigued her.

She glanced over at Agent Smith. "Have you been here before?"

He looked up from his computer. "Oh, yes. Many times."

Even though it exceeded their charter, she imagined that the Department of Homeland Security had a lot of interest in this centrally located US-friendly country. She glanced over as Agent Lewis sat in the seat next to her and held out a blue hijab covered in flowers.

"Time to get into character."

Lynda gave a tight-lipped smile. "Have I mentioned how much I hate having anything on my head?"

"Not even once. But I can tell. Which is why you need to put it on and keep it on all the time you're outside. Kuwait is a great training ground. It's the best way to condition you for wearing it in Turkey." She patted Lynda's hand. "I would be the one to do this mission if I had ever laid eyes on any of the suspects."

Lynda straightened the scarf. "You'd pass as a more authentic Muslim than me." Her hand circled her face. "White. Like vanilla ice cream. See that?"

Agent Lewis laughed. "Again, you're the witness. You'll be fine. And you won't be the first white woman in this mosque."

Lynda fit the scarf over her head so that it completely covered her hair and neck and draped loosely along the top of her chest.

Agent Lewis nodded. "You've been practicing. You move like you've been doing it since adolescence."

Lynda grinned. She'd spent hours putting the scarves on her head in three different ways, until she could do it without thinking. She had also practiced drawing her weapons in full garb.

The wheels chirped as the plane met the runway, and soon they walked down the stairs onto the tarmac. She squinted against the bright sunlight. At the bottom of the staircase, a man in an Army uniform with a small black eagle in the center of his chest greeted them. On his left sleeve, he had three stacked tabs that read "Special Forces," "Ranger," and "Airborne," all above a patch shaped like an arrowhead with a dagger and three lightning bolts—the emblem of the Green

Berets. On his right sleeve, he wore a scroll that said "1st Ranger Bn."

The man shook hands with Agent Smith, who turned and introduced Agent Lewis and Lynda. "Colonel Jenkins is commanding the team assigned to assist you in the mission," Agent Smith said.

"Your cyber guy's already here," the colonel said. "Got him set up yesterday."

Agent Lewis scanned the area. "We'd like to have some face time with the man assigned to assist Special Agent Culter."

The colonel nodded. "No problem. They arrived about two hours ahead of you. They just finished unloading their C-17, and I sent them to go grab some breakfast." He gestured toward the rows of tents. "I had food brought into the briefing room for us to save time. Drop your bags. I have a detail coming to collect them and deliver them to your assigned CHUs."

Lynda looked around as they walked to a desert-brown up-armored Humvee. She climbed into the back with Agent Smith while Agent Lewis climbed into the passenger's seat. The colonel spun them around and drove extremely slowly down the rows of tents. She peered over his shoulder and saw the speedometer hovering right around ten miles per hour. He turned three times until Lynda had no idea where they were or what direction the airfield was. Everywhere she looked, everything was exactly the same.

The colonel stopped in front of a large greenish-brown tent covered with a fine coat of dust like everything else here. He looked over his shoulder at her. "Hang tight. I'll get your door. Don't think I'm trying to be sexist or anything like that. They're really hard to open from the inside."

They went into a briefing room set up like a classroom. Rows of chairs faced a raised stage that consisted of a screen and a podium. The colonel led the way through the room and into a smaller back room that held eight chairs around a conference table. A large plate with about a dozen wrapped pastries and granola bars sat next to a silver bowl piled with apples.

Lynda gladly chose a bright red apple as she took a chair. She wanted to scratch her head but rolled the apple between her hands instead. Agent Lewis and Agent Smith selected pastries and pulled out seats around the table. The door opened, and a man in a military uniform with a red beard and green eyes came into the room.

"Ah, good, Captain Norton," Colonel Jenkins said. "I'll make introductions."

Bill kicked back in a wheeled desk chair and waited for all the special guests to arrive. He knew this mission had a different tone to it. Most of the time, they had weeks to prepare for a mission. This time, they'd barely had a week, and everyone had been hush-hush about everything surrounding it.

Despite the long flight and his nerves humming in anticipation, his mind wandered. He watched Specialist Calvin "Hobbes" Brock arm-wrestle with Sergeant Eric Gill. "Gilligan" hailed from Phoenix City, Alabama, and he and Bill had crossed swords over Alabama football.

Thinking of Alabama sent Bill's mind into the dark abyss of home and the single-wide trailer in Pelham where his mother lived, where a steady stream of the man of the month rolled through. The older and more haggard Charlotte Sanders got, the rougher and meaner the men she attracted. He shuddered at the thought of that dark hole and forced his mind out of it.

His gaze wandered over to Peña and Selah. They sat shoulder to shoulder, talking in low tones. Peña had once put his own life at risk, against orders, to save Selah's life. That provided the perfect example of why Bill didn't think people who did what they did should be tied romantically and emotionally to another person.

The side door opened, and Colonel Jenkins came through, followed by Rick, then a man in a short-sleeved shirt and khaki pants.

"Brown shirt alert," McBride murmured. The term came from, among other reasons, the inexplicable preference DHS agents demonstrated for a particular brand of khaki tactical gear whenever they came to the Middle East.

Bill almost rolled his eyes at the thought of having to work alongside DHS again. The last time the team had to go on a babysitting mission with DHS agents, things had gone sideways fast. McBride had ended up with a bullet through his bicep.

A woman in a blue hijab with pink-and-purple flowers on it followed the brown shirt. Bill straightened. Something about the way she moved looked familiar and put his senses on alert. In his peripheral vision, he saw Selah get up and approach the front of the room just as the woman slipped the hijab off—something he'd never seen a Muslim woman do. She rubbed at her scalp almost absently as she talked with Selah.

When he saw her rich auburn hair with the red-and-blond streaks, his heart started pounding. It couldn't be her. Flashes from his first year of college rushed through his memory: Psychology 101, study group, pizza and sodas in the dorm lobby.

What was Lynda Culter doing in Kuwait? More importantly, what was Lynda Culter doing in Kuwait wearing a hijab while consulting with his Special Forces A-Team commander?

She glanced over the occupants of the room. She made brief eye contact with him but didn't pause. Clearly, the thick beard and about a decade of separation kept her from recognizing him. Before he could say anything, Colonel Jenkins called the room to attention.

"All right, people, listen up. I'm sure you all remember the attack on the Alaskan pipeline last month. What we've learned since then is that the group who perpetrated the attack and who we thought was a domestic ecoterrorist organization known as Green War is in fact an international organization. They have staged attacks on no less than five different pipelines globally, and the fine analysts in our great capital have determined that the orders for at least three of those attacks came from Turkey."

He gestured at Rick, who stepped forward. "The vice president has asked us to lend our particular expertise to a joint task force, cooperating with various US agencies along with combined assistance from our allies at Interpol, to capture the head of this organization."

"Why us, sir?" Peña asked.

"Because it's what we do, Lieutenant." He turned to the brown shirt. "This is Agent Neil Smith with the Department of Homeland Security. He's going to give us some more information."

Agent Smith stepped forward. "We have reason to believe someone inside the Green War organization attends a mosque in Turkey. We've uncovered a few emails sent from the mosque's Wi-Fi on different dates. Your team will go into Turkey and establish surveillance of the mosque. If anyone asks any questions, you're just visiting the great city on leave. Plausible deniability. When we've identified all the key players, our task will be to capture them—alive—and perform tactical debriefs for information gathering."

Bill had a natural talent at reading people, seeing subtle variations in posture, tone, and countenance. While Smith spoke, he watched the man's facial expressions. He got the impression that despite his DHS title, Agent Smith was an honorable man who had every intention of doing the best job he could.

"Please disable any cell phones," Rick said as he turned on the projector.

Someone in the back of the room dimmed the lights. An organizational chart appeared on the screen, and "SECRET" was written across the top and bottom in red. The first slide was a photograph of the Alaskan pipeline blast. Rick used a laser pointer to indicate the Morse code symbol for W. The next slides showed the other blast sites. On each slide, Rick indicated the Green War tag. An organizational chart appeared, with black silhouettes in place of photos.

"Our biggest obstacle is the lack of information," Rick said. "We don't know much about the organization or how it operates."

Peña raised his hand. "Question, sir. How are we supposed to surveil and capture someone we don't know?"

Agent Smith gestured at Lynda. "This is Special Agent

Lynda Culter with the Bureau. As far as we know, she's the only person who has ever seen the members of this organization and can identify them. Agent Culter?"

The projector went off, and the lights went back on again. Lynda slipped her hands into the pockets of her khaki pants. "In May, my partner, Jack, and I were captured while serving a warrant on the leader of Green War, a man known as Damien Cisco. They murdered Jack, but our backup arrived and my life was spared. I saw Cisco and two other men. I'm here to help you identify them."

Bill studied her facial movements, her body language, the way her lips moved as she spoke. The slight hitch of breath at Jack's name, the pause before she said "murdered," a very faint trembling of her lip that he never would have seen if he wasn't watching so closely—he could tell that Jack had meant something to her, something more than a partner.

His heart twisted. Lynda had suffered enough pain at the hands of another man in her life. She deserved happiness, adoration, someone to lift her up and make her see the amazing woman inside.

Rick nodded. "We're going to pair her up with a 'husband,'" he said, using air quotes, "and have them attend the mosque. The women's prayer room is on a balcony overlooking the area where the men pray. She'll be able to observe and analyze from there." He pointed to Selah. "Selah will be with her," he said, then gestured at Ibrahim, "and Abe here will be her man."

Brock leaned forward and slapped Ibrahim on the shoulder. "Congratulations, man."

"Won't my wife be surprised?" Ibrahim muttered.

"Honest Abe, Peña Colada, and Chief MMMBop," Rick

said, "I need you to hang out here for another few minutes. The rest of you, go recover from your trip. The second our visas are secured, we're on our way to Incirlik. Plan to leave at first light. State is expediting those visas."

Before Bill could go to the front of the room and reacquaint himself with Lynda, she and Selah disappeared out the door, followed by Colonel Jenkins, Rick, and the DHS agent. Hanson and Peña followed.

Bill looked over at Fisher. "Dude, this is not what I was expecting today."

Fisher shook his head. "I bet Honest Abe's wife wasn't expecting it either."

Bill chuckled more in irony than humor. What kind of game had God pulled him into by bringing Lynda Culter back into his life?

Lynda walked alongside Emma to the mess hall. Born and raised in Alabama, she'd been to Florida every spring break on a family trip to the beach, to Quantico and surrounding areas to attend the FBI Academy, and to Anchorage to live. She could hardly believe that she now walked along a dirt road on a military installation in Kuwait, thousands of miles and oceans away from home, on a completely different continent.

Right now, on December 2 in Anchorage, the temperature hovered right around twenty-five degrees. She'd gotten a weather alert on her way to the airport advising that the expected snowfall through the weekend would exceed five inches. Now she walked down a dirt road in seventy-two-degree weather wearing a hijab.

"Where are you from?" Emma asked.

"Alabama by way of Alaska. You?"

"Afghanistan via Texas." She lifted her hand when someone walking by greeted her. "My father helped the Americans right after 9/11. He was granted sanctuary when his life was in danger."

"Wow. What a legacy." In a different environment, she'd want to sit down and spend time with Emma, learn her father's story and what it was like coming to the States. "Have you been to Afghanistan since?"

Emma smiled up at her. "I speak six languages fluently. The military has me all over the Middle East providing translation services. I have been to Afghanistan several times, but not since last year." Her face sobered. "I never got to see my family when I was there, though, because that would have put their lives in danger."

Even though Lynda lived thousands of miles away from her family, she went home as often as possible. She couldn't imagine not having the option to see them when she was there. "Oh, Emma, I'm sorry."

"One day it won't be so. That is my prayer."

Lynda hesitated before saying, "So, you don't wear a hijab. Is that because you're on duty?"

Emma shook her head. "No. I would wear one in uniform. I'm a Christian. That's a story in itself." She opened the door of the mess hall. "I think my husband might already be in here."

"Is he a soldier?"

"You met him. Lieutenant Peña."

"Oh! I knew your last name was Peña. It didn't occur to me you were married." Lynda thought of the man with the dark eyes and pointed stare. "He is an intense man."

Emma chuckled. "You don't know the half of it."

They got trays and worked their way through the food line. Once she had a plate loaded with meatloaf, rice and gravy, and carrots, she followed Emma to a table full of men she mostly recognized from the briefing room. Lieutenant Peña raised his hand. Emma sat next to him and Lynda sat across from her, next to Sergeant Ibrahim.

She bowed her head and silently asked God's blessing over her meal. When she lifted her head, Ibrahim said to her, "My wife will be amused by this situation."

She picked up the Louisiana hot sauce from the center of the table. "I think I'd be amused too. Are you Muslim?"

He nodded. "My family is from Jordan. My parents immigrated to Michigan long before I was born."

She doused her meatloaf with hot sauce. "Does it bother you that we're going into a mosque?"

He considered her for a moment. "You prayed over your meal. You're a Christian?"

She nodded. "I am."

He pursed his lips. "Would it bother you if we were going into a church?"

She thought carefully about the question, not wanting to give a flippant answer. "I think the idea that someone is using my church would bother me more."

"There's your answer."

She didn't necessarily enjoy the meatloaf. It had a salty taste and a dry texture, but she was starving, and the hot sauce helped. As she contemplated the piece of chocolate cake she'd picked up on impulse, Emma and her husband stood.

"Are you good here? Do you need me to stay?" Emma asked.

Lynda shook her head. "I'm good. We have a briefing at two, right?"

"Yes. Make sure your time is right. We're in an odd time zone."

Lynda looked at her watch. "I have 11:40."

"Good. And you know your way to the CHU?"

She thought of the turns and roads to get to her personal room in the little rectangular trailer and nodded. "Yep."

Smiling, Emma and Peña left, carrying their trays. Deciding to eat the cake despite the logical part of her brain telling her no, she picked her fork back up just as someone took Emma's chair.

"Hey, Drumstick. How you doing?" Ibrahim asked.

"Finer than a rooster with socks on," the man said in a rich Southern voice that made Lynda freeze. "It's meatloaf day. Can't hardly beat that with a stick."

She looked at his tray, at the large hands that worked the utensils. Her gaze slowly moved up his chest, past the thick black beard, and into the dark eyes of Bill Sanders.

How?

"Bill?" she asked on a breath. "What—?"

He winked at her. "Had about the same reaction seeing you. I've had a forty-five-minute head start to get over it, though."

Memories cascaded through her mind. College study groups, football games, stolen kisses, plans and dreams of their future, and so much laughter.

Then the December day he left college, his arm in a sling from a football injury that snatched away his scholarship. The same day that he crushed her heart and made sure she understood that she'd been a distraction, someone to help him study, nothing more than that. Thanks for the good times but won't be seeing you later.

Despite two years as a police officer in Birmingham and four years as an FBI agent, as she looked into Bill's eyes, she suddenly turned back into that whimpering little girl who got her heart broken by the school's quarterback.

"I see the shock is wearing off and the memories are rushing back," he said. "It was nice to not be hated for a couple of seconds."

How could he joke? Did he not know what he'd done to her? How he'd made her feel? What he had done to her psyche that had taken years to get over?

"What are you doing here?" she snapped.

He shrugged and scooped potatoes onto his fork. "Just, you know, defending liberty on the frontiers of freedom."

She opened and closed her mouth, then stood. "Excuse me, please. I need to go to my room before my next meeting."

He lifted a hand. "Yeah, good to see you again. Tell your mama I said hi."

She crossed the room on legs that shook, put her tray on the conveyor belt to the kitchen, and left the building. When the door shut behind her, she found a picnic table outside and leaned against it, pressing her hands against her stomach. Soon, the shaking, quaking feeling left her and she could walk. She promised herself that as soon as she had some privacy in her own room, she could have a real reaction—maybe cry, possibly break something.

CHAPTER

★

FOUR

He could have handled that better. He certainly could have treated Lynda with more kindness and understanding.

Bill mentally kicked himself for the third time in the last hour. He crushed his empty paper cup and slumped farther into the lounge chair in the corner of the rec room. Times of stress tended to bring out the sarcastic Alabama boy buried deep inside. In super stressful times, he couldn't seem to help himself. Through his miserable life, humor and sarcastic wit kept him sane, focused, and untouched by his surroundings.

Seeing Lynda had catapulted Bill back to that December afternoon when he'd sat in the orthopedic doctor's office and was told that he couldn't throw a football anymore. He'd tried shifting to his left hand, but it didn't have the same kind of precision, not enough to fake it for the purposes of a scholarship, anyway. He left college at the end of the semester and had to go back "home," to the place he had sworn he'd never return to.

Sitting in that nasty trailer, listening to his mother and her boyfriend of the month fight over the last can of beer at ten on a Sunday morning, he'd almost given up on life. Was this his destiny? To become like her?

He snuck out the back door and drove his motorcycle to his grandmother's nursing home. He hated that she was here, in a low-income home, but he didn't have two dimes to rub together, much less the kind of money he needed to put her somewhere else. The white-tile floors, the block walls painted a weird shade of green, the thin mattress on a narrow bed—all of it broke his heart. She never once complained, though.

She was coherent and alert, and he sat in a metal folding chair and held her hand while she searched his face with the same dark-brown eyes he had. "God has plans for you," she said in her strong voice. "But you have given up on Him. I'm sure that breaks His heart."

"Maybe He gave up on me, Meemaw," he said. "I don't know what to do next."

She smiled, revealing the ill-fitting, cheap dentures. "Ah, Billy, He knows. What, you afraid to ask Him? Afraid of what He'll say?"

He put his chin up. "Nothing scares me."

She patted his cheek. "Prove it." She looked at the clock on her nightstand. "Help me to the community room. It's time for church service."

He helped her into her wheelchair and wheeled her down to the community room. The hospital chaplain gave a sermon about gifts and talents. Bill thought it an odd lesson to teach to a geriatric population who had already lived their best lives. After watching her eat a lunch that consisted of peanut butter sandwiches and canned vegetable soup, he took her back to her room.

When he left, he sat on his bike in the parking lot and prayed, "God, if You're telling her something about me, I'd appreciate being in on the conversation. No fair talking behind my back. I need direction."

As he drove back to the trailer park, his bike stalled out. He wheeled it into a strip mall parking lot. As he knelt next to it, examining the V-twin and checking hoses and connections, the smell of pit barbecue filled his senses. He hadn't eaten since lunch the day before, and his stomach tried to gnaw its way out of his body at the delicious aroma. He looked up and saw a barbecue tent next to an Army recruiting truck.

Like a donkey being lured by a carrot, he wandered up to the truck. Over his third brisket sandwich—a gift from the recruiter who would trade him a barbecue sandwich for five minutes of his time—he made an appointment to take the Armed Services Vocational Aptitude Battery, known as the ASVAB. That began the process of Bill making the Army his career.

Because of Bill's living situation, the recruiter arranged for him to be on something akin to active duty orders, and that night he slept with a full stomach on a cot in an armory in exchange for four hours of guard duty a day and cleaning the latrines after dinner. He even got paid a stipend, which surprised him. Soon, he finished all of the requirements, took all the tests, signed on all the dotted lines, and entered basic training.

Once he started getting paid, he took every spare dime of his paycheck and put it into his grandmother's new facility. She thrived there and received good care, and he didn't mind paying for that. In fact, it honored him to have the opportunity. The Army fed him at the mess hall and housed him in the barracks, and quite often he deployed with his unit, so he'd had no need for many material things.

His meemaw had died this past summer. They'd come home from a deployment in Africa, and he made it back in time to tell her goodbye. He saw his mother for the first time in years at the funeral. He barely recognized her. She'd aged considerably more in the ten years since he'd gone.

He shook his head. Why had seeing Lynda taken him down that sad and lonely road?

Trying to pull his mind out of the past and back to the present, to the coming mission, he looked around. His unit had secured this rec room for their use during their time here. Fisher and Gill played a game of Ping-Pong in the corner of the room, and Brock sprawled in a chair with a suspense novel.

Bill glanced over at Ibrahim, who sat forward in his chair, clutching his stomach. "Yo, Abe, you okay?"

Ibrahim shook his head. "I'm suddenly nauseated. I hope the meatloaf today wasn't bad. That would make a long day for us all."

"Want me to see if I can find you a soda? Something to settle your stomach?"

"Thanks." He pressed a napkin against his eyes with a shaking hand.

Bill grabbed a can of ginger ale out of the fridge and brought it over to him.

Ibrahim stood up and shakily reached out to take the can. "I'm going to go to my room. Briefing at fourteen hundred, Daddy said?"

"Yeah. Fourteen."

When Ibrahim stopped at the doorway and leaned against the wall, Bill walked up to him. "Hey, man, I'm headed to my room too. Still need to unpack. I'll walk with you."

By the time they got to their assigned CHUs, Ibrahim was leaning completely against him. Bill stopped at his friend's room and took the key from him. "Would you rather go to the CaSH?"

"Nah. Just something I ate. I'll be okay."

When he shut the door, Bill hesitated for several seconds before heading to his own room. He would stop in and check on Ibrahim before the briefing.

In his quarters, he unpacked his footlocker. He pulled out his hammock and secured it to the rafters. He had a bed, but the idea that something could crawl into his sheets kept him awake at night. Sleeping in a hammock in a freshly unrolled sleeping bag kept thoughts of the critters pretty muted. Not entirely silenced, but at least muted.

It amused him, this phobia he had, because he could sleep on the ground in the jungle or the high mountains or even a swamp and never even flinch. But in the desert . . . He shuddered at the thought.

Everything essential unpacked, he sat on the bed and thought back to the lack of conversation with Lynda. He really ought to seek her out and have a grown-up talk. If she'd even entertain such a thing, especially after the way he'd talked to her today.

He needed to explain what happened, why he had done

what he'd done. She likely wouldn't understand, and she might not believe him, but he felt like he owed her an explanation.

And he loathed owing anyone anything.

At 1:45, Bill knocked on Ibrahim's door. When he didn't answer, Bill tried the handle, thankful to find it unlocked. He'd have broken it down, but he preferred not to.

He found Ibrahim lying on the floor by the bed, his face a scary ashen color. Bill rushed forward and put his fingers on his friend's neck. Ibrahim's heart raced, and sweat soaked his shirt.

"Hey, buddy," he said, rolling him over, "let's get you to the CaSH."

He got him to stand, then slung Ibrahim's arm over his shoulders. Securely wrapping his own arm around his friend's waist, he limped him out into the alley.

"Hey!" he yelled down the row of CHUs. "Help!"

Almost immediately, three doors opened. Waller, one of the two combat medics on the team, peeked out his door, assessed the situation, then rushed forward. "What happened?" he asked, lifting Ibrahim's eyelid.

"He didn't feel well after lunch. Thought he'd eaten something bad. That was just about two hours ago."

"Okay. I'll get his feet." Waller bent and grabbed Ibrahim by the back of the knees. Bill shifted and secured him under his arms. Together, they carried him to the medical unit.

Leaving Ibrahim with Waller and the doctor, Bill went on to the ready room on the other side of the base. The hot Kuwait sun beat down on his head. By the time he made it into the crisp air-conditioning of the briefing room, sweat had soaked the T-shirt he wore under his uniform.

He found Colonel Jenkins, Peña, Selah, Rick, and Agent Smith around the table. Lynda stood in front of a whiteboard, a red marker in her hand. Pictures of explosions and green spray-painted Morse code covered the board.

Rick raised an eyebrow. "Why, Sergeant Ibrahim, you've gotten about an inch shorter."

"Beard got thicker too," Peña added.

Bill smiled. "Honest Abe is lying on a cot in the med facility. Waller sent me here to tell you that he's calling in sick."

The colonel frowned. "Sick? Green Berets don't get sick."

Bill nodded. "Yes, sir. However, Waller and I carried the unconscious Green Beret ourselves. I can attest to you, sir, that if he's not sick he is most definitely unwell."

The colonel made a "humph" sound.

Selah frowned. "What does that mean for the mission?"

Rick rubbed his beard. "Abe is our only Arabic team member. We need someone else who can pass as a Muslim."

"Well, white people are Muslim, right?" Agent Smith asked. "I mean, it's a religion, not a race."

Selah shrugged. "Yes, but we want someone who won't stand out. I'm afraid Captain Norton with his Norwegian features and red hair would most definitely stand out. He'd be accepted, but he'd be noticed. We need someone who won't be noticed."

Rick looked at Bill, who immediately raised his hands in defense. "I am an Alabama boy, sir. I don't think I could pretend to be anything but."

"You wouldn't have to speak beyond simple greetings," Selah said.

Lynda's expression stayed neutral, but Bill could see the spark of panic in the edges of her eyes and the slight tightening of her mouth. "I'd prefer someone other than Bill," she said.

Rick raised an eyebrow. "Bill?" He looked from Bill to Lynda and back again. "Since you're obviously on a first-name basis, one of you better share the particulars."

Bill cleared his throat. "We, uh, went to college together."

When Bill didn't elaborate, Rick turned to Lynda. "I'm detecting an undercurrent of hostility. However, this mission is of the utmost importance and takes priority over college sweethearts." He pointed at Bill. "Sergeant Sanders is the most obvious choice. Pull up a chair, Drumstick. We have to get you up to speed. If Abe can't do the mission, you need to be briefed in."

Bill sighed. Rick was like a brother to him. He'd give a kidney to the man if he asked. But right now, he'd love to pop him in the nose just hard enough to make it bleed. If he'd ever explained about Lynda, let Rick in on those early days of adulthood as he navigated the waters of creating a new life away from the old one, maybe his friend would understand. But he never had, and Rick had always done well to put the mission above anything personal.

Much to Bill's surprise, Lynda took the lead. "We'll travel as husband and wife doing a tour of the Holy Land. Time is of the essence. The attacks have been on a regular schedule of every six weeks, and we're approaching the next anticipated date. Your team will follow via train or car. We'll stay in a hotel near the mosque and attend all of the prayer times." She pulled a photo off the whiteboard. "This is the view from the women's prayer room. Because it's a balcony of sorts, I should be able to see the men below."

"If she observes the men we're looking for, then the team will need to be ready to follow them," Selah said.

Bill studied the pictures. "How many men are we looking for?"

Lynda crossed her arms and sat down. "I can identify three, including the leader we know as Damien Cisco."

He thought back to the briefing earlier in the day. "You were taken captive?"

If he hadn't been watching her face so closely, he would have missed the fear and sorrow that played through her eyes. "My partner and I were serving a warrant. Until that moment, we thought they were peaceful types. Tree huggers. We had no idea what they had planned."

His imagination went into overdrive, and a surge of anger had him bite out, "And what have they got planned?"

"They've destroyed four oil pipelines in strategic areas in North and South America and one here in Kuwait," Agent Smith said. "Dozens of people have been killed, two towns destroyed in the wake of the bombings. Obviously, it has something to do with oil, but we don't know yet what the bigger picture is supposed to look like."

Bill flipped a page in the file he inspected, trying to get caught up on what Ibrahim already knew from the earlier briefing. "It looks like some arrests have been made."

Lynda shook her head. "Everyone we've arrested is exactly who we thought the group was initially. Peaceful lovers of the environment who had no idea what a blast of several hundred pounds of EPX would do to four kilometers of oil and natural gas pipeline. It's like there's a manipulation of the grunt soldiers in their army, but there's a different agenda at the top."

Bill laughed. "Sounds familiar."

Colonel Jenkins shook his head and smiled. "Let's stay on task here, people." He pointed at Lynda. "Why do you think this will work?"

She pulled on her right earlobe with a movement that Bill immediately remembered. "Honestly, Colonel, I don't. But it's all we have. This tiny little bread crumb of a series of emails coming from this mosque's Wi-Fi is our best clue. The imam and his staff look completely clean. Our best guess is that a phone tapped into the Wi-Fi to send the emails. The times corresponded to within ten to fifteen minutes of prayer times for those months. It's this or wait for the next explosion."

"What's the intel on the EPX?"

Agent Smith spoke up. "It's an RDX-based explosive like C-4 and Semtex. Light. Stable. Portable. Highly effective, especially when made into a shaped charge. The signatures we analyzed match a lot delivered to the French Foreign Legion three years ago, but every ounce of that lot is accounted for. Our best guess is the manufacturer made an extra lot that he sold off book. The CIA looked into it, but most of the players are dead or missing."

"The lot was manufactured in Turkey," Lynda added.

"Of course it was," Colonel Jenkins said.

Bill absently rubbed his beard. "I don't know anything about prayer calls or the culture inside of a mosque."

"This is all assuming Ibrahim can't go," Selah said. "If he's not feeling better, you could go see him after dinner tonight. See if he's up to talking. If not, we can do some internet research together and I'll do my best to explain it all to you."

He shook his head. "I also don't speak the language."

"That's okay. You being American won't seem odd if you're with your American wife and staying in a hotel. I'll teach you greetings and basic replies that you would have picked up attending your own mosque, but you won't need to be fluent to pull it off. You will need to memorize some of the prayers."

"The important thing is to have you there, present, ready to follow a man if need be," Lynda said. "Your looks allow you to enter without being obtrusive. Unless someone directly addresses you, there's no reason to think you're not of Arab descent."

No one really knew his ancestry, including himself, but he didn't throw that into the conversation. "You're not exactly a Persian princess."

She lifted her chin. "I'm a woman. My hair will be covered and I'll have makeup on. I can go unnoticed, especially if I keep my head down." She picked up a file box and riffled through it, then pulled out two thick manila envelopes. "These are our cover identities. You need to go to the State Department tent and get your new passport. Agent Smith has everything lined up there. They just need to add your photo. Please do that immediately so they have time to properly finish it."

She handed Bill the envelope, but he didn't open it. He needed time to digest it in private.

Colonel Jenkins tapped the table. "All right, folks. Wheels up at oh seven. Your team will go through Incirlik, then travel by civilian vehicles to Istanbul. It's a long drive. Sergeant Sanders and Agent Culter, your flight takes off at 10:40. Selah and Peña will also be on it. That way, you'll clear local customs in proper order and appear like a young Muslim couple touring the homeland, coming on a commercial flight from Kuwait." He stood. "Dismissed. Captain? I'd like to go into a more detailed mission briefing with you and Lieutenant Peña for your team as a whole at sixteen hundred."

Rick nodded. "Yes, sir."

After the colonel left, Peña dryly said, "He didn't clear sixteen hundred with me. What if I had other plans?"

Rick shook his head and laughed. "See you in an hour."

"Yes, sir." On his way out, Peña said, "I'll go get the scoop on Abe."

Bill stayed in his seat and watched Lynda pack up her notebook and file and walk out with Agent Smith, never looking in his direction. He wondered briefly what the next few days would look like.

Once the room emptied, he glanced at Rick, who hadn't moved from his seat and pretended to read the file folder in front of him. "You might as well ask me."

"Don't need to," Rick said, shutting the file. "You already know the question."

Bill sighed and sat back, draping his arm over the back of the chair next to him. "We went to college together. First semester, we were paired up in this psychology group, and man, she was so smart. Like, I couldn't believe she'd even talk to me kind of smart, you know?"

Rick nodded.

"When I was on that clean campus with those buildings and manicured lawns and quads and especially the football stadium, I could forget the dirt yard in front of my mom's trailer, and I could forget the things that scurried into the dark when you turned on the light."

Rick shook his head. "Bill—"

"I know what you're going to say. Where I come from isn't who I am. But, dude, there's a stink that I can never wash off. She didn't need to be a part of that."

"So you broke up with her?"

Shame burned in his chest. "I got hurt first semester of my sophomore year. Couldn't throw the ball anymore, so they dropped me from the team. I spent the rest of the semester trying to find a way to explain to her that I couldn't stay, that I had to go, but that I loved her and wanted her to stay and thrive and be amazing. I just lost my nerve."

"What? You just left?"

He slowly shook his head. "No. I said things, mean things. Things to make her hate me so she never came looking for me and thereby never got exposed to my world."

Rick stared at him for several seconds, his green eyes burning with intensity. Finally he said, "That's messed up."

"Yeah." Bill heaved a sigh. "I'll try to talk to her."

"You ought to." He tapped the table in front of Bill. "Oh, speaking of college, did you get your grades from your final before you left?"

Bill smiled, thinking about the last final that stood between him and his degree. He'd taken the test Tuesday. "Ninety-three."

"Bah. I'd fight it. No way you lost seven points." Rick laughed. "Well done, especially considering the timing. Congratulations. We'll have to have a graduation party for you."

"Don't you dare."

Rick winked and stood. "I have some things to do before my next briefing. You good?"

He thought back to Lynda. He was not good. Not even kind of. "Yeah, man. I'm good."

CHAPTER

FIVE

Lynda left the briefing to go back to her "room." The rectangular modular container Emma had called a CHU contained a bed, a mirror with a shelf, a locker, and a desk. The wall separated her from the other occupant who had her own access point.

Emma had shown her the bathroom CHU, so she'd inspected the eight stalls. Beside it she found the shower CHU, which had a small dressing area with lockers and six showers. Maybe the fact that she'd have to be here only until the morning made it all very new and exciting. She imagined that after a week or two, she'd definitely be ready for less spartan living conditions.

Her suitcase sat on her bed. Since they would leave in the morning, it made no sense to unpack. Instead, she decided to spend some quiet time with God. She left the room, following the directions she'd been given for the chapel tent.

She entered the tent, astonished at the difference the shade inside made. She was glad to see no one else there. The chapel was set up the same as the briefing room she'd been in before, with rows of chairs facing a raised dais. This one had a large wooden cross behind the platform and a table in front of the podium, much like churches back home.

She grabbed a Bible off the shelf near the plywood door, then took a seat and slipped the hijab off her head. "God," she whispered, "I wish I knew where You were going with this, because right now being distracted by Bill Sanders is the last thing I think I need. But obviously You know better."

She sat in silence for several minutes, meditating and contemplating. When she raised her head, her stomach growled, and she realized she was still inside the window for the dining hall dinner hours. She fingered the lanyard with her ID on it as she looked at the hijab, which she just didn't feel like putting back on. Tomorrow, she wouldn't have the freedom of choice, so she draped the hijab around her neck.

When she stood and turned, she faltered the moment she saw Bill sitting in the back row. When had he arrived?

Suddenly, she was nineteen again, in love, high on life, trusting her heart to someone she never should have trusted. When he'd left her standing there on that December morning, she had a hard time even understanding what he'd said to her. She'd never felt good enough for him, and his words just affirmed that.

Honestly, she'd never really gotten over it. Not until Jack, and then he . . .

"What do you need?" she asked.

"I, uh, saw you come in here. I need to speak to you. I

want to explain something." He made no attempt to stand or move closer to her.

Her stomach twisted into knots, but she had to spend the next unknown number of days with him, so clearing the air now might be wise. Despite her desire to just punch him in the nose and run away, she stepped forward and crossed her arms. "I only have a few minutes. I was on my way to dinner."

"Won't take long."

His presence filled the large tent. She resented his intrusion into this space where she'd come to seek a quiet moment alone with God but tried not to show it. Instead, she sat down across the aisle from him and said, "Fine. I'm listening. Explain."

He turned toward her with his feet in the aisle and put his elbows on his knees. He looked rough-and-ready with his thick beard and dark eyes. "I'm sorry for the things I said to you. You probably already know I didn't mean them."

His words did nothing to soften her heart. "That apology is about ten years too late. Nor is it an explanation."

He laced his fingers and stared at the floor. Though he sat completely still, she imagined he hummed with energy inside. In college, he could never stop moving. She admired the discipline he'd obviously achieved since then.

"I didn't know what my future was going to hold, but none of my options looked good," he said. "I didn't want to drag you down to my level in life. It's messed up, I know. But I was nineteen, scared to death, and angry at the world."

After several moments she asked, "That's it?"

When he raised his head, the look in his eyes took her breath away. "Best I got," he said.

She pressed her lips together and stood. "Thanks for taking

the time to 'explain.' I'm going to get dinner. Please excuse me."

She stormed out, then ducked into the shade of another tent. Pressing her hands to her mouth, she willed the sobs filling her chest to subside. She had cried enough tears over Bill Sanders in her lifetime and refused to shed another.

Feeling like she might have regained some control, she stepped back out onto the road. The hot sun burned her scalp through the part in her hair. As she glanced up at the shining blue sky, she understood why people in this region traditionally wore things on their heads. She couldn't fathom what life would be like without the air-conditioning units pumping cooled air into each of the tents.

"Agent Culter!"

She paused on the brown dirt path and turned. Agent Smith rushed toward her. "I'm headed to dinner," she said.

"Me too. Thought I'd walk with you." When he matched her stride he said, "I checked in on Sergeant Ibrahim. He is currently in surgery having his appendix removed."

She gasped. "Oh no!"

"Exactly. All I could think was at least it happened today and not tomorrow. Which is terrible to think, but I'll own it."

His candor impressed her. "It is better that it happened today," she said. "I'm glad they have the medical facilities to take care of him."

They reached the dining hall, and Agent Smith opened the door for her. "Are you nervous about tomorrow?"

She shrugged as she picked up a tray, skimming the monitor that gave the night's meal choices before choosing beef enchiladas. "I'm not nervous. I'm just anxious to be there and get started."

"Yeah."

She worked her way down the line, asking for enchiladas, corn, and tortilla chips. She added a glass of iced tea, then walked out into the tent area and glanced at the tables. Emma was sitting next to her husband at a mostly empty table.

Lynda approached them. "May we join you?"

"Sure." Emma patted the seat next to her. "How was your afternoon?"

"Full of information." Lynda bowed her head. When she finished her prayer, she lifted her head and caught Agent Smith staring at her. "What?"

"You're going to have to get out of that habit," he said.

She glanced at Emma. "Do Muslims not pray before eating?"

Emma shook her head. "No. They say the du'a."

"What is that?"

"It's supplication to Allah. Kind of recognizing that through Allah's provision, there is food. Before every meal, they say, 'Bis m'Allah wa'laa barak t'Allah,' which means, 'In the name of Allah and with the blessings of Allah.'"

Lynda frowned. "Do they bow their heads?"

"Not really. Cup your hands like this." Emma made the motion. "Just kind of look down." She took a sip of her soda. "And after every meal, they say, 'Alhamdulillah il-lathi at'amana wasaqana waja'alana Muslimeen.'"

Lynda's eyes widened, and Emma said, "But you can just say, 'Alhamdulillah,'" which means, 'Praise be to Allah.'"

Emma's voice rolled through the words naturally. Lynda barely recognized a syllable. "How am I going to pull this off?" she whispered.

Peña leaned around Emma. "It's just education. Memorize

it. Learn it. Practice it tomorrow morning at breakfast. I'll get with Sanders tonight and make sure he's schooled too, though he should be up to speed."

Emma added, "I'll write it down for you. It's not terribly hard."

Captain Norton and Bill approached, carrying trays. They sat across from her. Even though she kept her attention on Peña, in her peripheral vision she saw them pray over their food. Interesting. The Bill she knew didn't pray over food.

As soon as they raised their heads, Emma explained the du'a to Bill. He nodded and said to Lynda, "Will be interesting, don't you think?"

She opened her mouth, then closed it, trying to decide how she wanted to speak to him. Finally, she said what was on her mind. "It's going to be hard to do. How do we reconcile praying to another god before a meal?"

Bill cut his enchilada with his fork. "The Israelites sent spies into Jericho. Do you think they blended in as much as possible, or do you think they stood out as aliens?"

The muscles on the back of her neck tightened. Bill was the last person with whom she wanted to have a conversation about a biblical perspective. Well, any conversation at all. But she contemplated the question. "I think the term 'spies' probably answers that for me."

"Exactly." Norton pointed his fork at her. "I don't think you have to worry about saying the du'a at mealtimes. God knows what we're doing and why."

Lynda sat next to Agent Cartridge and watched him type. He filled in the holes of the couple they'd created for this mission. Since Sergeant Ibrahim would not pose as her husband, he had to be wiped from the generated social media account and Bill inserted.

As Agent Cartridge placed Bill's face in the wedding portrait and adjusted the size and shape of the groom, Lynda shook her head. "You are amazing, sir."

Agent Cartridge typed a little more, his head moving up and down to some tune she couldn't hear. After about ten more strokes, he paused long enough to pop the headphone off the ear closest to her and ask, "What?"

She smiled. "I said you're amazing."

He put the headphone back on and kept typing. "I just know what I'm doing," he said, casually dismissing her genuine praise.

She patted him on the back. He flinched away, and for the first time, his hands paused. He didn't look at her and remained motionless. She held up her hands, and as soon as she stood, he went back to typing.

When she turned around, Agent Lewis looked up from her laptop. "Try not to touch Mason. He doesn't like physical contact."

"I picked up on that."

"Is Sergeant Sanders clear on the mission?"

"Seems like. I know his team has been working with him all day." She thought about the praying before eating and said, "My biggest concern is that a little mistake will give me away. For instance, did you know that in occupied France, they could detect the British spies by the way they poured their tea? I don't want to pour my tea the wrong way and end up throwing the mission."

Agent Lewis shut her laptop. "The good news is you're

not going to insert yourself into their world. If that were the case, we'd have Emma Peña take that position. What you're doing is just being present so you can see who comes and goes. If it fails inside the mosque, we can always put you outside as a tourist and change your appearance every day so no one suspects."

Lynda screwed her face up. "It will be much easier from inside."

"Exactly."

The door opened and Agent Smith entered. "Kuwait authorities approved the visas. The only thing is that Lynda's passport photo needs to be retaken."

She pursed her mouth. "Why?"

He tapped his head, and with wide eyes Lynda looked at Agent Lewis. "How did we not think of that?"

Agent Lewis gasped. "Your head is uncovered!"

Agent Smith gestured at the door. "I'll walk you to the State Department. They're waiting for you."

"I have to go by my room first and grab a hijab," Lynda said.

"Okay."

She and Agent Smith walked along the dirt road. The sun had set a couple of hours ago, and she looked up at the sky. "Outside of the city in Alaska, the sky is incredible. The stars feel like they're sitting on top of you."

He nodded. "I've seen it. But I think this is more amazing. Alaska has trees and mountains. There is nothing to stop your view in the desert."

At her room, he waited outside while she grabbed a hijab and found a light on an elastic band designed to go over her head.

She went back outside, and Agent Smith pointed at the light. "My daughter got one of those for summer camp last year. She was the hit in the dorm. I bet next year, they all have one of those."

They made three turns, then went down an alley in a completely new part of the base. By the time they got to the CHU that housed the State Department, Lynda had no idea of their location.

Agent Smith paused with her outside. "I have to go to a meeting. You good?"

She looked behind her and back at him. "Can you give me directions?"

"Sure." He gestured with his arm, and she had a sudden flashback to Damien Cisco pointing on the porch in Alaska. The entire time Agent Smith spoke, she didn't hear a word. "Okay?"

Mouth dry, heart pounding, she licked her lips. "Sure. Thanks." She watched him as he walked away and made a mental note to head in that direction when she finished here.

After getting the photo retaken, she walked out of the office, slipping the scarf off her head. She stared at the road options. She could literally go in any direction. Anxiety filled her stomach with butterflies. Which way? Twisting the scarf in her hands, she closed her eyes and tried to remember the angle at which they'd approached this building. With the image in her mind, she headed off in that direction.

A blanket of stars hovered above Bill. He lay on top of the aluminum picnic table and contemplated the vastness of the universe and the splendor of the Creator. He had seen a lot of the world, and the more he saw, the more he understood the magnificence of God. And the desert sky never failed to bring him to a humble place with Jehovah. The God who had created him and could name every hair on his head had created this entire universe and could count every grain of sand on every beach on every planet in every galaxy in that universe. And He loved him, Bill Sanders, and chose him. It overwhelmed Bill, filled him up until it bubbled out of him, and he wanted to shout out the news about his God.

The second he identified the sound of a footstep, his body tensed, and he quit looking at stars and naming constellations. He listened. Someone light, inexperienced in the dark, hesitant. He sat up and turned his head, spotting Lynda on the path. She had a light strapped to her head. He thought about silently moving out of her line of sight but stayed still. When the light crossed over him, she visibly jumped.

"Lost?" he asked.

She pulled the light off and rubbed at her hair. "They needed to retake my passport photo. Somehow I got turned around in the dark going back."

"Easy to do. All of the buildings are either Quonset huts, tents, or CHUs. Giant tent city."

"I've never been good at directions in enclosed areas. I love Alaska, because everything is wide open, and I can picture the maps in my head with a compass." She lifted a finger and made a spinning motion. "Little paths and alleys get me confused."

"I never would have put you in Alaska." He sprang from the table and lithely landed on his feet. He pointed in a direction about ninety degrees from the one she'd been headed.

"Go that way and you'll walk straight into the dining hall. Will you know where you are from there?"

"Yes." She looked up at him and coolly said, "Thanks."

"We all get turned around sometimes," he said.

Once she moved out of earshot, he took a deep, shaky breath. They could do this. They could live in a hotel room and pretend to be civil and married in a way that would fool anyone who decided to take a closer look.

She hated him. It radiated off her. When he'd talked to her in the chapel, he saw the anguish his words had brought into her life. It made him hate himself right along with her.

Tears sprang to his eyes, tears he hadn't let out in a decade. He bowed his head and said, "God, I know You've forgiven me. How about You lead the two of us to forgive me too. That would be awesome."

When he finished praying, he walked over to the medical facility. As he stepped into the trailer, he blinked to adjust to the bright fluorescent lights. He nodded to the nurse on duty. "I'm here to see Sergeant Ibrahim."

The nurse gestured in the proper direction, and Bill walked to a curtained area. He found Ibrahim reclined with his head slightly elevated and his eyes closed. He had an IV drip going into one arm and a pulse oximeter on his index finger. When Bill stepped into his area, Ibrahim opened his eyes.

"This is a fine way to get out of duty," Bill said, grabbing a chair from against the wall and pulling it closer to the bed.

Ibrahim's lips moved in a slow, languid smile, obviously affected by pain medicine. "I just wanted a few days off."

"You headed home?"

"Yeah. Tomorrow. Going to be a long flight."

"Maybe you can sleep most of the way. How are you feeling?"

"Like I got in a knife fight and lost."

Bill shook his head. "Man, didn't your mama tell you to never get in a knife fight with a surgeon?"

Ibrahim smiled but then sobered. "I owe you my life. Thank you."

"I'm just glad I came across you, or you'd still be lying there."

"Likely." He slowly reached over and picked up a plastic cup with a bent straw. It took him a couple of tries to get the straw to his lips. When he put it back down, he adjusted his covers, smoothing them out. "Now I get to go home to my children and wife, and she can pamper me and my life will be perfection for a while." His smile left no room to doubt his sincerity. "You're going in my place, I heard?"

"Yeah. I hate to bother you with it, but I wanted to know if you have any elements I need to borrow or if there's anything I need to buy. I've not done any research before today, and I figured it would just be easier to come to you and ask rather than do too much or risk too little."

"You shouldn't need anything special. Unlike Agent Culter, you can wear anything you want, and Western clothes are perfectly fine." With slow and careful movements, Ibrahim reached over to the cart next to the bed and retrieved a notebook. "You can get my cap out of my room. My kufi." He made a motion around his head. "You don't have to wear it, but probably half the men there will." He ripped off a piece of paper and held it out. "Some basic Arabic to help you with greetings and prayers. Gilligan wrote it out for me."

"Thank you."

"You mean, 'Shukran.'" Ibrahim closed his eyes. "I'll admit I wish I could do this mission. To stop someone from perpetrating violence from a holy place." He sighed.

Bill smiled. "I'll admit I wish you could do this mission." He stuck the paper in his pocket. "Take care. Enjoy Rania spoiling you."

He slowly opened his eyes and gave a lazy smile. "She's quite upset that this happened here. It will be good to go home so quickly."

Leaving Ibrahim to rest, Bill left the building. Outside, he let his eyes adjust to the total darkness again before walking through the compound, easily moving along the road and through the shadows. He went into a large Quonset hut to his team's recreation room. On one end, McBride and Waller watched a movie. Morita and Gill played Brock and Fisher at pool. Hanson and Rick sat over a chessboard, but they talked in low tones instead of playing. Bill felt safe approaching them. Anything they'd needed to discuss in private they would have done, well, in private.

"Gentlemen," Bill said. "Lovely night out there."

"You can see the stars like they're right on top of us," Hanson said. "It helps to imagine what they look like outside of our atmosphere. It's incredible."

"Maybe you should join Space Force."

Hanson snorted. "Yeah. Not likely. I'm afraid the Green Beret is a permanent fixture."

Rick lifted his chin. "Were you able to get caught up with Ibrahim?"

"Yeah. All set." He rubbed at his beard. "I saw Agent Culter on the path. She had an issue with her passport."

"Yes. Last news I had was that it's all copacetic now."

The way Rick managed information and the team, always somehow knowing exactly what was going on with everyone, impressed Bill. Rick had natural leadership abilities that definitely had him in the right job.

"Hopefully, we'll be able to leave tomorrow," Bill said.

Hanson grinned. "You gotta trust more, man." He stood. "Twenty-one hundred. You're about to see me turn into a pumpkin."

"Bah. It's only noon at home," Rick said. "You can start the day over again."

"Or I can call my wife before the kids get home from school." He wiggled his eyebrows, and Rick laughed. "Plus we left day before yesterday, right?"

Bill shook his head. "Dude. You can't ask me to do math when I've been up for thirty hours. It's not right."

Hanson slapped him on the shoulder as he left. Bill took his seat and said to Rick, "We'll see you in Istanbul, I guess."

Rick grinned. "Like you'll see us."

"Heh."

Rick paused. "You work things out to her satisfaction?"

He smiled slightly at the image of Lynda with the light on her head. "I would have said no, but then I saw her a little while ago and she didn't try to knife me in the kidney, so I think we'll make it." He rubbed the back of his neck. "Going to be a long mission, though."

"Well, it's probably no less than you deserve. In all honesty."

"Ouch. But at the same time, truth."

Rick leaned forward, his eyes full of respect and wisdom. "You need to forgive yourself, you know."

Bill hadn't expected Rick to attack it so directly. Pain

twisted in his chest. If he'd had more sleep, he could have battled it. Instead, he looked down, unwilling to let his friend see the emotion that wanted to wreck him from the inside out. "You say that, but I crushed that girl. And I did it to protect myself."

"You did what you knew at the time—what you learned out of your childhood environment. You didn't know Christ until after you got home. You're a completely new person from your soul forward, and you know that. So put off the old, put on the new, and forgive that self-centered man you used to be."

Bill stared at the chessboard, not seeing it. When he felt like he had control, he sniffed and raised his head, then waved his hand over the board. "Up for it?"

"Nah. I'm wiped. Hitting the sack."

"Okay, brother. See you at oh six for chow."

"Yep." Rick stood and said to the room, "Try to sleep, boys. Jet lag plus an early day could lead to mistakes."

On his way out, he stopped and squeezed Bill's shoulder, conveying what Bill already knew without a doubt. Rick had his back, whatever that meant he needed.

Long after he'd gone, Bill sat there, staring at the black pawn, curious about what the next few days would look like for him. Going into a mission with clear rules of engagement, weapons ready, strategy mapped out, and defined parameters never gave him a moment's pause. A mission like this one, rife with uncertainty and shadowy corners, made him uneasy out of the gate, an uncomfortable feeling for sure.

He knew he could pull it off, because his team relied on him to and he'd never let them down. But he would really love to take a pass on this one.

Bill closed his eyes, fatigue making them burn, and decided to quit thinking about it tonight. Tomorrow would bring its own challenges, and he never liked to borrow tomorrow's troubles.

He stood and said, "Good night, my brothers."

A chorus of farewells followed him out the door.

CHAPTER
★
SIX

DECEMBER 3

While Captain Norton gave the final set of instructions to his team, Lynda sat in the back row and made notations about any pertinent information she thought she'd need. Most of it didn't apply to her. She glanced at her watch. It was 7:13 a.m. The team would board a C-130 and fly to US base Izmir, then take different civilian transports to Istanbul. Incirlik would serve as their base of operations.

"If you're driving, we have lists of safe places to stop. Check your phones," Norton said.

That reminded Lynda that she would have to remove her biometric locks from all of her devices. If she were captured or killed, the bad guys would have no trouble unlocking her phone or laptop using her face or severed thumb. She pulled her phone out and changed the settings to require a password instead of a thumbprint.

Norton continued. "I sent the list of coordinates to you this morning. Those of you taking the train, you should have car rental reservations built into your itineraries."

She wondered why some would drive, since the trip would take about ten hours. She looked over at Agent Smith. "Why are they going someplace so far from the destination?"

He leaned closer to speak softly. "Only US base in Turkey. Well, there's one more, but it's only for NATO use. Politically speaking, Turkey and America are not best friends at the moment."

She'd known the mission would be covert, but she didn't realize that it would go down without the cooperation of the Turkish government. That certainly added another layer of tension to an already stressful situation.

Norton mentioned her in the briefing, pulling her attention away from Agent Smith. "Drumstick and Agent Culter will fly in today around fifteen hundred on a commercial flight out of Kuwait City. By the time they collect their bags and get checked in to their honeymoon suite—"

A couple of the guys in Bill's group laughed and clapped. One whistled at him. Lynda pressed her lips together to keep from smiling.

"—the first wave will be arriving." Rick pointed at Hanson. "You're taking point on the train."

Hanson nodded. "Check, Daddy."

The nicknames intrigued and amused her. Emma had explained most of them, though Lynda couldn't imagine why they called Captain Norton "Daddy." But Bill's "Drumstick" had such a perfect ring to it that she thought she might just start calling him that.

Norton held up an envelope and looked at Bill. "I have

your new passports. State did a fine job on them." He tossed one of the envelopes at Bill, who caught it almost casually, then looked at Lynda. "Agent Culter, I have yours here too."

She lifted her chin so he knew she heard him.

He gestured at Emma. "Selah, you and Peña are booked on the same flight as Drumstick and Culter. You're also in the same hotel. We want you in the front of the plane, so you two get to fly first class."

This elicited catcalls and boos among the laughter of camaraderie. Peña held up his hands. "Guys! Guys! Someone has to take on the tough assignments while you guys get all the cushy jobs."

Norton grinned and looked at his watch. "Wheels up in twenty. Any alibis? Good. Go."

Bill's team stood as one and picked up their duffel bags before filing out of the room. Agent Smith left with them.

Norton approached Lynda. "You have a driver's license and two credit cards in your married name, Lydia Ahmed. Your passport has stamps showing you and Drumstick traveling from your home in Alabama to Saudi Arabia. You visited the holy cities there. Then you drove to Kuwait and spent the last week here, and now you're off to Istanbul."

She took the envelope from him and felt the passport inside. She knew the backstory because she'd been the one to put it together. "Thanks." She pulled a manila envelope out of her leather folder. "Here is my FBI ID, passport, personal cards, and such."

"And your cell phone. We have one coming for Mrs. Ahmed."

She should have thought of that. She pulled her cell phone out of her pocket and added it to the envelope.

"I'll keep them safe on me until you need them." As he slipped the envelope into his briefing folder, he held up a finger. "I have something else for you." He reached into his pocket, pulled out a ring box, and opened it, revealing a simple band of gold.

She frowned. "I beg your pardon?"

"On behalf of Drumstick Sanders, will you be his wife in public from this day forward until this mission ends?"

Feeling foolish, she laughed and took the box from him. "Of course. Sorry."

Bill walked up to them. Unlike the rest of his team, he wore civilian clothes. He had on a pair of khaki pants and a black T-shirt that stretched tight over his well-muscled chest. She looked away from him, wishing she hadn't noticed his physique.

Norton handed him a ring box too. He opened it, hooked the ring with his thumb, snapped the box shut, and tossed it back to Norton, who caught it fluidly without even glancing up. Bill slipped the ring into his pocket.

Lynda cleared her throat. "Captain, can I ask you a perhaps odd question?"

"You're free to ask me any question," he said. "But you only have twenty seconds because I have a plane to catch."

"Why do they call you Daddy?"

"Ah," he said with a wink. "SF tradition. I'm the team leader, the team daddy. Every team has one."

"Oh. Okay. That makes sense, thanks." She waited as Bill and Norton shook hands and Norton left, then she turned to Bill. "I have to meet with my team."

He replied with a stoic expression. "Right. See you at nine."

Following the directions she'd written down the day before, she headed to her team's CHU provided by DHS. She gave her name to the guard inside and signed the logbook. Then she walked past several towers of computers and through another door into an office where Agents Lewis, Cartridge, and Smith waited for her.

"All set?" Agent Lewis asked.

"All set." Lynda held up the thick envelope. "Captain Norton had my new IDs."

"Perfect." She gestured at the ring box that Lynda carried. "And the ring. That's great. They have tracking devices in them."

Lynda raised an eyebrow. "Seriously?"

Agent Cartridge slipped the headphones off his ears. "Seriously." He handed her an e-reader. "This has all of your mission briefs on it to read on the plane. When you get to Istanbul, push this button three times," he said, pointing. "The briefs will disappear, and a collection of murder mysteries will take its place."

This technology was fun. She felt like 007. "Thanks."

"It's a permanent deletion, so make sure you want it to happen." He held out a thin laptop. "Do you know how to use the portal?"

He meant the portal to her files on the FBI servers, she assumed. "Of course."

"Well, on your issued computer, I'm sure there's an icon you can click that will take you there. But on this one, you have to go to a command prompt and access it that way." He held out a sticky note. "I've written down the access for you, but it would be best if that note didn't get into the wrong hands. I'm sure you've already been briefed, but never use biometric locks."

"Right." She looked at the command stream and thought the logic in it would make it easy to memorize. "Okay."

"The rest of the time, the computer will look like it belongs to a typical American woman. Social media sites, shopping sites, email to all of your fake family and friends—that kind of thing."

"Wow. You've been busy."

"It's my job, you know." He stared at the floor.

Not wanting him to think she'd intentionally offended him, she said, "And you do it remarkably well."

"Just my job." He looked at the whiteboard behind him. She glanced back and saw a checklist for everything he'd addressed with her.

"Do you have a phone for her?" Agent Lewis asked.

"Yes." He handed it to Lynda. "It's set up for Mrs. Ahmed. Password is your badge number. No outbound calls. If there's some message we need to get you, we'll call you. I'll be in the warehouse in Turkey to provide technical support. That's it. Unless you have questions. I answer questions, provided they are, in fact, questions."

"No questions. Just gratitude," Lynda said.

Agent Cartridge turned his chair away, effectively shutting her out.

"Agent Smith will be your favorite uncle." Agent Lewis smiled. "We'll be local. My sources are setting up a home base in a warehouse on the river. We're also setting up a separate facility to house any prisoners. Once we secure the members of Green War, you'll have a place to take them. Captain Norton has those details and locations."

"So, this is it." Butterflies came awake in Lynda's stomach.

She gathered the phone, computer, and e-reader. "Guess I'll see you in Turkey."

★ ★ ★

ISTANBUL, TURKEY

"What are you reading?"

Lynda looked over at Bill. She held up the thin device. "An e-reader."

He raised an eyebrow. "Well, duh. I mean, what are you reading?"

"Oh." She held it out to him. Agent Cartridge had formatted the information on her screen to look like a novel in case someone glanced over her shoulder. She watched Bill's face and could tell when he realized it.

"Guess that's better than a stack of files," he said.

"Well, the jury's out. But it's more discreet. Right now, I'm just reading." She hit the button three times. "And now it's deleted in time to go through customs and security, and a murder mystery featuring a female detective in 1945 New York City is in its place."

"Fancy."

The flight attendant came by, collecting any trash before landing. Lynda handed her the empty miniature water bottle and a napkin, then pulled up an actual book on the e-reader. She scrolled to about two-thirds of the way through it, saved her place, and closed the e-reader, just in case someone checked it. After she slipped it into the pocket of her bag, she looked out the window and watched the shoreline of the Black Sea as they approached the airport. She expected a hum of nerves that had been present for two days, not this sense of calm covering her like a cloak. She felt like she could think clearly, observe, process. As she raised her seat back, she closed her eyes and said a silent prayer of thanksgiving for the clarity.

For three hours, she and Bill had sat next to each other and hardly spoken a word. She fiddled with the simple gold band on her left hand and had a passing memory of a conversation they'd had in the beginning of their sophomore year of college, weeks before Bill got injured. He'd told her he loved her, alluded to a future together.

She looked down at her hand, at the glint of sunlight on the band. What would have been different in her life if he'd stayed? Would they have gotten married? She looked at him out of the corner of her eye. The way he'd treated her after he got hurt made her glad that they hadn't stayed together. She wondered how much he'd matured emotionally in the last ten-plus years.

He turned his head and caught her stare. Instead of reacting, she simply turned to look out the window. He radiated intensity in a way that almost intimidated her. He always had. She knew a lot of it had to do with the coming mission, much like it had been with a coming game, but it didn't make her less aware of it. She had a feeling that no matter what this case brought to bear, Bill could handle it. Nothing about their history suggested that, but something about his countenance now gave her that impression.

She wanted to find out why he did this for a living, what had drawn him to Special Forces, what mental process had led him here, but she couldn't do it now. They both knew that their conversation, however low they kept it, could be heard by any number of people around them. While they waited to land, she mentally worded and reworded questions to ask if the opportunity ever presented itself.

The noise of the landing gear deploying briefly overtook any other sound, and the pitch of the engines changed. She glanced over at Bill again. He had his eyes closed and gripped his armrests. The knuckles on his hands looked white. Sweat beaded on his forehead.

"What's wrong?" she asked.

He opened one eye and looked at her, then at the window beyond her. "I hate landing."

Wondering if she should comment on the fact that he jumped out of airplanes on a regular basis, she slid the screen down on the window so he couldn't see the ground rushing up to meet them.

They took their time getting off the plane. Customs provided no issues. She felt a little silly about all the preparations they'd made to go through it. The officer stamped their passports, asked simple questions, and directed them through the appropriate gate.

Outside, they met up with Emma and Peña. The two men traded glances while the women hugged.

"Let's find a taxi," Emma said.

"How was first class?" Bill asked sarcastically.

"My butler was adequate, but we had to fire the downstairs maid," Emma said.

Their taxi pulled up, a beat-up four-door Toyota built at least thirty years earlier. The taxi driver loaded their bags.

Emma asked, "English?" He shook his head, and she said, "*Arabi*?"

He nodded and spoke to her in Arabic. She replied, and

they piled into the back of the cab, Emma on Peña's lap so they'd all fit.

As the driver shot out into traffic, Peña patted Emma on the thigh. "You don't speak Turkish?"

"Not enough to make sure the driver gets us to the right place." She adjusted the bottom of her hijab. "But I bet I speak better Turkish than you."

"You assume. You've never asked."

Bill chuckled. Since Lynda sat pressed up against him, she felt it more than heard it.

It didn't take long to get to the hotel. They'd chosen an American brand within walking distance of the mosque so they could come and go with ease. After they piled out of the taxi and the driver unloaded their bags, they walked through the revolving door into the luxurious blue-and-gold lobby. A spicy smell filled the air. Fresh flowers adorned the tables.

Lynda and Emma sat on a curved blue-and-gold couch while the guys checked them in. Emma looked at her watch. "Prayer time is in just under two hours."

Lynda scanned the room, glancing over people, appreciating the different culture here that she'd never had a chance to absorb before. "Perfect. Get settled, walk over."

Bill approached, a cardboard sleeve with key cards in his hand. He held it up. "Ready?"

"I am." Lynda stood and slipped the strap of her bag over her shoulder.

As the elevator took them to the twelfth floor, her stomach started to dance with nerves. For the next however many days, she would have to spend a lot of time alone with Bill. She wondered if it would have been any easier with a complete stranger but decided it would not.

He led the way to their room. After he opened the door, she waited one heartbeat, then another, before she walked in.

They had a suite with a separate bedroom decorated in the same lavish golds and blues that adorned the lobby. A smoke-colored glass table sat in front of a blue-and-gold-striped couch. A matching blue chair completed the living area. The kitchenette had a full-sized refrigerator and a small table that sat two. Beyond a glass door, patio lounge chairs flanked a table under a blue canopy and looked out toward the shining white-domed roof of the mosque and the flanking towers standing sentry. The bedroom had a queen bed with a gold-and-cream brocade cover. A cream chaise lounge sat at the foot.

Lynda wandered into the bedroom and set her bag on the bed as Bill followed her. She slipped the head covering off and set it on the dresser.

"It'll be nice to be here for a while," he said. "I'm looking forward to seeing the city."

She frowned and looked at him, and he held a finger to his lips. He set his backpack on the bed, pulled out a video camera, and pushed two buttons on it. A little door opened to reveal a rectangular device. He turned it on, then walked around the suite, running it over lamps, curtains, doorframes, and electrical outlets.

After several minutes, he said, "All clear," then put the device back into the video camera and returned that to the backpack.

"Why would you think they'd bug us?"

"Because it's an American hotel. You never know. Better safe." He pulled his phone out of his pocket. "I'll have to do that every time we come back from somewhere. Just so you know."

"Of course."

They spent the next few minutes unpacking. It felt strangely intimate to put her toiletries in the bathroom next to his. He had a dresser in the living room, where he'd sleep, and she used the dresser in the bedroom. Her hands had a slight tremor, and her breathing felt shallow. She needed that calm she felt on the airplane to come back to her.

Once she had done everything she could do in the bedroom, she went into the other room. In the kitchen area, she found an electric kettle and coffee and tea services. She filled the kettle with water and turned it on.

She could see Bill through the balcony window, so she crossed the room and slid open the door. He glanced at her before he looked out at the mosque again. He gestured with the phone in his hand. "Prayer time is in ninety minutes."

"Emma said that. What time do you want to walk over there?"

"I'll confirm with Peña."

"Do you want tea?"

He glanced down at her. "No, Lynda, thank you." His tone implied that right now they needed to focus on the mission and not niceties like tea.

Her lip curled as she spun on her heel and stormed back inside. Jet lag still moderately affected her, so she didn't feel the slightest guilt at helping herself to a cup of tea.

She slammed the cup on the counter harder than necessary, then ripped a tea bag out of the paper cover and sloshed hot water into the cup. She paced into the bedroom and sat down in a chair near the window. From this vantage point, she could see the mosque and, if she angled her head just right, Bill out on the balcony.

As she sipped her tea, she watched him send a text, then slip his phone into the cargo pocket of his pants and grip the railing of the balcony. Finally, he turned and went back into the hotel room. She heard the door sliding on the rail and the clink as it slid shut. Then he appeared in the bedroom doorway.

His mouth had formed a hard line. "So, me thanking you for offering tea causes you to get angry. Explain, please."

"I will not, because I'm not going to argue your tone with you. It would be pointless and exhausting." She dunked the tea bag up and down in the cup. "But I will ask if you think there's going to be this level of tension the entire time we're in this suite together. If that's the case, I'd like to prepare myself."

He crossed his arms over his chest and leaned against the doorway. The muscles in his arms bulged with the movement. "I would like to not have tension."

With a closed-lip smile she nodded. "Great. Let's make that pact." She gestured toward the window. "Were you texting your team?"

"Yes. They're on the road."

"And Peña?"

"Thinks we should start walking thirty minutes before prayer time."

"Probably wise." She took a sip of tea, watching him over the rim. "Anything else?"

"Yeah." He walked into the room and leaned his hip against the dresser. "Sorry if my 'tone' gave you the impression of anything other than the fact that I can't stand tea, and I processed that while trying to properly word a covert missive to my commander."

Embarrassment brought a flood of heat to her cheeks. "Oh. Okay."

"One other thing."

"Yes?"

He leaned down until she could almost feel his breath. "Whatever you think is going on in my mind, understand that it is nothing personal about you. Right now, I'm mission focused. I have other things to deal with than a December morning ten years ago."

She stared at him for several seconds, her heart pounding, until she finally cleared her throat and said, "Fine."

He straightened and started to walk from the room. "Glad we're fine."

After he left, she bowed her head and released a pent-up breath. "God," she whispered, "I need calm. I need center. Please help me."

CHAPTER

SEVEN

The mosque was exceptionally beautiful. The rich burnt orange–colored ceiling had gold accents. The same gold framed the arched windows and the screens that covered them. The design took Lynda's breath away.

She followed Emma through the women's entrance, mimicking the way Emma moved and carried herself. They removed their shoes, then went up the stairs into the women's prayer room. They'd gotten there early enough to secure a spot close to the black iron balcony so that Lynda could look over the railing. She stood in a corner, giving her a view of the entire floor below. When the prayer time began, she followed Emma's instructions and knelt on the markers on the carpet, remembering what to do with her hands and face, and when and how to do it. She could not see the men during the prayer. As soon as they finished, she stood and watched as they all milled around the room below.

She nodded hello to the women who made eye contact with her but did not try to communicate with anyone. She and Emma made their way downstairs as quickly as possible. Without being obvious, she tried to look at the face of every man she passed. When they reached Peña and Bill, she felt a little frustrated at the lack of success.

They went to a restaurant near the mosque and sat outside on the patio. Bill took a seat and pointed to the chair he wanted Lynda to occupy. In the US, he would have held her chair out for her, but in Turkey that would have stood out. Chivalry had never existed here.

Once she sat, he said, "This should give you the best view of the street."

With a nod, she focused on the foot traffic. She barely paid attention to the food they ordered and tried to casually take in everyone walking by. Very little conversation happened at their table, at least none that she really paid attention to.

At some point during the meal, a tone sounded on Bill's phone. He glanced at Peña and said, "They're here."

Peña nodded. "That's a relief."

Emma leaned close to her husband. She wore a purple hijab that made her brown eyes shine. Peña's coloring and her outfit helped them blend into the population. As they talked quietly, Lynda could see the love the two of them shared.

"Nice to know you're not the only backup, eh?" she said.

Peña looked around and nodded before he took a drink of his water. "In a word."

The waiter brought the check, and Bill pulled a folded stack of liras bound with a money clip from his pocket. He counted out the cash and handed it to the waiter, then they all stood.

He looked at Lynda. "Anything?"

She gave a brief shake of her head. "We'll try again tomorrow morning."

They walked back to the hotel. Lynda no longer felt conspicuous in the hijab. Traveling to Turkey, getting used to wearing it, she noticed a couple of stares in the various airports and sometimes on the base in Kuwait. Here she completely blended in. It fascinated her how much it detracted from her actual appearance. It hid the shape of her head and the color of her hair. She had enhanced her makeup and carefully lined her eyes. If she took the head covering and makeup off, no one would recognize her if they'd seen her today.

In the hotel lobby, they made plans to meet early to go to prayer at eight and to find some breakfast after. She and Bill walked to their room. As soon as the door shut behind them, she pulled the scarf off her head. Bill pulled out the bug finder and began sweeping the room.

Instead of trying to engage with him, she went into the bathroom and washed her face. Finally feeling like she could breathe again, she pulled her laptop out of her bag and took it into the front room. Bill sat outside on the balcony, having concluded his sweep.

She opened the computer and stared at the blank screen. She needed to type out her report for the day but couldn't compose her thoughts. She decided just to create a timeline of the day, from the briefing to the airport to the mosque. She made a couple of notes of key figures she'd seen during the prayer time and some of the women she'd observed in the prayer room. Before long, she'd written enough of a report to call it one, even if it wasn't in her normal style. Satisfied, she accessed her encrypted portal to the FBI server and submitted her report, then closed the laptop lid and stood, stretching.

Exhausted was too mild a word to describe her current state of being. Crossing multiple time zones in such a short span of time had thrown off her circadian rhythms. Her body had no idea of the time. Her stress level had ratcheted up three more notches, and the constant tension between her and Bill wore down any reserves of energy she had left. Determined to make a better go of it tomorrow, she went into the bedroom and shut the door.

She grabbed a pillow off the bed and put it on the floor next to the chaise lounge, then knelt on it. Propping her elbows on the lounge, she bowed her head and thanked God for the clarity and calm on the plane, then asked for guidance and wisdom on the mission. Then she said, "Please, God, release the hold on my heart as far as Bill Sanders is concerned. I want to forgive him without losing a part of myself in the process. I know from Scripture that Christ asked You to forgive the very soldiers who tortured and executed Him because He knew they didn't know what they were doing or why. I need to forgive Bill even if I don't understand why he did what he did to hurt me."

As she got to her feet, she heard the exterior door close. Frowning, she walked out of the bedroom and checked the patio twice. Bill apparently had left.

Her heart started pounding. What would she do if he didn't come back? Maybe he'd gone to Peña's room. She went back to the bedroom and grabbed the headscarf. She draped it over her head and tossed one end over the opposite shoulder. Gripping the neck of it to keep it from falling off, she dashed out of the room and ran to the elevator.

No one answered at Peña and Emma's room. Dejected, she went back to her room.

Likely, they'd gone somewhere to meet their team. Knowing that didn't make it easier to accept that she hadn't been invited along.

As she sat on the couch, she thought back to her and Bill's interactions. The times she'd maintained calm, so had he. Maybe if she treated him pleasantly, he would reciprocate and that would ease the tension. She could be the bigger person and make the change. Maybe it would stop the vicious cycle of anger and reactions, and now rejection.

Could she do it? Determined to try, she told herself no matter what, don't react, don't argue, don't accuse. Bill had made it clear that he was focused only on the mission right now, not the past. She needed to make that her focus too. She could treat him like she'd just met him yesterday in preparation for the mission, with a mutual respect born of a shared objective.

She would start with doing something for him. She had only ever seen him drink cola and water, so she called room service and asked for a six-pack of soda. About fifteen minutes later, a knock sounded at the door. She slipped the hijab on and answered it, accepting the drinks with a smile.

It felt good to put them in the refrigerator. Maybe Bill would accept her peace offering the way she intended it.

Bill had given it twenty minutes after Lynda went into the bedroom before he came in off the balcony. He glanced around, making sure all was in order, then grabbed the key card and left the room. He made his way downstairs and out into the street, blending into the crowds, and walked to the hotel three blocks away.

After making sure no one had followed him, he slipped into the staircase and ran up three flights of stairs. When he got to room 325, he tapped twice and waited. Almost immediately, Rick opened the door.

Bill slipped inside and spotted Peña sitting at the table with a steaming cup in front of him.

"Took your sweet time, Drumstick," Peña said. "I've been here twenty minutes already."

Bill shrugged. "Wanted to ensure Agent Culter got settled before I left. Didn't have the inclination to debate with her about coming alone." He didn't add that he also wanted some distance from her right now.

Selah came around the corner. "Why come without her?"

"Because she's not part of this team. Same reason Brown Shirt Smith isn't here," he snapped.

"I feel like there's more to the story of you two than you're letting on." Selah, the trained interrogator, raised an eyebrow, then quickly added, "But that's obviously none of my business."

"Obviously."

"Let's focus on the mission," Rick said, rubbing the back of his neck. "I'm tired and jet-lagged." He held out a holstered Sig Sauer P320 Nitron Compact to Bill. Out of habit, Bill pulled the slide back just enough to ensure a round had already been chambered, dropped the magazine to see that it held a full complement of rounds, then reloaded and safed the pistol. The action took just a few seconds. He then concealed the weapon under his shirt.

Rick handed Bill a box of ammo, which Bill tucked into

his backpack. "I already gave Peña Colada one. Selah has her standard arsenal of knives and her Glock. All set?"

Bill held out his hand. "I need a weapon and ammo for Agent Culter."

"Right." Rick gestured at the bedroom door. "Come with me."

Bill followed Rick into the bedroom. His friend shut the door and leaned against it, crossing his arms over his chest. "You need to vent or something? Maybe pray? You're practically vibrating with tension."

Bill let out a deep sigh. He did not want to vent or pray or do anything else. But Rick knew him better than any person on the planet. "I don't know if I can be in such close quarters with her."

Rick shook his head. "It's just the job, cupcake. Suck it up. We do jobs all the time. You think it was easy dragging an angry woman through the African jungle while you were dealing with a bullet near your heart?"

In an almost unconscious reaction, Bill rubbed his chest. He could feel the scar beneath his shirt. "Well, then you married her, so there you go. I have a really hard time with the disrespect Lynda shows me. It borders on contempt. I've had more than enough of that from women in my life."

"From what you told me, you earned her contempt, so you need to saddle up and ride it out, cowboy." Rick straightened and picked up a Glock subcompact off the dresser. He pulled the slide all the way back and then turned it toward Bill so he could see daylight through the empty chamber and magazine well. Rick then picked up a fully loaded extended magazine and slid it into the magazine well, chambered a round, and safed the weapon. He extended it to Bill grip first.

"Like Selah's," Bill said.

The weapon had a tan composite body and a black slide. It measured less than six inches and weighed less than twenty-four ounces fully loaded. Lynda should be able to hide it just about anywhere. Bill took the weapon and tucked it into his backpack without further inspection. He then accepted two extra loaded magazines and a second box of 9mm ammunition.

"Would praying about it help?" Rick asked.

"Probably." Bill rubbed his eyes. "I'll let you know tomorrow."

"Hey, man," Rick said in a quiet voice, "you need to get a handle on this. Right now, nothing is more important than the mission."

"I hear you." With the virtual arsenal in his backpack, he prayed no one would stop him on his way back to the hotel. "See you later."

"Much later. We don't want to risk meeting again in person while we're here."

"Yeah, you said that in the briefing yesterday." He knew what Rick didn't say. If he wanted to pray with his friend, he needed to do it now because the opportunity might not present itself again.

Rick stared at him for two heartbeats. "All right. I'll be seeing you, even if you don't see me."

He turned to open the door, and Bill said, "I appreciate your concern, brother. I really do. But I don't want to talk about it. I just need to process it and figure out a way to work past it."

"If anyone can, you can."

They stepped back out into the main room. Dave Morita

had joined them. Rick held up his hand in a casual greeting. "Mr. Miyagi, glad to see you made it."

Morita had been part of the team that took a train. "Thanks, sir," he said. "Anything to report?"

"Just that we are all in place."

"Yes, sir." Morita held his hand out to Bill. "How's married life?"

"Well, I'm sleeping on the couch already," Bill said with a forced grin.

Morita laughed and slapped him on the shoulder. "Begin as you mean to go on, brother." He looked at his watch. "I'm in a room with Brock in a hotel just east of here."

Rick checked his phone. "McBride and Swanson are there as well. Different floor."

"Yes, sir. We saw them coming back from dinner when we checked in."

"Good. Chief Hanson is at his hotel with Trout and Bourbon. He just texted and said he made it in."

"We were in the same train car." Morita looked at his watch. "With your permission, sir, I'll go get the report in."

"Yeah, knock that out."

"You have my local cell number if you need me."

As he left, Bill said, "It's weird to be using cell phones." In normal missions, cell phones were prohibited. They weren't secure forms of communication.

"It's okay for now, as long as we authenticate every time," Rick said.

As Bill headed toward the door, Peña said, "We'll walk with you." He looked at Rick. "Good night, sir."

"Good night, Lieutenant."

They went out of the hotel through the main entrance. Selah kept her arm through Peña's, walking slowly.

Bill's mind kept going back to the conversation with Rick. He rubbed his chest again. Earlier that year on a mission in Katangela, a jungle nation in Africa, he'd gotten shot—a lucky shot, really. The bullet entered his side, where his armored vest came together, and traveled through his lung and into his chest, lodging itself very close to his heart. Before he could fully heal from the surgery performed in a village clinic designed and stocked to deliver babies, his team had to make a harrowing journey through the jungle, over roads, down a river, and finally via helicopter. He remembered the feeling of utter helplessness and prayed he never found himself in that position again.

He looked up and realized he'd been in his head this entire walk. He needed situational awareness, to pay attention to his movements, instead of remembering a mission that had ended successfully almost a year ago.

In the elevator, he looked at Peña. "I'll see you tomorrow."

Peña and Selah stopped at their floor, and Bill lifted a hand. "Sleep well," he said, watching them walk down the hall.

On his floor, he got out of the elevator and fished his key card out of his pocket. As he swiped it, the door opened. Lynda glared at him, but he brushed past her.

"Where have you been?" she said.

"Connecting with my team." He pulled her weapon out of his backpack and extended it to her. "Here. Captain Norton brought you a present. It's loaded."

When she accepted the pistol from him, he was impressed when she cleared it by checking the magazine and the safety before focusing on him again. He held out the two extra magazines but not the box of ammunition. "We'll have to store our extra ammo in the room safe. Best we can do."

She accepted the magazines. "I realize I'm not in the clique, but a note saying you'll be back would be preferable to nothing."

Panic skirted her eyes. Nothing else about her countenance gave away how scared she'd obviously been. Contrite but unwilling to show it, he said, "Fair enough. Just remember that I will always come back. Always."

She snorted. "You say that, but you've left me before."

She turned to leave, and he grabbed her arm to keep her still. "Lynda, I already said I'm not playing college games with you."

Her eyes cleared, and a touch of temper replaced the panic. The index finger of her free hand moved from the slide of her weapon to the trigger. She may not have even noticed it. "Let me go," she said quietly. As soon as he relaxed his hand, she jerked free and stepped toward the bedroom. "I'll see you in the morning."

"Yeah," he said, his word reaching the just-slammed door. "You will. And the next and the next."

CHAPTER
EIGHT

DECEMBER 4

Lynda came out of her room at seven, dressed in a pair of khaki pants and a turquoise long-sleeved top, wearing a tan hijab with turquoise-and-purple flowers on it. A part of Bill worried how she would act, but she bade him good morning in a normal voice. Not normal like she normally hated him, but normal like a colleague with whom she had to conduct business. He wondered what had precipitated her complete change of attitude. But some instinct told him that if he asked about the change, it likely would cause the previous attitude to reappear, and he'd rather just keep it simple.

She went straight for the kitchen and added water to the kettle. "I know you said you don't like tea. Do you drink coffee?"

"No." He cleared his throat and tried to sound a little less abrupt. "I drink Coke or Pepsi or RC, or whatever dark cola is handy. I grew up on the Piggly Wiggly store brand, so I've learned not to be picky." He smiled. "As long as it's dark, sweet, and caffeinated."

She walked to the refrigerator and opened it. A six-pack of Pepsi cans sat on the shelf. Unexpectedly touched, he glanced at her as she grabbed one and held it out to him.

"Thanks. Appreciate that." He accepted it from her, and the sound of the carbonated air releasing when he popped the top made his mouth water. "That means a lot to me."

"I determined yesterday that I would get along, not react. Last night, I immediately reacted. I apologize."

Nothing in her eyes or expression suggested anything but sincerity. "I accept your apology," he said.

She smiled and started to tug on her ear, then awkwardly lowered her hand when she encountered the silk scarf. Bill watched her make herself a cup of coffee, enjoying the way she moved. He could tell the head covering bothered her, that it inhibited the way she maneuvered around the kitchen.

After she poured hot water over the instant coffee, she added a packet of sugar and some cream, then carried her drink outside. He followed her out onto the balcony. The sky had turned a deep indigo, but the stars had disappeared as the city slowly came awake. The world felt still in preparation for the coming dawn.

"The mosque is such a beautiful building." She took a sip of her coffee, looking at the building's exterior lights shining just a few blocks away.

"Did you know it's the first mosque to have a woman design the interior?" he asked, perching on one of the chairs.

She turned and smiled. "I did. Discovered that during my

research. I think that explains the openness of the women's prayer room, don't you?"

"Probably."

For the next several minutes, he watched Lynda work her way through the morning, mentally preparing herself for the mission. He appreciated her diligence. And he'd really appreciated the subtle clues from Peña during yesterday's prayer time. As much as he'd learned and practiced, when he was in the crowd of men during prayers, it occurred to him how little he knew about this religion.

He sipped his soda and checked his watch. "We need to head downstairs."

"Yup."

Making sure he had his room key, that his shirt didn't cling to show the outline of the gun at his back, and that he had his phone, he let Lynda precede him out the door. He studied her as she walked ahead of him to the elevator, trying to guess where she had hidden the tiny Glock but unable to find even a hint. They rode down in silence and stepped into the busy hotel lobby to find Peña and Selah waiting for them.

Bill shook hands with Peña. The smell of breakfast enticed him. "Ready?"

The sun had just started to tease the horizon when they walked out of the hotel. Despite the early hour, traffic already jammed the street. The smell of car exhaust and old cooking grease assaulted Bill's senses. A man on a bicycle buzzed by them. A restaurant employee lifted the wooden shutter for the storefront.

"Welcome to morning chaos," Peña said under his breath. "It wasn't like this yesterday afternoon."

"Everyone was probably exhausted from the morning," Selah said with a smile.

Lynda rubbed her arms. "I don't know why I thought it would be warm here."

Bill smiled. "You're from Alaska. How is forty cold?"

She batted her eyes at him. "Must be my cold heart."

He chuckled, which made her smile and caused her eyes to light up. "Must be."

At the mosque, Lynda and Selah left them and went to the women's entrance. He and Peña took their shoes off, then headed into the main hall. The sound of the prayer call being broadcast to the city filled the room. More people attended this morning than they'd seen yesterday. He wondered if that had to do with the time of day or the day of the week. He glanced at faces as they walked to their places, looking for a white man who might not belong, while also being careful not to look like that one white man who didn't belong. He never glanced back to the women.

He surreptitiously shifted his pistol to his hip so that when he got on his knees to pray, it wouldn't stick out of his back. The call to prayer came, and they faced Mecca, bowing and touching their foreheads to the ground. As he bent down and sat up, he realized he needed to do something different. Maybe a pocket of his cargo pants would provide better concealment? He'd have to work it out.

His phone vibrated in his pocket: two quick successive texts. He put his hand down with his thumb tucked under, giving Peña the cue that Lynda had signaled him. His neck muscles tightened and his vision tunneled. He wanted to spring to his feet and act, but he didn't know who or what had garnered the signal, so he just waited, his entire body taut, humming with energy.

Lynda stood next to Emma and scanned the faces of the men as they came into the room below. She heard Emma talking to someone and pulled her gaze off the crowd to focus on the woman next to them. She wore a coral-colored hijab that made her brown eyes shine. Lynda guessed she was maybe twenty-five. She carried a little girl in her arms.

Emma spoke in low tones to her. The woman didn't speak Arabic, but she spoke scattered English. She pointed at Lynda. "America?"

She smiled and nodded. "Alabama." Her team had agreed not to get too extreme in their background stories so they wouldn't trip up with the details. Keeping as true to her actual life as possible, she had created her cover identity. She pointed to her chest and said, "Lydia Ahmed."

The girl said, "Zehra." She patted the baby on the back. "Eylül."

Before they could speak more, the prayer call sounded. As they turned to face Mecca and begin their prayers, Lynda glanced down and froze. One of the men from Alaska walked next to another man. He wore a kufi, but she recognized the shape of his eyes and his pointed nose and chin.

Lynda excused herself and rushed out of the room before the prayers began. At the bottom of the stairs, she almost ran into the imam. He spoke Turkish to her, and she covered her mouth and belly as if sick. He made a disgusted scoffing noise and pointed toward the courtyard in the direction of the restroom.

Barefoot, she rushed out. As soon as she went into the bathroom, she shot Bill two texts. After a few minutes, she felt safe enough to go wait in the courtyard near the fountain. Making a quick stop to pick up her shoes, she headed that way. When people started coming out, she partially turned and kept her phone ready to snap pictures.

The man from Alaska slipped the cap off his head as he walked outside. He wore a dark-blue T-shirt and worn jeans. Lynda casually held her phone up to her ear, took a picture, and texted it to Bill. When the man broke away from his group, she followed him and managed to get two more pictures before he got into a car.

As she turned to go back to the building, Bill rushed up. "Red car," she said.

He lifted his phone to his ear and started talking as he walked to the parking lot. She gasped when he placed himself behind the car as it started to back out.

"Hey!" he yelled, slapping the trunk.

The car came to an abrupt stop, and the man angled his body out of the window. Bill spoke to him, the man waved, and Bill stepped out of the way. The man backed the car up, and as he drove off, Bill lifted a hand to wave at him. He turned and trotted back to Lynda just as Emma walked up.

"Did Peña get on his tail?" he asked Emma.

She nodded and pointed at a scooter turning a corner a block away. "Not sure who the scooter belongs to."

"We all have to sacrifice for the cause." He turned to Lynda. "Send us all the photos you took. Let's get back to the hotel."

★ ★ ★

Before Lynda could swipe her key card, the hotel room door opened, startling her. She stepped back, running into Bill's chest, and found herself staring at Captain Norton. She carefully placed her Glock back on safe and replaced it in the hidden slot in her purse. She barely remembered drawing it.

"Hello," she said, pushing away from Bill and past Norton. "You just let yourself in?"

"It wasn't that hard."

Bill looked at the ceiling and drew a circle with his finger. Norton shook his head. "I cleared the room." As the door shut behind Bill, he said, "Peña lost him. He got on the ferry to the Asia side. Peña couldn't get a ticket."

"Rush hour," Bill said. "Well timed."

"Left the car, though."

"Will a license plate help us here?" Lynda asked as she slipped the hijab off.

Emma had followed them into the room and said, "Only if we have a way to hack their database." She looked at Norton. "Do we have a way to hack their database?"

He shrugged. "There are cyber guys here from more than one agency. Pretty sure they could if we needed them to, but I'd rather wait. Peña is meeting Hanson and Fisher at the ferry parking lot to tag the car. Then we can follow it remotely."

Lynda's phone chirped. Since she'd put in the local SIM card, the phone hadn't made a sound. Even though she didn't recognize the number, she answered. "Hello?"

"How's my favorite niece, Lydia?" Agent Smith asked.

She held up her hand to silence the room. "Missing my favorite uncle."

"Check your email. I sent you some pictures from our trip."

"Oh, fun! I can't wait to see them." She hung up and tossed the phone onto the couch. She went into her room to retrieve her laptop from the safe in the closet. "Sounds like Smith has news," she said, coming back into the room and powering on her computer. "He wouldn't call unless it was major."

Bill frowned. "He wouldn't know we've made contact yet."

"No. I obviously haven't filed a report yet." She accessed the secure portal and logged into her email. Three files waited for her. The first one was about an explosion at a refinery in Venezuela, reporting seventeen dead and damages that required them to shut down the building. Another file contained photos of the area around the explosion.

Bill looked over her shoulder. "Where?"

"Carabobo. An hour ago." She zoomed in on a photo. "They arrested one of the perpetrators. The other died." The edge of a piece of metal showed a streak of green spray paint.

An instant message from Agent Lewis popped up on her screen.

See the paint? Likely the Green War tag.

Lynda looked up at Norton. "Refinery explosion in Venezuela. Seventeen dead, including one of the bombers."

He crossed his arms over his chest. "So, Agent Culter sees one of our targets in the mosque, and then an attack happens halfway around the world. That timing is too good to be coincidence."

"I don't believe in coincidences," Bill said. "I think you nailed it. He was there to coordinate the attack."

They all were silent for a few moments. Lynda looked through the photos but didn't see another possible Green War tag. Unfortunately, it was after midnight in Venezuela, and all the photos were dark or distorted from the flash.

"I'm going to get with State and send Hanson and Fisher to the Asia side," Norton said. "We have a photo. State might have some friendly assets on that side. They can monitor the ferry traffic. You all keep going to the mosque. He may be back, or there may be more." He looked at Lynda. "Good work, Agent."

She simply nodded, but inside she smiled. As Norton slipped out the door, she replied to Agent Lewis's message.

> It depends on how they identified tanks and such at their site. Might be coincidence. If we have someone there, then that's easily discovered. As soon as it's light outside, I'd like pictures of everything in the parking lot as well as any surrounding structures. Anything on social media?

Emma sat at the table. "Looks like the mosque was the right call."

"Looks like." Bill leaned against the counter. "Will hubby call you or just show?"

Lynda read Agent Lewis's reply as she listened.

> You've got mail. Photos and early witness reports. I'll keep sending more as we authenticate and attribute.

"I imagine he'll show here." Emma looked at her phone. "It's nine. Do you want me to go to the bakery downstairs and get us some food?"

As soon as she said that, Lynda realized how hungry she was. Her body still worked to adjust to the different time zone. Skipping breakfast wouldn't be a great idea. "That would be amazing."

Bill nodded. "Thanks."

Lynda went back to the email and found the third file. It showed the man who had been arrested and his deceased partner. "So young," she said. "What a waste." She messaged Agent Lewis again.

> I don't recognize these perps. Either they weren't in Alaska or they were kept out of my sight.

After a brief moment, she had a reply.

> Didn't think you would. Suspect is typical of the others. Indoctrinated. Thought he was doing the world a favor.

Lynda sat back and was about to rub her eyes before she remembered the heavy makeup. She settled instead for pressing her fingers against her forehead. "How can someone convince these college kids to blow things up? They're not violent. They're not even fringe thinkers. They're kids who get folded into the idea of leaving a better earth than what they started with. How does that equate to explosions and death?"

"There's no reason to think they knew people would die," Bill said. "The average college kid doesn't know bombs or explosives, or the destruction that can possibly happen with even a small amount of ordnance. They just know what Hollywood and video games have taught them. Maybe they thought they were just doing enough damage that production would stop for a single day, and they could then claim to have saved the earth by an inch or two." He shrugged. "I don't know."

Notifications came with more pictures. Lynda spent the next several minutes studying them closely, zooming in, zooming out. Emma came back with cheese and bread, and Lynda ate without paying attention to the food as she dug deeper into the pictures. She tried to zoom in on a truck in the parking lot, but it pixelated too much. Finally, she sent Agent Lewis a message.

> Sending this back for analysis. Looks like this truck's right front tire may have the painted tag.

Hours later, Lynda stood and stretched. At some point, Peña had returned. "Hi," she said, rubbing her neck. "How is the tracking going?"

He pulled out his phone and accessed a screen, showing a map of sorts with a green dot. "If the car is theirs, we'll be able to track it. Hopefully it's not stolen." He slipped the phone back into his pocket. "So, another explosion on the day we see your guy in the mosque. What do you think the mosque has to do with it?"

Her computer chimed, so she glanced at the incoming message, then said, "We found the Green War symbol. It's confirmed." She focused on Peña again. "Lieutenant, I don't know that the mosque has anything to do with it. As far as we know, the guy is there every day for the morning prayer, then gets in his car and drives to the ferry to go to work in Asia. We cannot possibly begin to make assumptions yet."

He rubbed at his short beard. "You don't need to convince me. I'm not an investigator. I'm a man of action."

"And yet you're intelligence."

"Well," he said with a grin, "someone has to be the brains of this outfit."

Bill's laugh boomed around the room. "Yeah, that's what you are." He shook his head. "The point is, Lynda, that we do better when we have something to do. I honestly don't know how you can dig and look and dig some more until you form a hypothesis and then dig into that. I'd go crazy. But whatever you need from us, we're here." He looked at his watch. "And starving. I vote lunch, and maybe the team in Venezuela will have more information for you by the time we finish eating."

"Okay," she said. "Let me close this up." She sent a missive signing off, then logged out of the server and shut everything down. She secured the computer back in the safe in her bedroom, then grabbed her hijab. She checked her eye makeup and came back into the front room.

Emma and Peña went to the door. "We're going to have lunch in our room. I have some reports to write," Emma said. "We'll see you before the one o'clock prayer."

"See you then." Lynda put the hijab back on and strapped a small purse over her body. She walked to the door and waited for Bill to finish a text. "Did you let Captain Norton know about the confirmation intel?"

"Yeah. He wasn't surprised." As they walked down the hall, he asked, "What are you hungry for?"

"Shawarma and pita," she said. "My mouth is watering just thinking about it."

His grin was infectious. "Well then, let's get you fed, wife."

CHAPTER

★

NINE

DECEMBER 8

Bill sat at the table, a lukewarm can of cola at his elbow, and scribbled in his journal. He had just finished reading the book of Judges on his Bible app. While he wrote, he tried to process the imagery, the emotion, the raw humanity that the book projected. His heart hurt at the things he personally knew about savagery, desperation, and hate. He needed to find a way to word it all.

He also needed to find the fortitude to continue day after day with Lynda Culter in close proximity. She had warmed up to him, and the feelings he'd had for her in college had come back full force. He remembered how much he'd enjoyed watching her brain work. She now spent hours a day investigating pictures, reading reports, analyzing all of the data. It made his neck hurt just to watch her sit so still for so long. He had a feeling that half the time, she even forgot about his presence.

Every morning around eight, every afternoon after lunch, and every evening before dinner, they went to the mosque. Every other day they went to a popular tourist location so they could return to the hotel sunburned and sweaty and carrying bags, continuing the facade of an American couple visiting the Holy Land.

They had spent five nights in the hotel. If they had to stay another two days, they'd have to find a different hotel. Any longer than that in the same location, even a tourist spot as active as Istanbul, and they would start drawing too much attention. Fortunately, they had plenty of hotels from which to choose and a certain anonymity due to the heavy tourist trade.

He finished writing, venting his angst onto the page. When he capped the pen, he felt calmer, more in control. He picked up the leather-bound journal and slipped it into his backpack as Lynda came out of the bedroom. She wore a pair of white jeans, a long-sleeved white T-shirt, a denim jacket, and a pink hijab with blue-and-white flowers on it draped around her neck. Over the last several days, he'd gotten used to seeing her like this.

"Good morning," she said, her lips gleaming with lip gloss. "How was your night?"

"Restless." He dug through the dresser and grabbed clothes. "I'm not sure how much longer they'll keep us here." He walked to the bathroom door. "I'm going to take a quick shower."

Usually, he finished getting ready for his day long before she woke up. He had spent way more time than normal

journaling today. He'd found over the years that the journal
helped him analyze his thoughts and focus his prayers. He'd
started doing it right after he joined the Army. While he lay
in his barracks room, he would fill page after page of legal
pads he purchased at the military supply store. When he
finished filling a pad, he'd destroy it.

He still did that. His journals were to help him sort his
thoughts, not to be read later. The idea that some of the extremely personal things he'd written over the years would
make it to someone else's hands made it easier to destroy
the journals. But he did it in a cathartic way, thanking God
for the process as the pages burned in a fire.

After his shower, he realized that he'd grabbed a shirt with
his Special Forces unit insignia blazoned across the back. He
didn't even know how he'd managed to pack that. It must
have already been in the bottom of his duffel bag when he
transferred everything to his suitcase. Irritated, he globbed
toothpaste onto his toothbrush, then ripped open the bathroom door.

Lynda sat at the table, her laptop open. When he stormed
out, she looked up at him. Her gaze roamed over his chest,
and her eyes widened. She was staring at the ugly, jagged
scars there. At least he had a toothbrush hanging out of his
mouth so he didn't have to say anything to her. He shoved
the SF shirt deep into his suitcase, went to the dresser and
pulled out an insignia-free shirt, and headed back to the
sanctity of the bathroom.

He finished brushing his teeth and gripped the counter,
looking into the mirror. He glared at the thick scar that the
bullet had made on his ribs and the long, jagged scar on his
chest where Cynthia, an obstetrician, had cut him open to get

at it and save his life. In the mirror he met his own eyes, steeling himself to face Lynda's questions. Finally, he knew he'd dallied long enough and went back out in the main room.

Instead of asking him what happened or how it happened, she simply asked, "When were you shot?"

The simplicity of her query stopped him. "This past February. Nearly a year ago." Absently, he brushed his thumb over the scar on his chest, feeling the ridge on his skin through his shirt. "In Katangela."

"Wow. In the chest. How scary." She closed her laptop and stood. "Were you already a follower of Christ when it happened?"

The question threw him off-balance. "Why?"

She laced her fingers so tightly together her knuckles turned white. "I, well, I'm sorry to pry. I just wanted to talk about it. I, uh . . ." She pulled the hijab off and ran her fingers through her hair. Then she started twisting and squeezing the scarf. "I wondered how you felt."

He frowned. "Felt?"

Unexpectedly, tears filled her eyes.

He stepped toward her, completely confused. He tried to answer her question as honestly as possible. "It hurt. The whole time."

She quit wringing the scarf to death and looked at him. "In May, when I was taken captive by Green War, they had me tied up. They were threatening us. Poured gasoline on us."

He waited a reasonable amount of time before prodding. "Us?"

"Me and my partner, Jack. We were there together, serving a warrant. One moment we're standing on the front porch supposedly getting directions to the proper house, and the next moment I wake up with a killer headache and we're tied to chairs in a barn."

His heart started beating a little faster. Despite his knowledge of what happened, he hadn't allowed himself to think about it on any level. Now she was forcing him to. Anger sent little shocks through his system, making his hands tingle and his mouth go dry. "What happened?"

"They wanted us to read a statement. Jack didn't hesitate to say no. They threatened him, beat him, hit him in the knee, doused him with gasoline, dragged him out of the chair." Her breath hitched. "And then just shot him. Dead. And they set his body on fire." A single tear escaped her eye. "When they turned to me, pointed the shotgun at me, I knew they were going to tell me to read this statement they'd prepared about the tyranny and destruction of capitalism. I didn't want to, but I thought I might just to live a little longer. I knew they would kill me either way. I'm still not sure what I would have done."

He moved toward her before he could stop himself. As if of their own accord, his hands started rubbing up and down her arms. "What makes you say that?"

She stared up at him, her eyes wide, filled with pain. "I was just frozen. Jack was laying there dead, burning, and Damien Cisco turned to me and I was just stuck. What was I going to do? Did I have the courage to stand up to him? To take the beating and the gasoline? To get hit in the kneecap? I'll honestly never know."

"How did it end?"

"We had called for backup, but we were a long way from any kind of civilization. It took them a while to get there. As he started coming toward me, the police arrived. The men escaped and left me there." She swallowed, seeming determined to beat the emotions back. "I was tied to a chair and couldn't get to Jack. His body was burned completely by the time they put out the fire."

Instinctively, he pulled her to him. He hadn't held her in over ten years, but she fit as perfectly as she had before. Her body quivered and she hesitated before putting her arms around him, but once she did, she gripped him like her life depended on it. For several moments, they stood like that. Finally, he stepped back and set her away from him. She hadn't cried or wailed, but her face looked wrecked.

Quietly, he said, "I've faced death more than once. The first time, I couldn't sleep for weeks. I just kept thinking, you know, what if I'd died? The more I thought about it, the more I was able to separate myself and analyze it. What if I *had* died? Then what? What does the Bible say about that? Am I ready to face Jehovah and meet Christ? Eventually, I realized that yes, I am. That removed the fear of death. Not the respect of it and the desire to live, just the fear." He cupped her face with his hands. "You are here. You're here ready to face the men who did that to you. I think you know deep in your heart that you would have stood up to them. It takes a special kind of courage to do what you do. Even if you're not sure about before, I think you know your own certainty now."

Before she could reply, a knock sounded at the door. He hesitated, not wanting to break the contact but knowing he had to. Lynda escaped into the bathroom as he let Peña in.

"Morning," Peña said. "Emma's on the way."

"Got a text from Daddy," Bill said. "He wants to see us sometime today."

Lynda came out of the bathroom with all signs of distress

gone from her face. She looked normal—alert and relaxed at the same time. She'd put the hijab back on and freshened her makeup. "Good morning. Any movement on the car?"

"No."

She sighed. "I feel like we're missing something here."

"We're going to meet with the captain later today. We'll know what the plan is by dinner."

A tap on the door brought Selah. She carried two coffees and handed one to Peña. "We ready for morning prayers?"

Lynda slipped the strap of her purse over her head and put her room key into the side pocket. "Let's do this."

Lynda sat across from Bill. They had a corner of the restaurant to themselves. They'd come for an early dinner to avoid the crowds.

Since their conversation that morning, the dynamics around them had shifted. The underlying hostility and anger that had become more muted over the course of the week had faded away. She felt a tinge of embarrassment at her reaction upon seeing his scars. Despite analyzing it all day, she still didn't know what had possessed her to ask him those questions. Perhaps the realization that another man she once loved had faced death too?

As soon as she made certain no one could overhear them, Lynda asked, "What did Norton say today?"

"The powers that be don't want us to be here much longer, but Selah convinced them that tomorrow is an important day for the mosque."

She broke off a piece of pita bread and dipped it in tabouleh. She enjoyed the bite of flavor in the fresh parsley and garlic.

Tomorrow was the weekly service for the mosque, more than just prayers. "So if the men haven't come to the prayer times, they might come to the Friday service?"

"Right." He used his straw to move a chunk of ice around in his drink. "But I don't know how we can put them off much longer after tomorrow."

"We should give it one more week."

"I agree. However, Norton is answering to people with much higher rank than mine. I'm just the grunt who follows orders."

She lifted her chin. "I haven't heard such orders."

With a chuckle he asked, "So you'd stay even if DOD pulls us out?"

Deflated, she looked down. "Probably not. Unless it was to take pictures so that someone other than me knows who we're looking for."

"I think we take one day at a time." He looked over her shoulder and lifted his chin, indicating that the waitstaff approached their table from behind her.

"I want to go to the hippodrome tomorrow," she said in a normal tone of voice.

"There isn't much to see there."

"I know. But I can't go back and face my mom unless I've seen it."

She sat back as the waiter placed a plate in front of her. She waited until Bill got his, then followed his lead as he went through the motions of giving thanks for the food. In her heart, she prayed and thanked God for His provision. Then she picked up her fork and speared a falafel.

Once the waiter had left, she lowered her voice again. "If only that car would move. Then we'd have more data."

"Any more news come through on your end while I was out today?" Bill asked.

"They traced the email with the go order back to the mosque again. Same as before." She pursed her lips. "I'm beginning to wonder about that. There's no attempt to hide it. Why do you think that is?"

The muscles on his neck tightened. "You think they're intentionally pointing at the mosque?"

"I don't think anything. I'm simply pondering the question." She put the falafel on a section of pita bread, then topped it with a creamy garlic sauce and a pickled turnip. She took a bite, the strong flavors complementing each other in a very pleasant way on her tongue. After washing her food down with a minty lemon tea sweetened with honey, she speared another falafel. "It's dangerous to make assumptions right now."

He plucked an olive out of a small bowl and popped it into his mouth. The way he stared at her with his dark eyes made her heart beat faster. "I kind of like the lack of hostility," he said.

Heat flooded her cheeks. "Maybe I should have cried on your shoulder earlier."

He gave her a quick, infectious grin. "Maybe." Then his face sobered. "I don't know why they're not hiding it. Maybe they don't realize we can track that kind of thing."

"I think someone with this kind of organization would know." She added some of the parsley salad to the falafel. "But I don't understand how all that works, so I can't answer you with any kind of personal knowledge."

He sliced into his beef. "You have instincts, though. Sharp instincts. Let them work."

They ate the rest of the meal in silence. As they walked back to the hotel, they intercepted Emma and Peña. A cold breeze blew under Lynda's hijab, making her thankful she'd worn a jacket tonight.

"Where'd you go for dinner?" she asked.

"We went to McDonald's," Emma said with a smile. "My poor husband is missing his fries and strawberry shake."

Peña rubbed his stomach. "Nothing makes me happier than golden arches."

Lynda glanced up at Bill. "What do you miss?"

"Burgers, but not like Peña. Norton and I always try to find the best burger wherever we end up. Thick patty perfectly cooked, medium-rare, fresh ingredients, a bun that complements the meat." He lifted his nose slightly. "I'm afraid it wouldn't compare to what pleases Peña's palate, but it makes me happier than a fresh-bathed hog in a mud puddle."

They laughed. Lynda wondered how long it had been since she'd actually laughed out loud.

Emma looped her arm through her husband's. "I always just miss my house. The home that Jorge and I created. It's our haven from the rest of the world. I have my reading nook and my garden."

"It's my garden, actually," Peña said. "She claims it even though I do all the work."

Emma's laughter carried in the air. "It's true." She looked at Lynda. "What about you? You've been gone long enough to have an idea."

She felt silly but answered honestly. "Baseball right now."

"Really?" Bill asked. "Interesting since it's not baseball season."

"I know. But I have a cable channel that plays games 24-7, on or off season." She made a swirling motion around her head. "It's how my brain relaxes."

"What would you do without that channel?" he asked. "Does any other sport do the same thing for you?"

"Football and soccer. But they're not as good."

"Hey, now. You can take that back," Bill said. "Nothing's better than 'Bama football. Not cherry pie, not corn pudding." He wiggled his eyebrows. "Roll Tide."

Lynda laughed and swatted at him. They entered the hotel and headed up to their room. Peña and Emma followed them in. As Bill searched for bugs, Lynda opened a tea bag and looked at Emma. "Tea?"

"Sure," Emma said. As they waited for the water to boil, she leaned her hip on the counter. "So, tell me about you two."

Lynda slipped the head covering off and absently tugged on her ear while she tried to find an answer to the question. "Us two?"

Emma simply lifted an eyebrow.

Finally, Lynda said, "We were college sweethearts."

Emma gasped and clapped her hands together. "I knew it! I could see it. What happened?"

Lynda looked around and made sure neither of the guys could hear her. "He was the quarterback of the football team. I was a nerd, a math major with a focus on statistics. What could he possibly have seen in me?"

Emma gave her a knowing look. "You've clearly never seen the way he looks at you."

Heat flushed her cheeks, and she fiddled with the tag of the tea bag. "When he asked me out, I couldn't believe it. He was so charming too. I mean, you can probably imagine."

With a grin, Emma said, "A very Southern gentleman."

"Yes."

"And muscles like iron."

"Exactly." Lynda poured water over the tea bags. "And then he broke up with me and I saw him years later in a briefing room in Kuwait." She didn't know what else to say. "It was hard to have all of that young adult angst come rearing back up."

Emma glanced at the two guys as they came toward them. "Glad to see it's fading." She smiled at Peña. "Would you like a drink?"

Bill opened the refrigerator. "We have Pepsi and water."

"Water's good," Peña said.

They walked out onto the balcony. Emma and Peña sat on the same lounge chair, and Bill stood at the concrete wall. Lynda stood next to him, looking at the setting sun reflecting off the roof of the mosque.

"I hope something happens tomorrow," she said. "I'd hate for this week to have been a waste."

He looked down at her, his eyes dark in the dim light. "I don't think it's been a waste," he said quietly.

CHAPTER

TEN

DECEMBER 9

At 6:30 the next morning, Bill tied his shoes, then grabbed a bottle of water. Before he started from the room, he went to the bedroom door and knocked. Seconds later, Lynda opened the door. She had on a pair of yoga pants and a tank top. A yoga mat was behind her on the floor near the dark window.

"I'm headed out for a run. Would you like to join me?" When they'd dated, they jogged together all the time. Right before he got injured, they'd run the Birmingham marathon together.

She raised an eyebrow. "Your run is your escape from me and this room."

He grinned. "Would you like to join me?" he asked again.

She shook her head. "I'd love to join you. But running in a hijab does not appeal to me. They make special sports ones and I don't have one." She gestured behind her. "I'm making do with yoga."

"Hardly the same thing. Do you still run?"

"Like marathons?" She crossed her arms and casually shrugged her shoulder. "I did a couple in college, but not much since then. The joy in running a marathon came from training with you."

He studied her face, could see the edges of pain in her eyes. "If I could take back the way I handled things, redo it, I would."

"Yeah? Well, unfortunately, we can't go back." She lowered her arms and stepped backward. "I'm going to get back to it while my muscles are still warm. Have a good run."

He turned away as she shut the door, wanting to react but choosing not to. What would he do differently if he could go back? Standing here—a thirty-year-old man, a member of an elite fighting unit, a recent graduate with a master's degree in psychology, and more deployments than he cared to admit—he knew without a doubt that the William L. Sanders of those days had not had the maturity to deal with the facts of life.

It didn't make what he did right. But at least he understood the psychology behind his actions. He would love to be able to change it, but like she said, they couldn't go back.

He grabbed his phone and earbuds, loaded a really pumping playlist, and left the room. In lieu of the elevator, he ran down the stairs and out the stairwell door into an alley. He glanced around and headed in the direction of the Bosporus strait. The circle he made to the water and back around gave him a good five-kilometer run.

Most deployments came with a heightened sense of awareness that made him able to act or react without thinking.

The brain and muscles that had received countless hours of training would take over his consciousness, and when the dust settled and the smoke cleared, he saw how he performed as if through someone else's eyes. Here, though, he had so many sensory things to keep up with—sounds, views, smells. Millions of people occupied this space with him, and he had no idea which of them he should consider a threat. Green War did not walk into a battlefield in uniform in a way that allowed him to pick them out as bad guys. He found that rather disconcerting.

He also didn't normally sleep on a comfortable couch with a belly full of good food in a safe, clean hotel. Typical deployments offered nearly opposite accommodations. It kind of messed with him and kept him on the verge of being on edge and just slightly less than hyperaware.

He had a feeling the rest of his team felt very similarly. He knew Peña did.

The marketplace had just started to come alive in the predawn hour by the time he made it to his hotel's street. He walked through the vendors, then paused to watch a woman setting out hijabs. Thinking back to his conversation with Lynda, he picked out a gray one with an American sports logo on it. Even though the woman hadn't officially opened for the day, she agreed to sell it to him. He probably paid a little extra for the convenience.

Back in his room, he found Peña and Selah eating pastries and drinking coffee. "Morning," he said, grabbing the water he'd set out. "Get anything besides sugar?"

"Have you checked the ingredients in your preferred drink?" Selah asked, grabbing a foil-wrapped sandwich and tossing it to him. "Chicken sausage biscuit."

"Ahh, Selah, my friend, this'll do." He inhaled the smell of the biscuit, and his mouth immediately started watering. He held it up. "Put this on top of your head, and your tongue would beat your brains out trying to get to it."

Peña shook his head, used to Bill's Southern quips. "You're missing out. I've eaten pastries on the Seine in Paris, and they pale in comparison to the bakery we found down the street."

"Flour was invented as a transport system for meat, not sugar," Bill said. He slid open the door to the patio, stepped outside, and watched the morning traffic below. On a Friday morning in a mostly Muslim country, traffic was much thinner than the other mornings he'd been here. He likened it to a Sunday morning back home.

The cold air didn't bother him. He just zipped up his sweatshirt and leaned against the stone wall. As he bit into his sandwich, Lynda came out of the bedroom. Through the door, he saw that she'd changed into a skirt and a long-sleeved shirt. She grabbed a coffee out of the carrier on the table and said something to Selah, then joined him on the balcony, leaving the door open.

"Sorry if I sounded rude earlier," she said softly.

"You weren't rude." He held out the hijab package. "I don't know if that was your excuse or if you meant it, but if you're wanting to go for a run, here."

Her face softened, and she held the plastic packet like he'd given her the most precious jewel on earth. She blinked back tears and opened the flap. "Thank you. I would love to go with you tomorrow." Her eyebrows drew together. "Have you seen women jogging?"

He shrugged. "Haven't looked."

"Hmm." She called out to Selah, "Can I jog?"

Selah walked to the doorway. "If you're covered."

Lynda's face lit up in a smile that made Bill's mouth go dry. "That's exciting."

"And stay with Drumstick. It's not always safe."

"Fair enough."

Peña joined them at the doorway. "You want to go to prayers this morning?"

After a pregnant pause, Bill said, "No, but we ought to. It's why we're here, after all." He took another bite of the biscuit and held it up. "If all assignments came with this level of pampering, I'd never consider retiring."

"No kidding. Less than a year ago, we were eating MREs in the jungle of Katangela," Peña replied. "Well, I was eating. You had a bullet in your chest. You weren't eating much."

"Bless your heart, Peña Colada."

Lynda chuckled, and Peña looked at her. "Why was that funny?"

"One, because 'bless your heart' is a feminine saying, so it sounds funny coming from the bearded giant in front of me. Two, it means the opposite. It's how a Southern lady would cuss someone out."

Peña grinned in a way that transformed his usually serious face. "I may start calling him Lady Drumstick from now on."

Lynda laughed. "Do it."

"Yeah," Bill said. "Do it. I dare you."

Peña snorted. Selah held up her wrist and pointed at her watch. "I hate to bust up the party, friends, but prayers await."

Lynda prayed as she wrapped the purple-and-pink scarf around her head and neck. She asked God to give her wisdom, help her recognize the people they sought, and protect her team.

She checked the mirror. She wore a jersey fabric skirt the same color purple as the scarf, with a long-sleeved light-pink T-shirt that fit tight on her arms and did more to highlight her thin frame than hide it. When she came out of the bedroom, she could smell the evidence of Bill's shower. The clean, completely male scent did funny things to her pulse.

He had an apple in one hand and his phone in the other. His black hair looked damp and his beard gleamed. He glanced at her as he slipped the phone into his pocket. "Ready?"

"Yes."

"Peña and Selah are already there. She wanted to get some pictures of people arriving under the guise of playing tourist."

"Smart." Lynda grabbed her purse and slung it over her body, feeling the weight of the pistol inside the concealed carry pocket. "Why do you call her Selah?"

"It's what we've always called her."

"I'm guessing it's her call sign, her nickname. Like Drumstick. I'm just curious why it was chosen."

"Before they got married, that was her last name," he said. "It's a biblical term that often ends a psalm. It's beautiful and lyrical and stuck as her nickname even after she legally changed her name to Peña."

She grinned. "Thanks, Drumstick."

His answering smile made her heart skip a beat. "My pleasure," he said. "We need to come up with a name for you."

"Yeah?" She shot him a look out of the corner of her eye. "What name would you pick for me?"

"Hmm." He tilted his head side to side. "I'll get back with you."

She slid her room key into her purse and followed him to the door. At the elevator, another hotel guest joined them as they chatted about where they'd like to eat breakfast. He had gray hair and wore lime-green shorts and a yellow-gold shirt. He spoke in English with an Australian accent.

"Where are you two from?" he asked.

Lynda let Bill answer, because that was what a proper wife would do. She stayed silent by his side. While Bill chatted with him, she pretended to check a message on her phone and took his picture.

The man bade them farewell as they got out of the elevator. Once they walked alone toward the mosque, Lynda glanced at Bill. His face had taken on the familiar stern look, his mouth a hard line, his jaw set.

"It's easy to forget we're on a mission," she said quietly.

He nodded. "Best to remember."

When they reached the mosque, Lynda saw Captain Norton and Sergeant McBride. The captain held a tourist's map and had a camera bag slung over his shoulder. Lynda made eye contact with him as she turned to go to the women's entrance, but he didn't acknowledge her.

Up in the women's room, she found Emma standing alone. She joined her, moving close to the balcony so she could observe the people coming in, trying to see every face. Not as many people attended the prayer time this morning, and she wondered if the afternoon service would make up for it.

When she and Emma finished their prayers, they quickly made their way downstairs so she could watch the men as they left. Soon after, Lynda and Bill met in the courtyard and walked together down the street. They stopped at a coffee shop with outdoor seating, where Bill and Norton sat back-to-back. Lynda glanced around, seeing no one observing them.

"We'll have the mosque inside a perimeter at noon," Norton said.

Bill nodded but didn't speak. The waiter brought Lynda her latte, and she took a delicate sip.

"Wear the earpiece," Norton said. "I want constant communication today."

The waiter brought Norton his coffee and left. The captain didn't speak to them again.

After about five minutes, Bill looked at Lynda and, as if speaking to his wife, said, "Ready? We don't want to be late."

They stood and left the café. Back at their hotel, Lynda pulled off the hijab the second Bill cleared the room. She ran her hands through her hair and asked, "Am I wearing an earpiece too?"

He nodded. "Probably better for you anyway. Your ears are covered."

"Tell me about it. They seem pretty certain that something will happen this afternoon."

Bill nodded. "Norton texted me at the café. Car is on the move. Brock and Morita are following it, but the hope is that it will go to the mosque. If it doesn't, we'll take you to wherever it stops."

Her adrenaline started pumping, and her heart picked up its cadence. After nearly a week they would finally have a chance to get eyes on the man from Alaska again, maybe even follow him.

She got her laptop out of the safe and accessed the secure server. As soon as she had a connection, she sent a message about the car to her higher-ups and started working on her morning report. Once she submitted it, she checked the incoming reports from the Venezuela site and systematically went through the incident board she'd created. At one point, she realized that Bill stood behind her. She looked over her shoulder and raised an eyebrow as if asking if she could help him.

"What's this?" he asked.

"My investigation into the attacks on the oil pipelines." She zoomed out and slid over so he could see the whole screen. "The only thing they all have in common is this symbol," she said, pulling up a photo of the spray-painted tag. "And our mosque."

"W."

"Right. We assume for war."

He pointed at the screen. "Who are the men?"

"Soldiers in the Green War army." She clicked on the face of a young dark-haired man who had attended the University of Alaska Anchorage. "Environmentalists who are drawn into this organization, not understanding that the end result is that they're going to kill people." She pulled up the video of his interrogation. "Like the other one we arrested, he knows nothing. He had no understanding. He was completely ignorant about the materials he'd placed along the pipeline." She closed the video and went back to the full board. "It's very frustrating to have a lead like an eyewitness instigator and have it be a complete dead end. Worse when it happens over and over again."

He crossed his arms. "That's a pretty impressive board, Agent Culter."

She turned to face him fully. "Well, Sergeant Sanders, it is what I do. I gather information and analyze it." She waved her hand around the room. "I'm not a covert agent. I walk into a place with my badge out and announce who I am and what I'm doing. This is all new to me, and I don't have a full understanding of what is expected of me and how to handle myself."

"Well, you could have fooled me. You appear very comfortable and calm."

Heat crept up her neck and into her face. "I appreciate that. Thank you." She turned back to the computer and looked at the clock. "What time do you want to leave?"

"Twelve thirty." He pulled his phone out of his pocket. "I'll let Peña and Selah know we'll meet them there." He started texting, then stopped. "Clever."

"I beg your pardon?"

He winked at her and gave a heart-stopping grin. "Agent Lynda Clever Culter. That's your nickname."

Her face heated up again. "I like that."

"Yeah? Me too."

She felt a silly, giddy excitement at getting her own nickname. Right now, though, she had twenty minutes before she had to put something back on her head. She stood and stretched. "Let's check out these earpieces."

CHAPTER
★
ELEVEN

The number of people coming to pray had varied through the week, but the crowd for the one o'clock service surprised Lynda. It shouldn't have. People could pray anywhere, but this service came with a teaching from the imam, making it similar to Sunday morning services in the Christian faith.

Women filled the balcony prayer room. Lynda and Emma worked their way through the crowd to try to secure a spot next to the railing so Lynda would have a view of the men below. Inside the prayer hall, people typically remained silent. It felt odd to experience so many people milling around without the buzz of conversation.

As she watched the crowd below, she wondered how she could possibly identify anyone in the mass of men. She could barely make out Bill and Peña, and only because she knew what their clothes looked like.

In her ear she heard the conversation between Norton and

his team. She loved listening to the way they communicated, understanding now more than ever the teamwork they displayed out of long habit.

The chatter of the team increased as the car they'd tagged pulled into the parking lot. Peña moved toward the front entrance, then signaled he had made it to the courtyard by the fountain. The confirmation came that the target had entered the building. Lynda looked down, recognizing the man she'd seen here before.

Peña followed close behind and situated himself next to the man for the service. The imam stood in front of the men and began his teaching. He spoke rapidly in Arabic, and Lynda couldn't even pick out individual words. After he talked for about thirty-five minutes, the prayer call sounded. Lynda gave a silent prayer of thanks to Jehovah God for the technology that allowed them to track the car and communicate with each other. While she went through the motions of the prayers, she focused on her God, asking Him to guide their movements, to help them uncover the evil that had become a global danger.

As soon as the service ended, Lynda pushed her way through the women and dashed down the stairs to the women's exit. She quickly slipped her shoes on, then ran around to the courtyard, searching the faces of the men until she finally found her target. The second she located him, she looked at the ground, not wanting him to see her eyes.

"I see him," she said quietly.

"Right behind you," Bill replied seconds before he touched her elbow. He steered her to the parking lot.

A car pulled up, and the rear door opened as they approached. Bill followed her into the back seat. She recognized the man driving but didn't remember his name. Norton sat in the passenger's seat.

In her ear, Peña said, "He's headed to the same car."

The driver of their car said, "Roger. I have the signal locked."

Lynda looked at the dashboard and saw the screen of a map. A flashing dot signaled the location of the car.

"He's driving now."

Norton patted the driver on the shoulder. "Go, Gilligan," he said, jogging Lynda's memory of his name—Eric Gill.

"I'm on it." Gill slowly pulled out into traffic and followed the car at a surprisingly leisurely speed.

Norton looked back at them. "Recognize anyone else?"

"No," Lynda said. "There were so many people, though. If the women didn't have to go in and out of a separate entrance, I might have had a better chance."

In her ear, Emma said, "He just picked someone up from the corner."

"Got it," Peña said.

A moment later, Bill's phone vibrated. He held up a photo, and Lynda recognized the tall Black man from the barn. He wore the same wire-framed glasses he'd had on that night.

"Yes," she whispered, remembering the fear she had experienced while tied to a chair, the smell of gasoline, the bright light in her eyes.

Bill swiped a couple of times on his phone, and her phone vibrated in her pocket, pulling her out of her thoughts. After she slipped her phone out, she forwarded the photo to Agent Lewis and copied Agent Cartridge.

"If he's in a database, Mason will find him," she said.

"The question remains whether he launched another attack today," Norton said.

"That is the question." She watched with fascination as Gill stayed ahead of the car but managed to track it. He had to double back once, but most of the time he turned in the same direction the car turned, sometimes even two or three blocks ahead of it.

Soon, they drove slowly past a café. Lynda recognized the car parked at the curb. Her stomach danced in nervous anticipation.

Norton radioed McBride and Hobbes to take up position behind the café, then turned to look at Bill. "We'll go in first and secure a table with some concealment in defilade or enfilade. Wait three mikes, then find a position by the entrance with clear lines of sight. On my signal, fetch some recon. You up?"

"Up," Bill said, tapping the side of his pants with his index finger. He had stowed his pistol there this morning, and Lynda suspected he kept his extra magazines handy as well.

Gill parked the car up the street from the café. After he and Norton got out, Lynda glanced over at Bill. "Was he asking if you were armed?"

"Of course." He grinned. "Why?"

"Why didn't he just ask you in English?"

"That was English." He checked his watch. Then he looked at her, really looked at her. "You're a little pale. Are you up for this? If you aren't, things could go south quick."

She nodded. "I'm up for it."

"Cool." He didn't look cool. He looked very tense. "Then do me a solid and hold off on the superfluous questions for the next little while. If you don't understand something, fake it till you make it. And if things go badly, just do what I tell you instantly—and without second-guessing me—even if I tell you to stand on your head. Trust me. You'll live longer that way."

These men ate together, slept together, lived together, trained together, and fought together. They moved and thought the same way. They saw things untrained civilians routinely ignored. She was the fly in the ointment among them, the unknown quantity that could get someone killed because they could not perfectly predict what she might do or say.

"Bill, I trust your team." She hesitated, her mouth closing on the next words before she let them escape. "I trust you too."

He nodded absently, the significance of her admission lost on him as he obviously processed higher priorities. "Give it another full minute. I don't want them to realize we're all together."

Nervously, she twirled the wedding ring on her finger. Maybe she could remove herself from the equation. "What if they recognize me?" she whispered. "Maybe you should just go in and take pictures."

He tugged at the corner of her hijab. "With the heavy eye makeup and your head covered this way, there's no way they can recognize you. I have a hard time recognizing you, and I've been living with you for the last week." He put his hand on the car door. "Ready?"

No. No, she wasn't ready. "Sure." Letting out a slow breath, she pushed open the door and waited for him to join her on the sidewalk. "Let's do this."

He stopped her from stepping forward by tugging on her arm. "Hey."

She turned and looked up at him. "Yes?"

He pulled her closer to the building they'd parked in front

of. Her eyes skimmed the window front, and she saw office supplies and copy machines. Because it was Friday, they were closed, much like a Sunday morning back home.

Inside the door's alcove and out of the line of traffic on the sidewalk, he switched off his earpiece. He slipped his fingers under her scarf, and her eyes widened as he did the same thing to hers.

"Listen," he said, putting his hands on her shoulders. She could feel the strength of them through the thin material of her shirt. "I believe in you. You can do this. I'll be right there with you."

She looked at him, reading his eyes, drawing strength from the sincerity backing his words. With their history, his words shouldn't have such an encouraging effect on her, but they did. The nervousness faded away and confidence pushed forward.

She nodded and turned her earpiece back on. He winked at her as he did the same. "Shall we?" she said.

"Attagirl," Bill murmured, leading the way to the café.

"Welcome back, you two," Peña whispered. "Enjoy your little break in the middle of this covert operation? Did you miss us?"

Lynda kept her eyes on the floor as they went into the café. She wanted to stay unnoticed until they secured a table. All her senses had kicked into high gear. She felt like she could hear every conversation, smell every scent. Her heart beat rapidly, and her eyes darted around the floor, looking at shoes, trying to picture the men wearing them.

They finally reached a table, and she slid into a chair with her back to the wall. As she picked up the menu, she glanced over the top of it and quickly took in the room.

This late in the afternoon, much of the lunch crowd had

dissipated. People occupied only about half the tables. Norton and Gill sat at a table near the wall. The smell of meat roasting on an upright turnspit filled the room. She glanced toward the kitchen and saw rows of kebabs on the grills. The glass counter displayed the salads and sides available.

Her eyes roamed over the tables nearby. Just as she started to scan faces, a waiter appeared. Lynda looked at Bill, who ordered coffee and a hummus tray. When he finished speaking to the waiter, he shifted so that his body filled her vision, and he took her hand beneath the table. "Relax," he said. "We're just here to identify and observe. Calm down. I can hear you breathing through my earpiece."

She stared at his face, finding no condemnation there. Instead, as she focused on his eyes, she saw support, encouragement, and a hardness she hadn't witnessed before. She breathed in through her nose and out through her mouth, forcing herself to attain a calm she didn't feel, and nodded. "Yeah," she said in a low tone. "I'm good."

He sat back again, and his hand abandoned hers. She saw the Black man with wire-framed glasses and gestured with her chin. "He's right behind you. I can only see his back, but he's the man Peña photographed."

Norton replied in her ear. "Do you recognize anyone else?"

She shrugged instead of answering. She slowly looked again, focusing on the shoulders and necks of the six men at the table, trying to take in as much detail as possible without actually looking anyone in the face.

Fear filled her mouth with a bad taste. What was she doing here? She didn't belong in the field, surrounded by covert operatives. She belonged in a cubicle with her notes and her diagrams.

Bill surreptitiously grabbed her hand again. "Slowly," he said. "We're all just as normal as bumps on a pickle."

The waiter arrived, two tiny cups of coffee in his hands. He set them down in front of them and started to back away when one of the men at the other table turned in their direction and called him over. As soon as the waiter moved out of earshot, Lynda softly said, "Black hair. Blue top. He's one. The two who look Middle Eastern and the two white men with blond hair—I don't recognize them."

"Roger."

"So we can assume this is a meeting of the minds?" Bill said.

"Looks that way."

"I got pictures," Norton said, his phone to his ear.

As the team talked to each other, Lynda half listened until she realized they had plans to follow the two men she'd identified. "We're not detaining them?" she asked Bill.

He shook his head. "They're not the big fish. We're going to follow the little fish upstream to Cisco. Understand?"

"I don't understand," she said. These men were directly connected to Jack's death! How could they just let them walk away?

He shrugged slightly. "It's not in our pay grade to understand. I'm paid to say, 'Yes, sir,' and 'No, ma'am.' That is where I begin and end." He pushed the untouched coffee cup out of his way. "Feel like I'm at a kid's tea party."

She sat back in her chair and crossed her arms. "Fine," she said for the benefit of the microphone in her ear. "But I am going to get clarification from those sirs and ma'ams."

"You have fun with that, Agent," Norton said. "You might have a little more luck than we would. We have movement."

"Roger," someone replied.

The two Middle Eastern men stood and headed in the direction opposite of the front door. They were young, their eyes burning with purpose. They talked excitedly to each other in a language she didn't speak.

"Maguire. Hobbes. Report," Norton said.

"In position, Daddy," came the whispered reply from Mc-Bride.

"Two of our guests are leaving by the back door."

"We got 'em," McBride said.

The waiter bringing their food distracted Lynda. After he set the plates on the table, Bill thanked him in Arabic.

Lynda took a sip of coffee simply because she wanted something to do with her hands. She leaned closer to Bill. "The blond man at that table over there—the one in the red shirt, not the one with these men but sitting with his back to us. Something about him is familiar."

He didn't look in the direction of the table. "We'll see if we can get his face."

She nodded.

"Affirmative," Norton said.

Her phone vibrated, so she slipped it out of her pocket. An incoming text from Agent Lewis informed her that the picture Lynda had forwarded her didn't help identify the man with the wire-framed glasses. She slid her phone back into her pocket. "No luck with facial ID from earlier."

"Probably a bit much to hope for," Bill said. "What fun would it be if we could open the phone book and find him?"

She propped her chin in her hands and looked at him as a wife would a husband, but she kept glancing to the group over his shoulder. "I wish I could see the blond man's face."

"Selah," Bill said, "can you hear them?"

"Negative."

He shook his head. "I can hear them, but I don't understand them. They're speaking Arabic, maybe. Or Farsi."

"I can only hear you," Emma said. "These mics are good and bad that way. No background noise. Would be nice if they'd pick up a sound or two."

"Technology makes everything easier," Bill said.

Despite the circumstances, Lynda smiled. Bill had always gotten very funny, even silly, right before a big game in college. Clearly, he used humor to cope with stressful situations. "You don't happen to have a bug you can stick to someone's jacket, do you?"

"If only." He broke off a piece of bread and held it out to her. "You're the one with the CIA connections."

"Watch the chatter, children," Norton said. "Keep your mind where you are."

Bill mouthed, "Daddy's mad," and Lynda put a hand over her mouth to keep from laughing out loud.

The two blond men Lynda had not recognized stood.

"MMMBop and Bourbon," Norton said. "Report."

"Up," Waller replied.

"On point," Norton said.

"Moving."

Lynda felt pretty confident Norton had just told Hanson and Waller to follow the men. She prayed for their diligence and safety.

The two remaining men at the table had been in the house or barn in Alaska. One of them called the waiter back over and spoke to him in rapid Arabic.

"I heard that one," Emma said. "He ordered a lamb platter and pomegranate tea."

"Thank goodness," Bill said. "The pomegranate here is much better than the mint."

Lynda chuckled, plucking an olive out of the bowl. "Take what we can get," she said.

A flash of light came from the reflection of the glass door opening. Another man walked into the café, and at first her brain didn't process what she saw. As everything clicked into place, she forced her head down, staring at the wooden table.

What? How? Blood roared in her ears, and her mouth went completely dry.

Bill leaned forward. "What?"

She shook her head. It couldn't possibly be true. But she dared not risk looking up again. She gripped the table so hard her fingers ached. The chair behind Bill scraped across the floor, and the man sat down.

She leaned forward, talking as low as possible. "Jack Haynes just sat down behind you."

His eyes widened. "Your partner?" he whispered.

She nodded.

"Not dead, then?"

"Died right in front of me."

"Apparently, he's feeling better now," Bill said.

"Bill," she whispered, "what if he sees me?"

"Is he looking at you?"

"No, his back is to me."

He spoke low and certain. "If his back is to you, right now we're golden. Daddy will get things sorted." He paused. "What's the plan, Cap?"

"Wait one," Norton said.

CHAPTER

★

TWELVE

Bill's first thought was to get Lynda out of there. They could not risk Jack Haynes recognizing her, and the longer she sat there, the more likely that would happen. She sat completely still, staring at the table. What he could see of her face made a red haze flash across his vision. Everything about her countenance screamed a woman utterly crushed.

This man had elaborately set her up in a way that made her look professionally like a fool and personally like a sap. It took a lot of willpower not to just reach behind him and slam the man's forehead into the table.

Even as he thought it, Rick spoke into his earpiece. "Slow is smooth. Smooth is fast. Get her out of there."

He had to be more careful than before. Due to his FBI training, Jack Haynes would have more finely tuned observation skills than the average ecoterrorist. Right now, in this setting, he had likely slipped into hyperalert mode, focusing on everything he could see in the restaurant. Bill had to remove Lynda in a way that wouldn't draw the agent's attention.

Using his body to block his hand motions, he got Lynda's attention and pointed behind her. Hopefully, she understood that if she headed toward the restrooms, she'd see a rear exit and take it.

She gave a slight nod and stood, keeping her head down, letting the hijab shield the sides of her face. For the first time since they got there, he was glad she wore it. She moved around their table and headed in the direction of the restrooms as he waved down the waiter to pay the bill. In his ear, McBride confirmed that Lynda had gone out the back and that he had eyes on her.

After settling the bill, he followed through the rear door. He'd say that he went that way because he didn't want anyone at the table beside them to think it odd that he and his companion had left the restaurant via different doors. However, he really went out the back because it was the straighter path to Lynda.

He didn't even acknowledge McBride for fear someone observed them. Lynda stood at the edge of the back lot, looking out over the water. As soon as the café door shut behind him, she turned slightly toward him.

She lifted her chin. "What now?"

"Now we get you out of here," he said. "Let the team do their thing."

"We aren't going to haul him back home and make him pay for what he's done?"

"Lynda, if it were up to me, I'd be hauling him in. Of course, I'd have to type a dozen reports about how he happened to encounter bodily injury along the way." He put his hands on her shoulders. Ordinarily, he would never touch her in public like this, but something told him she needed that touch. "But it ain't up to me. Our orders are to follow, observe, report, and await further orders. And I don't ever disobey orders. Not ever."

He ran his hands down her arms and stepped back, intentionally opening the space between them. "Now, let's get back to the rally point."

He wanted to make sure no one followed them, and she needed to move. Bundling her into a car right now wouldn't help her.

They walked to the docks, then followed an alley to a warehouse. There Swanson kept watch, wearing a blue button-down shirt, a pair of brown slacks, and sunglasses. He sat on a bench and had a paper coffee cup and a phone. By all appearances, he looked like a businessman on a break, except that it was Friday, so this cover was not so great.

"Pot Pie," Bill said as he passed him.

"Drumstick," he replied. "Drama, drama."

"At least it ain't boring."

Bill had been to the warehouse once before, but only to observe the location and mark the route to it in his memory. When they went into the building, Lynda stopped short and he whistled under his breath.

Six large screens with various live feeds from the streets around the mosque took up a portion of one wall. One of the screens showed the GPS location of the car they'd tagged. Four computer terminals sat side by side on a long table. An incident board filled an entire wall with images from different pipeline attacks. The photos they had acquired in the last week hung on the board with question marks beneath them.

Bill turned off his earpiece so as not to distract the team. He pointed at his ear so Lynda would do the same. She slipped out her earpiece and handed it to him.

A woman with light-brown skin and hair stood at the incident board, taping up the new photos of the men taken in the café. She glanced over her shoulder at them. "Ah, Agent Culter. Welcome to our command post."

Lynda stepped all the way into the room. She slid the hijab off. "Wow." She looked at Bill and back at the woman. "Natalie Lewis, Bill Sanders."

She lifted her hand in greeting. "Sergeant."

He raised an eyebrow. Lynda hadn't introduced her as "Agent," so he asked, "And you are?"

"Glad to meet you."

He smiled. "Ah. Agency. Got it. Nice to meet you as well."

Agent Smith raised his eyebrows, then smiled and stood up from the computer terminal. "Well done, Lynda."

"Yeah? What part? The part where I facilitated the faking of the death of an FBI agent?" She wandered over to the incident board and tugged on her ear.

Agent Smith looked at Bill with a raised eyebrow. "Well, at least we found him." He gestured to another terminal, and a young man with curly brown hair looked up. "Sergeant Sanders, Agent Mason Cartridge. Cyber weapons."

Bill nodded. "Lynda has good things to say about you."

Agent Cartridge threw a thumbs-up, then slipped the headphones from around his neck to cover his ears and went back to his terminal.

Bill spotted a familiar face. Fisher sat at a computer terminal opposite Cartridge. He had three computer screens in front of him. One showed a GPS location, one showed an active audio spectrogram with the sound waves moving up and down, and another had a transcript. Arabic words were generated on the screen, so he assumed an AI program was translating and transcribing the speech.

When Bill approached, Fisher looked up and flipped one of his headphones off. "Hey, Drumstick. Peña managed to bug the car. Can you believe it?" He tapped his headphone. "I don't understand a word of it, but Selah will get the written report."

"That's all good." Bill leaned his hip against the table and shifted so he could keep an eye on Lynda. She stood in front of the board, unmoving. Her arms were crossed, and her headscarf dangled from her fingers. "Chatter sounds like everyone has an assigned follow."

"Roger. Daddy will be here soon as he has everyone dispersed."

Bill gave Fisher a good-natured slap on the back and walked over to Lynda. She glanced up at him. Her eyes stood out in her pale face, and her lips formed a tight line. She gestured at the board. "I wish we could have been coming in here daily. I would have felt more in control."

"I know." He pointed at the scarf in her hands. "At least we're done with the ruse. You won't have to wear that much more than the time it takes to check out of the hotel."

She glanced around. "Will we come here, then?"

He shrugged. "More than likely. They have bunks upstairs."

Agent Lewis chuckled. "He says bunks. It's cots behind screens. And that one snores." She pointed at Agent Smith. "Loudly."

Bill lightly punched Lynda's shoulder. "Looks like we've not had it so bad."

"Yeah," she murmured. She turned back to the board. He wanted to shake her and tell her to scream and cry and get it out, but he didn't know how helpful that would be.

"We're moving," Fisher said.

Bill turned his earpiece back on. He listened as his team followed the two men Lynda had identified from Alaska, the two Middle Eastern men, and the two blond men. Peña and McBride tag-teamed following Haynes.

About five minutes later, Rick and Hanson walked through the door. Rick pulled his earpiece out. "Agent Culter. I need you to tell me again exactly what you saw in that house in Alaska. I need some more detail." He grabbed a metal chair, carried it to the center of the room, and set it down. He gestured at Lynda and said, "Have a seat, please."

Energy vibrated off Rick. Bill couldn't tell if he was angry *at* Lynda or *for* her, and he wanted to intervene. Clearly, Rick could tell because he held up a single finger in Bill's direction as a warning.

Lynda carried her own chair over, set it down facing Rick, and sat in it, then gestured at the other chair as if inviting Rick to sit.

Attagirl, Bill thought. *He's not your commander.*

Rick spun the chair around and plopped down with his arms across the back of it to accommodate the weapons strapped to his back and hips.

Lynda took a deep breath through her nose as if recentering herself. "We were serving a warrant in rural Alaska. Not everything is clear about addresses and street names. We were where we thought we ought to be and approached the door of the house. A man answered. He was super nice. He said we needed to go further up the road and pointed in a direction that had me turn away from the door. As soon as I turned, I felt pain and the world went black."

"What next?"

"I woke up zip-tied to a chair. Jack was in a chair behind me."

"Where were you? In the house?"

She shook her head. "No. I found out later we were in the barn on that same property."

Rick scrubbed at his beard. He was processing all the information, putting it into a logical order that would allow him to make the next decisions. "Jack's hands were zip-tied to your chair?"

"Our hands were zip-tied together. Behind our backs." She laced her hands in her lap, squeezing them until her knuckles turned white. "I came to but realized I was in a situation, so I kept my head down. Everything hurt. I could feel Jack shifting in a chair behind me, so I touched him, like to let him know I was fine."

"Right. You're concussed, scared, and have no reason to think things aren't what they seem. It was a total hood-wink."

"Hoodwink. That's the word I've been searching for." Her cheeks turned red and her eyes filled, but she took a shaky breath and blinked back the tears. "They asked me to read a statement."

"What did the statement say?"

She shook her head. "I have the whole thing in the file. The gist of it was 'I'm Agent Lynda Culter of the fascist bureau of investigation.' It's very countercultural. If you want to read the profile report from the BAU on the language of the statement, I can get it for you."

He smiled. "I would appreciate that. What happened next?"

"I told them I was a federal agent and to let me go. Jack got their attention. He said something that made them go to him. Instead of reading the statement, he said something about being a federal agent and they hit him in the kneecap."

"He was behind you. Did you see him get hit?"

She closed her eyes. "No. I heard it. And felt his body move. I also heard him cry out."

"Okay. Good. Next?"

"He said something else and they splashed him with gasoline."

"How do you know it was actual gasoline?"

"Because some of it also got on me."

Rick looked at Bill, then back at her. "You keep saying 'they.' Why?"

She shrugged. "Because there were three of them and I don't know who did what."

"All men?"

"Yes." Lynda gestured at the ready board. "We have pictures of all but one."

"So Jack is covered in gasoline now and you assume he's down to one useful leg."

"And all I can think is that we're going to burn to death." Her breath hitched.

Bill started to take a step forward, then turned his back so he could get a handle on his emotions.

"They cut Jack free, and my hands were suddenly freed as well. But my legs were zip-tied tightly to the chair and I couldn't get them loose. While I struggled, two of them dragged Jack past my line of sight."

Rick nodded. "Now, what happened next?"

"They dragged him to another room. He couldn't walk. I thought it was because they hurt his knee."

"Could you see him the whole time?"

She closed her eyes. "No. He fell inside the doorway. Damien Cisco, the one in charge, stood in front of the doorway and shot him. When he moved out of the way and came walking toward me, I saw Jack's body less than a second before they set it on fire." She opened her eyes again. "Then he pointed the gun at me. Just then, I saw the lights of our backup arrive."

"Who called backup?"

"I tried but didn't have a signal. As we walked up onto the porch, Jack said he would, but I don't remember hearing him do it." She let out a breath. "Since we left the café, I've been trying to remember, and I never actually heard him call. When we woke up—or rather, when I woke up—he said he'd called for backup and I just believed him. And they arrived. So, in hindsight, I never doubted that he had."

Rick stood and put a hand on her shoulder. "Thank you for going over the details with me." He slipped his hands into his pockets and looked at Bill. "Chances are good she started to come around and they had the backup timed perfectly. For instance, if it takes twenty-four minutes from police station to location, that was how long they had."

"Especially if they had someone watching and reporting," Bill said.

"Exactly. Perfect ruse." Rick looked down at Lynda. "One final question. How long were you two romantically involved?"

She gasped and met his eyes. "Six months."

With a nod of acknowledgment, he stood and walked over to the command board. "So, Jack Haynes is in on it. Who is he in the organization, and why did Green War pull him out of the Bureau?"

Agent Lewis grabbed two papers out of the printer and stuck a picture of Haynes up on the board. She carried the other paper over to Lynda.

Lynda gasped again. "That's him! Damien Cisco."

"That was the man in the café sitting away from everyone," Rick said.

"We finally have a picture." Agent Lewis placed it over the shadow outline in the top tier of the organizational chart. "Well done, Agent Culter."

"Do we have his location?" Lynda asked.

Rick shook his head. "He didn't get followed. I think Jack Haynes threw everyone off."

Bill couldn't stay away from her another second. He took Rick's seat and reached over to take Lynda's hands, closing his fingers over hers to try to warm her ice-cold skin. "You okay?"

Her fingers trembled against his. "I'll be fine when we can bring him in."

"Okay."

Jack Haynes had clearly used her to establish a level of trust that came with a romantic relationship. He'd needed her emotionally attached to him so that when she remembered the events of the hostage situation, her emotions would override her ability to properly assess everything she'd seen. He'd used her and discarded her for his purposes.

Even though Bill hadn't actually done that to her, he'd told her he had in order to make her hate him. In her mind, in her emotions, it had happened to her twice with men she loved.

He rubbed his fingers over her knuckles, then released her hands and gestured at the setup. "This is where you can do what you do best, right? Analyze? Process?"

She nodded, then stood and walked over to the board. The defeated slump of her body gradually went away as she pushed her shoulders back and lifted her chin. When she looked at him again, the fire in her eyes made him catch his breath. "Yes, Bill, this is where I do what I do best." She looked over at Agent Lewis. "Can you give me everything we have on Jack Haynes? Can you access his FBI files and all of his background and security checks?"

Agent Lewis nodded. "What I can't get, Agent Cartridge can. We already have a FISA warrant."

Cartridge gave a thumbs-up and went back to typing at his station.

"The important thing is that we keep it as quiet as possible. It's likely he has an alert set up for anyone searching his record," Rick said.

"Not a problem," Cartridge replied.

Lynda crossed her arms over her chest. "Good. Let's find out what he's up to."

CHAPTER

★

THIRTEEN

Lynda rolled her head from side to side, then took a sip of the tepid coffee. She made a face and tossed the half-empty cup into the trash can. The images on the board in front of her had started to blur together. She focused on her watch—6:17. She'd been working on this for about four straight hours.

She'd started another board, this one set up her way to massage her brain, and left the other one alone. That one belonged to Agent Lewis.

Rubbing her neck, she turned as Bill appeared from a back room. He carried the hijab that she'd taken off hours before. "We need to go to the hotel, pack, and check out."

She scowled. "Why do I have to put that back on?"

"You know why."

She did. A Western woman walking down the street might draw someone's eyes, which meant that if they crossed paths with Jack again, he'd definitely recognize her. In the hijab, she gained anonymity. Resigned, she took it from him and put it on.

"I hate things on my head," she said, securing it properly. "Cap, hat, scarf, it doesn't matter. They all make my head hot and my hair itch."

"There's worse things." He shrugged. "This will be the last time, I hope."

Outside, Sergeant McBride looked up from his newspaper and nodded at them. Lynda glanced around. "Wasn't Swanson here before?"

"They rotate out." As they walked away from the warehouse, Bill said, "Sorry you had to go through that. In Alaska, I mean. Sounds like it was an ordeal."

Ordeal. What a word to describe terror followed by grief followed by utter betrayal. "It's clear he used me. I don't like being used."

She had a puzzle to solve. That helped her push to the background thoughts of Jack using her and then setting her up. Instead of wallowing, she was working through the puzzle of who they dealt with and analyzing their motivations in order to put a stop to them.

"Did you get the file on him?"

"Agent Lewis has someone compiling it and will deliver it as soon as it's ready." They came out of the warehouse district and walked to the shoreline. "I skimmed the early electronic stuff, but it was making my eyes blur."

"What does your gut say?"

"I don't know if I can trust my gut," she snapped. She stopped and looked up at him. His expression indicated that he understood, that he didn't take it personally. "Sorry. It's not your fault. I think the first two men who left the café are important. I'll be interested to read about their movements."

"So far, they're just typical college students from Yemen."

"Yemen?" She pressed her lips together. "I think they're important," she said again. "I think we need to bring them in and question them."

"Why?"

"Because Jack didn't show up until after they left. So what does that mean? He didn't want them to be able to identify him? Are they about to be used to blow up an oil pipeline somewhere in this part of the world?"

"Good question." For several moments, he didn't speak, then he said, "And what do you think about Jack faking his death? What does your gut say about that?"

Pain stabbed at her stomach, and she absently rubbed it. "I don't know. Why go through such an elaborate ruse? What did he gain?" She pressed her hands against her eyebrows. "Why be with me? It wasn't like he was able to learn anything from me. He was my superior. He fed *me* information."

"Hmm." They turned onto a busy road, and he said, "We can look at it closer another time."

She knew he meant that he didn't want them overheard.

In their hotel room, they made short order of packing. When she finished, she joined Bill at the patio railing. "I'm kind of going to miss spending all of this time with you," she said.

He looked her up and down, then turned and faced her fully, surprising her when he slipped the hijab off. She started to lift her hand to brush her hair back, but he beat her to it, running his fingers along her scalp. A tingling sensation ran from the top of her head down to her toes.

"Bill?"

He shook his head and closed his eyes for a moment. His hands fell to her shoulders. She stepped forward and his arms came around her. She wondered how a decade could possibly dissolve into nothing.

"I'm sorry I hurt you," he said. His voice rumbled in his chest, and she felt it almost as much as she heard it. "I'm so sorry."

She looked up at him. She could read the pain in his eyes, the regret, and believed him. What had he overcome to become the man who stood here with her today? His excuse for breaking up with her in such a final way made her heart break for the boy from Alabama she used to know. He hid his pain and stress behind humor. Who remained when all of the coping mechanisms got stripped away? She'd like a chance to get to know that Bill, the real Bill.

The chirp of his phone broke the spell. She took a step away from him and held her hand out for the hijab. "Sounds like our cab is here."

"Sounds like." He rubbed his eyes with his thumb and middle finger. "Let's roll like a one-pin spare."

She narrowed her eyes as she put on the hijab. "When was the last good sleep you had?"

"Suddenly you're mothering me?" He spoke in a light, teasing tone as he pulled his phone out of his pocket. "I'm not here to rest. I'm on a mission. Let's get down to the cab so we can end this charade and get back to work." He sent a text, probably to a member of the team. "Ready?"

"As ever."

They went back into the room. She slung her backpack over her shoulder and grabbed her suitcase handle. In the hall, he took the handle from her and wheeled both of their suitcases to the elevator.

They didn't speak as they crossed the busy lobby. Their cab waited for them outside the main doors. Bill loaded their suitcases into the trunk and said, "Havaliman."

The driver nodded. "Airport, yes."

As they drove past the mosque, Lynda saw the black-haired man she'd identified earlier. She tapped Bill on the leg and subtly pointed. He nodded and pointed as well, keeping his hands below the window. She looked in the direction he indicated and saw Sergeant Morita a few paces behind the man.

The driver made quick work of the journey. Lynda's stomach dropped at a couple of precarious turns, but they arrived in one piece. Once the cab rolled away, they went into the airport and out a door near the baggage claim. As they walked down the sidewalk, a cab pulled up next to them. Peña sat in the driver's seat.

Lynda got in the back seat and slipped the hijab off. There might come a time during this mission when she would have to put it on again, but she prayed that wouldn't happen, that they could do everything they needed to do without her having to pretend to be someone else.

"How's things?" Peña asked.

"Fine as a tick on a buck's behind." Bill pulled a water bottle out of his backpack and took a long drink. "Saw Morita tailing one of our friends."

"Yeah, at the mosque. He said he saw you looking."

"Our eyes met across the crowd. We had a moment. It was magical."

Peña snorted. "I bet." He met Lynda's eyes in the mirror. "Your package came."

Jack's FBI file. Her heart started a frantic beat. "Yeah? Anything in it?"

He shrugged. "I skimmed it. Nothing set off any alarms. It doesn't mean as much to me as you, so I figured you could do the heavy lifting and brief us with more context."

"Fair enough." She clasped her hands together because she wanted to beat on Peña's seat and tell him to drive faster. "Where'd you get the cab?"

"Apparently your agent has some local resources," he said, referring to Agent Lewis. "I don't know. I just know what papers to flash if something happens." He looked at her reflection again. "Not that anything is going to happen."

She chuckled and looked back out the window, already planning how she would lay out the contents of Jack's file.

Bill carried his bags up to his assigned area in the warehouse. The upstairs offices had been converted into sleeping quarters, and each one had cots and privacy screens. He dropped the suitcase at the foot of the bed, shoved the backpack underneath, and crashed on top. He needed sleep. For the last week, he'd been on high alert. Being without his team made him feel like he couldn't risk fully shutting down. Three, four days like that, he had no problem. On day eight, today, it had become a problem.

His chest hurt. He hated admitting that. It had been less than a year since a bullet had lodged itself next to his heart. Ironically, getting shot hadn't hurt much. In fact, until he collapsed from a tension pneumothorax, he hadn't even been aware that the discomfort in his armpit had originated due to a stray round. The removal of a bullet near his heart by a doctor who wasn't a surgeon in rough conditions in an African village . . . now, that was another story.

He'd sat back when his unit deployed without him once. When the chance came to go on this mission, he hadn't hesitated. He had no desire to be left out again. He looked forward to the day that the pain became a distant memory. He wanted everything back to normal with his body at 100 percent peak performance.

Bill pushed the thoughts aside and focused on sleeping. He woke up at three the next morning. He'd had seven solid hours of deep, purposeful sleep and felt refreshed for the first time in days. He could hear McBride breathing in the cot next to his. As quietly as possible, he gathered his boots and left the office. When he reached the top of the stairs, he sat down and put on the boots.

The teams worked in shifts to follow all of the suspects. They also had limited support from some CIA assets for extra manpower. Bill needed to check with Rick and make sure that he was added to the rotation.

At the bottom of the stairs, he walked down the corridor and found the break room. Someone had stocked the refrigerator with Pepsi. He would have to find Rick and thank him for that. Maybe even hug him. As he cracked open one of the cold drinks, he pulled a microwave meal out of the freezer. He couldn't read the Turkish writing on the package, but it looked like some sort of chicken and rice dish.

While his food cooked, he leaned against the counter and thought about yesterday. It meant a lot to him that Lynda admitted she didn't want to lose their private, intimate time. As much as he had dreaded being stuck with her at first, he treasured that time now. What a difference a week made in the scheme of life.

Before, she'd absolutely hated him with a passion and stubbornness he could understand and even respect. Now she trusted him, relied on him. More importantly, he trusted her. Outside of his team, he couldn't say that about another person in his life—not without a caveat.

He used a folded paper towel to pull the meal out of the microwave, then opened drawers until he found forks. When he sat down in one of the four chairs around the table, he bowed his head and took a moment of silence. Then he thanked God for the food and said, "And forgive me for crashing before I properly thanked You for Your hand of protection earlier."

As he dug into the chicken and rice, Rick walked into the room. "Good morning, sleepyhead."

Bill smiled. "I suspect I feel a whole lot better than you look. Might be your turn to go count some sheep."

"Already did. Got about four hours." He turned on a kettle and put a tea bag into a cup. "Just finished supervising shift change and getting reports from details."

"Did you add me to the rotation?"

Rick nodded. "Three p.m. You're on Haynes."

That made Bill smile. He was sure it didn't look like a kind smile. "Be still my heart." He scooped some chicken and rice into his mouth and tried to ignore the gummy texture.

"How is that meal? Smells pretty good."

"Are we comparing it to an MRE or Hammerhead Bar and Grill?"

Rick laughed. "Fair enough." He poured hot water over his tea bag, then pulled out the chair across from Bill.

"Not hungry?" Bill asked. "Doesn't taste terrible. Texture's off. Like eating shawarma that got jammed into a blender and then made into a waffle."

"I'll hold out for the breakfast run." Rick stared at him. "Overall, how did the week go? Off the record."

Bill washed the mouthful down with the sweet carbonated water before he said, "We accomplished the mission in a week. I think there's a lot to be said for that. Lynda knew who she was looking for and didn't hesitate."

"Sounds like you made up."

"I like to think some of the past was forgiven." His pulse rate picked up a little at the mental image of Lynda standing in front of that incident board, tugging on her ear. He had always found her brain incredibly attractive.

"Maybe rekindled?"

Bill felt a flush of heat on his neck. "I beg your pardon?"

Rick grinned. "Come on. You can tell Daddy."

Bill snorted. "Is this what it's going to be like now that you're married and living happily ever after? You feel like you have to start playing matchmaker on me?"

"Oh, my friend, if only you knew the bliss that can come." He stood. "Going to grab a shower. See you in a bit."

Bill threw the empty container in the trash and the aluminum can in the recycling, then headed into the main room to seek out a computer terminal. When he saw the far wall, he stopped short. A grid made up of different colors of tape separated the sections. Some contained printouts of graphs and timetables. Others had pictures of all the known players with colorful strings connecting different people. One entire side showed a timeline with photos and charts of the different pipeline attacks.

When he walked closer to examine the grid, he found Lynda on a green couch. She lay on her stomach, her face pressed into a pillow, her arm dangling down. On the floor in front of the couch, the grid continued—more pictures, more charts, more lines making connections.

He silently walked along the grid on the floor and then to the wall and tried to follow the path of her reasoning, but he could see no logical course. As much as he wanted to ask her to explain her brilliant mind and show him what she'd done, he decided she needed the sleep more. If she had done this amount of work in the few hours he had slept, she hadn't been down for long.

As he turned away from the wall, Agent Smith strolled into the room. With tousled hair and a half-tucked shirt, he looked like he had just gotten out of bed.

Bill moved farther away from Lynda as Agent Smith gestured at the wall and said in a quiet voice, "Fascinating to watch her put the puzzle pieces together."

Bill studied the grid again. He turned his head and relaxed his mind and started to see what she'd done. "I can see where she's drawing correlations. I'm just missing the conclusion."

Agent Smith agreed. "There's mountains of information she pulled all of this from. It is truly a gift."

"What's a gift?" Lynda asked.

Bill turned as she sat up and brushed her hair away from her face. "Your ability to problem-solve," he said with a smile. "Rather early, sleepyhead."

She glanced at her watch and stretched her arms above her head, yawning. "I crashed like three hours ago. I don't even remember getting to the couch."

"Well, in all fairness, you've been going for a couple of

days." He pointed at the kitchen area. "Buy you a cup of coffee? I'd love to hear what you're thinking."

Soon, they sat at the table. Agent Smith had left to take a shower.

"Did you find anything useful in the Jack file?" Bill asked.

Lynda shrugged. "What's interesting is what isn't there. It's all very squeaky clean. Perfect boy next door, college honors, spotless police record." She sat back in her chair and propped her arm along the back of it, rubbing her forehead. "He joined the Violent Gang Task Force. He had some language skills that got him placed undercover in a cell with a Russian mafia group. Stayed under in deep cover for five years. When he came out, they arrested the boss, Kirill Volkov, and prosecutors are building a tight case. So Jack fulfilled the mission just as it was written. I don't even see anything dirty inside."

Bill thought about that, then asked, "Where did he go after that?"

"Straight to me." She took a deep breath and blew on her coffee. "The next assignment was heading up the task force investigating Green War. There had been some rumors and some chatter that was picked up that led us to information to generate a deeper investigation of the organization. The first bombing was just one month after Jack died in Alaska." After taking a sip of her coffee, she said, "In the early days, we tried to infiltrate the organization but couldn't. Now I can guess why."

He stared at her for several seconds. "It's been a little while since you saw Jack in the restaurant. How are you doing with that?"

Her mouth tightened. "What do you need me to say? I'm angry. And I'm humiliated. I'm filled with questions, and I want to grab him by the collar and shake him while I ask them." She took another sip. "If you're waiting for me to cry like a wounded schoolgirl, I don't do that anymore. You cried me out of that habit, I think."

Guilt landed a painful blow. "I would never suggest you have yourself a good cry," he said.

Rick walked in. "Good morning, children." He set Bill's Bible on the table.

Bill looked up at him. "You, sir, are a gentleman. And a scholar, but a gentleman first."

Rick scuffed Bill's hair like he would a puppy. "Sure thing, brother."

"I didn't think to give mine to someone else," Lynda said. "I just didn't bring it." Before she touched it, she asked, "May I?"

Bill shrugged. "Sure."

As she thumbed through it, he remembered all of the highlighted sections, the scribbled notes in the margins, and all the incredibly personal stuff he'd written. Suddenly, he wished she hadn't taken it.

She had the book open to Psalm 131. She ran her fingers over the words on the thin page. "What a treasure you have here. The Bill I knew didn't have a Bible like this."

He roughly cleared his throat as Rick left the room. "I had a moment with God that brought me to this job. I figured, the way He arranged things for me told me He obviously cared. Even though my entire life I never felt like He did, at that moment I felt it in my soul. I bought that Bible with my first Army paycheck."

She closed the cover and slid it back toward him. He breathed a quiet sigh of relief.

"I invited you to a Bible study once," she said. "Remember?"

He shook his head. "Not really."

"It interfered with football practice. So I told myself I would press after football season was over." She smiled. "And football never ended. If it wasn't preseason, it was the actual season, then postseason. Kinda crazy the way it was all-consuming."

He smiled. "Until it ended in an unexpected way."

She nodded. "And you left. I never heard from you again." She paused. "But I think you would've liked my Bible study group."

McBride appeared in the doorway and knocked on the frame. "Drumstick, we've got movement. Daddy's calling."

Immediately, the relaxed feeling left Bill's shoulders, and his senses engaged. His heart rate picked up, and adrenaline started pumping through him. He stood and looked down at Lynda. "I'd like for you to explain your process I saw out there when I get back."

"Oh!" She looked toward the door and then back at him. "Sure. If I'm able to explain it. Usually, I just work through it and then people are interested in the results."

He winked at her. "I'm interested in you. How your brain works."

Color filled her cheeks as he left the room.

CHAPTER

★

FOURTEEN

DECEMBER 10

Lynda stood in the back of the room as Norton addressed the group. The other governmental agencies had relinquished tactical control of this mission to the DOD and Norton's team.

Someone had placed a screen against the wall, and Peña worked the computer that projected a map onto it. The team had filed into the room wearing military combat gear over civilian clothes: vests with mounted cameras, belts, and holsters. They carried their helmets and weapons.

Everything about them had changed as day turned to night and they finalized the mission details. Even the energy emanating from them had changed. Lynda sensed an intensity here that she never had before and could almost feel them mentally and physically preparing for battle. They were an imposing group. It certainly made her glad they were on her side.

Norton explained the location, the area where the mission would take place, and the terrain they might encounter in detail. He pointed out buildings, cameras, likely civilians. He highlighted the cars that hadn't moved in several hours and showed videos of the targets going in and out of the buildings.

"We need to move now," he said. "Everything tells us they're planning to strike again soon." A sky view with infrared dots appeared on the screen. "This is real time. There are seven known targets. The two that Agent Culter identified, the man we know as Jack Haynes, and four others, two of which we'll call subjects theta and sigma. Theta and sigma have not left this other building on the college campus since we began surveillance." He circled the building with a laser pointer, then slipped it into his pocket. "We're going into the building blind. We have no idea what their weapons or munitions capabilities are, so we're going to assume the extreme. They have used rare military-grade explosives in every pipeline sabotage attributed to them, so we can assume they have access to additional military-grade weapons." He pointed at Agent Smith. "Anything to add?"

Agent Smith stood and walked to the front of the room. Lynda could feel a different kind of energy coming off him too. "I'm not unfamiliar with the differences between our two agencies. However, I hope you can listen and understand. These men must be brought in alive and able to speak. I don't believe Jack Haynes is the head of this organization. We need to find out who is. Is it Cisco? Or does he answer to someone? Attacks have happened globally, millions of dollars in critical infrastructure have been lost, causing a ripple effect of supply issues throughout the world, and hundreds have lost their lives."

He nodded at Peña, and the screen changed. Pictures of two of the men from the café appeared. "Theta and sigma are students. Both are Yemenis. In the class system in the Middle East, people from Yemen are treated like the proverbial redheaded stepchildren. They have a hard time getting good jobs, they're talked down to, they're less than." The pictures of all the men who had perpetrated the attacks on pipelines joined the images of the other two. "Every one of these bombers was radicalized on an emotional level first. Then they were indoctrinated about environmentalist causes, big-bad-wolf corporations, and finally, how they could make a statement for all the disenfranchised countrymen who work like slaves in the oil business. They've been coerced, manipulated, and prepped."

"How were they going to college, then?" Peña asked. "Does Turkey offer some kind of Yemen incentive?"

"No." Agent Smith slipped his hands into his pockets. "It looks like an anonymous donor paid their tuition and living expenses. These two men are brothers. They lost their father in an accident on an oil rig, leaving their family destitute."

Lynda sat up. "So, you think they were handpicked and groomed?"

"That's the guess, yes. Agent Cartridge is trying to trace the money, but he keeps hitting dead ends."

Agent Lewis straightened from where she leaned against the wall. "Were the Yemenis about to bomb a pipeline?"

He nodded. "Yes. When we searched, we found the materials in their living quarters, along with the plans and specifications of a pipeline in Saudi Arabia. We left them there but will collect them tonight when we collect the brothers."

Lynda frowned and shook her head. That didn't make sense. Why would these pipelines be disrupted on such a global scale? Until the team understood the true intent, she didn't think they'd ever really find that elusive "man in charge."

"The need to bring these men in and interrogate is essential." Agent Smith pointed at Emma. "We can play rough, but leave something for Ms. Peña to deconstruct."

An amused murmur ran through the room.

Norton took over again. "I'm going to remember that phraseology as it pertains to Selah," he said with a grin. Then he surprised Lynda by pointing at her. "Agent Culter, I want you on the ground with us. No one in the room knows this case better than you. You may recognize someone you didn't know was a key player before."

She crossed her arms. "Like Jack Haynes?"

With a nod Norton said, "Exactly like Jack Haynes." He gestured toward her but looked at Emma. "Selah? Gear her up, please."

The image on the screen changed to an overhead of the location again. Norton began to go over the tactical aspects of the mission while Lynda went with Emma to a far corner of the room.

Lynda sat on a chair and pulled her boots on. "Doesn't he think I need to hear the mission details?" she asked, trying to see the screen.

Emma stuffed plates into her ballistic vest. "You'll stick next to Drumstick."

Lynda slipped the vest on, adjusting to the weight and

feel of the heavy armor. "I'm not some damsel in distress. I know how to plan and prep for a raid."

"It's not that, Lynda. Captain Norton and the team respect your skills, I can assure you. Otherwise you would be nowhere near the mission tonight." Emma fastened the camera to the vest. "But 'team' is the operative word. That unit out there moves like one. They have trained, fought, bled, and sometimes died together. As many missions as I have been on with them, I'm still just assigned to Jorge and told not to leave his side."

Lynda glanced at the group. "Died?"

"Yes. Not long before Jorge and I got married." She held up a leg holster. "Which side do you prefer?"

As Lynda finished gearing up, she continued to study the group. She hadn't experienced them the way Emma had. So far, they had done almost everything separately. She looked forward to seeing them in action, literally and figuratively.

Her gaze finally rested on Bill's profile. Something had softened in her broken heart over the last week. She had a feeling if she gave him any hint of something romantic, he'd consider that an open door and an invitation. Did she want that?

"How do you stand it?" she asked.

Emma's eyes widened. "Stand it?"

"Knowing what kind of dangers they face."

Emma held up the helmet, and Lynda reluctantly took it. She'd already started mentally prepping herself to wear it.

"This world is full of evil people," Emma said. "My family had to leave our home, my aunts and uncles, all of my cousins, and flee to a foreign land. That group of highly trained soldiers has fought together to rid the world of evil. Every time they win, we all win." She tapped her own vest over her heart. Her gloved hands thumped against the armor plate. "I can live with that knowledge and do whatever I need to do to support my husband's part in it, as he does the same for me. This is the life God gave us, gifted us for, prepared our hearts and minds for. I'm okay with that."

Energy hummed through Bill's veins like a circuit turned on between his brain and his circulatory system. Everything heightened—sight, sound, smell. The world moved more slowly around him, giving him ample time to assess situations, decide on courses of action, analyze reactions—all before anything happened.

He'd never been able to put into words the way his mind shifted into that special tactical mode at the start of any mission. He'd tried to talk to Rick about it once, but the memory of how he felt never fully lingered after the fact.

Long missions exhausted him because of that mode. Nothing turned it off until the mission ended. Tonight, though, he could just let it hum.

Agent Lewis had secured vehicles. They loaded up and headed to the target house.

Bill slowed his thoughts, closed his eyes, and focused on his heart and soul during the drive over. He said the silent prayer that he always did, whether jumping out of an airplane or heading into a firefight. *God, I love You. I long to hear, "Well done, good and faithful servant." Please search my heart and forgive me of any iniquities. Protect me and keep me focused and courageous.*

When he opened his eyes, the vehicle came to a stop. He

got out, rallying with the rest of his team well away from the building.

He saw Lynda pressed up against the building, weapon ready. He felt a burden of responsibility for her like he never had before. But that did not change how impressed he was with her skill. This was not her first raid. She moved with efficiency and silence and obeyed orders without question.

If they didn't need to make sure that they captured key players, they could have gone in, guns blazing, blowing through doors and generating shock and awe. A snatch and grab like this one required more finesse, so Bill stood by as Brock used his mad skills to soundlessly open the door.

Agent Lewis spoke in their ears, directing them to the heat sources in the building. Bill moved low and quickly, as quietly as possible, through the large house, past a dark and empty living room and up the staircase, right on the heels of Fisher and Swanson. At the top of the stairs, he banked left as they turned right, moving silently down the hallway.

He and McBride worked their way down the hall, clearing doorways and entry points. At the last door, they stopped. McBride reached out and checked the handle. It turned smoothly. He pushed the door open and they went in, weapons up and ready. Bill spared one quick glance to make sure Lynda had followed him.

They wore night-vision goggles and used infrared flashlights mounted on the barrels of their weapons to light up the room like green-hued daylight and pick out any humans. As he and McBride entered the room, they yelled, "Hands in the air!" and the figure on the bed jerked awake, sitting upright.

McBride rested the muzzle of his weapon against Jack

Haynes's temple and stopped him from reaching for the pistol on the bedside table.

"Evening, Jack," McBride said. "Let's go. You know the drill. Nice and slow."

"I got him," Bill said, keeping his weapon trained on Haynes. "Go ahead and secure him."

McBride let his weapon swing on its attached sling and used a zip tie to fasten Haynes's hands behind him. Then he lifted Haynes by his arm and propelled him toward Bill, who took control of the package.

He gripped Haynes's arm tightly as they marched through the hall, down the stairs, and into the main room. They slid their goggles up, and Peña flipped on the light. According to Agent Lewis, they'd secured everyone in the house.

Haynes's steps faltered when he saw Lynda. Bill wanted to kick the man forward and force him to land at her feet. Instead, he just made eye contact with her and tried to encourage her with his eyes. She made him proud when she looked Haynes up and down as if inspecting him, then said to Bill, "He can go over there," pointing at Peña. Bill did well not to chuckle out loud.

Peña took photographs and tagged each prisoner with a plastic bracelet and a barcode printed from a label maker. Haynes didn't speak the entire time.

Bill heard over comms that Fisher and Hanson had captured the Yemeni students in their dormitory. He imagined the two had quite a start waking up to fully loaded United States Special Forces soldiers. If he hadn't had this weasel to collect, he might have volunteered for that mission.

In the main room, he counted five prisoners. None of them spoke a word, but he didn't expect them to. Right now, the prisoners had to mentally shore themselves up, formulate what they would say in interrogation.

Outside, Bill's team put hoods on the heads of the prisoners before loading them into vehicles. Each prisoner was assigned a guard.

They took the prisoners to a building near the docks on the other side of the city that the CIA had converted into a holding facility, complete with interview rooms equipped with cameras and microphones.

"Let's go, Box of Underwear," Bill said to Haynes, taking him by the upper arm.

He wanted Haynes to mouth off, say something. But he didn't. He just got out of the vehicle and let Bill guide him inside the building. In the cells section, Bill read the serial number on his wristband to Agent Smith, who checked him into the system, scanned the bracelet barcode, and put Haynes into the cage.

As soon as the door locked, Smith said, "Take one step backward." He reached through the bars and took the hood off Haynes's head. "Lift your arms." Haynes complied, and Smith used a pair of cutters to clip the zip tie. With his arms free, Haynes stepped forward into the cell but did not turn around. Bill guessed he took his time assessing the single cot in one corner and a toilet in another.

Bill bit back a dozen things he wanted to say to the guy and instead just walked away. On his way out of the room, he passed Fisher bringing in one of the students from Yemen. The kid looked terrified, and tears and snot poured down his face. A part of Bill felt sorry for him. He couldn't imagine having to interrogate him.

In their ready room, he pulled his helmet off and grabbed

a bottle of water. The door opened and Lynda came in. He raised the bottle toward her in a mock toast. "Well done, you."

She nodded. "Feels good. How are you?"

"Fine as a frog's hair split four ways."

She grinned. "Can I ask you a question?"

He shrugged. "Sure."

"Why Box of Underwear?"

He raised both eyebrows. "Jack."

After a long pause, she said, "In the box?"

"Exactly. And I don't think I need to explain Haynes."

Her smile warmed his blood. "You know, one could easily describe you as incorrigible."

After downing half of the bottle, he wiped his lips. "What's stopping you?"

Chuckling, she grabbed a pack of peanut butter crackers and a water and walked over to the couch. As she opened her laptop, Agent Smith came into the room.

"Have you discovered anything more about the students?" he asked Lynda, nodding a greeting to Bill.

"Yeah. I think we can come at them from this angle," she said, scooting over for him to sit and see her screen.

Bill watched her work, not even necessarily hearing what she said. He studied her face, the intensity of her concentration, the intelligence as she processed information. Suddenly he realized how those feelings he'd had for her in college had been just the beginning of his journey to falling entirely in love with her. As she brushed a piece of hair off her forehead and looked at Agent Smith, smiling at something she'd just discovered, he found himself tripping and falling into a chasm from which he didn't think he could return.

Nor did he want to.

CHAPTER
★
FIFTEEN

Lynda stood in front of the monitor and watched the young man on the screen. He was thin and gangly with dark tan skin, close-cut curly hair, and brown eyes. He wore a T-shirt with the logo of the Yemen national soccer team. His student records listed him as Kadeem Nasser. She and Agent Smith would interview him together, but she'd requested just a few moments to observe him.

"He's very scared," she said.

"Terrified," Agent Lewis said. "But of them or us?"

"That is the question." Lynda looked at Emma. "Ready?"

They had not yet discovered whether the students spoke English. Emma would serve as their translator.

Lynda stood in the corner of the room while Agent Smith and Emma sat at the table. "Good morning, Mr. Nasser," Agent Smith said. Emma quickly provided the greeting in Arabic. When Kadeem's eyes went to Emma, Agent Smith said, "You will look at me when I speak. Not at her. She is not here."

He kept his gaze on Emma until she relayed the message, then his eyes flew to Agent Smith.

His desire to comply twisted Lynda's heart. She began to suspect he did not speak English. "Where are you from, Kadeem?" she asked through Emma.

He looked back and forth from her to Emma. "Ma'rib," he said, a bead of sweat sliding down his forehead.

"Look at me, Kadeem." When he looked at her again, she asked, "What does your family do in Ma'rib?"

"My mother is a cook," he said. "My uncle owns a restaurant."

"What kind of restaurant?"

"Falafel. Soldiers like to eat there."

She knew the answer to her next question, but she needed to ask it to put him in the right frame of mind. "What about your father? What does he do?"

His face fell, and tears filled his eyes. "He died."

"He died? How?"

"An accident. At an oil refinery."

She paused, and Smith stepped in. "When did he die?"

"Three years ago."

"I bet that was hard," Lynda said. "You were a teenager. What happened to your family when your father died?"

A muscle in Kadeem's jaw ticked. "My mother and sisters moved in with my uncle."

"And you and your brother?" Smith asked.

With impatient movements, he swiped at his eyes. "There was no room."

Smith opened the file folder in front of him. Kadeem's

photo could clearly be seen. "Tell me about coming here to go to school."

His shoulders straightened. "We applied."

While Smith turned the pages in the folder, Emma took a quick sip of water. Lynda observed Kadeem's interest in her water bottle.

"What did you apply for?" Smith asked.

"There was a scholarship for boys. We thought we could go to school here, in Turkey, and then get good jobs and our mom and sisters wouldn't have to work for my uncle anymore."

"How did you hear about the scholarship?" Lynda asked.

"We were in an orphanage. A man came."

"So, a man spoke to you about the scholarship."

Kadeem nodded.

"How many of you applied?"

"All of us."

Smith sat back and tapped his finger on the arm of his chair. "How many got scholarships?"

Kadeem shrugged. "Just Samir and myself."

"Kind of interesting how you and your brother both received scholarships when all of you applied."

"We are very smart. Our father was very intelligent. He was an engineer and a good man."

Lynda noticed a tone of pride, almost self-righteousness, in his voice when he spoke about his father. Something important was there. She decided on a different tactic. "What were you studying?"

He looked at her with wet eyes for several seconds before he replied. "Accounting."

"You haven't asked why you're here," Smith said.

Kadeem looked at Emma for several seconds before he looked at Smith. "What good would it do to question the American imperialists?"

Smith shut the folder and stood, the cue for them all to leave the room. In the observation room, Peña, Norton, Hanson, and Lewis sat around the monitor. Bill leaned against the wall underneath a bank of monitors that captured the holding cells.

Norton spoke first. "Impression?"

"He's angry." Lynda rubbed the back of her neck and shook her head. "Something with his father." She picked up the file on Samir Nasser. "I want to get a feel for the brother. I want to see if it's the same with him too."

"He's a year younger," Hanson said. "Might affect something."

Bill gestured above him. "Why start with them? Why not go to the top?"

Her eyes roamed the screens until she found Jack. He lay stretched across his cot, arms behind his head. "I'm not sure. Something is off here." She looked at Emma and Smith. "Ready?"

Soon, they took up their same positions in a different room, this time facing Samir. He had very similar features to his brother but was slightly more filled out and had a close-cropped beard.

"Please," he said in perfect English. "I don't understand why I'm here."

"You speak English," Smith said, opening his folder to the page that listed Samir's education. "Where did you learn?"

"I fed American soldiers."

"In a restaurant?"

"At their base. Where they were. Locals worked. I worked there for two years before coming here to university. It was not hard to pick up the language."

Lynda nodded. "Tell me about your dad."

Samir looked from her to Smith to Emma and back to her. "What about him?"

The look of terror that crossed his face surprised her. "Well, let's start by telling me what you immediately thought of when I asked you that question."

"I don't understand."

Emma didn't need prompting to translate. After she finished speaking, he licked his lips and looked down at the table. "He is dead."

"Why?" Not how. She knew how.

"He told them that the pressure was too high and that the valves weren't correct. He requested that the valves be replaced but was told to make it all work. An explosion killed him."

Smith picked up the pace. "You said 'them.' Who do you mean? Who did he tell?"

Samir spoke in Arabic. Emma translated, "Saudi Arabian officials."

Smith turned a page in the file. "Why did you flee to Turkey instead of joining the Army?"

Samir's eyes bugged out of his head. "Flee? I don't understand."

"Why did you escape to Turkey?"

"I won a scholarship. If I go to college, I can help my mother and sisters."

Lynda crossed her ankles and leaned against the wall in a relaxed pose. "What are you studying?"

"Mechanical engineering."

"Like your father?" Smith asked.

Samir lifted his chin. "I will be proud to be like my father."

Lynda tapped the wall and straightened. Smith shut the folder, and they left the room without another word.

In the observation room, Peña looked at Lynda. "What?"

"He's the one," she said.

"What one?"

"The one that convinced his brother to do this. He's running on emotions. His motivation for whatever they were going to do is based on his father's death. The first time his father was mentioned, he was terrified. Terrified that we knew. He's going to play innocent, and he'll likely throw his brother under the bus, but he's the one."

Lewis looked at the monitor. "Do you think the Nasser brothers were the ones who blew up the Kuwaiti pipeline?"

"Likely. And we know they're going after a Saudi one. The question is which." Lynda's fingers itched for a map of the region. "Can we get a map of the pipelines and refineries within a day's travel of here?"

Smith raised an eyebrow. "Are you serious? Do you know how many there could be?"

She ignored him because they both knew the answer to that. "And their passports. Have we finished searching their rooms?"

Lewis nodded. "Boxes are in the ready room."

"Did the brothers go to Saudi Arabia?"

"Yes," Lewis said. "But during the hajj."

Lynda shook her head. "Hajj?"

Emma answered. "The hajj is the trek to Mecca, following the path that Mohammed took. All Muslims are expected to do it at least once in their lifetime. No matter your nationality, your status, or your sex, if you're a Muslim you must be allowed into the country for the hajj."

Lynda tugged on her ear and watched the monitor. "I'd like to see those passports."

"What about our other guests?" Norton asked.

"I think they're okay to sit for now," she said, glancing at Jack. He hadn't moved. "I'd rather go into their rooms with all the intel. They don't know we have the Nasser brothers. I'd like to make that a special surprise."

DECEMBER 11

Bill leaned against the kitchen counter, his nerves still slightly humming from the action a few hours ago. Agent Smith used the counter as a desk as he made notations in a file folder. The silence in the room grew heavier.

Finally, Bill spoke. "How did you end up at DHS?"

Smith stopped writing and looked up at him. Their two organizations had a lot of historical hostility. Bill could tell he measured his answer. "I was Secret Service. I stayed when we got put under DHS from Treasury. Then I got injured on the job. I thought about going to one of the other branches, but I didn't have the criminal law background for the FBI. I would have joined the CIA, but I didn't want to end up in, you know, Turkey."

Bill laughed, which seemed to make Smith relax a little more.

"So, I just stayed DHS, and I'm riding out to my retirement."

"That's tough."

"What about you?" Smith closed the file folder and slipped the pen into his pocket. "Why SF?"

Bill thought about it, carefully formulating his response. "I joined to escape my life. I wanted to do more than survive. My recruiter kind of slotted me and had it all set up for me, and I didn't even care. I just signed on the dotted line and did whatever they told me to do. Go to this school, do that thing, take this test. Found out I was pretty good at it." He scratched at his beard. "Strange how God works all that out."

"It is that." Smith crossed his arms over his chest. "Do you have a family?"

The thought of his grandmother made his heart ache. "Nah, man. Just my team. You?"

Smith gave a sappy smile. "Yeah. A wife of ten years and two little girls."

"I bet it's hard to be away from them." Bill could see Smith with a houseful of little girls.

"Well, it's rough to be surrounded by men instead of women." Smith laughed. "I'll be glad to go home." He scooped up the file folder and left the room, passing Hanson on his way in.

"Chief," Bill said.

"Drumstick." Hanson filled a paper cup with coffee. "I am ready for good coffee again."

Bill held up his soda. "Consistently the same everywhere I go. Amazing how that works."

"Dude. Do you know what that stuff is doing to your gut?"

Bill slapped his flat stomach. "This gut here?" He winked, and Hanson laughed.

Rick came into the kitchen, followed by Peña and Mc-Bride. He sloshed some coffee into a cup and said, "We're cleared to go back to the headquarters." He pointed at Peña. "You too. I know Selah is staying for language services, but you need to go back and rest. I need you in the interrogation room tomorrow."

"Yes, sir."

Rick looked at Bill. "You're coming back tomorrow too. I want you in the room when we make our go at Haynes. You're the one who arrested him, so your presence will provide a bit of intimidation whether he realizes it or not. It could be used to our advantage."

"Yes, sir." Bill dumped out the rest of his soda and tossed the can into the recycle bin. If he wanted to sleep, he didn't want the sugar or caffeine. "We leaving Agent Culter?"

"We are. She's with Smith and Lewis. When they finish with the two brothers, they'll follow." He raised a finger and made a circling motion. "Let's go. Tomorrow's just a few hours away."

Bill looked at his watch. That little hand hovered dangerously close to the number four. "It's actually already tomorrow. Unless you're talking about the next tomorrow."

"Can it, Drumstick," Rick said with a smile in his voice.

"Yes, sir. Sorry, sir," Bill said in his best junior-ranked-soldier voice.

Lynda stared at Kadeem. He licked his lips and finally said, "Could I have some water?"

She opened the bottle in front of her and poured a little into a clear plastic cup. She wanted to feel sorry for him, but she pushed that back and focused on the bigger picture. "Your brother speaks English. Why don't you?"

He looked at Emma, waiting for her translation. She repeated the question, and he shifted his gaze back to Lynda. "I didn't work where he worked."

"What did you do?"

"I worked for a . . ." Emma paused and asked a question in Arabic, then continued. "A mason. I hauled bricks."

Lynda pulled a passport out of the file folder. "Saudi Arabia this past July, huh? Let's talk about that trip."

Kadeem licked his lips again and drained the water. "I went on the hajj."

"You know what I think?" She laced her fingers and leaned forward. "I think you entered Saudi Arabia during the hajj because they're not allowed to tell you that you can't." She spoke with confidence, certainty. "Then you got in a car driven by one of your contacts here in Turkey. You went to the site of a pipeline. While there, you talked about the plans to blow it up and all of the damage that would do to the Saudi Arabian oil industry—the same industry you blame for your father's death."

Eyes wild, Kadeem looked from her to Emma to Agent Smith, who stood behind them, then back to her. A bead of sweat slipped down his temple. "How . . . ?"

Smith spoke. "How did we figure it out? Because your brother told us. He also told us that it was your idea."

"No! No!" He pressed the heels of his hands against his eyes. "I don't believe you. My brother would never do that." He lowered his hands. The wild look had gone out of his eyes. "I have nothing else to say."

Lynda nodded and stood. "Great. We'll get someone to take you to your cell."

With a frown he said, "Cell? I am being arrested?"

Smith stepped forward. "You are detained. Now, I can zip-tie your hands again, or you can be a good boy. You decide."

Kadeem held up his hands as if in surrender.

"Good choice."

Lynda and Emma followed Smith to the wing that housed reinforced cells. A CIA agent opened the door to Samir's room, and Smith gestured for Kadeem to enter, putting the brothers together for the first time. The agent shut the door behind him, and it automatically locked.

In the observation room, Emma sat down next to Agent Lewis and slipped on a pair of headphones. "I'll give you a typed transcript, so you don't need to hover."

Lynda smiled. "I kinda do." She could learn as much from their body language as from their words.

As Emma translated, they watched the silent scene play out on the screen.

"Kadeem: 'How could you tell them?'

Samir: 'Tell them what?'

Kadeem: 'About the plans in Saudi.'

Samir: 'Brother, I told them nothing. They're tricking you.'

Kadeem: 'They knew. The only way they knew was if you told them. No, don't touch me, don't talk to me. I told you this was wrong. That it was a bad idea. And now Mother and the girls will never be free of that man.'

Samir: 'You need to rest and relax. They're tricking you. I promise.'"

Kadeem lay on one of the two cots and turned to face the wall, pulling his knees up and wrapping his arms tightly around himself. Samir looked at him for a moment, then sat back down on his cot and crossed his legs. He rested his palms on his knees and closed his eyes.

For several moments, no one moved, then Lynda said, "I think we should call it done tonight." She looked at her watch. "Well, this morning. Get some rest. Let's convene back here at ten." She looked at Smith. "Do we have a way back to our HQ, or do we have rooms here?"

"I have a car. They're expecting us back at HQ."

Outside, the cold air sat silent, as if waiting for the dawn. Emma looked up at the dark sky. "I love this time of morning. This heavy silence descends, and it's like the cusp of everything becoming new."

Lynda breathed in the air, smelling the sea. "I know what you mean."

They drove through the quiet city, keeping parallel to the river. When they reached headquarters, she felt the adrenaline fade like a stopper had been pulled from a drain.

As soon as she got to her room, she grabbed fresh clothes and her shower kit and went to the women's shower room.

It felt good to rinse away the last twenty-four hours. So much had happened. Her mind swirled with information, puzzle pieces, cogs, and gears. She wanted to sit down and analyze it all, but her brain needed sleep before she could make sense of anything.

When she walked out of the bathroom, she ran into Bill in the hallway. It was silly to be self-conscious of her wet hair and loose-fitting tank top and shorts, but she found herself tugging on the hem of her shirt anyway.

"Hi," he said quietly, leaning against the concrete wall. "Everyone tucked in for the night?"

"Uh, yeah. We're all meeting back at ten."

He raised an eyebrow and gave a pointed glance at his watch. "Not much downtime."

"Should be enough. If I can shut it all down." She tapped the side of her head. "Lots of information swirling."

"There's no telling what your subconscious will percolate on while you're sleeping."

"True." She stepped to the side. She felt too tired, too punchy, to have any kind of meaningful conversation with him right now. "Well, I'm going to try to get a little sleep."

"Sweet dreams." He straightened. "I'll see you later this morning."

CHAPTER

★

SIXTEEN

Bill stood with his back to the wall of the interview room, center of the table. Peña and Hanson sat at the table to his left, facing the man whose passport said Antoine Bishop of the United States. Lynda had identified him as being present in the barn in Alaska. He had dark-brown skin, a shaved head that shone in the lights of the room, and broad shoulders. He wore a pair of gray, short-sleeved scrubs issued to him by the CIA, which showed the classic Russian mafia tattoos running down his arms. His wire-framed glasses lay folded on the table in front of him.

Peña was a master at tactical debriefing. He could convince a subject that he was their best friend or their worst nightmare, sometimes both in the same conversation. By the time he finished what he did so well, the subject usually begged to tell him everything. Bill didn't have half of Peña's patience and would probably launch into the worst-nightmare scenario long before he had successfully primed the subject for it. He typically provided silent intimidation during the debriefings. The subject had no idea of the level of psychological insight Bill gained from them while standing silently in the back of the room.

Right now, Peña worked in his best-friend mode. He smiled, he laughed, he joked, he called Bishop "brother."

"So, you're the good cop," Bishop said after about five minutes. "When does the bad cop come in?"

"Nah, man," Peña said. "I'm just trying to get to the heart of it. I got no skin in this game. I recycle. I drive an electric car. I can understand the passion. We're good, you and I."

"If we're so good, you can let me go. I haven't done anything wrong, and you're illegally detaining me."

"Illegally?" Peña pursed his lips. "I'm not sure where you got your law degree, but one does not kidnap and torture a federal officer and then cry foul with detainment."

"Federal officer?"

"Sure. Agent Culter. You remember her, don't you? Tied to a chair, bleeding from the head, psychologically tortured."

Bishop sat back and crossed his arms over his chest. "I have nothing to say."

"No? I think you have lots to say. So does she, starting with a positive identification." Peña clicked his pen. "I got nothing but time. Go ahead and don't say a thing. No one knows where you are. We got time." He stood. "I, however, have a lunch date, so I'm going to leave you to stew. You just holler out if you need anything."

Bill opened the door for Peña, and they headed to the observation room, where Rick watched the screen with Agent Lewis.

"Feelings?" Rick asked, staring at Bishop. A CIA agent had taken up the guard post.

"He's going to take time," Peña said. "He's trained for this, somehow. I'm going to need a couple of days."

Rick looked at Agent Lewis. "What have we got from their residence? Anything good?"

"There's so much to look through," she said. "Agent Culter is doing that now."

"I say we take them out of Turkey," Rick said to Hanson. "The longer we're here, the greater the chance of discovery."

Turkey did not enjoy an American military presence on its soil. Capturing and interrogating citizens or guests of the country would not go over well with the government.

"I concur," Hanson said. "Every minute here is a risk. How do you want to do this?"

Rick looked at Bill. "You think boat?"

Bill scratched his chin. "Boat to Greece? Then back to Kuwait?"

"Kuwait or Djibouti."

"Can I vote?" Peña asked.

Rick chuckled. "Let's pack everything up. Selah can continue to work the brothers. Shut down HQ and let's head back to base. We'll debrief them all there." He looked at his watch. "Call Brock. Have him call for a boat. I think that's the most efficient way out of here." He turned toward Agent Lewis. "You joining us?"

"Let me get with command. I'm thinking probably."

"Okay. I want to clear the buildings by twenty-one hundred."

Lynda packed the last of four suitcases and stepped back. Morita and Fisher stood by, ready to take them. Bill walked into the room, dressed in full tactical gear. She glanced at the clock on the wall above Agent Cartridge's computer terminal. Ten minutes until nine. Norton wanted everyone cleared out by the top of the hour.

"Is that the last of it?" Bill asked.

"Other than what's in my backpack." She slipped the strap over her shoulder and walked to Agent Cartridge's work space. "Need help?"

The IT marvel tapped on his keyboard and shut the laptop's lid as he shook his head. He disconnected all the cords and put the computer into his bag.

Bill said to him, "Go with Sergeant Fisher. He's your travel buddy."

Fisher walked up. "Mason, can I help you carry anything?"

Agent Cartridge gestured at a large, hard case. "Please be careful. The case is waterproof, so we should be good to get onto a boat." He walked a step behind Fisher out of the room.

Lynda grinned at Bill. "Are you my travel buddy?"

"Yes, ma'am. I am at your disposal." He pressed the button on his mic and said, "Roger, sir. They are en route. We are right behind." He looked back at her. "Prisoners are on the boat. You and I are turning off the lights and shutting the door behind us."

She glanced around the room. The giant warehouse had been stripped of everything mission-oriented. Some computer screens remained, but all of the hard drives had left with Agent Smith an hour ago. "It's incredible to think that we got into the country just eight days ago. It feels like a lifetime."

"Time flies." He paused. "You did good work here."

Her chest swelled with pride. It shouldn't matter to her what Bill Sanders thought of her, but it did—very much. "Thanks. You too."

"Me? I'm just the muscle." He put his finger on the light switch. "It's time to put the chairs on the wagon."

Lynda giggled.

They walked out into the cool night to the rental car Norton had driven from the American base days ago. Lynda put her backpack into the back seat and slid into the car.

Bill glanced over at her as he started the car. "I really enjoyed working with you. I'm sorry for the circumstances, but I think it turned into a good thing."

She wanted to reach out and touch his hand but instead clasped her hands together. "I agree. It was hard at first, but I'm happy it got smoother."

"I just wore you down with my charm. You can admit it."

"It is the only answer." She rubbed the back of her neck.

He backed the car out. "Have you spoken to Haynes?"

Her stomach clenched at the thought. "No. I don't think anyone has at this point, other than an initial attempt at information gathering."

"Do you want to be part of his tactical debrief?"

A part of her wanted to raise her fist and yell, "Absolutely!" Another part wanted to hide in a dark room and hope she never laid eyes on Jack again. "I don't know yet. I'm still information gathering." She looked at Bill. "I feel like if I could dig into the why and what, the how would make more sense. Then I could let some of it out of my mind." She turned to look out the window so he couldn't see the tears glistening in her eyes. "I don't like being used. I don't like knowing I was a victim. It's been a hard couple of days as I've been working through it."

"I don't pretend to understand how you're feeling, but if you need to vent or even punch someone, I'm available." He hit the button on his mic. "Roger. ETA four minutes." He glanced her way. "Cartridge, Morita, and Fisher just got to the boat."

"That seems fast."

"Morita is a master. He could probably draw a perfectly detailed map of the city right now. I'm sure he found forty-seven shortcuts to our extraction point."

"Only forty-seven, huh?"

He grinned at her in a way that made her heart skip a beat. "Well, I might be exaggerating slightly."

"Not you."

His face grew serious as he looked in the rearview mirror. "We have company."

He turned suddenly. Lynda braced herself to keep from sliding across the seat, while using the side mirror to see the car turn with them. "Looks like a police car." He accessed his mic. "Six, this is Backstrap. We have detected an observer. Advise you depart and we regroup at the RP. How copy?"

"Good copy," came the instant reply.

He turned sharply again, and the car turned with them. Suddenly, the sky behind them lit up in red-and-blue lights.

"Whose car is this?" Lynda asked.

"I'm pretty sure it's a rental, but I wouldn't put money on the name on the contract." He hit the radio again. "Apparently we have attracted the interest of the local gendarmerie. Should I stop or evade?"

A moment later, he got his answer. "Evade if possible."

After a few seconds of glancing at the buildings surrounding them, he glanced over at her. "Buckle up, Buttercup."

As she checked her seat belt to ensure it was tight, Bill downshifted, and the car darted forward.

It fascinated her how everything slowed to a crawl, but her mind kept thinking at its normal pace. Bill calculated turns and movements with a precision that impressed her. He sped up. He slowed down. He darted over curbs and down alleys.

She stayed as still as possible so as not to distract him and tried not to visibly react to the speed and impending objects or barriers, praying the entire time. She begged God to keep them safe, to let them evade capture, and to get them home.

Bill whipped into the left-hand lane. Oncoming headlights glared in the windshield as he passed three cars then jerked back into the right lane. He downshifted and shot ahead, shifted up again, and took a sharp right down an incline. He killed the lights and turned on a residential road. He quickly parallel parked in between two cars and shut the engine off. "Let's move."

She grabbed her backpack as they got out of the car. Bill took her hand, and they ran in between two villas. The smell of roasting meat carried to them on the breeze, and the sounds of a game show came from an open window. As they ducked behind a building, the police car stopped at their newly abandoned vehicle. Bill's hand tightened on hers as they ran between the houses to the next street, turning the opposite direction of the main road.

He helped her over a stone fence, then vaulted over it and knelt beside her. "If we get separated, go to the American consulate. Do you know where that is from here?"

They weren't going to get separated. Lynda would make sure of that. "I have the address."

"Perfect." He took her hand again. "Let's go."

They ran along houses and darted in between alleys. The police presence in the neighborhood grew. At one point, they ducked behind a hedge near a bedroom window. Eventually, they found themselves out of the residential streets and into a more business-centric area.

"Change clothes if you have them," Bill said as he pulled his vest open. "Put your vest under your shirt."

Leaning against the alley wall of a curry restaurant, Bill turned his back while she pulled her shirt off and put the vest on over her tank top. As quickly and modestly as possible, she changed into a long skirt and wrapped a scarf around her head.

Bill stripped off his vest and shirt. Even with his back turned, she could see the scar from the bullet wound along his rib cage. He covered it when he put the vest back on, then put his shirt over it.

They looked a little less out of place as they reentered the pedestrian traffic. She glanced up at him, her mouth dry, her heart pounding. "Do they know who we are?"

"You have as much information as I do, darlin'," he said, looking down at her but cutting his eyes to glance behind them. "Let's just keep moving. I'll know in a minute if we're good." He pressed the button on his mic. "Talk to me. Get us out of here."

They walked hand in hand down the street. At one point, they darted into a shop and moved to the back, then turned to watch the doorway. After several moments, they went out the back exit onto a different street. They did this a few times, then finally called for a cab and gave instructions to go to the docks.

They rode in tense silence. Lynda's neck muscles tightened with every passing mile. She wanted to rub at her head and pull the constricting fabric away, but she just sat perfectly still and watched the city go by.

The second the cab dropped them off at a marina and drove away, Bill tugged on the hijab. "You can lose that."

Relieved, Lynda slipped it off and put it into her backpack.

"I have coordinates to meet a boat."

"Are we swimming?"

He grinned down at her and shook his head, then took her hand again, and they walked along the dock to slip number forty-seven. A small motorboat bobbed on the tide.

Bill glanced all around, then reached down and untied the rope. He hopped on board, held a hand out, and said, "Let me have your bag first." Once he set that to the side, he took her hand and helped her onto the boat.

"Whose is this?" she asked.

"I'm guessing one of the agents'. Rick relayed information from Lewis."

Thanks to the combination provided by Agent Lewis, a lockbox inside the cockpit revealed a key, and the boat started right up. Bill carefully backed out of the slip, then they quietly drifted out of the marina. A couple of times, he talked to his team on his radio. Lynda sat on the seat next to his captain's chair and closed her eyes, shivering slightly in the cold wind.

Once they got out on the open sea, Bill cut the engine and pulled his earpiece out. He turned toward her, resting his arm against the top of the fiberglass canopy. "You did well out there."

She shook her head. "I'm not a field-trained operative. Undercover is not my thing. I back up raids and filter through information. They probably should have put someone else with you and used cameras and—"

He leaned down and cupped her cheek, cutting off her statement. "You did really well out there."

She stared up at his face bathed in moonlight. Her breath caught at the intensity glowing in his eyes. "Bill, I don't know if I can do this again with you. I don't know if I'd survive you a second time."

He removed his hand, and she missed his touch. "Lynda, I'm not a scared nineteen-year-old kid anymore. I'm a man, all grown up and much more emotionally stable. I'd go back and change what I did if I could. But I can't. I just know that this last week with you opened something up inside me that I don't think has ever seen the light of day. And once I realized it, all I could think about was getting you somewhere safe so I could kiss you."

Heart pounding, she stood. She looked all around, then back at him. "Looks pretty safe to me."

His arms came around her without her knowing which one of them moved first. Nothing about the feel or taste of him reminded her of the boy she'd known. His beard felt soft against her cheek and tickled her palm, his lips velvety and warm. She forgot the cold, she forgot the danger, as her entire world became the feel of Bill's body and the way his mouth moved on hers.

He gripped the back of her head in his strong hand, and his other arm wrapped around her waist, pulling her even closer. The blood roared in her ears, and all her senses became consumed by him.

Eventually, he quieted the kiss, pulling back slightly, until it became just a mingling of breaths and a brush of lips. When he loosened his arms, he pressed a kiss to her forehead and then released her.

She melted back into her chair, and he propped himself up with his forearm against the canopy. He cleared his throat, then put the earpiece back in. "Okay, give me those coordinates again."

CHAPTER

★

SEVENTEEN

KUWAIT
DECEMBER 12

Bill sat on the leather sofa in the ready room. Morita walked in and said, "I never thought I'd be glad to be back in Kuwait."

Bill tapped his boot. "I think it's less Kuwait and more American soil. Besides, I've always liked it here." He took the last bite of his apple. "Last night was crazy."

"Did Lewis ever say what happened?"

"Someone on campus saw us putting the brothers into the car we were driving. There was the Turkish equivalent of an APB put out on that car. Just bad timing."

"Bad timing." Morita shook his head. "Dude." He said it like all of the night was conveyed in one word.

"Tell me about it." Bill stretched, then tossed the apple toward the trash can. It went in after bouncing off the wall.

"I'm just thankful we evaded capture. I can't imagine explaining everything to the Turkish authorities when we weren't supposed to be there and we had fake passports."

"No kidding." Morita opened a bag of popcorn and put it in the microwave. "I'm sure Agent Culter has had her share of excitement this week."

Bill had managed to go the last two minutes without thinking about Lynda. Suddenly, the thought of her flooded his mind. His mouth went dry and his heart rate accelerated as he remembered their kiss. "She, uh, told me on the boat that she prefers being an analyst to a field agent."

"I'm the opposite. I don't know how they stare at information all day. I just want to do something." Morita watched the spinning bag until the pops started to die down, then pulled it out of the microwave. The room filled with the buttery smell of popped corn. "But I guess we need analysts to tell us what to do, am I right?"

"I hear you, brother." Bill chuckled, then looked at his watch. "I'm due back in debriefing. Catch you later."

He walked to the CHU where they housed the prisoners. After he signed in, the duty sergeant directed him to the appropriate room.

In the hall, he found Agent Lewis with Rick. "Daddy, Lewis, howdy."

"Get some rest?" Rick asked, securing his earpiece.

"Slept like a bedbug snuggled into Granny's back. What do we have going on in there?" On the monitor, he saw two of the men they had captured with Jack Haynes.

"Trenton Phillips and Shane Franklin," Agent Lewis said. "They appear to be your typical Southern California natives. Clean-cut. No records. They have also been talking their heads off. Either they have no idea that we've been listening to them since day one, or they are plants and are feeding bad information. Either way." She gestured with her chin at another monitor. The man with dark hair sat immobile on his cot. "In there is Leonard Popov. Only he told us his name was Mohamed Zaahid. His fingerprints popped on Interpol's database."

Bill frowned. "Why would a Russian pretend to be Turkish?"

"That is certainly the question." Rick tapped his ear. "We're ready."

Peña and Selah came from around the corner. Bill shook Peña's hand. "Hey, man."

"Glad you made it. Sounds like you had a ride."

"Better than the county fair." He looked at Selah. "Are you ready to translate Russian?"

"Da." She winked at him. "Don't underestimate me." She looked at Rick. "Jorge said that we're going with ignorance at first?"

"Yeah. He doesn't know we know who he is."

"Perfect." She glanced at Lewis. "Does Agent Culter know about the positive identification?"

Lewis nodded. "I've sent his file to her."

"Where is she?" Bill asked, trying to be casual, but a small smile crossed Selah's lips.

"She has our briefing room," Lewis said. "She needed the space. Agents Cartridge and Smith are with her. They're trying to put it all together."

Peña clapped his hands together. "So, let's get them some more information. Who's going in?"

"Me," Bill said.

Rick pointed down the hall. "I'll be observing." He glanced at Lewis. "Ready?"

Lynda pinned a chat transcript from one of the recovered cell phones onto the bulletin board. She stepped back, surveying the progress on the information gathering. In the background, she listened to Emma's transcript of the conversation the two brothers had during transport and once they arrived here.

She rolled her neck and closed her eyes. Something was here. What could she not see?

She started back at the beginning—the explosion of a pipeline in South Dakota, followed by one in Alaska a week later. That explosion killed twenty-seven and destroyed fifteen thousand acres. Then ones in Colombia, Kuwait, Venezuela, and the planned target in Saudi Arabia. Why? She believed their motivations had nothing to do with the environment. There was another reason.

"Have we ever been able to locate the person who sponsored the Nasser brothers? The one who gave them their scholarship?" she asked Agent Cartridge.

His fingers never stopped clacking on his keyboard. "Sort of. I traced everything to a Russian bank, but I haven't been able to get any further than that."

"Russian? Hmm." She walked along the timeline that stretched around the wall. At the capture and arrest of Jack, she stopped. Russian. "I need Jack Haynes's record of service while he was undercover with the Russian mafia," she said. "Did that come with his records?"

Agent Smith nodded and opened a box. He dug through it

and pulled out a thick file folder. "Here are all of his reports and the subsequent investigations."

Jack had spent five years under deep cover. Maybe something had happened during that time.

An hour later, Bill strolled into the room. Lynda tried to ignore the way her pulse rate increased at seeing him, the way she suddenly lost her place and concentration. But she couldn't help smiling because she was so glad to lay eyes on him.

He winked at her and said, "You'll never believe this about our prisoner Mohamed Zaahid."

"Hmm." She grinned. "He's actually Russian?"

Bill's jaw dropped. "How did you know that?"

"Because I'm good at what I do." She pointed at the newest section of her board. "And I got the fingerprint reports too."

"Very sly, Agent Clever."

"We all have our strengths." She made a notation on a notepad. "What did you get out of him?"

"So far, nothing. Peña was at it for two hours. I think they're regrouping to determine how best to address it." He pointed at her. "They're wanting you right now."

"Good. I was about to go join them." She picked up her notebook and rolled-up map and left the room. Bill followed her. She found Peña, Emma, Norton, and Lewis sitting around a monitor in the observation room.

When Norton saw her, he sat up straighter. "What do you have?"

"It has to be Russian mafia connected."

Emma shook her head. "Why would the Russian mafia blow up oil pipelines?"

Lynda unrolled the map on the table, showing the global

oil pipelines. Using a red marker, she made an X over Alaska, South Dakota, Venezuela, Colombia, and Kuwait, then circled Saudi Arabia. "There are a lot of pipelines in the world. Millions of miles."

"Are they wanting to destroy them all?" Emma asked.

"I don't think so." She drew a big circle around Russia. "I think that they're wanting to corner the market. Drive prices up in the larger supply areas so they can sell their oil."

Peña traced the red circle. "So, it's all about money and not about the environment?"

"I think." Lynda opened a file folder. "I also think they were using the mosque to make us look to Muslim extremists instead of anyone else. Agent Haynes was undercover with the Russian mafia for five years. It's possible that he's still linked to them." She found a report that included information about Leonard Popov. "Your Mohamed Zaahid, as I understand you've discovered, is Russian. He is part of the organization that Haynes was investigating. I think that's a bit of a coincidence, don't you?"

"I don't believe in coincidences." Norton pointed at a screen. The Nasser brothers sat facing each other. "Why the college students? What do they gain?"

Lynda shrugged. "They're young, passionate, able to be manipulated. Feed them environmental propaganda, tell them the world will end in their lifetime if they don't effect change, and make them believe that they'll be heroes as they avenge their father's death. It's not that far-fetched."

Norton looked over at another screen. "The question is, how far down does the mafia go, and where does the environmental activism start?" He pointed at the screen with Popov and said to Emma, "Let's talk to him. Start off in

Russian. See how he reacts." He looked at Lynda. "Do you want to sit in on it?"

She shook her head. "No. But I would like to talk to the Nasser brothers some more."

"We'll get there." He glanced at their screen again. "We offered to send them to the Saudis, but they've agreed to stay with us for the time being."

Lynda shuddered and rubbed her arms. She couldn't imagine the punishment for two Yemenis who planned to blow something up in Saudi Arabia. "We're also finding hints about something big about to happen in the States. I've dug and dug through correspondence, emails, texts, but it's all just alluded to. No specific information."

"You think there's a bigger network in the States?" Peña asked.

Lynda nodded. "I think there's an entire organization. But it's just guesswork."

"Well, your guesswork is better than anything else we have." Norton stood. "Drumstick, Selah, Peña Colada, go find out what's going on. We'll be watching." He tapped his ear. "Keep your earpiece on. Agent Culter might have something to say to you."

Lynda sat in the empty dining hall and watched a replay of an Atlanta Braves and Miami Marlins game on her phone. She was always glad when she found a game she'd never seen before. A cold cup of coffee sat in front of her. Her mind swam with information and ideas and plots and—

She pressed the heels of her hands into her eyes and willed her brain to stop. She looked back at the game, analyzing it, strategizing like a coach, hoping that would get the attention of her thought processes. Baseball gave her brain an out when work overwhelmed her.

For some reason, though, it didn't help tonight. Maybe it just all made her miss home that much more.

When Bill scooted a chair out and sat down across from her, it startled her. She looked up from her phone and smiled at him. A warmth started in her chest and spread through her body. "Long day."

"Long couple of weeks," he said.

Last night on the boat felt so far away, so long ago. Sitting here, in the reality of their world, she wondered what they could possibly have been thinking.

"Don't do that," he said as if he could read her mind. He opened a can of soda and poured it into a paper cup. "We knew that this assignment would be hard on this budding romance. Let's just keep it cool in that complicated mind of yours."

Heat filled her cheeks. "How did you know?"

"Because I have been paying close attention to you under close quarters for several days." He picked up her hand. "I'll forgive you for being a Braves fan. It's not what's going to break us."

She chuckled as his touch chased away the lingering doubts and fears. "Fair enough. Who would you suggest I root for?"

"Well, 'Bama, baby. Of course. No need to leave the state."

"I've seen every single 'Bama game ever played. I needed one I'd never seen before. The Braves are second best."

He grinned. "Fair enough." He gestured at the phone. "Why did you need one you'd never seen before?"

She opened her mouth and closed it again, trying to formulate an explanation about how the game helped her mind. "Using strategy and statistics to determine what will happen next in the game, adjusting that strategy and those statistics as things happen during the course of the game—all of that helps me shut my mind off."

He stared at her for several moments. "You are incredible. I hope you know that and never doubt it." He released her hand to take a long drink of his soda. "Can I buy you lunch?"

She wrinkled her nose. "I tried. They closed service an hour ago and will open it back up for dinner at five."

He wiggled his eyebrows as he reached into his pockets and pulled out two packaged sandwiches from a vending machine and two bags of chips. "Your choice is turkey on wheat or egg salad on white."

She considered his size, his caloric needs, and picked the egg salad. "You are my hero," she said, bowing her head to ask God's blessing on the unexpected meal. When she raised her head, he slid a package of cheese-flavored potato chips her way. After eating half of the sandwich, she lost the inner battle with herself and blurted out, "I'd like you to talk to me about something."

A guarded look crossed his face, which made her courage falter. "What's that?"

She took a deep breath and plunged forward. "What was it about me that made me undesirable outside of the college environment?"

He blinked. "I beg your pardon?"

"Well, it was obviously something. We were together for over a year, but only on campus. Never off. Explain that to me."

He picked up one of the sandwich halves and took a bite,

which was about a third of it. After he washed it down, he said, "I didn't want you to see my home. So, as a coping mechanism, I compartmentalized. In school, you were this incredible, smart, sexy, wonderful person who didn't know anything about that part of me. Outside of school, I couldn't have hidden it, so I made sure there was never an opportunity for you to see it."

She analyzed what he said, then closed her eyes and shook her head. "Hide what? I don't understand."

He tossed the rest of his sandwich down and leaned back. "I grew up in a roach-infested single-wide trailer with a woman who traded food stamps and other favors for beer money. Which meant that the only meals I got were in school. That made the summers rather long and tedious. I have no idea who my father is. I doubt he even knows of my existence." He rubbed his beard. "When I got hurt and had to go home at the end of that semester, the idea that you might see me there . . . It was better to hurt you than to suffer that shame."

Her heart immediately broke for the boy he used to be. "How awful for you. That explains your depth of character."

"You can't be serious."

"I'm not going to argue about it." She stood, walked around the table, and leaned back against it, facing him directly. "Bill, even then, if I'd seen you in that environment, it wouldn't have meant that that's how I would forever see you."

His eyes grew hard. "You say that in hindsight."

"That's fair. I do." She leaned forward and cupped his face. His beard tickled her palms. "I was in love with the man I saw. The strong, funny, capable leader who made life brighter for me."

He closed his eyes and released a long breath. "And now?"

She straightened and let him go. "And now I'm worried that this is like campus. Once we leave it, you're not going to want me outside of it, in your real life. I don't know how to trust you." She walked back around the table and picked up her remaining sandwich. "I do want to. I just don't know how."

He ripped open his bag of chips. "I guess I'll just have to prove to you that you can trust me."

"I retain my right to keep myself emotionally safe until then," she said. "You don't fully understand what your words did to me and the negative impact it had on my self-confidence. You didn't just break up with me. You annihilated me. For years." When he opened his mouth, she held her hand up. "I know. I understand now why you did it. You just have to give me time."

"You can have all the time you need."

CHAPTER

★

EIGHTEEN

Lynda held a cup of coffee while she made notes on a white-board. In the background, the recorded interview with Trenton Phillips played. He was one of the blond men and had been in the house when their team raided it.

Jack and two of the men from the barn that night remained very reserved. They had no opinions to give on the state of the world on any level. They didn't answer any questions, and they didn't have much to say. Despite cells next to each other, they didn't speak to one another in any apparent way.

Trenton Phillips and Shane Franklin acted differently. They were Americans, passionate about their views on the West's fossil fuel consumption, the state of the polar ice caps, the depletion of the ozone level, and even the presence of cattle to feed the fat Americans and Europeans. They came across as angry, enraptured, and overzealous.

They probably sincerely believed what they said. They did not believe that there was anything wrong with their mission to disrupt the use of fossil fuels. The end justified the means, so to speak.

In the middle of a rant about the US news not reporting Green War's activities, Phillips said, "They will. You'll see."

She quickly hit the pause button on the recording and capped the dry-erase marker. Why would they? What did that mean?

She grabbed the binder of the text messages and flipped to the section with the phone found on Phillips. Frowning, she scanned his texts, looking for one that felt out of place. She hadn't been able to pinpoint the specifics when she'd read it before.

There. That one. A text to Shane Franklin, sent last Thursday.

> They'll have to pay attention next Wednesday.

The reply came minutes later:

> You know it. But, dude, keep it on the down-low.

She ripped out the page and rushed out of the room. Thankfully, she found Peña and Norton in the observation room. "I'm positive something is going to happen in the States."

Peña put down his pen and stood. "What?"

"Something bigger than a pipeline. Something that the press can't ignore." She waved the paper. "Phillips texted his buddy, the one you have him in a cell with. Look at it." When Norton took the paper, she continued. "He said something very casually in one of the interviews that reminded me of this text." She walked to a phone and started dialing the complex series of numbers. Within seconds, someone answered. "Director Blake, please." At the prompt, she added, "Agent Culter."

Norton handed the paper to Peña. "What's your next step?"

Lynda turned away from Norton, wanting to speak to her deputy director without distraction, and explained what she'd found.

"No idea what yet?" Perry asked.

"No, sir. I'm going to leave them here, let them continue their interviews, and make my way back to the States."

She could hear paper rustling, and then he said, "Go to DC. I'll meet you there tomorrow."

She hung up the phone and turned to Norton. "I need to go back. If you can continue to work Trenton Phillips and Shane Franklin, maybe they'll shed enough light that I can actively handle it on the ground end."

He nodded. "How long do you need?"

"Twenty minutes."

"We'll get you transpo." On her way out of the room, he added, "Well done, Agent Culter."

She paused at the doorway. "We haven't stopped them yet."

"We will."

She turned and faced him fully. "I would like to talk to Jack before I leave."

He raised an eyebrow. "Is that going to be helpful to the mission or helpful for you?"

Good question. "Maybe both. What I want to do is see how he reacts. I want to analyze his body language. I think Bill would be able to give me a lot of insight with it too."

He paused, clearly contemplating it. "Fair enough. I'll have him brought to a room. I'm going to put Peña and Hanson in there with you, but you can lead."

Lynda wished that she'd brought a file folder with her. At least then she would have something to do with her hands while she thought about what to say and how to say it. Instead, she sat across from Jack and just stared at him.

She noticed right off the bat that he needed a shave. In all the time she'd known him, he had always paid careful attention to his appearance.

"Hello, Jack," she said.

He stared at her with a stony expression. She had a hard time reconciling the man she'd known with the person in front of her. Her Jack always had a ready smile, a loving touch. She had fallen fast and hard for him. Within just weeks of dating, she couldn't imagine spending her life without him.

He sat with his hands laced on the table and finally asked, "How many laws have you broken to keep me here without counsel, Agent Culter?"

It didn't surprise her that he'd decided to start off as the aggressor. They had not observed him speaking a single word since his capture. He'd had plenty of time to decide his angle of attack.

"Terrorism has a different due process," she said. "I don't need to explain that to you. However, if you would rather, we could turn you over to Saudi Arabia. You could spend a year in a dungeon before they cut your head off for planning a terrorist attack against them."

If she hadn't been watching him so closely, she would have

missed the flash of fear in his eyes before it was replaced with contempt. "What do I have to do with Saudi Arabia?"

"You mean other than the plan to blow the pipeline? The one that we stopped with the arrest of the Yemeni students?"

His mouth gaped. "How did you know—?" After stuttering a moment, he said, "You wouldn't."

"Hand you over? Whether I would or not is truly of no consequence. It's not up to me, is it? That's a matter for the State Department to decide. I'm just a cog in a wheel." She paused. "Probably better for you that it's not up to me, if you want the truth."

His upper lip twisted in a snarl. "Then why are you in here with me if you're just a cog? Want to know all about why I used you? Blubber, blubber, sob, sob. Want me to tell you all about what my endgame was in romancing you? Curious about how I could stand pretending to fall in love with the cold fish that was you?"

Her throat started to close in embarrassment as she thought about the people watching this interview in the other room. "Not particularly. I've figured the romance part out. My emotional involvement with you clouded my memory of the event, kept me from analyzing it too deeply, while I was still a valuable witness to your demise."

"Always analyzing, always one step ahead."

"Clearly not always." She tilted her head, tried to get into his brain. "I'm headed back to the States. Your minions have provided us with information about the attacks coming on Wednesday. I personally just wanted to let you know that you've failed, and I'll be handing you over to the proper authorities."

When he slammed his fist on the table, she jumped. Annoyed at herself for reacting, she laced her fingers together and kept her expression stoic.

"You cannot possibly stop it," he said. "It's out of your hands. The pieces have been set into motion."

"Did you ever learn Newton's first law of motion?"

"What are you talking about?"

"In part, it states that an object in motion stays in motion with the same speed and in the same direction unless acted upon by an unbalanced force." She stood and leaned forward, close enough to smell his breath. "Consider me the unbalanced force. All of those pieces and parts you've set in motion? I will stop them."

She straightened and turned to leave the room. As she put her hand on the doorknob, he said, "You were the hardest cover job I've ever had to do."

Without another word, she ripped open the door and exited. In the hall, she leaned against the wall and pressed the heels of her hands to her eyes.

Suddenly, she felt Bill's presence. Without even looking, she leaned into him and let him put his arms around her.

"You did well in there," he said.

"I reacted. I shouldn't have."

"You did well." He pulled back and put a finger under her chin, tilting her face up to his. "I'm proud of you."

"I have to go," she whispered. "If I leave now, it will be Tuesday morning when I get there. That gives me just a day."

"I know. Rick told me. Go be that unbalanced force."

DECEMBER 13

Bill rapped on Lynda's doorframe. She opened it seconds later, her eyes widening when she saw him. "I just barely finished packing," she said. "What are you doing here?"

They'd already said their goodbyes. He could tell she hadn't expected to see him again so soon. "Pilot's ready. You're going straight to Dover, Delaware. Do not pass go, etc. Should land seven a.m. Tuesday morning. Which is lots of fun if you consider that it's one a.m. Tuesday here. So, you're almost flying backwards in time." He held up the keys to the vehicle. "I'm driving you to the airfield."

"Perfect." She zipped her backpack shut. "I have so much reading to do on the plane. I'm glad I didn't have to get a civilian flight."

He cleared his throat. "I realize the circumstances weren't exactly anyone's consideration of ideal, but I have really enjoyed working with you and having you nearby."

She stepped into his arms and hugged him. He closed his eyes, relishing the feel of her. Too soon, she pulled back just far enough to look up at him. "I'm happy God brought us together again."

He pushed his fingers into her hair and lowered his mouth to hers. Everything about kissing her felt right. It stilled his mind and soothed his soul. As he drew her closer and wrapped his arms around her, he couldn't help but feel the finality in her touch, in her kiss. He pulled his mouth from hers and pressed his cheek to her head. He had things he needed to say before he lost the chance.

"I love you," he said, desperately wanting her to hear and believe him. "I don't think I ever stopped."

His arms felt empty the moment she pulled away. She slung her backpack over her shoulder and picked up her suitcase. "I want to believe that."

His heart twisted. Did they have hope? He couldn't help but think about the way Haynes had spoken to her, the things he'd said to her. He didn't blame her for keeping a bit of distance between them. Did she put him in the same category as Haynes? Was it too late for them?

He refused to believe that. He stepped forward and ran a hand from her shoulder to her wrist, then took the handle of her suitcase from her. "Ready?"

They didn't have far to drive, but the silence weighed heavily between them. He didn't know what else to say. When they got to the airfield, he shifted to face her. Before she could open the door, he grabbed her hand. "I don't know how to make this work on my own."

"Bill, you aren't alone." She took his hand in both of hers and put it against her cheek. "I'm going to miss you."

He pulled her close and kissed her one more time, and then she got out of the car. He could barely see her until she got closer to the plane that lit up the tarmac.

Long after the plane took off, he continued to sit there, but he didn't know why. Did he expect her to cancel the trip and come running back into his arms? A ridiculous thought considering everything going on in the world.

Once he turned the vehicle in and went into the headquarters building, he sought out Rick. Thankfully, his friend sat alone in the observation room. The monitors showed the prisoners in their various cells. It looked like a very quiet night.

"Lynda get off okay?" Rick asked.

"Yeah." Bill sat down next to him. "I'm not sure letting her leave was the right thing to do."

"For you. But for the mission, which is our current and most important focus, it was." Rick tapped the screen of the environmentalists Phillips and Franklin. "These men here. Their passion for the environment is real. I don't believe that the Russians are truly connected to Green War. I think they were using them."

Bill shifted mentally, pushing his personal woes and angst to the side and bringing the mission to the forefront. "To what end?"

"Troops on the ground, maybe. Manipulative passion? I don't know." Rick slid a photograph toward him of an elaborate tattoo of an eagle with spread wings on a man's back.

"Who is this?"

"Popov. Kinda screams mafia, doesn't it?"

"Yeah. But for sure? I mean, it could just be a tattoo, right?"

"Not according to Culter or Smith." Rick sat back and pulled a packet of peanuts out of his pants pocket. "Add in Jack Haynes's experience with the Russian mafia and his sudden resurrection, and I think Agent Culter was right. I think we're looking at something with a few more layers than some wacky environmentalists."

"So what's next?"

Rick held out the nuts, but Bill shook his head. "We have thirteen hours until Culter lands in DC. Now we pray with desperation that we can crack those two right there and find out exactly what kind of attack is being planned on the States." He gestured at the photograph. "The Russians, Popov and Bishop, aren't talking." He pointed at another screen, and Bill looked at the Yemeni brothers. "Those two don't know anything."

Bill crossed his arms, sat back, and looked at the two American environmentalists. Their interviews had been interesting. Bill's experience had always involved combat enemies of the state. He'd never encountered this specific kind of passion and purpose.

"How are we going to do this?" he asked.

Rick grinned. "Selah is going to go in and work her particular brand of magic."

Bill snorted. He'd seen all five feet two of Selah go into a debriefing and come out hours later with the information needed and the subject in a confused state, not entirely certain how she'd extracted said information. Until now, Phillips and Franklin had only talked to Peña. "I don't envy them."

"No. She's doing research right now," Rick said. Selah would pull all the personal information she could find about the two men so she could go in fully armed. "We're going to let them eat breakfast and then hit them after."

Bill stood. "I'll go find her, see if she needs help."

"Sounds good." As Bill started to walk out of the room, Rick said, "When this is over, take some time and go to Lynda. Work out logistics of Alaska and Kentucky. Until then, try not to get bogged down mentally with it. I need you here with me."

Bill looked at his best friend. "Understood."

CHAPTER

★

NINETEEN

Military aircraft were loud and uncomfortable. Lynda learned this quickly on her thirteen-hour flight to Dover Air Force Base. She put on noise-canceling headphones and played classical music. Music with words would distract her mind.

Because she had the back of the plane to herself, she spread out. Along the backs of one bank of seats, she taped pictures of the people she knew to have a part in the operation. She generated a timeline along the floor. Details that she'd grabbed from Jack's reports in deep cover went on the other side of the plane. His timeline got laid out above that of the attacks.

The more she looked at the pieces and parts, the more she thought there were two entirely separate groups operating. One was Green War, an ecoterrorist organization bent on destroying the world's reliance on fossil fuels. They were violent, angry, and desperate to be heard. They recruited college kids to do their dirty work and hid behind anonymity and misdirection.

From the other group, she could see connections going back to the Russian mafia boss Kirill Volkov. The FBI had arrested him last year, and he currently faced trial for numerous crimes. Why use Green War? What did they provide?

She ate a cold MRE as she walked along the timelines. Green War's activity had ramped up when Jack arrived in Alaska. Clearly, his new position had served as a catalyst for the organization to step up its game. But why?

She got out a notebook and a pen and made some notes. *Passion. Funding. Disposable "minions."*

She paused, pen over the paper. Could it be that simple? Why not? Sometimes the simplest, most obvious answer was the right answer.

After several minutes she set the notebook to the side. Right now, she needed to focus on the alleged imminent attack.

Bill took the sentry position in the back of the interview room and stared at Trenton Phillips. He had blond hair, blue eyes, and lean features. He looked like he belonged more on a surfboard in Malibu than sitting in an interrogation room in Kuwait.

When Selah came into the room, Phillips looked from her to Bill and back to her before he sat back and scoffed. "I hate to break it to you," he said, "but they shoulda started with you. If that guy before you couldn't scare me, what makes you think you will?"

She set her tablet on the table and swiped across it. Soon, an image appeared on the wall next to Bill. Inside a large stadium, a man in white knelt on a black pad, while another man in a white robe and a red-and-white-checkered headdress approached him with a sword.

"In Saudi Arabia, they do public executions," Selah said. "Most of the prisoners are drugged. That way, they don't try to get up and run away. I think it's rather a nice concession, don't you? I mean, I'm sure they could tie them up to keep them from running away, but this is much more humane."

Phillips stared at the image, opening and closing his mouth like a fish gasping for air. He looked at her and said, "I'm an American citizen."

"You are indeed. I know everything that there is possible to know about you. But what you probably don't know is that we're in Kuwait right now. You know, where you blew up a pipeline six weeks ago? And the Yemeni brothers we arrested have already admitted to us your plans to blow the pipeline in Saudi Arabia. So the fact is, we can just let Kuwait and Saudi fight it out over who gets you first. Of course, the one who gets you first will have you last."

Tears spilled out of his eyes. "What can I do?"

"Well, I imagine you'll have to tell me why America would want you more. Since, you know, possession is nine-tenths. And we currently possess."

He searched her face. Bill could tell that he tried to gauge whether she would actually turn him over to the local authorities. His partner did not believe she would. He had called her bluff. When Bill had left that room three hours ago, he'd wondered if the State Department would make good on its threat and hand Shane Franklin over to Kuwait or Saudi Arabia, or if they would still send him to the States for prosecution.

Selah left the image on the wall and began her line of questioning. "Who is Cisco?"

Phillips's gaze darted between her face and the image. "Our leader. The leader of Green War."

"How long have you been with Green War?"

"Seventeen years. I was recruited my senior year of high school."

She nodded. "Thank you for telling me the truth. Now, let's dig into things a little further." She swiped on her tablet again, and a grid of images appeared. They all showed destruction. Some were pipelines, others manufacturing facilities. "Tell me which of these nine attacks were not done by Green War."

He looked at the wall. His eyes moved rapidly from one square to another. "The center one."

She raised an eyebrow. "Anything else?"

He shook his head.

"Why do three of them not have the Morse code tag on them?"

"They were the early days. Cisco started the tag when there wasn't a lot of media attention about the bombings. He thought if they were all tied to the same organization, then people would start paying attention."

The image of the beheading replaced the picture of the pipeline attacks. "Your partner had a lot to say about what's happening this week. I'm not sure if it's enough to get him a ticket home, but it was a start. Why don't you fill in our gaps?"

"I can't do that."

"Why not?"

"Because Cisco will kill me."

She gestured behind her. "Are you saying he'll publicly execute you by beheading? Is that what I'm hearing? Because, Trenton, my boy, let me get something through that blond head of yours. This here, this is a sure thing. You getting a chance to ever see home again? It isn't."

He slapped the table. Bill stepped forward and glared at him. A look of fear crossed Phillips's face. "Why would you do that to me?"

"I'm not doing anything," Selah said. "I didn't break any laws. I didn't blow anything up."

Bill stayed in the forward position, ready to intervene in case Phillips went after Selah.

She asked again, "What gaps can you fill?"

As an inhuman-sounding wail left his mouth, he pressed his palms against his eyes. Then he hit his forehead over and over again with the heels of his hands. "Okay," he said, sniffing and wiping his eyes. "Okay. Look, what if I tell you where there's a clue? Will that help? Then you finding out isn't my fault."

Selah glanced at Bill and rolled her eyes. He couldn't believe how quickly this man had caved. "Sure," she said. "Let's see what kind of clue you're willing to give."

"Right, okay. Hidden in my apartment is a composition notebook."

She shook her head. "We've been in your apartment. There is no composition notebook."

"Yes. Yes. Yes, there is. One of the fireplace bricks is removable. It's there."

She lifted her chin and studied him. "Okay." She picked up her tablet and glanced at Bill. "Put him back for now."

They would keep him quarantined from Franklin since they couldn't risk the other man shoring Phillips up not to tell them anything more. They would place him in an isolated cell, where he would not be able to get the image of the beheading out of his mind.

Bill gripped Phillips's upper arm and said, "Let's go, sunshine." At the door, he squeezed tight. "I can cuff you, or you can be good. Let me know."

Phillips looked at the floor. "You don't need to cuff me."

"Great," Bill said with a smile. "Step to your left."

★ ★ ★

WASHINGTON, DC

A courier with a photocopy of Phillips's composition notebook found in the fireplace met Lynda at the airport in Dover. During the helicopter ride to Washington, DC, she studied the contents. She could ascertain chemical formulas, but not what they meant. Scrawled in the margins of one of the pages, she made out a name, Roman Hansel.

She pulled her phone out of her bag and dialed Perry Blake's direct number. He answered before the first ring finished. "Did you figure out the notebook?"

"Not more than the reminder of how poorly I did in chemistry. Did you see the name?"

"Yes. A chemist in Columbus, Ohio. He should be here by the time you get here."

"Has anyone analyzed the formulas?"

After a pause, he asked, "How far out are you?"

"Fifteen minutes."

"I'll see you here."

For the rest of the flight, she read about Roman Hansel, professor of chemical engineering at Ohio State University. She dug around in his social media and his affiliated organizations, but she could find nothing to link him to Green War or the Russians.

The helicopter landed on the roof of the FBI. She worked her way down to the floor where Perry had set up a command center and found him with his hip against a table and his arms crossed over his chest, watching one of the recorded interviews of Trenton Phillips. When the door shut behind her, he looked up.

"You made good time," he said.

"Not bad when you don't have to fly commercial."

"True. In-flight service isn't as good, though." He gestured to the screen. "What have you figured out?"

"Doctor Hansel is clean as a whistle."

"Until you dig into his computer. That's where it all comes out." Perry beckoned with his finger to Dan Tanaka, one of the cyber forensics agents from Lynda's home station.

Dan picked up a file folder and came across the room. "Lynda," he said.

"Good to see you, Dan. How's the new baby?"

"Cutting teeth. Fun times." He opened the folder and pulled out a sheet of paper.

She scanned the list on it, raising an eyebrow as she processed all of the names. "This is like the checklist for environmental organizations. Everything from Al Gore to Green War."

He nodded and shifted his glasses to the top of his head. "Exactly. Hansel's internet search history reads like someone doing a term paper on the environmental impact of the twenty-first century."

She frowned. "How does one go from a chemical engineer to an ecoterrorist?"

"You're assuming that he is one," Perry said.

Lynda raised her eyebrows and looked at him. "Are we saying he isn't?"

Perry shook his head. "Not at all. I'm just saying don't make assumptions or jump any guns. At least, that's what you always tell me."

She nodded and tugged on her ear. Her exhausted mind had started skipping steps. Looking back at Dan, she asked, "Any catalysts?"

He grinned and pulled a newspaper clipping out of the folder. "You mean like a wife who committed a murder-suicide by carbon monoxide poisoning?"

Her heart rate increased. "Yes. Kind of like that." She snatched the article from him and skimmed it. A two-year-old baby had died alongside the mother in the car kept running in the garage.

"Got it!" an agent at one of the tables said. She waved in Perry's direction. "Director."

They walked over to her station. "It reacts chemically with fuel," she said. The screen in front of her showed an animated three-dimensional model of chemical compounds coming together.

Lynda frowned. "How does it react?"

"Well, based on the analysis of the formula by a chemist from MIT on the other end of this teleconference, this compound will solidify fuel into a thick gel."

Perry gestured at the screen. With a few mouse clicks, the

agent removed the animation, and a man with gray hair and wide, black-framed glasses appeared. "How does it turn fuel to gel?" Perry asked.

The chemist pointed at his chest. "I cannot tell you that," he said in a thick Eastern European accent. "I have to study it more."

"What kind of fuel?" Lynda asked.

"Kerosene."

Lynda rubbed her forehead with her thumb and forefinger. Kerosene? She gestured at the next terminal over. "Can I use this?"

"Of course," the agent said.

She went through the protocol for a video conference and soon faced Bill. Seeing him made her heart skip a little beat, brought a smile to her face. "Hi there. I didn't expect you to answer."

He gave a sleepy grin. "I'm holding down the fort. We knew you'd be calling. You've only been there forty minutes. Little slow on the draw, aren't you?"

She chuckled. "Well, I'm running on really bad instant coffee and a chicken à la king MRE, so you have to give me some grace."

The look on his face made her think he'd give her all the grace she ever needed. "What do you know, Clever?"

"What we've found has something to do with kerosene. Something about a chemical compound that jellifies it."

"Kerosene?" His frown drew his eyebrows together. "Like jet fuel kerosene?"

Her heart started pounding and her mouth went dry. "Jet fuel?"

The chemist on the screen next to her said, "Of course! That explains these numbers. Give me just a moment."

Behind her, she heard Perry on the phone. "I want the locations and travel of every known member of Green War." He paused, then said, "I realize it. Now, please."

Lynda met Bill's eyes on the computer screen. "I have to go. My phone is on. Keep in touch."

He nodded, already standing up. "Roger."

CHATER

★

TWENTY

Lynda sat next to Perry, examining Doctor Roman Hansel, trying to get a read on him. She wished Bill was in the room. He could analyze someone just by facial tics.

Doctor Hansel was young for all of his accolades. His file said he had just turned thirty-seven. He had shaggy black hair, gray-green eyes hidden behind thick, black-framed glasses, and long limbs. He gave off a very bored countenance, as if planning what he'd have for dinner tonight instead of worrying about his arrest and interrogation in FBI headquarters.

"Doctor Hansel," Lynda said, "I'd like to talk about your work with Green War."

"What about it?"

Her eyes widened. She'd expected him to deny knowing anything about the organization. "You provided them with a chemical formula."

He nodded. "Yes. I developed it about a year ago. I chartered jets and took containers of jet fuel up to different altitudes dozens of times in the last year testing it out. I finally perfected it."

Perry took over. "The formula turns fuel into gel?"

"Yes. Exactly. Once the fuel solidifies, it won't go back to a liquid and can no longer power the aircraft. Then . . ." He lifted his hand, palm down, and wiggled it back and forth, then slammed it onto the table. He laughed and sat back with his arms crossed.

He's insane, Lynda thought. She looked over at Perry, then back to their very amenable suspect. "What is your endgame?" she asked.

He clasped his fingers together and rested them on the table. "I went into this with the insane idea that I could affect this society's reliance on fossil fuels. However, I've figured out that they're so integrated into almost every single aspect of our civilization that it would be impossible to affect anything. Instead, I decided to shed light on the issue. Green War was very welcoming to the idea."

After a moment of silence, Perry asked, "And when a plane goes down and people die, does that mean anything to you?"

Doctor Hansel didn't even blink. "Of course not. No one seemed to care when my family died. Why should I care when others die? Don't want to die in a plane crash? Don't fly."

"How is the compound getting into planes?" Lynda asked.

"I created tablets out of the powder. Wrote out careful instructions. Green War activists took over the details."

"What airports?"

He gave an empty, emotionless smile. "I have said all I intend to say."

241

"What airports, Doctor Hansel?"

"I refuse to speak another word, and I demand to speak to an attorney."

She glanced at Perry, who said, "Okay, Doctor Hansel, we are done here. I need to get with Homeland Security and find out exactly what all of the charges against you are going to be."

He nodded as if implying he understood, but he did not speak again. Instead, he picked at his front teeth with his fingernail and looked at the ceiling.

Back in the situation room, Lynda faced Perry, leaning against the wall and slipping her hands into her pockets. "What do you think?"

"I think we've gotten all we're getting out of him."

She hated to agree with that. "You're probably right. I think he's telling the truth, though."

He rubbed the back of his neck and pointed to a closed door. "I had your bag put in there. Sleep. There's an attached bathroom. I don't want to see you for at least three hours."

She couldn't possibly. "But, sir—"

"Three hours, Agent Culter. Not a minute sooner." When she opened her mouth again, he said, "I will contact Kuwait and give them the information we've obtained. I will also put the team on tracking all of the known Green War associates and discover what airports might possibly be affected. There isn't a single thing you can do at this moment. It's the perfect time to close your eyes."

He made sense. She had pushed fatigue back one too many times. Other people could continue to do the grunt work right now. If she rested her mind and gave her brain some much-needed sleep, she'd be sharper in the end, more able to draw lines and connections.

She went into the assigned office. A brown leather sofa sat in front of an empty desk. In the adjoining bathroom, she washed her face, brushed her teeth, and paused to look at herself in the mirror.

Her pupils flared, and her exhausted mind swirled with so many details and so much information. She thought about the last two weeks, preparing to go to Kuwait, flying in with the CIA and DHS, reconnecting with Bill. Her thoughts stopped on Bill.

Despite everything that had happened in the past, she believed he had completely changed. She could see him living for God, loving God. Observing the respect with which his team and leaders treated him, the same people who had served in combat with him in the direst of circumstances—that told her so much more than a conversation with him.

Could she loosen her grip on protecting her heart against him? Could she trust him with it again?

Did she want to?

Yes, she very much wanted to.

Could she love him again?

No doubt. She absolutely could. The question existed, however, of logistics in any kind of relationship with him. He lived in Kentucky. She lived in Alaska. She would not compromise her career to be with him. What she did, how she did it, was too important in the scheme of the world. And she could say the same for him.

So would they exist like Emma and Peña? See each other on the odd week of some months and then go their separate ways as their careers demanded? Or would one of them have to make a sacrifice in order to preserve their relationship?

She pushed her fingers over her eyes. This kind of deep thinking shouldn't happen minutes before she wanted to go to sleep. She had to reset and wake up, ready to face whatever Green War brought next. Bill would have to wait until another time.

A pillow and a wool blanket lay at the foot of the couch. She lay down, covering her head with the blanket, and closed her eyes. Exhaustion made the room spin until her thoughts faded to nothing.

KUWAIT

Even though he strove to appear neutral, Bill had a hard time looking at the sniveling figure of Trenton Phillips. He tried to pretend the man's lack of fortitude didn't disgust him. Someone willing to kill an unknown number of people should have a little more gumption, in his opinion. Not that anyone ever asked.

"So, we have a product that turns jet fuel into a gel. Why don't we talk about that a little more?" Peña said.

"I can't tell you anything! Cisco will kill me. And he'll enjoy it." Phillips brushed at the sweat-matted hair on his forehead. "Come on, man, have a little mercy!"

"I'm pretty sure that my counterpart indicated the amount of mercy you'd receive at the hands of the local authorities," Peña said. "The goal is to make the State Department want to go through the trouble of extraditing you to the US. So far, I'm not seeing a great effort on your part."

"I've told you all I know."

"Then I can't help you."

Bill took the cue and stepped forward. Last time, he'd given Phillips a choice of having his hands bound. This time, he picked the man up by his collar and laid him across the table, securing his hands behind him.

After Bill signed Phillips back to the guards, he went to the ready room to meet with Rick and Peña. Agent Smith had updated the command board with the information about the chemical compound. Bill pulled up a chair next to the terminal that accepted incoming calls from Lynda.

"What are we going to tell the local authorities?" Peña asked. "We have the Nasser brothers, Phillips, Franklin, and Haynes. Who gets whom?"

Agent Lewis rubbed the back of her neck and rolled her head around. "I don't know. I'm waiting to hear from Washington. It's going to be a diplomatic nightmare, especially since we have them in custody and took them out of one country and into another."

"Best wait until we're all the way done with them." Rick scooted down in his chair and crossed his ankles. "The Nasser brothers will be a different story entirely."

They had no reason to take the brothers to the States. However, to hand them off to Saudi authorities might as well mean signing their death certificates.

"Indeed. I have sympathy there, but our hands will likely be tied." Lewis looked at her watch. "I have to shut down for a few hours."

"What about Guantánamo?" Bill asked.

Smith shook his head. "They didn't perpetrate an attack on us. They planned an attack on Saudi Arabia. Not even close to something that would justify containing them in Guantánamo."

The computer made a blip. Bill glanced over and saw an instant message from Lynda.

> Hansel confirmed only what we know. Lying down for a couple of hours. Nothing new on this end.

He leaned over and typed,

> Roger.

"Agent Culter says they got nothing new out of Doctor Hansel, but he did confirm what we know." The knowledge that she wouldn't return for several hours made all the excess energy he'd stored up drain out of his body. He rubbed his beard and stood. "I'm going to catch forty." He looked at Rick, silently conveying that his friend needed to rest too.

"Now's probably our only chance for a while," Rick said.

"It's early afternoon in DC," Smith said. "They have a lot of personnel covering a lot of territory. I say we meet back here in six hours and see what new developments have occurred."

Rick looked at his watch. "Zero three thirty. I'll get Mc-Bride in here to monitor communications. He'll wake me if something comes in."

Bill left the CHU and walked down the dark street to his own CHU. Even though the slightest chance of missing any communication from Lynda did not appeal to him, he was running on about three hours sleep in the last forty-eight. He needed to shut down just for a little while.

He'd actively pursued terrorists for years. He'd shot at bad guys, been shot by bad guys, even had a harrowing escape through the jungles of Africa just two days after a bullet was surgically removed near his heart. But he'd never really worked with stopping a terrorist attack at home. Everything happened over here, away from home. That's why his team came all this way and lived for months in tents, eating government-issued meals packaged in green plastic—so they could keep terrorists away from home.

But now terrorists from his own nation were intent on harming human beings. He had a hard time reconciling that. These weren't soldiers of a nation-state at war with his country—these were citizens from his homeland.

Exhaustion fueled his thoughts, so he tried to push them from his mind. In his room, he grabbed what he needed and then took a quick shower in the nearby CHU. When he finished, he stared into the mirror, then closed his eyes and said, "God, we need Your guidance right now. So many issues, so much confusion. What is a red herring, and what is the proper path of investigation? And how can I personally help? What insight can You give me? Use me, Lord. Make me Your weapon."

Back in his CHU, he climbed into his hammock. Before he dozed off, he said Psalm 91 out loud. It was nicknamed the soldier's psalm. Whenever he faced an uncomfortable or frightening situation in his job, he recited it.

He fell asleep whispering verse 5. "You shall not be afraid of the terror by night, nor of the arrow that flies by day . . ."

WASHINGTON, DC

When Lynda woke up, her watch said 8:00. Focusing on the window and seeing the dark sky made her realize it was eight at night, not in the morning. She had slept for six straight hours.

Her head ached a little. The combination of dehydration and fatigue contributed to that. While she freshened up, she talked to God. "I'm not sure what the plan here is, Father, but help me keep my eyes open and see the dangers for what they are. Keep me from getting confused by false trails and intentional misdirection. Let me do good work here with the gifts You've given me."

As she came out of the office, her sleep-muddled mind took in the organized chaos around her. The corner of the room that Perry had occupied had spread to the entire floor and become a full-fledged command center. The sound of ringing phones and buzzing conversation provided the background music to dozens of agents who took up work spaces. The very real threat against the airlines on a global scale, including the United States, had increased the personnel on the task force.

Lynda found Perry in the same spot as when she'd first arrived. He looked her up and down and nodded. "Good. Ready to work?"

"Yes."

"MIT worked out that if you add this chemical compound to kerosene jet fuel, then once you get to 30,000 feet, it jellifies and no longer will fuel the aircraft. We found records of Doctor Hansel chartering over fifty flights in the last year."

She opened her mouth, then closed it, unable to decide what question to ask first. Finally, she asked, "How many airports are in the United States?"

"Over five thousand. Public. That doesn't include private."

She let out a long breath and slipped her hands into her

pockets. Needing to move, she paced to the wall of information someone had compiled. Notes, pictures, diagrams, formulas . . . Her mind swirled as she tried to put it all into a logical order.

She turned to Perry. "Can we test for the chemical compound?"

He nodded. "Yes. The FAA is expediting testing."

"How is Green War distributing the chemical?"

"We don't know. We don't even know if they did."

"Sir?" a man said loudly from across the room.

Perry looked at the screen the agent gestured to. The room fell silent as the news report of a 757 that had crashed in Utah filled the screen. Lynda recognized the delivery-service logo on the plane. The crew of three was confirmed dead.

Perry turned and pointed to a woman with black hair and red-framed glasses. "Find out what airport they flew out of and ground all of the planes there."

"Yes, sir."

"And issue a notice to the FAA. Keep flights below twenty-five thousand feet."

Lynda shook her head. "It was supposed to be tomorrow."

Perry had a phone to his ear but said, "It is tomorrow in Turkey. Isn't that where they were?"

Of course! Her throat tightened. She hadn't been fast enough. She went to an empty terminal and accessed the server to video conference the team in Kuwait. Her heart skipped a beat when Bill answered with a smile. He looked more rested and alert than the last time she'd seen him.

"Well, don't you look fresh as a daisy on Easter morning," he said. "Looks like someone got some sleep."

"I could say the same about you if I'd understood what

you just said," she replied with a smile. Then she sobered. "A parcel-service plane went down. Killed the three crew members. Have you been briefed on what the team on this end has learned in the last couple of hours?"

He looked away from the screen and gave a sharp whistle, then focused on the screen again. "Last we heard was from you."

"Okay." Perry must not have connected with them to brief them. She organized her thoughts. "The scientists at MIT think that this chemical compound will cause jet fuel to gel up, freezing the engines, and the planes crash. But the trick is that it has to get above thirty thousand feet to do so."

Lewis appeared on the screen and asked the same question she did. "Can we test for it?"

"Yes, and the FAA is expediting tests. We're finding out the origin of the plane that crashed and grounding the flights that haven't taken off yet. I think I heard someone telling air traffic control to keep the flights already in the air below the threshold."

Lewis nodded. "We'll see if we can get some intelligence gathered on this end."

CHAPTER

★

TWENTY-ONE

KUWAIT

Selah stared hard at the stoic man who sat across the table from her. Bill's team believed that his partner had given them all of the information he possessed. Fisher had taken him away, sobbing so hard he could barely walk, about two hours ago.

Peña, Rick, and Selah brainstormed the best way to break Franklin right now. Selah agreed to do the interrogation. They all wondered if he would call her bluff again.

Bill sat next to her. Rick had asked him to sit close so he could read Franklin's facial expressions, the slight nuances of nerves, tells, and giveaways of stress.

Selah swiped at her tablet, and a news article about the horrific conditions in Venezuelan prisons filled the wall behind her. Franklin glanced at it, then looked at the table. Bill could see a bead of sweat appear at his temple.

"Your partner gave us the information that led us to arrest Doctor Hansel and avert the calamity planned for the United States," Selah said.

His head flew up, and his eyes bugged out. "You're lying."

"Shall I play his interview back for you? I have it right here."

He glanced up at the camera in the corner of the room. "Then why am I here?"

Bill spoke. "We need Cisco."

Franklin snarled. "You need him for what?"

Selah gave a lazy smile. "We have something personal to discuss with him. Where can I find him?"

"It wouldn't matter what I tell you. By now, he knows we've been captured. Where he would go and what he would do is nothing I'd know."

"Try me," Selah said. "Let's start with a phone number."

Franklin rattled off a number. "Like I said, it won't work anymore."

Another swipe closed the projector down. "Why are you suddenly so cooperative?" Selah asked.

Franklin sat back in the chair. His leg moved up and down like a piston. "I would rather be tried on US soil. Whatever you need from me to make that happen, I'll give you."

"Sorry you blew up a pipeline in Venezuela, are you?"

He shrugged. "No. But I also blew up pipelines in the States. I'll confess."

"Colombia?"

He nodded.

"Kuwait? 'Cause that's our current host country, and it would be a matter of driving you half a mile and dropping you off outside a very ornate gate."

His cheeks turned bright red. He stared at the table and nodded again.

Bill appreciated a man who knew when the game was up. "What about the Russians?"

Franklin made a casual motion with his shoulders, almost a partial shrug. "That was Cisco's deal. They did some heavy funding for us to disrupt the oil production globally. We just couldn't touch their new pipeline."

He'd started to relax. Selah asked him several other questions, but he provided no new information. Eventually, she had him taken from the room. Bill looked up as Rick and Agent Lewis came in.

"Thoughts?" Rick asked him.

"He was scared. He obviously didn't want to be extradited to anywhere but the States."

"Can we believe him?"

"It all comes down to who he's most afraid of, Cisco or our allies here." Bill rubbed his beard. "It's a balancing act."

Peña came into the room. "Haynes is ready." He pointed at Bill. "Sit with me? I want your impression."

"Yes, you do," Rick said, slapping Bill on the back as he left.

Brock escorted Haynes in. The man looked from Peña to Bill and back again. "Where's Lynda?" he asked as he sat down.

Bill breathed slowly, refusing to show any kind of reaction to the punk. He kept calm and collected. His emotions for Lynda would not play a part in harming their investigation.

"I ask the questions," Peña said.

Haynes gave a very charming smile full of straight white teeth and good humor. "By all means. Please, ask me questions."

Peña started right up front. "Why the mosque?"

He stared for a moment, then blinked. "I beg your pardon?"

Typical delaying move. He wanted more time to formulate a believable response.

"You are not Muslim," Peña said. "Your counterparts are not Muslim. Why were you directing your minions through the mosque?"

Haynes sat back in the chair, then leaned forward again. "I don't know what you mean."

Peña tilted his head as if to look at him from a different angle, then glanced at Bill. "Am I speaking English?"

Bill nodded. "With that cute little Los Angeles accent."

Peña redirected his stare to Haynes. "I think you know what I mean. Why the mosque?"

Haynes took a deep breath and let it out. "I don't have anything to say to you about that."

"No?" Peña grinned at Bill. "He doesn't have anything to say about that."

Bill chortled. "You mean, he doesn't have anything to say about the fact that the Russian mafia was trying to pin the explosions perpetrated by Green War on the innocent men worshiping in their holy place? I am astounded at his lack of words. I'm sure his superiors would love to know everything we do and wonder how we could have possibly found out."

Haynes's Adam's apple bobbed up and down. Beads of sweat formed above his eyebrows. "I have nothing to say to either one of you."

"That's fair," Peña said. "I get it. I mean, any word out of your mouth might lose you a finger or eye. The damage that could be done to your body would be horrible to live with,

I'm sure." He stood. "I'll just go write an unsecure report and broadcast it over the airways."

Bill stood as well. When Peña reached the door, Haynes said, "Wait!"

Peña paused, hand on the doorknob, and turned. "Wait?"

"I, uh, look, I might have information. But I need protection."

Peña turned fully around. "That's the kind of thing you discuss with federal prosecutors. That's not me. Right now, you're being held as a terrorist under an entirely different set of laws. Get me through now, and I'll see if we're willing to hand you over to the feds or if you get to stay here and face the local governance." He turned again and opened the door. "I don't care which one."

"Okay!" Haynes started to stand, but Brock grabbed him by the shoulder and sat him back down. Hard. "I will cooperate."

Peña looked him up and down, then walked back into the room. "In what way will you cooperate?"

"I know how this goes. I'm a trained interrogator too."

Bill chuckled. "Son, you couldn't pretend to be on our level."

Haynes held up his hands. "I understand. You're right. But I will cooperate as long as you or the FBI or Homeland Security or whoever is in charge of this show understands that in the end, I'm going to need protection."

Peña tapped Bill's arm with the back of his hand. "It fascinates me, really, how people integrate themselves with bad guys, then when they get caught, it's all about wanting protection. Suddenly, they're not the bad guys, they're just the soon-to-be victims."

"We're like three for three here," Bill said. "You'd think we could find someone in charge."

Haynes crossed his arms over his chest. "I'll wait. I have all of the information." He tapped the side of his forehead. "All right here. Names, dates, plans, executions. And I have a lot more time than you do."

Peña nodded. "I'll get back to you."

As they left the room, Brock took Haynes back to where they'd held him.

In the observation room, Agent Lewis said, "He has to be playing us. Why would he turn without you even trying?"

"Because he knows where we are," Bill said. "And he'd rather not contend with the government of Kuwait."

Rick rubbed his chin. "Is that enough to make someone who turned against his country flip again?"

"Depends on his motivations." Bill leaned against the counter and slipped his hands into the pockets of his uniform. "What was he after before? Money, power, stick it to the government? If it was money or power, that's gone now. He knows he'll never get it back."

Lewis pulled a phone out of her pocket. "I'll call DC, see what they're willing to give him."

"He's going to want it in writing," Rick said. "I can taste it."

Agent Smith had just come into the room. "I already called. They want him extradited. The offense on behalf of the FBI is rather great. They'd rather have hold of him than give him over to another country for prosecution."

"Kuwait is going to want something," Lewis said. "Their facility is still not up and running."

"Well," Rick said on a sigh, "we have the Nasser brothers,

who took direct orders from Trenton Phillips, who was in possession of the phone that sent the go orders. That would satisfy Kuwait immensely."

Lewis nodded. "That works. I'll call my contact and get them off our hands, and we'll hand the rest over to you, Smith."

"Roger." Smith walked over to a computer terminal. "I'll start getting paperwork together for Haynes."

WASHINGTON, DC
DECEMBER 14

No other planes had gone down. Initial testing at major airports revealed that Green War had so far contaminated four other fuel supplies. The State Department had placed Homeland Security and the FAA on a high-level alert in an attempt to ensure that no more fell victim.

Lynda looked at the photo on the board in front of her. The man she'd labeled "Cisco" stared back at her. She turned to Dan Tanaka. "Have we gotten anything from facial recognition?"

"I've run it through social media, military, and police. Right now, we're doing universities. Give it another hour, maybe two."

"You're my favorite, you know?"

He winked and returned to his terminal. She went back to arranging her board, then took red and black markers and drew lines from event to person to event. Once she had it all complete, she took a step back so she could see the entire board at once.

Studying the layout, she let her mind relax and look for the patterns. Faces, words, data rose above the board. She could visualize the history of Green War from what they knew after interviewing the Nasser brothers, and she saw the escalation of violence while the mission degenerated under the leadership of someone seeking to do harm instead of affect the environment.

She rubbed the back of her neck and contemplated walking away long enough to get a cup of coffee when Dan interrupted her thoughts. "Got him."

She rushed to his workstation, where he'd pulled up a student ID for Georgetown. The name on the ID said Adrian Cissell. But the picture was definitely Cisco's.

"Can you get his records?"

"Got 'em." Dan slipped one headphone off. "Homeschooled. Testing is off the charts. Perfect scores on the SAT and ACT. Entered Georgetown at sixteen with a declared major in environmental science. Was asked to leave three years later when an investigation into complaints of assault from a girlfriend brought another ex-girlfriend forward. No charges were ever filed, but his scholarship was revoked."

"Family?"

"Only child. Looks like his mom and dad died in a plane crash when he was eighteen. Father owned a Cessna 172 that he kept on a private airfield in Virginia. Investigation revealed a blown fuel line."

Little jolts of energy ran down Lynda's back. "I don't suppose you could find an address?"

He clicked and typed and finally said, "I can give you the address of one of the women. As for him, no. He's a ghost.

Not that I won't keep looking, but I'm getting absolutely nothing on that name or Damien Cisco."

Perry came into the ready room just as Lynda updated the board with the student ID of Adrian Cissell. He looked at the board. "Agents in Omaha arrested a Green War activist scaling the airport fence. That makes a total of six caught in airports and now in custody."

"Plus what we have in Kuwait."

"And Doctor Hansel. I think we got way ahead of this and stopped it."

"I hope so."

Perry pointed at the picture of Cisco. "Thoughts?"

Lynda turned and faced him fully. "I think I want to go talk to one of the women. She's local. Maybe she knows something that can put us on a path."

He screwed up his face. "It seems a stretch to go back ten years to a college incident with an ex-girlfriend."

She nodded. "It is absolutely a stretch. But it won't take long and helps provide some additional groundwork. Plus I could use some fresh air. It's been a while."

He looked at his watch. "Okay. It's worth checking."

Lynda walked up the steps of the brownstone. She pressed the button and stepped back so that the camera near the doorbell would capture all of her. After several seconds, a voice came over the speaker. "Can I help you?"

She held her badge up to the lens. "Special Agent Lynda Culter. I'm looking for Debra Cassady."

"What's this about?"

"I just have a few questions for you," Lynda said. "It shouldn't take long."

"One moment." About a minute later, the screen door opened. A young woman with bright red hair came onto the porch, her vivid blue eyes filled with fear. "I'm Debra Lucas now, but my maiden name is Cassady." She gestured at the chairs on the porch and sat down. "My husband is on a call inside. It's better if we sit out here."

Lynda settled into a wicker chair. "No problem. It's beautiful out here."

"It is in the summer." Debra plucked a dead bud from a flowerpot on the porch railing.

"I'm here about Adrian Cissell," Lynda said.

Debra's fingers froze in the middle of pinching off a dead leaf. Her freckles popped out as the color fled from her face. She lifted her gaze to Lynda's. With wide eyes, she slowly shook her head back and forth. "I'm not going to talk about him," she said in a whisper. After another heartbeat, she surged to her feet and put her hand on the door. "I need you to leave now."

"Wait," Lynda said. "Please. I need help. He's hurt a lot of people, and we're just trying to get enough information about him that will help us find him."

Debra looked all around them. "He said he'd kill me."

Lynda stood and very slowly and calmly walked forward. "When?" She tried to look over Debra's shoulder into the house. Her hand hovered over her weapon. "Debra?"

"On his way out of college. He stopped by my dorm to tell me that he would be back to kill me, to make sure I waited up for him. I put in another complaint, but I never heard from him again. It's been ten years, and I can just now sleep with only one light on."

A man walked down the hall toward the door. Lynda took a step back and rested her palm on the butt of her gun. Her heart pounded. It felt like sawdust filled her mouth.

When the door opened, a man who was not Adrian Cissell/Damien Cisco stepped out. "Deb? Everything okay?"

Debra pressed herself to his side. His arm came around her and pulled her close. "FBI is looking for that creep from college. Remember?"

He picked up her hand and turned her wrist over, exposing what looked like a cigarette burn. "Yeah, I remember." He pressed a kiss to her wrist, then looked at Lynda. "We can't help you. It's been ten years since either of us saw him."

Lynda kept her attention focused on Debra. "Did he ever mention owning any property, especially after his parents died?"

Debra shook her head. "Sorry. He was never very chatty. I didn't know much about him at all that wasn't related to the school."

Lynda pulled a business card out of her jacket pocket. "If you can think of anything, please call me. I appreciate your time." She looked at Debra's husband. "Mr. Lucas."

He inclined his head, then steered his wife back into their home. Lynda didn't feel like she'd accomplished anything at all except wasting the time it took to interview Debra.

She pulled out her phone in her car and was patched through to Kuwait. Bill answered within seconds.

"Well, aren't you pretty as a picture?" he said with a smile. "You just brightened this whole dreary place."

A flush crawled up her neck. "Bill, ever the charmer. Why are you always the one who answers?"

"Because I sit next to this terminal so I don't miss you."

She couldn't stop the grin that covered her face, despite her reason for calling. "Damien Cisco's real name is Adrian Cissell. We had a couple of leads in this area, but they didn't pan out well."

"Have you heard from Agent Smith?"

"No. Well, not since I left the office."

"He's processing the paperwork to demobilize and bring our friends back to the States. We hope to leave tomorrow sometime."

She thought about the men they had captured. "Including the Nasser brothers?"

He pressed his lips together and shook his head. "The Kuwaitis are getting them. They destroyed the pipeline here, killed seventeen. As sweet as I'm sure their mama thinks they are, the end did not justify their means."

Though the brothers had retaliated against their father's death, they had also killed several fathers in the process. She hated the world that generated the kind of desperate revenge they sought. "You're coming too?"

He shook his head. "Well, yes, but not to DC. I'll go on to Kentucky with my unit. But Smith is coming straight to you with Haynes. The other prisoners will be taken into custody in Dover and detained in the appropriate facilities. I'm not sure if they're going to be tried federally or in each state. That is way above my pay grade."

"Yeah. Mine too." She couldn't stop the disappointment she felt and wished the Army had stationed Bill a little closer to her geographically. "At least we can get our hands on Haynes and continue to question him here."

"Exactly."

Bill looked above his camera, then nodded to someone out of her range of sight. "I think Selah will also come to DC. She's a contractor for the FBI too, so she'll be able to be part of that." He narrowed his eyes as if trying to get a closer look at her. "You okay?"

"Sure. Tired. I'll sleep a week when this is over."

"You and me both." He grinned. "Talk to you soon."

"Count on it."

CHAPTER

★

TWENTY-TWO

Lynda set the pizza box on the desk in her hotel room. While her laptop booted up, she washed her face, brushed her teeth, and changed into a comfortable sweatshirt and a pair of yoga pants. She really should exercise. In the background of her exhaustion, her muscles ached to move. But more than anything, she needed to unwind.

She patched through to the terminal on the other side of the world. Within seconds, Bill's face filled her screen.

"Well, aren't you a sight for sore eyes?" he said.

"I could say the same for you. I'll be much happier when you're not in an eight-hour time difference." She grabbed a slice of veggie-loaded pizza and took a bite.

He narrowed his eyes. "Now that's just mean."

With a grin, she glanced at the time. "It's seven in the morning there. You hardly want fresh Piazza's Pizza."

"You don't even know." His teeth flashed white against his black beard. "I've spent so long and at so many places eating horrible food that when an opportunity to eat good food comes my way, I don't mind the time or hour."

She washed her bite down with some sparkling water. "Is it quiet there right now?"

He nodded. "Permission to transport the prisoners just now came through. As soon as everyone finishes breakfast, we'll begin demobilization. We're leaving early tomorrow morning now." He took a drink of his soda. "How are things on that end?"

"Lots of details. Sorting it all out." She didn't want to talk about the case since her brain needed a break. She wanted to talk to Bill. "Do you still follow football?"

She watched the expressions cross his face as he shifted gears from work to sports. "Only the SEC," he said.

"You mean only 'Bama football?"

He grinned and kicked back in his chair. "And any team playing Auburn."

"It's a wonder my daddy ever liked you," she said, putting on her Alabama accent. "War Eagle."

"You can just shush your lips." His laughter belied his words. "It's too bad football doesn't do for you what baseball does. That would make you the perfect woman."

"Well, I enjoy it, but it doesn't relax me the way that baseball does." She took another bite of pizza. "I can't believe I was there just a couple days ago. It feels like a lifetime."

"That's because you miss me."

Oh, she did miss him. So much more than she thought she would. "I'm glad you think so highly of yourself."

"Well, I know I miss you."

Pleasure spread from her heart and through her chest.

He cleared his throat and leaned forward. "I've never been distracted on a mission before. But I'm distracted by you, Agent Clever."

"Sounds like you need to keep your head in the game."

"Sounds like."

They flirted like that for several minutes. Gradually, the tensions seeped out of Lynda's shoulders, and the puzzle pieces in her mind stilled and rested. Flirting with Bill had proven much more successful at turning her brain off than watching a baseball game.

"I'll have leave coming up at Christmas," he said. "I'd like to spend some time with you that isn't directly involved in an ecoterrorist organization."

What would it be like to be with Bill away from work and school? "I'm willing to try that," she said, covering her yawn with her fingers. "But for now, I'm full of pizza, and my brain feels relaxed for the first time in days. I need to sleep."

"Sweet dreams, Clever. I'll talk to you later."

**KUWAIT
DECEMBER 15**

Bill sat in the dining hall and swirled the soda in his glass, watching the remaining slivers of ice quickly dissolve. Fisher stood to move away from the table and jostled Bill's arm, splashing some of his drink. "Sorry, bro."

"No worries." Bill glanced at him. "It's been a long couple of weeks."

Fisher left, and Bill wiped up the spill then went back to contemplating his glass. He kept thinking about his conversation with Lynda in the quiet early morning just twelve hours ago. Besides suddenly craving pizza, which made him smile, he realized how easy he found just relaxing and flirting. With his job, he'd felt like he couldn't have a relationship. He came and went too often on too short notice. And, quite frankly, as the scar on his chest would attest, he worked a very dangerous job.

He couldn't believe it when Rick got married and worried it would affect how the team daddy handled everyone. However, Rick hadn't changed a thing in the way he led or how he made decisions. So maybe Bill's simple jealousy of his best friend's newfound happiness had turned to judgment. He didn't like that idea.

As if he could hear his thoughts, Rick slid into the chair across from him. "Hey."

Bill took a sip of soda. "Hay is for horses."

Rick snorted. "Nah. Donkeys like it too."

It took a minute for him to realize what Rick said, then he threw his head back and laughed. "Good one. I'll have to remember that."

"I aim to please." Rick pulled a small green notebook out of his front pocket. "Can you aid in prisoner transport?"

"Of course."

"With five prisoners, Agent Smith is uncomfortable doing it alone."

"We're all going to be on the same plane anyway, right?"

"True. But that ten-hour nap you're sitting here counting on will no longer exist. Unless someone spells you, you'll be on."

Bill shifted his plans in his mind. He needed to move the goalpost of the expected end of the mission mentally. "Then I guess I better make it an early night."

"Yes. You're released until zero four. The rest of the team can finish demob." Rick stared him down, his green eyes shining. "You planning to spend time with Lynda when we get back?"

Bill raised an eyebrow. "If I were?"

"You got no worries from me. I've learned the value of the love of a good woman."

"You sound like a proverb," Bill said with a grin.

"The words just flow."

Bill sighed and pushed his tray aside to cross his arms on the table. "It's an impossible situation."

"What is?"

"Me and Lynda. She lives in Alaska in a job that she's designed to do. I'm in Kentucky in a job that takes me across the world at a moment's notice. Not exactly geographic allies."

For a moment, his friend studied him. "Is that an excuse or a real issue?"

He took the question seriously, mulling it over. "I don't know."

"Sounds like you need to know that answer before you can truly go forward." Rick tapped the table with his palm and stood. "I'm glad I know how to focus prayer for you, brother."

Bill stood as well and picked up his tray. "Me too. Thanks for the clarity."

Rick chuckled at his sarcasm.

Bill carried his tray over to the conveyor belt that would

take it back to the dishwashing station. "How can I pray for you? It looks like I'm about to have several hours available to me."

He and Rick went outside. Bill pulled his cap out of his cargo pocket and put it on.

Rick did the same, then slipped his hands in his pockets. "I need some clarity for what's next. And wisdom always helps."

The sound of boots hitting gravel came their way, and they both turned. Gill jogged toward them. As soon as he saw Rick, he slowed down and said, "Sir, Colonel Jenkins asked me to find you."

"On my way, Sergeant," Rick replied. He turned back to Bill. "I'll see you in the morning, brother. Thanks for your prayers."

Rick turned and jogged in the direction of headquarters. Bill looked up at the blue sky. He had about nine hours of unexpected downtime. He didn't know if he liked having so much alone time with his thoughts right now.

He walked back to his CHU, closed his eyes, and sank into a chair. As he started to doze off, he realized that he had an opportunity to shower without fighting for a stall with five other guys. But first he would start a load of laundry.

After his shower, he met his reflection in the mirror. "Decisions," he said quietly, thinking about the completion of his master's degree and the reenlistment packet he needed to decide what to do with.

Back in his CHU, he picked up his worn Bible and sat back in the chair. He still had twenty minutes before the dryer finished, so he flipped the Bible open to where he'd left off in Isaiah 30. He paused on the verse that said, "Your ears shall hear a word behind you, saying, 'This is the way, walk in it,' whenever you turn to the right hand or whenever you turn to the left."

The words stood out to him. Using his finger to mark the page, he closed the book and leaned forward on his knees. "God, please, whisper in my ear. Give me direction."

CHAPTER

★

TWENTY-THREE

WASHINGTON, DC

The predawn sky was lit with a silver line on the horizon as if heralding the coming sun. Lynda had managed to sleep about three hours. Once she woke up, she was unable to fall back asleep. She pulled her chair to the window and looked out at the sky, letting her mind relax, trying to pull the puzzle together, trying not to be distracted by the conversation with Bill last night and how good he'd made her feel.

She could see clearly the two different organizations that had once worked together with differing objectives. The Russians wanted to drive the market to their oil by disabling or disrupting the other players in the market. The Green War soldiers wanted to disrupt the use of fossil fuels to have an impact on the modern way of life. If they managed to ground the planes, everything would stop, if only for a few hours or a day.

She believed those in Green War didn't understand their leader's narcissism and his stumbling into insanity. Wanting to effect change by bringing down planes carrying innocent passengers indicated a mind that did not function properly, a mind that existed in extremes that didn't bode well for anyone who got in his way.

A task force inside the FBI was handling the Russian mafia angle. Once Lynda spoke with Jack, she would gladly give them all the information she'd gathered and let them handle the incoming prisoners tied to that cell.

She glanced down at the Bible open in her lap. Her daily reading had taken her through Lamentations. She found the book hard to read while working on such a tough case because lamenting is the act of expressing grief and sorrow. Despite that, something this morning had filled her with such hope that she thought it might burst out of her chest in physical form. In the midst of lamenting over all the terribleness going on in his world at the time, Jeremiah penned in the third chapter, "Through the LORD's mercies we are not consumed, because His compassions fail not. They are new every morning; great is Your faithfulness."

Lynda's breath hitched at the reminder of God's enduring faithfulness, His love for His children, and His mercies. As a tear slipped down her cheek, she closed her eyes and bowed her head, thanking God for His presence and asking Him for His help in this case.

She hadn't turned to God enough in her career. She'd taken the gifts He'd given her and run with them. Yes, she'd acknowledged the Giver, but she'd always relied on herself in problem-solving, in solution-finding. She needed to remember that it all came from Him and was for Him, and that to truly be able to utilize what He'd gifted, she needed to lean into Him and let Him take the lead.

After a few moments of meditation, she stretched her arms toward the sky, working out the tightness in her lower back. Maybe a shower would help relax her enough so she could sleep for a little while longer. Setting her Bible aside, she stood. The vibrating of her phone stopped her. With a frown, she glanced at the incoming call. No good news came at 6:50 in the morning. She didn't recognize the number, but it had a DC area code.

"Culter," she said.

"Agent Culter, this is Detective Watson from DC metro. We found your card in the pocket of a homicide victim last night and wondered if you had a few minutes to answer some questions."

Nerves had rolled themselves into a tight knot in Lynda's stomach. She had walked up the steps of this brownstone just yesterday, determined to find out more about Damien Cisco. Instead, she'd gotten a woman killed—a woman who only wanted the man out of her life completely.

Lynda showed her badge to the uniformed officer at the door. He opened the screen door for her and told her to go through to the kitchen. She took in the small living room with a white couch on top of a white-and-gray rug. In the kitchen, brushed-nickel appliances and a wooden table broke up the white. She wondered if she would find the rest of the house so devoid of color.

At the kitchen counter, a man with a badge around his neck typed on a laptop. He looked up as she came in. He stood about five seven and had straight brown hair and watery blue eyes. He lifted his chin in her direction as he finished typing, then shut the laptop. "Agent Culter? I'm Detective Watson."

"Yes, Detective," she said, shaking his hand. "Thank you for calling me."

"I'd love any insight you have." He gestured, and she followed him out of the room and onto the teakwood porch, which fed out into a well-manicured yard.

Lynda glanced over as two people laid a sheet over the body of Mr. Lucas. Next to it lay another body covered in a sheet.

"I was investigating an environmental group responsible for that downed transport plane," she said. "Mrs. Lucas once dated the head of the organization."

The detective pulled a folded index card out of his jacket pocket and scribbled a note onto it. "Any idea who did this?"

She looked around. "Have you found any kind of green mark anywhere? A dot with two dashes, perhaps?"

He raised his eyebrows. "Possibly. Why?"

"Because that's the tag of the organization. If you found it, then I know who is responsible."

The detective walked over to the body next to Mr. Lucas and lifted the side of the sheet enough to reveal Debra's arm. Someone had written the Morse code symbol for W in green marker on the inside of her wrist.

Lynda blinked back tears. "The man most likely responsible for this goes by the name Damien Cisco, but he was born Adrian Cissell." She pulled a photograph out of her coat pocket. "This is him. She told me that he threatened to kill her in college if she ever told anyone about him. When I questioned her, she wouldn't speak to me about him."

He took the photo from her and slipped it into his pocket. "Any other insight you can give me would be fantastic."

She considered what information she could share. "He has a network. We're just scratching the surface of how big it is. I have a feeling you won't find him if he doesn't want you to."

The detective gave a cold smile. "And if I do find him, will you guys swoop in and take him from me?"

She bent down to take a picture of Debra's wrist. As she stood and slipped her phone back into her pocket, she said, "Detective, you can count on that."

Perry was waiting for her when she got off the elevator. He immediately said, "This isn't your fault, Lynda."

"Perry, a woman who voiced fear about speaking to me was found shot to death a few hours later. Her husband too. I feel like that's partly my fault."

They walked together into the big room that served as their temporary command center. "We're certain we're looking at Cisco for this?" he asked.

She pulled out her phone and opened the photo of Debra Lucas's wrist. "If it wasn't him, it was someone who worked for him." She slipped the phone back into her pocket. "Maybe I should have listened to you and left that line of investigation alone, huh?"

His phone chirped, so she left him to the call. After dropping her purse at an empty workstation, she splashed coffee into a paper cup and carried it over to the Green War board. Debra's face smiled back from her student ID photo. Lynda closed her eyes and rubbed the bridge of her nose, thankful for the time of meditation she'd had this morning to help steel herself for this day.

"Morning, Agent Culter," Dan said, walking past her. He had his messenger-style bag slung over his body and carried a paper coffee cup with their hotel name branded across it. He looked fresh and rested, likely because he had slept alone in a hotel room last night instead of sitting up in Alaska with a teething toddler.

She kept herself from scowling as she said, "Morning."

For some reason, her eyes focused on the hotel logo on his cup. He looked down and put his hand on his chest. "What? Did I spill ketchup on my shirt or something?"

"No," she said, then looked back at the board. Hotel. Someone out of place, away from home. "Why is he here?"

"I beg your pardon?"

"Sorry. I was talking to myself."

Why was Cisco still in DC? And how did he know she'd interviewed Debra? Was he watching Debra's house, or was he following Lynda?

Perry hung up the phone. "Prisoners will be here tomorrow afternoon. Sometime after two."

She pushed her fatigue to the background and faced him. "Is it possible to ask part of that team to come here for the interview with Jack Haynes?"

Perry's eyebrows drew together. "Why?"

"They're exceptionally trained and have been working with him for a few days."

He shook his head. "They can't have anything to do with him once they're on American soil. Haynes knows that, so we'd run the risk of sabotaging his prosecution if we did something like that."

Lynda pursed her lips, thinking fast. "But one of them is not military. Emma Peña. She's a contractor and has worked for us before." She turned to Dan. "Could you wire the room so they could see every angle?"

He shrugged. "Absolutely. No one would even know I'd done it."

Refocusing on her boss, she said, "They could just observe in a different room. And share their observations with Emma."

Perry's eyes crossed over the board before he looked at her again. "I'll see what I can do."

"Thanks." She turned back to the board. "Why is Damien Cisco here?"

"Do you think he's planning something in DC?"

"He's either planning something or he's following me. But why would he be following me?"

She glanced his way, saw the darkened expression on his face. "I'm not crazy about that idea."

"Nor am I," she said. "But if he knows I spoke to Debra, then he was either watching her or following me."

Perry crossed his arms over his chest and leaned against a table. "Or he has someone else doing that. I have a couple of techs pulling traffic cam footage around the area where you were yesterday. We'll get them to analyze whether someone was following you."

"That would be great to know. Good idea." She rubbed the back of her neck. "How did your call with the FAA go?"

"Good. They're testing fuel nationally, and airports have

heightened security. Beyond that, there isn't much more they can do."

"I'm just thankful no more planes went down."

"We all are. We need to look at what we've accomplished here and recognize that we've done a remarkable job."

"You're right," she said. If only they could stop Damien Cisco. "We have a team meeting at eleven. Are you running it or do you want me to?"

"I'll do it. I'll go get my notes and see you in there."

CHAPTER

★

TWENTY-FOUR

DECEMBER 16

Usually when he returned to the States after a deployment, Bill slept for about sixteen hours, then went to a restaurant for the biggest, thickest burger he could find. This time, he changed into civilian clothes while on the plane. Once they landed in Maryland, he and Rick rented a car and followed Peña, Selah, and Agent Lewis to DC. Despite the fact that the uniformed services never served as law enforcement officers or had any authority with civilians on domestic soil, the FBI had requested that Bill's team work with the domestic agents while they tactically debriefed the prisoners.

Once they checked into the FBI headquarters building, they walked through a maze of hallways and into a room filled with screens and speakers. Three of the screens showed an interview room from different angles. A man with tan skin, straight black hair, and glasses sat at a console wearing headphones. He glanced in their direction when they came in but didn't speak.

Bill leaned toward Peña. "I'm not too comfortable with this, brother. What do you think?"

Peña had his arms crossed and lifted a shoulder in a shrug. "Emma's a contractor. She has all the freedom to do what needs to be done. We're just observing."

"Haynes knows the law."

"That's why he won't see us."

The door opened, and Bill's heart skipped a beat when Lynda walked in. She saw him and grinned broadly, then hugged Selah.

"We're bringing Jack in now," she said. "My director wants everything we can get on the Russians. Jack's admitted to very little. He's hard to break because he knows how we work."

"As soon as our plane took off, he quit acting like he wanted to cooperate. I think he was just playing us to get him out of the country." Bill slipped his hands into his pockets and wiggled his feet inside his hiking boots. It felt good to be out of his uniform.

"I guess we just need him to want to help us more than any other alternative," Lynda said.

"Why do you want us here?" Rick asked.

"Because you've had him this whole time. You've got a feel of his rhythm and moods. We need to find Cisco. And we'd really love to, you know, break down that whole Russian cell."

"Just the easy stuff," Bill said with a wink.

Her cheeks reddened. "Exactly." She opened a small cardboard box and handed out earpieces. "I want you all in Emma's ear. We have cameras at every angle. You'll even be able to see his feet or lap. Agent Dan Tanaka here"—she pointed to the man at the computer console—"wired the entire room. Jack is going to be cocky and arrogant, especially now that handing him over to the Middle Eastern countries is apparently off the table, but there has to be a way to make him break."

Selah looked at her husband. "Jorge is a better interrogator than me. You really should put him in there."

"That would break several laws, and Jack knows the law." Lynda set the empty box on a desk. "Ready?"

Selah took a deep breath and inserted the earpiece.

Lynda gestured to Agent Tanaka again. "Dan is going to be your tech support. Just ask him for angles, sounds, whatever you need. He's the master."

She and Selah left the room. Bill walked over to the screen and asked, "I can see his lap?"

Tanaka slipped one headphone off. "Yeah. There's a camera under the table."

"Give me that angle and one of his left side."

"Roger."

Bill stood back and observed Haynes's demeanor when they brought him into the room. He sneered at Lynda, licked his lips. She didn't even flinch. Bill's fists ached to teach him a lesson.

He observed Haynes's body language as he sat down. A moment later, Selah began talking to him in Russian. That seemed to throw Haynes for a loop and knocked the arrogance down about 5 percent. His hands clenched and unclenched even though his face stayed neutral. A couple of times, he gripped his pants leg and even pinched himself as he answered.

Bill ran his hand down his beard a few times before he spoke. "Selah, whatever you just said, he pinched himself to keep his face straight."

Rick walked over and looked at his angle. "Thoughts?"

Peña shrugged. "He's terrified. I mean, he's a cop, a terrorist, and part of the Russian mafia. He's not going to live a week in prison."

"Selah, he did it again," Bill said. "Stay on that track."

"He doesn't know we can see his hands, does he?" Rick asked Tanaka.

"No reason he would," the agent replied. "I mean, what weirdo puts cameras on the underside of an interview table?"

Peña chuckled. "I'm guessing you?"

"You betcha. The other option was a glass table, but it was disallowed. Some silliness about safety."

Bill grinned. He liked Dan Tanaka. "There. Again, Selah." Haynes's face remained calm, charming. He occasionally smiled in such a way that Bill assumed he practiced. "Agent Tanaka, you deserve a prize, brother."

On the screen, Selah said something in Russian, and Haynes pushed away from the table. The agent guarding the door stepped forward. Haynes jerked the guard's hand away from his shoulder and started to sit down, then lunged at Lynda. She and Selah stood so fast that their chairs flew out behind them.

Peña started toward the door. Rick stepped in front of him. "Stay in your lane, Lieutenant."

The guard wrestled Haynes to the ground and secured his wrists. For ten more minutes, Haynes and Selah talked. Bill watched the man's face, but his expression gave nothing away.

"It would be nice to still have his hands," Bill said.

"Not necessary," Selah replied. She looked at one of the cameras. "We got it."

A few minutes later, the door opened and Selah walked in. "We have his agreement to turn state's witness against the mafia in exchange for protective custody."

"Fantastic," Bill said with a grin. "Did we get Cisco too?"

"No, but Haynes confirmed his identity through the photos."

Selah never ceased to surprise him in an interview. Often, when he was present, she spoke a foreign language. So even though he never understood what she said, he could see the results as men twice her size buckled in front of her.

This time, though, he wanted to know. "What did you say to him?"

She smiled. "I promised him that we'd accidentally put him into the general population in Sing Sing after we had federal indictments handed down with his name listed as a main witness."

He chuckled. "You don't have the power to do that. And you have a boatload of morals that would keep you from sending him to the dogs that way."

"Well, I know it and you know it. But Jack there, speaking in Russian and already trying to reckon how he's going to survive prison under protection, didn't know that."

He shook his head. "Never let me be on the opposite side of the table from you."

Peña slapped him on the back. "I say that to her regularly."

Selah slipped the earpiece out and put it in the cardboard box. Everyone else followed suit.

"Where'd Lynda go?" Bill asked.

"Went to call her boss and get protection going."

Peña put his arm around her shoulders. Bill rarely saw public displays of affection from either one of them. "Well done."

"You know, when you learn from the best . . . ." She grinned at him and jerked her head toward the door. "Ready to go? You have all of my attention for the next two weeks, then I have to go to Syria." She held up her badge. "My pass doesn't require an agent to escort us around the building, so we don't need to wait."

Peña looked at Rick. "Sir?"

"You're officially on leave. Enjoy your holidays. Merry Christmas. See you in Kentucky in two weeks." Rick turned to Bill. "What about you?"

"I think I'm going to stay in town for a couple of days."

"Fair enough." He looked at his watch. "I have to go to my in-laws' for dinner. I think I'll walk with Selah and let her be my escort out of the building. I'll see you later."

Just when Bill tried to decide if he should wait or leave with the group, Lynda came through the door. A glow of happiness seemed to light her up from the inside. "You all are a fantastic team. Thank you for your help."

"Our pleasure." He looked at his watch. His body ached with fatigue. "I need to go sleep off some of this jet lag. Could we meet tomorrow? Maybe midmorning?"

She hesitated only slightly before she grinned up at him. "Yes. I think I can swing taking tomorrow off. It's Saturday, after all."

They walked out of the office and down the hall. "Good job, Agent Clever. I remain impressed at your ways."

"I couldn't have done anything without your team. Seriously."

"I'll let the captain know."

In the elevator, she put a hand on his arm, and he looked into her eyes. "I'm really happy you're here right now. I'm glad Captain Norton put you on this detail."

His blood roared in his ears, and he gently brushed a strand of hair off her forehead. "Me too, Lynda."

While guards processed Jack for transport, Lynda leaned against her desk and observed. For the last two hours, she and Perry had worked with Jack to craft a very long and detailed statement about the mafia cell for whom he worked and his relationship with Green War. She had that statement tucked under her arm.

Once the guards went through the explanation of what would happen next, they cuffed Jack's wrists and ankles. When he turned and saw her, he glared for a moment, then grinned. "Well, my dear, looks like you got me now."

She gave a closed-lip smile. "Looks like."

"Do you have nothing to ask me? Did I ever really love you, that kind of thing?"

She walked up to him. "Jack, I am many things. A simpering fool is not one of them. There are a lot of emotions I've had to deal with in the last several months. But make no mistake, I've dealt with them." She glanced at the US marshal to his right and asked, "All set?"

"Yes. Just sign here." He held out his phone. She skimmed the open document and signed with her finger.

Lynda followed the marshals while they walked Jack to the parking garage and loaded him into the back of an SUV.

They started to drive away as she swiped herself back into the building.

While she waited for the elevator, an explosion knocked her to her knees. The metal garage door crashed into the wall next to her, and she covered her ears and ducked. As soon as she could catch her breath and get to her feet, she rushed through the door.

Her steps faltered as a rush of emotion surged through her chest, momentarily freezing her in place. Flames engulfed the SUV. It took a moment for her brain to kick in and realize that a car bomb had just gone off. In the parking garage of the FBI building! How could this have happened?

When the heat of the fire reached her, she lifted an arm to shield her face. Acrid smoke burned her eyes and nostrils. Alarms went off, and the sprinkler system engaged. She held her arm to her nose and tried to get to the burning vehicle to see if anyone was still inside, but it was too hot. She looked around, looking for any other witnesses, but saw no one.

Lynda took a sip of coffee. Her throat still burned from the fumes she'd inhaled, but the doctor at the scene had cleared her. An agent had gone to her hotel room and retrieved dry clothes for her.

She was still trying to process everything that had just happened. If she had been a second later in turning around, she would have been caught in the blast and likely killed.

She thought of the two US marshals who had treated her kindly and with respect. They had done their jobs with precision and professionalism. One of them had worn a wedding ring. She wondered about their families, possible children, and her heart clenched. To lose a parent would be so hard. To lose a parent the week before Christmas seemed like an extra dose of pain.

Her mind walked through Jack getting into the vehicle and his last words to her. So many things she could have said to him, so many ways she could have put him in his proper place, and now she'd never have a chance. Had she gotten over the vile words he'd said to her in Kuwait, the ways he'd used her? She hoped so. And she hoped the finality of his time on earth would help her in the healing process.

He'd used her, but it didn't have anything to do with her. She was just a pawn in his larger scheme. Understanding that would go a long way in helping her heal.

Now she sat in Perry's temporary office with his senior director next to her on the couch. "Did the bomb come from the mob or Green War?" Director Evans asked.

"How would they know we were transferring him today?" Lynda asked, rubbing the tense muscles on the back of her neck.

Director Evans tossed his empty coffee cup into the trash can. It hit the rim and slid in. "They always know."

An agent appeared in the doorway. "Bomb had Volkov's signature, sir." He held up a file. "Do you want details?"

Perry nodded and held out his hand. As soon as the agent gave him the file, he looked at Lynda. "Do you want in on this?"

More than anything. "Yes, sir."

He held out the file. "Compare and contrast."

"Yes, sir."

"I want to know how closely embedded the two organizations are."

"Understood."

He was giving her a new puzzle so she could get her mind off the explosion, and she appreciated it. She stood, and Director Evans looked up at her.

"All the resources you need, Agent," he said. "Just say the word."

"Thank you, sir."

She went back to the situation room, grabbed a new whiteboard, and lined it up with the other two she'd set up. Methodically, she read the file on the bomb and added notes, images, and details to the whiteboard. She pinned Jack's picture to the board and used red string to connect him to both the Green War terrorists and the mafia.

Next, she analyzed the bomb. She had only preliminary reports from that afternoon, so she dug into the reports about the bombs used on the pipelines and in the attacks by the mafia.

At some point, Dan handed her a hamburger. She sat in a chair, her legs propped up on the table. While looking at the pictures and lab reports and technical specifications, she slowly ate the burger. She tried to pull everything together into a single, cohesive story.

When she realized she had emptied her water bottle, she straightened and glanced at the clock, not surprised that it was almost nine at night. She grabbed another bottle of water and found Perry in his office. He looked up expectantly when she knocked on his doorframe.

"Well?"

"The last three bombings that we could attribute definitively to Russian mafia influence used the same signature. This is different from what Green War was using on the pipelines, but I don't think that's significant because you'd use a different bomb on a pipeline than a car. I'm feeling confident that it was the ecoterrorist organization trying to look like the mafia."

Perry pursed his lips and sat back in his chair, tapping his mouth with his finger. "They've been in bed together. Do you think this was a joint thing?"

She shrugged. "I don't have enough information to analyze that."

"Agent, there are times hypotheses are acceptable and even expected."

She sighed. "I'm wondering the same thing. We know someone is here, right? Maybe it's Cisco, maybe it's a soldier. But Debra Lucas was killed and directly tied to Green War. I think it's probably safe to say that Jack knew too much about both organizations, and that made him dangerous. It would make sense."

"Very good." Perry checked his watch. "The director still wants us to leave tomorrow. Take all of this back to Anchorage with you, Tanaka, and me."

"Even with the murders that happened today?"

He pressed a button on his phone to silence an incoming call. "Local homicide is working the murder and feeding information to us. The bombing is being handled by an entirely different department that is feeding information to us. Despite it all being part of a bigger picture, we can do what we need to do from our home base. We will be more efficient in our own homes than in hotels away from our families."

"I would like to fly out of Birmingham, if that's okay."

"Of course. Oversee boxing up your boards and then

consider yourself off duty until a week from Monday, the twenty-sixth."

"Thank you, sir."

She and Dan waited while a team checked over her assigned vehicle thoroughly. Even so, she cringed as she started the engine and let out a breath she didn't realize she was holding when nothing happened.

As they drove to their hotel, she said to Dan, "I'm glad you were here this week. Your cameras helped us get that statement from Haynes. Even with his death, we still have the names and details of some pretty big players. We wouldn't have had that without his statement. The organized crime unit was giddy over what we sent them."

"Hmm," he said. "I wonder if the mafia knows how much we know now, or if they were hoping to get him before he said anything."

"I can't even pretend to know." She turned into the parking garage and found a spot that fit the big SUV. "You'd think they would have given me a sedan. It's just the two of us."

"At least you got assigned a vehicle. Us cyber guys don't get such luxuries."

She chuckled as they got out of the car and walked to the hotel lobby. "Stick with me, kid. I'll take care of you."

"Yeah, right." He looked her up and down. "Are you okay?"

She shrugged. "My ears have finally quit ringing." She put a finger into her ear. "I keep thinking if it had been one second sooner . . ."

He nodded as they stepped into the elevator. "That's scary. I'm glad you're okay."

"Thanks, Dan. Give my love to your wife."

"I will. I'm looking forward to going home." He got out on his floor, and she went up two more.

In her room, she checked the bathroom and the closet, nervous and paranoid in a way she'd never been before. After she cleared the room, she saw a light blinking on the phone, indicating a message.

With trembling fingers, she dialed the number to retrieve her messages. When she heard Bill's voice, she almost sobbed out loud. What had she expected? Damien Cisco to leave her a voice mail?

Sniffing back tears, she shook her head and felt the exhaustion of operating on high alert for the last couple weeks. She focused on the message and wrote down the number for his hotel, then immediately called it. It took about six rings for him to answer the phone.

"Sorry to call so late," she said.

"You never have to apologize for calling me," he replied. "I called your cell but didn't hear back from you."

"Yeah. It ended up being a long day at work." Her voice broke. She put her hand over her mouth to hold back a sob.

"Hey, Lynda, what's wrong?" He instantly sounded awake.

"There was a bomb. In the car transporting Jack. He and the two marshals transferring him are dead." She let out a shaky breath. "I was right there. If I hadn't just gone in the doors—"

"You're okay, though? Not hurt?"

"No. I'm good."

He paused. "I'm sorry about Jack."

Her breath hitched. She looked out over the city. "He was a bad man who did bad things. I'm sorry he died, but it's not like he didn't know something like that could happen when he started working with them."

He chuckled. "Touché, Clever. Do you know who did it?"

"Green War, trying to frame the Russians, as far as I can tell." She cleared her throat. "Enough of that. I'm glad you answered your phone. I'd love to get away from this case for a while. What do you want to do tomorrow? Maybe we could sightsee. I haven't been here since I graduated from the Academy."

"Of course. What time?"

She looked at the clock beside the bed. "Ten is good for me. At the Lincoln Memorial?"

His deep voice sent shivers down her spine. "I'll see you there."

CHAPTER
★
TWENTY-FIVE

DECEMBER 17

Bill waited on the steps of the Lincoln Memorial. He thought back to the phone conversation last night. The idea that Lynda had nearly been killed in a bombing took his breath away. He wanted to shield and protect her from any harm. How would he have reacted if she'd been injured?

He looked at his watch for the fifth time. Why did he feel so anxious?

A group of young teenagers bounded up the stairs. Half of them had their noses buried in their phones. He shook his head. So much life was missed today in society's tendency to make what happened inside the little boxes more important and more interesting than what happened around them.

"Why are you frowning?" Lynda asked from above him.

He looked up and watched her descend. His heart felt

lighter at the sight of her. "Thinking of missed moments because we're focused on other things."

She grinned and slipped her arm into his. "Well, we finally have nothing else to take our focus. It can just be me and you and this beautiful city."

The sunlight shone down on her, bringing out her red-and-blond highlights. She'd left her hair down, soft and feminine around her face. He hadn't seen it like that since Turkey. His fingers itched to bury themselves in it.

She looked happy, fresh, seeming nothing at all like the shaky person he'd talked to last night. Should he bring it up or let her remain separated from it for a while?

He decided to let her be the one in charge of that conversation. He turned and gestured toward the sidewalk. "Where shall we start?"

They walked through the Vietnam Memorial. It fascinated him how marble slabs containing thousands of names would create such peaceful, silent surroundings. Even the birdsong he'd heard earlier didn't penetrate the memorial.

From there, they went to the WWII Memorial, then strolled down the National Mall. By then they both were hungry, so they slipped into a ramen restaurant and soon found themselves at a corner table.

Lynda shifted her eyes to the doorway three times in a way that made him lean forward and ask, "Are you okay from yesterday?"

She lifted a shoulder. "I don't even know how to process what I saw. It was terrible. But Perry let me work on it, and I think I was able to help." She squeezed lemon into her water. "We head back to Anchorage now. They want us working on our own turf. I have to report a week from Monday."

He tilted his head to look at her. "How does that make you feel?"

"I don't like handing over the bombing to a different team. I feel like it belongs in our investigation, and I intend to keep working on it. Thankfully, I have access to the data." She ran her fingers through her hair and told him about the murder of Debra Lucas.

His eyes narrowed. "What are they doing to protect your team?"

"We're being more hyperalert than usual. I had a team check my car, then it got placed under tight surveillance before I drove it last night and again this morning. Once we're back home, I think we'll all feel a little better."

That didn't sound like enough. "Are you checking to see if you're being followed?"

"I am now. But since yesterday, I've been to my hotel, work, and here, so it's not like there's been a lot of opportunity to check." He opened his mouth to say more, but she reached out and covered his hand with hers. "I am a good agent and I have a good team, Bill. Please don't worry."

He let out a long breath, then smiled. "Worry's what kept the cat out."

She stared at him for a moment, then threw her head back and laughed. "Oh! I've missed those sayings of yours. Every time I heard one over the years, I thought of you." She looked around. "I've loved being here. I'd like to come back and work here."

"As an analyst?"

"Yeah. Damien Cisco is still out there, and Green War is only a drop in the bucket. There's so much I can do." She propped her chin in her hand. "And you? Back to Kentucky?"

"That's where the unit is. We're all on leave right now." He thought about the possible mail waiting for him at home. "I've been doing school online. I just finished my master's thesis, took my last final before I left Kentucky."

Her eyes widened. "You never said anything about that!"

"Well, I don't yet know what I want to do about it."

"What are your options?"

He shrugged one shoulder, acting more casual about it than he felt. "I could go to a special school and become an Army officer."

"Wow. Is that what you want to do?"

"That is an unknown. I like my team. I don't know if I'd like the military as much as I do now if I was away from them."

She nodded. "I can understand that. What's your degree?"

"Master's in psychology."

With a smile, she folded her arms on the table and leaned toward him. "That's kind of a launchpad, isn't it? From there you could do so many different things. Are you looking at something where you can use your natural insight into the character of people?"

Rick often mentioned his ability to read other people, but he didn't really focus on that trait in himself. He simply found it useful in a tense situation or in a tactical debriefing. But in the day-to-day, it was a part of him, of how God had made him. "I use that already," he said.

The waiter brought their food, and Bill shifted his soda out of the way of the big, steaming bowl. The smell made his stomach growl, reminded him of a place he'd frequented during a training exercise in Okinawa.

They bowed their heads. Bill silently asked God to bless

the food and open his mind and heart to what He would have him do now that he had time to stop and think about it.

"When I was stuck in that jungle in Katangela, I just wanted to get out and get home," he said. "Which is funny, because home was a barracks room." He picked up the chopsticks and ceramic soup spoon before digging into the bowl of ramen. "Now the idea of going back has zero appeal. I feel restless, like someone put a cage around me and I need to break free."

"Maybe that's God telling you it's time to look at other opportunities," Lynda said.

"Maybe." He took a few bites and sipped some broth. "I'm sure it's one of those things that when God shows me, it will be quite clear what I'm supposed to do. And if I don't get that, I can always reenlist."

They ate for a few more minutes. Then she said, "I'm going to Alabama tomorrow. I need to see my parents and hug them. I've learned what a gift I have in them and want to take an opportunity to show it."

The thought of parents and Alabama made his heart ache. He didn't think he could say he had a gift in his mother, at least not with a straight face. "Have a good trip."

"Why don't you come with me?" She stared at him, her eyes insistent, her expression neutral. "Christmas at my parents' is great."

He set his spoon down and leaned back in his chair. "Lynda, there is nothing great for me in Alabama."

"So let's give you something good there."

He sighed and rubbed his chin. He missed his beard. "I have to be back in Kentucky." He glanced around the busy restaurant and thought about Alabama, the stench of the trailer that followed him wherever he went, then looked back at her. "What are we doing?"

She raised an eyebrow and set her spoon to the side. "Eating ramen."

"We can't be together, Clever. We live four thousand miles and three time zones apart. Your career is going to bring you to the upper echelons of government service. Mine is going to let me retire in ten more years with pretty good health care and some VA benefits."

She opened and closed her mouth, then said, "Bill—"

"We have never belonged together. I knew that back then. I know that now."

"Just stop." Lynda held up a hand. "Stop. It's absurd, this thing you're doing. So what if your childhood was super terrible and your mother is some awful person? I mention Alabama and all of our options go away?" She pointed at him. "That makes it so you don't get to be with someone you love? That doesn't even make sense." She reached out and took his hand. Just her touch, casual as it was, calmed him, soothed him. "I'm not asking us to solve the logistics over this delicious meal. I'm just asking you to want to."

"I do, with all my heart. I just—"

"Then that's all that matters. Don't you think God can work out the details?"

He smiled as the tension left his shoulders. "Well played, Clever."

She picked up her spoon. "Better eat. There's more to see."

They strolled to the parking garage, Bill's arm slung over her shoulders, her arm around his waist. Here, away from the day-to-day, being with him made her feel complete, whole. But, like him, she didn't see how they could be together.

Why did it have to be so hard? What if they'd stayed together all through college? Wouldn't they have worked it out then? Two intelligent, capable adults should have the ability to manage the details.

The problem remained that one of them would have to make a sacrifice career-wise. Would either of them be willing to do that?

She thought back through the day. Peace and contentment flowed through her after being with Bill away from work, away from terrorists, away from agents and directors and uniforms. Just the two of them.

They slowly stopped walking about twenty feet from her car and turned to face each other. The look in his eyes told her that he'd make the sacrifices and being together would be what mattered in the end.

Wordlessly, he cupped her cheek. Her lips tingled for his kiss. As he lowered his head, she rose up on her toes to meet him, but then he stopped.

She felt a change go over his body. His muscles tensed, his eyes hardened, his hand lost its gentle caress. Adrenaline flooded through her as she pulled her phone out of her pocket and took half a step away from him. He looked above her right shoulder, and she turned. Her heart leaped.

Damien Cisco walked on the level above them.

Bill moved past her faster than she could comprehend his intentions. She quickly called 911 while she pulled her gun out of her purse.

Bill grabbed the handrail above him, then easily pulled himself up. As she ran up the ramp to join him, Cisco stopped and spun around. He reached behind him and pulled out a gun, pointing it at Bill.

Lynda's breath caught in her throat. She knew without a doubt that Cisco would not hesitate to pull the trigger.

"Stop right there," he demanded.

Bill stopped. Lynda tried to sneak in behind him, but Cisco turned, bringing both of them into his view.

"Don't think I won't kill lover-boy," he said to her while keeping his eyes on Bill.

"It's the only shot you'll get," she said. She fervently prayed, *God, help me make a good decision here. Please, Father, keep me strong, brave. Don't let me fail.*

"It's the only shot that will matter." He spared her a glance.

Bill took the chance to silently come forward one step.

Cisco immediately turned back to him. "I'm not even kidding."

Lynda took a step sideways. If Cisco couldn't see them both at the same time, one of them could make a move. She kept her eyes trained on him and tried to anticipate what he would do next, her heart racing.

CHAPTER

★

TWENTY-SIX

Bill held up both hands. "Look, Damien, let's just sit down and talk about things."

The other man stared at him, his eyes hard, emotionless. Why wasn't he reacting more to getting caught? He'd managed to elude them for months. "You can't play games with me. You're not going to fool me."

"I don't want to do that, man," Bill said. "Really. I just want you to step back and think about your situation." Keeping the gun on him and away from Lynda was his priority right now. Even if it meant getting shot again. He started mentally shoring himself up for that possibility.

"The only situation I see is you at the end of my gun," Cisco said. "You're going to let me go."

"I can't do that, man."

"Yes—"

"No. It's not up to me." Bill gestured with his head at Lynda, who had her gun trained on the terrorist. "I'm just here for the scenery. She's calling all the shots."

Cisco's gun wavered.

She stepped sideways, and Cisco turned his gun on her. "Stay put, Agent Culter. I don't want to shoot you."

Bill nodded. "You're right. You don't. Because then you'll have to contend with me, and you really don't want that." Ice dripped from his voice. "I'll take a long time with you, and it will hurt the entire time."

Cisco turned to Bill again, so Lynda sidestepped and said, "You know, getting in bed with the Russians is what caught you. I guess even ecoterrorists need funding these days."

He spun toward her. His knuckles turned white on his gun. "Sometimes we have to make compromises we wouldn't otherwise make. So many ideas that would have crippled the country's reliance on fuel make people reexamine their priorities."

Crazy, Bill thought. *Insane*. Which meant Cisco couldn't be reasoned with and would have to be taken by force.

Lynda had moved far enough to the side that Bill could step closer without being seen.

Cisco started to turn toward him again, but Lynda interceded. "Still, if they hadn't started blowing up pipelines, you might have brought down way more planes than just the one. Now no one will ever know who you are and what you did. It will all be kept quiet."

His laughter echoed around the garage. "I still have people. The word will get out."

Bill stepped closer, and this time Cisco spun fast. The second the gun moved from Lynda, he charged, bending low and going in for a tackle. Before the man could adjust his aim, Bill's shoulder made contact with his chest and they landed on the ground.

Bill grabbed Cisco's wrist, forcing his fingers to loosen their grip on the weapon. Lynda kicked it out of the way, and Bill shifted to get the upper hand and restrain Cisco.

He pinned Cisco to the ground as Lynda secured his wrists, then hauled him up. Just as he pressed Cisco against one of the concrete columns, the garage filled with flashing red-and blue-lights. Seconds later, a DC police car flew onto their level, followed by two black SUVs.

Lynda held up her badge and her gun until the police officer acknowledged identification. Then she approached the first SUV. Perry Blake got out of the driver's side.

The police officer took over custody of Cisco. Bill's hands were trembling, so he shook them and huffed out a breath, resetting his brain and calming himself. He sauntered over to Lynda, catching the end of her sentence.

". . . like back in his college football days."

Blake chuckled and held out his hand. "Well done, Sergeant Sanders. The country owes you a large debt."

Bill shook his hand, then slipped his arm over Lynda's shoulders. "Just in the right place at the right time, sir."

It took a couple of hours before she could break free. The federal team had to cordon off the scene, collect any evidence found in the area, and interview Bill and Lynda, then finally released them.

Bill leaned against the concrete column by her car. "Where were we?" he asked with a grin.

She smiled up at him, her heart picking up speed. "You were about to kiss me goodbye."

"Oh, right, I remember." He slipped his hand behind her neck.

She met his kiss easily. Right now, all of the logistics she'd worried about didn't mean anything. The taste, the feel, the smell of him . . . She could stand here all day and just kiss him until they both turned into puddles on the floor.

They eventually pulled away. She leaned her forehead against his chest and said, "I wish we didn't have to go our separate ways." She looked up at him. His eyes had softened, and he brushed a strand of hair behind her ear, his fingertips leaving a tingling trail on her cheek.

"You and me both." He stepped back and patted the roof of her SUV. "Best get in before you miss your flight."

She opened the door and got into the driver's seat. His eyes widened and his hand shot out, catching her door.

"What?" she asked as he knelt next to her, looking at the base of her seat. His entire countenance had changed. She could feel the intensity radiating off him. When he raised his eyes to meet hers, her mouth went dry. "What?" she repeated.

"Just sit still," he said. He put a hand on her thigh. She didn't know if he intended it to comfort or restrain her. "Call your boss back. Tell him to get bomb control here."

Her heart beat so hard she wondered how she could hear his voice over it. With shaking fingers, she called Perry and put the phone on speaker.

"Agent Culter?" he asked.

When she opened her mouth, no sound came out.

"He rigged her car," Bill said. "You need to get a team down here."

If Perry said anything else, she didn't hear it. She sat perfectly still as Bill investigated her seat and under the car. Finally, he crouched next to her again. She focused on the grave determination on his face. "It's bad, isn't it?" she whispered.

He cupped her cheek. "I won't leave you."

"Bill!" His name came out in a gasp of air. "Can't you stop it?"

"I can't see it. You'd have to move, and I get the distinct impression that would be bad."

"How did you know?"

"I heard the click." He looked beyond her as she heard the unmistakable sound of tires on the parking garage floor. "Listen. I'll stay right here, okay?" He looked back at her. "We're in this together."

A bead of sweat ran down the center of her back. "Don't be ridiculous. You need to be safe." She didn't like the resignation lurking in his eyes. She reached up and touched his cheek, missing the feel of the beard that used to tickle her palm. "Do you know when I fell in love with you?"

He grabbed her wrist, pressing her hand against his cheek. "Lynda," he said in a quiet voice.

"Let me." She wanted to turn toward him but didn't know if shifting her weight would cause the bomb to go off, so she stayed still. "We were in, like, the third study session our group had. We'd already been on two dates. One of our group came in super hungover. Remember? And you said, 'He looks like ten miles of bad road.' It was so ridiculous and made me laugh, and suddenly, I couldn't talk to you enough. You smiled that charming smile of yours, and the dimple showed in your left cheek, and your eyes lit up. And

I just thought, 'Man, if I could make him happy like this all the time . . .'"

He chuckled and shook his head. "You cannot possibly mean that."

"It's true. We hadn't been together long. What, maybe two weeks? I knew it was over for me." A tear slid out of her eye. "We've lost so much time."

"I've done a lot of things in my life, Clever, that I should probably never have done. But what I said to you—I'd take it back this second if I could." He kissed her palm. The touch of his lips radiated through her arm. "I didn't need to wait as long as you. I just had to see you, hear your voice, watch that brain of yours function. I'd never been so enamored in my life. Nor since. You've always had my heart, Lynda. You always will."

Perry got out of his SUV and started toward them, but Bill stood and held up his hand. "I don't know if it's on a timer. I can't see it."

"How do you know it's there?"

"I know. Just keep a perimeter. Get a bomb unit here."

"They're on their way."

Bill ducked his head and looked at her, hesitation on his face, before he spoke to Perry again. "We aren't going to be able to defuse it. I need them to bring us protection, and you need to clear the building."

Her breath hitched. She felt like she couldn't get enough air.

He knelt back down. "Listen," he said, his once soft, loving voice taken over by clipped tones and rapid speech. "Anything we do to try to get to this thing might make it go off. I think the best bet would be to get you behind this column. It will protect us best it can from the blast."

She knew two things for certain. If they didn't try anything, she'd die. And Bill would do anything and everything to save her.

"Okay." She licked her lips, wishing her mouth didn't feel so dry. "Just tell me what to do when."

He looked through the passenger window. "Well, Clever, right now we're going to pray. Close your eyes."

Hot tears burned trails down her cheeks as she complied.

His voice moved around her. "Father, we love You. You know that. We seek to do Your will, to follow You, to be shining lights for You. Right now, we need Your divine hand. Protect us from the blast so we can continue doing good works. And if that's not Your will, God, then we look forward to seeing You in a minute."

When she opened her eyes, he winked at her. "I feel better already," he said, standing as a bomb squad officer approached with protective gear.

Soon, Bill had fully suited up. Under his instructions, she carefully moved so he could help her put the heavy jacket on.

He held up the head covering. "I know you don't like things on your head."

"I'll live," she said with a breathless chuckle. "Just do it." She plugged her ears with the hearing protection, then sat still as he slid the helmet over her head.

The bomb squad officer said they couldn't risk putting the pants on her. They removed the steering wheel to give her more maneuverability, then Bill directed everyone back. He hooked the handle of a long shield in his right arm and held out his left hand. "We're going to need to make it one movement," he said. "I don't know how long we're going to have. Releasing the pressure on the switch might cause an instant explosion, or it could set off a chemical reaction that will buy us a split second or two."

His voice came through the speaker in her headpiece. Everything they said could be overheard by the team outside the perimeter.

"Understood," she said, trying to keep the wobble out of her voice.

She'd been this scared once before. That night in Alaska, when Cisco had trained his shotgun on her, she had frozen in fear. She couldn't freeze this time. Any hesitation would harm Bill. So she focused on saving him instead of herself.

"Please, God," she whispered. She left off the rest. God knew. Please save them. Please don't let this hurt too much. Please don't let Bill die because he was too stubborn to leave her side.

"As I say three, I'm going to pull," Bill said. "You need to shift your body out, and as soon as your feet hit the ground, jump and let me take your weight and haul you."

"Got it."

"One." She shifted one leg out. "Two." She took a deep breath and held it. As he said, "Three," she turned her body and lunged out of the car. The second her feet touched the ground, she sprang up and his arm came around her, putting her behind the shield. He spun and crouched behind the pillar, placing the shield between the concrete and their bodies.

As he crouched, the explosion ripped through them. She screamed as something crashed into her leg. The oxygen was sucked out of the air, and she gasped for breath. Her ears rang and nausea swirled in her stomach.

Later, she couldn't remember anything clearly or in its proper order. Bill falling limp against her, the helmet pressing against her head, the pain in her leg almost as overwhelming as the steady, muffled ringing in her ears.

Someone pulled Bill off. Hands clamped on her leg. Perry stood over her, directing people. She tried to get up, to check on Bill, but hands held her down. She tried to talk but couldn't tell if the sounds coming out of her mouth made sense.

Finally, someone took the helmet off and she could breathe again. Her first breath filled her nostrils with acrid smoke, burning the back of her throat, making her vision wobble. Someone placed an oxygen mask over her mouth and nose, and she took a good breath, then another.

At some point, they moved her onto a gurney, but she didn't know how or when. She'd lost sight of Bill. As she tried to pull the mask off to ask where they took him, her vision turned gray. Even as she muttered his name, everything went black.

CHAPTER
★
TWENTY-SEVEN

A hazy memory of danger tickled the corner of Bill's brain. Something . . . What had happened?

Lynda. An explosion.

His eyes flew open. Oh. Bad idea. Light pierced his eyes, making the dull ache in his head sharpen. His mouth went dry, his stomach swirled.

"You're an idiot. You know that, don't you?"

Ah, the voice of reason. He carefully turned in the direction it came from and opened one eye halfway. Rick stood near a window.

"I guess you're wondering why I've called us here today," Bill said in a weak voice.

"At least I know you'll live." Rick plopped into a chair. "I'm getting a little tired of visiting you in hospitals."

"At least this one isn't a maternity ward."

Rick chuckled. "You have a bad concussion. Somehow, despite it all, that's it." He rubbed his face. "No crush injuries, no impalement. Just a crack at that hard head of yours. You've slept about twelve hours."

"What about Lynda?"

Rick shook his head, and Bill's entire world fell out from under him. But then Rick said, "They won't give me any information. Last I heard, she was still in surgery. As soon as Director Blake clears it with her parents, I'll know more."

Relief flooded every pore of his body. Surgery meant living. He thought back to yesterday's events. "I thought he was just following us, but he must have just finished installing the bomb when we happened on him."

"Sounds like." Rick stood. "You're going to live. I'll go see if I can find food and information. Do you want anything?"

The idea of putting food in his stomach held absolutely no appeal. "No. I'll wait for our post-deployment burger when I can sit upright."

With a smile, Rick slapped his shoulder. "Deal. Get some rest."

After he left, Bill closed his eyes again, but in his mind's eye he could see only the terrified look on Lynda's face right before he put the helmet on her. What kind of surgery? What damage had the force of the explosion done to her body? Had he not moved fast enough to save her from the detonation?

His head pounded. He looked at the bed railing and hit the button to call a nurse, then covered his eyes with his arm.

"May I help you?" a nurse said.

"Do I have an order for pain meds at all? My head hurts."

"One sec, hon."

He heard the squeak of shoes and carefully lowered his

arm. The nurse who entered had rich brown skin, blond braids, and a kind smile.

"Just acetaminophen, I'm afraid," she said. "I'll leave the light out." She handed him a little paper cup with the two pills in it, then poured him water from the plastic pitcher by his bed. Once he took the medicine, she asked, "Are you hungry?"

"No, ma'am," he said. "I can't imagine ever being hungry again."

She tsked under her breath and adjusted his blankets. "Stay still. Be calm. Those are the things that will help you get better."

He wanted to reply with something witty, but nothing came to him, so he just closed his eyes and willed himself to sleep the headache away.

DECEMBER 19

Lynda opened her eyes and found herself looking out the window. From her hospital bed, she had a perfect view of the bright blue Maryland skies. She knew that the morning air would be crisp and fresh. She could see the dichotomy from the winter weather in Kuwait.

She slowly turned her head. Bill sat in the chair next to her bed, reading a book. She hadn't expected to see him. Her heart started pounding and she tried to sit up, but the weight of the cast on her leg made everything harder. As she struggled, he lifted his head.

His dark eyes focused on her face, and the harsh expression softened. He had the heavy shadow of a beard on his chin, giving him a rugged, devil-may-care appearance. A white bandage covered his right temple.

"Well, don't you look brighter than a daisy in full sunlight."

"I'm so happy to see you," she said. "I couldn't get any information about you and my phone was in the car."

"They wouldn't let me out of my room until the doc cleared my concussion." He reached out and brushed her hair off her forehead. "How are you feeling?"

"Fine for now. A piece of the car went into my leg and lodged itself in the femur. The impact also broke my hip. The doctor said they have to do one more surgery. I think I'm going to be grounded for a while."

He nodded. "I think you're quite blessed to get to keep it."

"Thanks to you." She looked over his shoulder as her mom appeared in the doorway. "Mom." When she looked back to Bill, his face had lost the relaxed look. He was guarded, careful.

He straightened and stood. "Mrs. Culter. It's good to see you again."

"It's been a long time, Bill." She held up two cups of coffee. "If I'd known you were here, I would have brought you a coffee."

His smile had very little warmth. "That's okay, ma'am. I never touch the stuff." He looked back at Lynda and squeezed her shoulder. "Take care, Clever."

He started from the room, and she called out, "Bill!" As he pivoted to look at her, she didn't know what to say.

He smiled. "It's okay. Just concentrate on getting better." He brushed by her mom with a soft, "Ma'am," and then went out the door.

"He looked a little rough for wear. I'm surprised they let him up and around," her mom said, coming fully into the room. She held out the coffee, but Lynda shook her head, so her mom set it on the table next to her and took a sip of her own drink.

"He came to say goodbye." She picked at a fray in her blanket.

"Would that be so terrible?"

Lynda shook her head and tried to see the blanket through her tears. "He saved my life, Mom. And he loves me."

"Baby, I know that. I just don't want to pick up your pieces again because of him. So forgive me if I'm hyper-protective of you as far as Bill Sanders is concerned." She put her hand over Lynda's, and Lynda's fingers stilled as she met her mom's gaze. "But I will let you guide your own heart."

"Thanks, Mom," she whispered.

Her mom patted her hand, then pulled a newspaper out of her bag and handed it to her. The top half was splashed with a picture of Perry leading Damien Cisco into the federal building. Agent Smith walked next to them.

Her mom settled into the chair that Bill had just occupied and pulled her crossword book out of her bag. "What now? Do you know?"

"Mama, I'm so good at what I do. I can't imagine giving it up."

Her mom paused with her glasses halfway to her face and stared hard at her. "Who in the world said anything about you giving it up?"

Confused, Lynda said, "I thought you didn't like—"

"Didn't like my daughter getting taken captive, then chasing terrorists to the Middle East, getting threatened by the

Russian mafia, and getting blown up? Yeah, not a fan." She set her glasses on her nose and opened her book. "Darling, God has gifted you with a tremendous ability to analyze and figure things out. There is no reason on this green earth why you should ever let that go."

An image of Bill ran unbidden through her mind. If she wanted to be with him, she'd have to. His job took him from duty station to duty station. The FBI would accommodate in reason, of course, but for her to continue doing the job she did, she needed continuity. She had a reason, but she didn't think it was enough. Besides, Bill had never asked her to let anything go. They'd made no plans, offered no promises.

"Okay," she said, reaching for the coffee. "I thought you were going to ask me to find something else to do."

"Goodness, no." Her mom settled back against the chair. "I'd never presume to come between you and God's plans."

FORT CAMPBELL, KENTUCKY

During the flight back to Kentucky, Bill tried to leave the past behind. With every mile, he made the honest effort just to let it go. He and Lynda Clever Culter could not be together. He'd known it in college. She'd been a silly dream, and he knew better now.

He got home midafternoon. After he let himself into his apartment and tossed his keys on the kitchen counter, he looked around. This was his first home. When he'd joined the Army, he'd used any available money to pay for his grandmother's care, which meant he lived in the barracks, didn't own a car, and ate at the mess hall. When she died, he'd signed his first lease, bought a car, and started furnishing the apartment.

He had no specific dreams about what he wanted to call home. Clean and bug-free topped his list of requirements. Beyond that, he didn't care much about size, wall color, location. This one-bedroom apartment had a simple layout and served all of his needs. He liked the porch because it could hold a full patio set. He spent a lot of time out there when he could.

He'd gradually furnished the place. The day he moved in, he had a bed and a couple of bar stools. So far, he'd managed to add a couch and a dresser.

He had last been home the week after Thanksgiving. Right now, Christmas loomed. Barely three weeks had passed, and yet so much had changed in that time.

In the stack of mail Rick had picked up for him, he found a thick cardboard envelope and opened it. "William Sanders, MS, Psychology in Applied Behavior Analysis," the diploma read. He ran a finger over the gold embossing and smiled. Somehow, through God's grace, he'd managed to turn a six-year degree into twelve years of hard work.

He opened the curtains to his balcony and slid the door open, hoping to bring some fresh air into the place. The plant that Rick's wife, Cynthia, had bought him sat on the patio table. He couldn't believe it looked so good. He'd set it outside on his way out the door to Kuwait, thinking it would get a better chance with the elements than in his dark apartment with no one to water it.

On his porch, he looked out over the wooded lot, listening to the sound of children's laughter floating on the breeze.

He ran his hand over his cheek, feeling the rough whiskers. It was always so hard to go back to shaving every day.

He thought back to Lynda seeing him freshly shaved and grinning as she put her hand on his smooth cheek. He closed his eyes, trying to recapture that moment.

His soul longed to be with her. No matter what he told himself or all the different ways he tried to convince himself otherwise, he believed God meant for her to be the better part of him. She always had been.

Before he could talk himself out of it, he called her hospital room. She answered on the second ring. "Hello?"

"Hey."

"The ringer scared the life out of me. I didn't even know I had a phone until it rang."

"Well, you said yours was in the car."

"It was. Daddy's getting me a new one. I'll have it tonight."

"Can I call you tonight?"

After two heartbeats, she said, "Bill, you can call me anytime."

He squeezed his eyes closed. "Likewise."

"Oh, let me get your number. Yours was in my phone."

He gave her his number and hung up. Overwhelmed with emotions, he went into his bedroom and dug through his dresser until he found running shorts and a T-shirt. After a good stretch, he left his apartment and headed toward the jogging path.

He ran slowly, paying attention to how his head felt. As he passed marker after marker, he thought back through the mission, the clues they'd missed, the mistakes they'd made. But they'd also had successes. They'd stopped the terrorists in the Middle East, broken up the Green War organization until Damien Cisco had no choice but to fight back or fade into obscurity, and stuck a boot deep into an organized crime syndicate that tried to affect the world petroleum market.

All in all, the simple mission of going undercover as a married couple touring the Holy Land had been a stunning success. Lynda and her team, he and his team—all of them should feel nothing but pride in what they'd accomplished.

No one could have foreseen what Damien Cisco did later. As hard as they'd worked to gather information and arrest suspects, they had no control over the people who'd died in the process of Cisco's acting out his insanity. But Bill refused to let Cisco's final acts diminish the triumph of the overall operation.

Feeling like he'd mentally sorted that out the best he could, he refocused his thoughts on Lynda. Seeing her lying in the hospital bed had ruined him. He thought he'd been prepared, but when he walked into the room, his stomach had fallen and nothing felt right since.

Had he missed something with Cisco that would have given him a clue to the bomb? He analyzed every nuance of expression, every word Cisco had uttered. Cisco had given absolutely nothing away.

After a single lap, Bill's legs turned rubbery and sweat poured down his face. He slowed to a walk, putting his hands on his hips. His head hurt. Maybe he should have waited another day or two before running.

He walked the second lap as the sky turned a vibrant pink with the setting of the sun. The air had cooled significantly with the dimming light. Deciding he'd shower and then call Rick to see if he wanted to meet for their traditional post-deployment-hamburger meal, he headed back up the hill to his building.

It shouldn't have surprised him to see Rick sitting on the stairs. His friend looked up at him, his green eyes filled with understanding and sympathy. "That good, huh?"

Bill whipped his shirt off and used it to mop his face. "Good?"

"You hate running."

"I do not hate running. I love running. I hate running in a PT formation." He thought of 5:00 a.m. morning runs, counting cadence, having to match his pace with all of the people around him.

"Is it not the same?"

"Of course not."

Rick stood and they went up the stairs.

"Not that an officer would really ever understand."

Rick snorted, as if to say he understood all too well on his own level. "I thought we could grab a hamburger."

"Your new wife isn't demanding your attention?" Bill asked with a grin.

"Dude, I've been home since yesterday."

"True." He unlocked his door and led the way inside. "Give me ten minutes."

By the time he got out of the shower and dressed, Rick had opened all the curtains and some of the windows. "Your plant survived."

"Only because I put it on the porch. There must have been a lot of rain for it to have survived a Kentucky autumn without any care."

"No, Cynthia came and watered it."

Bill looked at the plant, then back at Rick. "Cynthia?"

"I gave her the key you gave me and asked her to water it."
He should probably be upset at his friend's presumption, but instead, he felt very cared for and loved. "Well, I guess there are advantages to you being married after all."

Rick laughed. "Let's go. I am starving."

Soon they sat at a table in a bar and grill with fat hamburgers in front of them. Bill's dripped with honey mustard and grilled red onions. As he sliced through the brioche bun, he said, "Lynda will keep her leg."

"That's amazing." Rick wiped his fingers on the black cloth napkin. "Is she still in the hospital?"

"Yeah. They have to do a second surgery."

"How's she doing?"

"She'll heal." Bill put his knife down and picked up his soda, sitting back against the booth. "She seems very fragile."

Rick raised an eyebrow. "How are you doing?"

"Got my diploma and transcripts in the mail. The semester just ended last week. I'm surprised it was there."

A big grin covered Rick's face. "That's fantastic. Well done." He raised his glass of water. "To the psych major. May you go far."

Bill chuckled. "Yeah. I can now freely analyze you."

"Your lack of degree never stopped you from doing that." Rick pointed at him. "Your ability to read people is a gift, man. It's served the unit well, but it doesn't have to be used as a military tactic. There are other jobs out there."

"What, are you firing me?"

"I know that your enlistment is up in a few weeks. Time to sign again on the dotted line—or not."

With a sigh, Bill set his plate to the side. "I only know this," he said, waving his finger in a circle. "It's what I do."

"Is that supposed to stop you?" Rick picked up a sweet potato fry and dipped it in ketchup. "Abraham only knew Ur. It didn't stop him from going where God directed." He bit into the fry and waved the other half in Bill's direction. "You were meant to be more than an A-Team grunt."

"Says you."

"There's a reason you pursued your degree." Rick shook his head. "I am doing exactly what I'm meant to be doing. This is who I am in my soul. Can you say that?"

His words twisted Bill's heart. He could not say that. "I'm really good at what I do."

"Brother, you are the best. I wouldn't want anyone else. But you and I both know that my father-in-law being the nation's vice president will limit my ability to continue to run this team. If the danger from Green War hadn't been so imminent, we never would have been chosen."

"Are you being transferred?" Bill asked.

"It wouldn't surprise me if I rode a desk for the rest of his term. But I went into marriage with Cynthia knowing that her father might be my commander in chief. I don't know if they'll transfer me or not, but deploying me might not be in anyone's best interest, especially if I could potentially be put at risk and therefore put the team and country at risk." He bit into his burger. After washing it down with some water, he said, "I'd encourage you to give your reenlistment some prayer and attention instead of just assuming that you're to carry on."

The idea of serving without Rick did not have the same appeal. Bill would have to think about it, seriously pray about it. "I appreciate your candor."

Rick smiled. "I will always supply you with candor, brother."

CHAPTER

TWENTY-EIGHT

Lynda stared at the night sky outside of her hospital room. On cue, her new phone rang. She didn't need to look at the clock to know it was exactly 9:00 p.m.

For six days now, Bill had called every night at exactly this time. The first day, they'd talked for twenty minutes. He told her about his plant surviving his deployment, and she told him about the nightmares she had about the bomb. He talked her through it, explained the tools he'd learned to cope with post-traumatic circumstances, and gave her mental exercises to work through. Their conversations went from minutes to hours.

She swiped up, and his face came on the screen. "Hey," she said, shifting her pillow behind her.

"Well, aren't you a tall glass of lemonade?"

She chuckled. "You don't drink lemonade."

322

He shrugged. "True. But I am more likely to drink it than iced tea, and that is the proper saying." He narrowed his eyes. "Looks like you got more sleep."

"Yes. No nightmare last night."

"Well done, you. Doctor Drumstick at your service. That'll be a nickel."

She grinned. "Come and collect."

"Oh, the temptation."

She could see his clean-shaven face and the burgundy V-neck sweater he wore. "Did you make it to Christmas Eve service?"

"I did. This was my first year at this church for the holidays. They had a beautiful candlelight service with carols and a very solemn quiet. I enjoyed it."

She suddenly missed her family and had to blink back tears. "I watched my parents' church on their website. It was wonderful to connect remotely."

"I know you're looking forward to seeing them this week." He walked through his apartment and out onto his balcony.

"It's still warm enough to go outside?" she asked.

"It's forty-nine. But I wanted to show you this." He reversed the camera so she could see his living room from the balcony. A sofa and a low coffee table faced a television mounted on the wall. Bookshelves covered the back wall. A bar separated that room from the kitchen, and high-back chairs sat at the bar.

The Christmas tree in the corner stood out the most. It had white lights and red-and-white bulbs the color of Alabama's Crimson Tide. A red star painted with the scrolling white *A* topped the tree.

The phone moved closer to the room, and she heard the

door shut before he turned his camera back to himself. "That is some tree," she said.

His grin lit up her hospital room. Her heart felt lighter when she saw it, and the love she had for him tried to beat itself out of her chest.

"Did you know it's my first Christmas tree ever?"

That took her breath away. Every time he revealed a part of his childhood and adolescence, her heart broke a little more for the boy he used to be. "Well, you know, begin as you mean to go on."

He laughed. "Exactly."

"So even in your barracks rooms, you never had a tree?"

He shrugged. "Why? I mean, my meemaw would have a tree in her room. Usually this little plastic thing she got at the dollar store. She'd tie ribbon bows all over it. And I always go to Rick's for Christmas. His parents outdo themselves with decorations. So there's never been a reason for me to have a tree."

A warm glow lit her up from the inside. He had a reason this year. "I can't wait to see it in person."

"I'll see you tomorrow."

"Yes, you will."

"It will be the best Christmas gift ever."

She hung up the phone with a silly smile.

The doctor had released her to an orthopedic surgeon in Anchorage. He'd do the third and hopefully final surgery on her leg. Before that, she wanted to spend several days at her parents' house. She hadn't been there in over a year and missed the home she'd grown up in. She wanted to eat her mother's cooking and visit her aunts and uncles and see a couple of cousins who still lived in the area.

But more importantly, she planned to stop and visit Bill on her way to Birmingham. She'd stay the night with Rick Norton and his wife, who was a doctor, in Fort Campbell, then Bill would drive her to Birmingham the next day.

Carefully, she swung her legs over the side of the bed and reached for her crutches. She had a hard time accepting how weak her body felt. With trembling arms, she got out of the bed but had to pause and take a few deep breaths before she could hobble out of the room.

She made it to the hallway and started down her route.

"You're early tonight," the nurse on duty said.

With a grin, Lynda said, "Short phone call."

"Those can be good too."

She chuckled. "By the way, Merry Christmas."

The nurse glanced at the clock. "Few more hours. I'm excited to have the night shift tonight. I'll be home in time for my kids to wake up."

Lynda smiled, remembering Christmas mornings, and kept going, making the full circle of the floor. It was slow going, but at least now she could do the whole way.

Back in her room, she glanced at her suitcase and smiled. Other than what she'd need first thing in the morning, she had packed everything, ready to get on a plane. Perry had helped expedite getting her driver's license and FBI identification replaced. She had new credit cards waiting at her parents' house, and her mom had given her a debit card and some cash before she left.

As she lay back down in the bed and adjusted her covers, she smiled, thinking about tomorrow.

FORT CAMPBELL, KENTUCKY
DECEMBER 25

Bill handed Lynda a glass of water, then sat on the couch. He'd bought a recliner to give her a place to sit and elevate her leg. For the last three hours, they'd simply enjoyed being in the same room again. He did not look forward to dropping her off at her parents' tomorrow.

"When is the final surgery scheduled?"

She thanked him for the water. "It'll be in Alaska in a few weeks. That way, all of my follow-ups will be with the doctor who did the final surgery." She pressed on the cast that went from the tops of her toes up to her hip. "The doc in DC put my leg in a hard cast so I could travel more safely."

He frowned. "I wish he'd finished with you there."

"I requested it this way." She set the glass on the table next to her. "I'm going to go back to work as soon as I can."

He understood her desire to get back in the game. Right after he'd gotten home from Katangela, his unit had deployed without him, and watching them go had hurt him in his soul.

She shifted her body and propped her chin in her hand. "What have you decided to do?"

He knew what she was really asking but said, "Eat a Christmas turkey with all the trimmings. Cynthia has teamed up with a couple of the other wives, and they're putting on a spread."

"Very cute."

"I thought so." When she just raised her eyebrow, he took a deep breath and slowly let it out. "I think I'm going to get out of the Army. What I'll do after that, I have no idea. My enlistment will end in May."

She reached her hand out. He didn't even hesitate to take it. "Have you talked to Rick about it?"

"I haven't talked to him specifically, but he knows I'm struggling with the decision and is praying for me about it." He put her hand against his cheek and closed his eyes at the touch of her skin. "I wasn't sure until I got home from DC. But every day, the insistence in my heart is stronger and stronger, so I think I'm making the right decision."

He looked at her again. She had her hair pulled back in a ponytail, and her face was scrubbed clean of makeup. He thought her the most beautiful woman he'd ever laid eyes on, especially like this.

"So, I'll be unemployed in a few months. That'll be fun." He kissed her palm and released her hand.

She smiled. "You are the most intelligent man I've ever met. Now you have your degree and years of experience in the military. I doubt it will be hard to find a job."

"You're probably right." He looked at his watch. He hated to take their alone time away, but it was Christmas. "Are you ready to go to the party?"

She glanced down at her leg. "I don't know. Do you think it will be okay?"

"I know it will. Cynthia's a doctor. She'll hover. You should have seen her with me when I was shot." He stood and reached for her crutches. "Do you need anything out of your suitcase?"

"No. I'm good like this."

He couldn't agree more. He grabbed the Christmas present he'd gotten Rick and held the door open for Lynda, then slowly walked next to her to the end of his breezeway. In the elevator, he put his hand on the back of her neck and leaned down to give her a warm kiss.

When he raised his head, she asked, "What was that for?"

He winked. "Proximity."

Soon, they pulled into the drive behind Rick's car. Bill hopped out and helped Lynda from the front seat.

She looked around, smiling. "I love how all the houses look the same."

He wiggled his eyebrows. "That's the Army for you. Dress 'em the same, house 'em the same. Nothing to distinguish one from another." He grabbed her suitcase and paced her as they walked up the drive.

Before they could get to the door, Cynthia opened it. She wore a red sweater and a green-and-white-checked skirt and had her blond hair pulled back with a gold bow.

"You look like a Christmas present," Bill said.

She ran her palm down her skirt. "I was on call today. Thought I would cheer up the women having babies on Christmas Day."

Bill introduced the two women. Cynthia stepped away from the door to give Lynda room to maneuver. "I'm so happy you're here." She gestured. "Go inside and to the left. First door on your right."

Bill could smell the turkey cooking, making his mouth water. As he carried Lynda's suitcase in, she sat on the end of the bed while Cynthia explained where the bathroom was and where to find fresh towels.

Cynthia tilted her head to the side, studying Lynda's face. "You need to rest." She turned to Bill. "You come with me."

Lynda laughed. "I'll be fine. She's right. I'm exhausted and my leg hurts." She dug through her purse and pulled out a pill bottle. "I haven't taken a pill since six this morning when I got on the plane. I think I'll take one and close my eyes for a few moments."

Cynthia pulled back the covers on the bed. "Take all the time you need. The guys who are coming aren't due for at least another hour." She looked up at Bill. "Rick's on the back patio cooking some veggies on the grill. I'm sure he'd love the company."

Bill brushed his lips over Lynda's cheek and left her in Cynthia's hands, then walked to the glass door off the living room and slid it open. Rick stood at the grill, gazing out at the yard with a heavy look on his face.

"Merry Christmas," Bill said, grabbing one of the chairs and sitting down. "Why the long face?"

Rick focused on him and his eyes cleared. "Merry Christmas." He looked at the door and back at Bill. "Just got word that they're pulling me from the team."

"On Christmas?"

He shrugged. "Her dad called me personally. He felt like he needed to explain, despite my insistence that he didn't."

Bill whistled under his breath. "'Hey, go do this super crazy covert mission in Turkey first, then we'll pull you.'"

Rick chuckled. "Pretty much." When he opened the grill, savory smoke billowed out. "It's not like I didn't know it was coming."

"What's the date?"

"Sometime in February."

Bill thought back through all the missions they'd accomplished as a team. He could attribute the cohesiveness to the quality of men he served with and not to any one man, but a new leader would provide an entirely different feel to it all.

"Glad I've already decided not to reenlist."

Rick turned to face him completely. "You seriously decided before now?"

Bill shrugged. "Ask Lynda. We were just talking about it."

Rick grinned. "Changes coming."

"And we all know change is always fun," Bill said, making Rick laugh.

★ ★ ★

ANCHORAGE, ALASKA
JANUARY

Lynda fought the fog of the anesthesia. She hated the stuff, and since she'd had three surgeries in the past month, she felt that hatred on a very personal level.

It was exhausting trying to wake up. She ended up dozing fitfully. The badgering by the nurses in post-op made it all worse. Every time she roused, someone tried to speak to her, to ask her questions. She couldn't tell how she answered or what she said.

She gave up fighting the anesthesia and let her body relax. The next time she tried to open her eyes, they stayed open. She looked over and saw Bill sitting in the chair next to the bed.

He looked up from his book. When he saw her eyes open, he smiled. "Well, now, this time it looks real."

She looked around. She lay on a bed in the bright outpatient surgical recovery area. "It feels like it's been hours."

He shrugged. "Maybe an hour since they brought you back here."

She wiped her face with her hands. "I hate anesthesia."

He chuckled. "Yes, you've said that a few times and to every nurse or doctor who has come to see you."

Heat crept up her face. She reached down and felt the wrap on her leg. "Did it work?"

"The doctor thinks so. You officially have a bionic leg. He installed the rod in your femur and all of the screws and braces required. You won't be going through a metal detector anytime soon."

"Titanium doesn't set off metal detectors," she said. She held out her hand, and he enveloped it with his warm, strong one. "Thanks for coming."

He lifted her hand and pressed a kiss to the back of it. "I couldn't miss the chance to see Anchorage in January. Come on. What Southern boy doesn't want that?"

He had come because she didn't want her parents traveling in the winter weather. He'd taken leave even though he had only a few months left before getting out of the Army entirely.

At least he had the chance to see the winter weather firsthand. She wanted to ask him to move here so they would be in the same time zone, but she didn't know how to. Instead, she just let him talk to her when he needed to and ask her opinion when he wanted it. Thankfully, he did so often and kept her in the decision-making process.

"Is the snow bad for you?" she asked.

He raised an eyebrow. "Like, could I exist with the snow?" He shrugged. "Sure. I mean, the love of a good woman can take me so many places."

She chuckled. Her voice sounded funny through the drug haze. "I do love you."

"Yes. And you're a good woman. Win-win for me." He reached over and brushed her hair off her cheek. She felt the touch through her whole body. "I'm going to call your mom and let her know you're awake and will live. Can I bring you anything?"

"No, I'm golden." She licked her lips and laid her head back. "I can't even feel my leg."

He pressed a kiss to her forehead. "Enjoy that while you can."

CHAPTER

TWENTY-NINE

PELHAM, ALABAMA
APRIL

Bill stared at the two metal steps that led up to the dented
and rusted trailer door. Nerves danced in his stomach. He
had no idea what waited for him on the other side of that
door, but he couldn't go forward with his future until he
dealt with this part of his past.

The grass had long quit trying to grow around the trailer.
A rusted-out 1972 Chevrolet Camaro sat on blocks exactly
where it had sat his entire life. A bush grew out of the back
window. Trash littered the yard. Fast-food wrappers, beer
cans, cigarette packets—just strewn wherever without regard
to anyone else.

Shoring up more courage than he'd needed that time he
went into a bunker in northern Iraq, he fisted his hand and
pounded on the door, then took a step back. He could hear

the thud of footsteps moving toward the door before it was flung open.

A shirtless man with a shaggy gray beard and a large belly hanging over dirty jeans glared at him with bloodshot eyes. "What do you want?"

The smell of stale cigarettes and rotting food wafted from the open door. Bill took another step back. "Charlotte around?"

The man glanced over his shoulder toward the kitchen. "Some dude's here for you."

He moved out of the doorway. A cockroach ran across the square of light on the floor cast by the open door. Beyond the light was the same furniture that had always been in that room. Then his mother filled the doorway and blocked his view.

She wore a red tank top, revealing her beefy arms, and denim shorts. Her bare feet were black with dirt. She had more gray than black in her hair now and had it pulled back in a greasy ponytail. A lit cigarette hung from her mouth.

"What do you want?" she demanded.

"I just wanted to see you." His stomach clenched and his jaw tightened. *I wanted to face you and tell you that you're a horrible human being.*

As she dragged on the cigarette, the tip glowed bright red. She ripped it out of her mouth and tossed it on the ground. "Is that it?"

"No." What else could he say? *I don't much like you, but I do forgive you for every terrible thing you ever did to me.* "I wanted to let you know that if you ever want to seek the forgiveness of God, then I'm happy to walk you through that process and introduce you to my Lord and Savior, Jesus Christ."

When she opened her mouth to cackle, he saw gaps from quite a few missing teeth. His nose twitched in disgust at his heritage. What had God saved him from by giving him his grandmother?

"You're just like her, ain't you?" she said. "I didn't need her God and I don't need yours."

He fisted his hands and slipped them into the pockets of his jeans. "That's all I wanted to tell you."

She spat in his direction. "Good riddance."

As soon as he drove clear of the trailer park, he pulled to the side of the road and leaned over a ditch, bile rising out of his stomach. He'd known better than to eat beforehand. He wiped his mouth, then leaned against the hood of his car and looked up at the sky, taking slow and deep breaths.

Only one more thing to do.

He got back in his car and took a long drink of water, then popped a mint into his mouth. It helped settle his stomach as he drove from Pelham to Birmingham. The Alabama sky shone bright blue.

It took him only half an hour. Fresh butterflies established themselves in his gut as he pulled into the neighborhood. Brick homes sat nestled behind giant live oaks that arched over the road, creating a canopy.

He turned into the drive and parked behind a black pickup truck. He turned the car off and bowed his head. "God, just, You know. Please."

After he got out of the car, he stood back from the brick steps. They led to a red door decorated with a wreath made from white lilies. His mouth went dry and his fingers felt cold. He had no idea what waited for him on the other side.

Finally, he walked up the steps and rang the bell. Lynda's

dad, Doctor Gary Culter, opened the door. He was tall and thin, with graying red hair and wire-framed glasses perched on his nose. "Bill, we weren't expecting you this early." He opened the door wider. "Come in."

Bill gestured toward the porch. "Could we talk out here for a moment?"

Doctor Culter looked behind him, then stepped out and shut the door. He led the way to the rocking chairs that flanked a table with a bright green fern. Bill perched on the edge of his chair.

Doctor Culter took his glasses off and stuck them in his shirt pocket. "How can I help you, son?"

Bill laced his fingers together and cleared his throat. "I am here to apologize for the way I treated Lynda in college and to ask you for your forgiveness."

Doctor Culter's cheeks reddened. He started rocking his chair. "I don't think I'm the one who needs to forgive you."

Shaking his head, Bill said, "You are, sir. You and Mrs. Culter. Lynda and I have had a lot of intense conversations over the last few months. I love her deep in my soul, and her forgiveness freed me up inside. But I hurt you by hurting your daughter, and I know that my future with Lynda could be in jeopardy if you didn't find it in your heart to forgive me."

The rocking chair stilled. "Do you know what motivated your words that day?"

Shame closed his throat. "Yes, sir. I was ashamed of where I came from. I thought she was too good for me, and I wanted to make sure she knew it."

Slowly the rocking resumed. "What have you learned in the meantime?"

Bill smiled. "That I am fearfully and wonderfully made.

I am not a product of my upbringing. Instead, I am a new creature in Christ."

Doctor Culter stared at him for several moments, then gave a brisk nod and held his hand out. "On behalf of my wife and myself, we accept your apology."

He gripped Bill's hand strong and sure. A weight Bill didn't realize he'd carried fell from his shoulders at the touch. Then he spoke the words that terrified him. "I plan to ask her to marry me."

After a brief, stern stare, Doctor Culter said, "You better. It's been over ten years coming." He gestured toward the door. "Lynda won't be here for a few hours, but you're welcome to come inside."

Relief made Bill's hands tingle. He shook his head and stood. "No, sir. I have other plans. But I look forward to sitting at your Easter table."

"We look forward to having you."

Lynda watched a duck bump against a turtle, sending it shooting down under the water to escape. It made her chuckle.

She closed her eyes and lifted her face to the sun. She'd left thirty-seven-degree weather and come home to seventy-eight degrees. Often, she had a hard time remembering the distinction in the weather when she shoveled snow from her driveway in October. It always became more apparent on this end of it.

The sound of feet on the gravel path made her turn. When she saw Bill, she leaped to her feet and ran up the path. He pulled her close.

His arms felt right and good around her. She breathed in the smell of him, soaked in the feel of him, and hugged him back as tightly as she could.

He pulled back enough to look at her face, to brush her hair off her cheek. "You shouldn't be running on that leg, Agent Clever."

He spoke the truth, but she wouldn't admit that to him. "I've had my cast off for two weeks."

"Mm-hmm." He slipped an arm over her shoulders, steering her back to the picnic table. On top was a sack lunch from a local café. He sat next to her on the bench, facing the water.

"I've missed you." She hugged his arm and leaned into his side.

"I've missed you too. It's good to see your face in real life." He put his arm behind her and drew her closer. "How was your trip?"

"Fine. Got in about an hour ago. How was yours?"

"I drove straight to Pelham."

When they'd talked about it this morning, he didn't know if he would go through with it. "How did that go?"

He shrugged. "'Bout as good as I anticipated. I did get to tell her Jesus loves her."

For a moment, she thought he had made a joke. He'd planned to confront his mother, forgive her, and walk away. Evangelizing her had never come up in any conversation. "What made you change your mind?"

He turned to look at her, his dark eyes serious and contemplative. "Because He does. And now I can die knowing I told her." He touched her cheek. "I saw your dad too."

She gasped, her eyes widening. "Where?"

338

"At his house. I had some air to clear with your parents. Some truths needed to be told."

"Heavy morning." She shifted to face him, straddling the bench. "You okay?"

"Darling, I have honestly never been better." He reached out and cupped her cheek. She leaned into his hand. "I'm on terminal leave with the military, I have a beautiful woman who claims to love me, and the burdens I carried for years have been shed. I'm lighter than I was two hours ago, and now I'm touching you and looking at you in person. This is the best I have ever been."

A tear slid out of her eye, and she leaned forward, pressing her lips against his.

Before the kiss deepened too much, he pulled back, breaking contact. "I would like to marry you."

Suddenly, she couldn't move. She could only stare at him. He slowly smiled. "I see you weren't expecting that."

Her heart started pounding, and the blood roared in her ears. She had to clear her throat twice to reply. "I, uh, no. Not this soon. I mean, yes, eventually."

Bill took her hands in his. "Yes. Eventually. I just want you to know that's my endgame. I've already talked to your dad about it."

She pulled her hands free and ran them across his shoulders and down his strong arms. When she reached his hands, she gripped them and leaned forward until their noses almost touched. "What's stopping you?"

"Well, you know, it's only been a few months."

With a smile, she shook her head. "Bill, it's been ten years. I think you need to quit dragging your feet."

The grin that spread across his face lit his eyes in a way

she'd never seen before. "Lynda Clever Culter, will you do me the absolute honor of becoming my wife?"

She pursed her lips. "I don't know. Can I see the ring first?"

He grabbed her and started tickling her ribs. Laughter bubbled out of her, and she fought to get free but had no power against him.

Finally, around a laugh, she said, "Yes, yes! Of course I'll marry you."

His hands stilled and he pulled her close, wrapping her against him. She stared up at him and cupped his cheek in her hand as his eyes darkened. He lowered his head to kiss her, sealing the deal.

Discussion Questions

Bill prayed for God's direction in his life, and immediately after, his motorcycle broke down in front of the Army recruiting station.

1. Do you think that God directs our lives in such specific ways? Why or why not?
2. Can you think of a time when God was so blatant in His direction of your life?

As part of their undercover assignment, Bill and Lynda have to attend regular prayer times in a mosque. They also must say a ritual blessing at meals to Allah.

3. Do you think they are somehow dishonoring God during this assignment? Why or why not?
4. Do you think they're being disrespectful to the Muslim believers attending the mosque? Explain.
5. Lynda asks Sergeant Ibrahim, who is Muslim, how he feels about them going undercover as Muslims.

Ibrahim uses an analogy of people going undercover to stop terrorists hiding in plain sight in a Christian church. Do you think that's a fair analogy? Why or why not?

Bill treated Lynda in a horrible manner in order to protect himself from the shame he felt about his home.

6. Do you think his motivation was justified? Why or why not?
7. In Romans 8:28, God promises that all things work together for good for those who love Him and are called according to His purposes. Do you think the ten-year separation of Bill and Lynda could have been in God's plan to set them up for this mission? In what way?

In the tactical debriefing of the terrorists, Emma makes the suspects understand that public beheading would likely be the punishment for their crimes in Saudi Arabia.

8. Do you think this method of debriefing is ethical? Why or why not?
9. Knowing the way things work in Saudi Arabia, do you think that releasing the Nasser brothers to the Kuwaiti authorities was the humane decision? Explain.

Lynda claims she has forgiven Bill for the things he said to her that hurt her so deeply, but she admits that she doesn't know if she can trust him or not.

10. Do you think that what Bill did is forgivable, or do you think Lynda would be justified in holding on to the pain in order to protect herself from him in the future?

11. Considering Bill's obvious deep and abiding faith and the way Lynda admires his dedication to his team, do you think her uncertainty is justified? Why or why not?

12. When we accept Christ as our personal Lord and Savior, our sins are forgiven, wiped away as if they never existed. The Bible tells us to forgive others as Christ has forgiven us. Do you think Lynda's hesitation in trusting a brother in Christ diminishes her forgiveness of him in any way, or do you think that her experience with him justifies her hesitation?

Recipes

Falafel

1 cup	dried chickpeas (not canned)
1	shallot (or ½ sweet onion), diced
3 cloves	garlic, diced
1 cup	fresh parsley
½ cup	fresh mint leaves
½ cup	fresh cilantro
1 tsp	salt (kosher or sea salt is best)
1 tsp	ground cumin
½ tsp	ground coriander
½ tsp	ground cardamom
⅛ tsp	cayenne pepper
¼ tsp	ground black pepper
	vegetable oil, for frying

Cover the chickpeas with about 3 inches of water and soak overnight. Rinse and pat dry.

Place all ingredients except the oil into a food processor. Pulse the mixture until it's well minced and mixed. You're not looking for a puree.

Cover and refrigerate for about 30 minutes. You can make the falafel ahead of time and refrigerate for up to 3 days.

Fill a pan with at least an inch of oil. Heat to 375°.

Scoop out 1½ tbsp of the mixture and shape into a ball, then flatten into a thick disk. Gently slip into the hot oil and cook until the bottom and sides are brown, about 3–4 minutes. Turn and cook another 2–3 minutes until the other side is brown.

Remove from oil and drain on a paper towel–lined plate.

——— Perfect Pocket Pita Bread ———

1 packet	active dry yeast (or 2¼ tsp)
1 tbsp	honey
1 cup	room-temperature water
3 cups	flour (I use fresh-ground hard wheat)
1½ tsp	salt
2 tbsp	olive oil

Mix yeast with honey and water. Let stand 5 minutes.

Sift together flour and salt. Add to yeast mixture. Add olive oil. Stir with a wooden spoon until it forms a ball. Place on lightly floured surface and knead for 10 minutes. (If you are using a stand mixer, use a bread hook and mix for 3 minutes on speed 2.)

Place dough in greased glass bowl and turn it so that both sides are greased. Cover with a towel and let it rise in a warm spot free from drafts until doubled in size (about 60 minutes).

Punch dough down and divide into 8 pieces. Roll each piece into a ball. Cover with a towel and let rest for 20 minutes.

While the dough is resting, preheat oven to 400°. Put either a baking stone or an upside-down cookie sheet on the middle rack of the oven while it's preheating.

On a lightly floured surface, roll each ball of dough out to ¼-inch thickness.

Open the oven and place as many pitas as will fit on your baking surface. Bake 4–5 minutes. They will puff up and turn crispy and brown.

Tabouleh

2 cups	fresh curly parsley, finely chopped
1 tbsp	fresh mint leaves, finely chopped
¼ cup	fresh lemon juice (1 lemon)
2	Roma tomatoes, finely diced
¼ cup	red onion, finely diced
¼ cup	extra virgin olive oil
1 tsp	kosher salt
1 cup	quinoa
1½ cup	boiling water

In a small bowl, mix the parsley and mint with the lemon juice, tomatoes, onion, olive oil, and salt. Cover and refrigerate for at least 2 hours.

Cover the quinoa with boiling water. Let stand at room temperature for 45 minutes. Drain and refrigerate until cold. Combine with the herb mixture.

Tzatziki Sauce

1 cup	plain yogurt
⅓ cup	grated English cucumber (keep the seed and peel)
½ tsp	salt (kosher or sea salt is best)
½ tsp	dried dill
¼ tsp	garlic powder
¼ tsp	ground black pepper

Mix all ingredients. Cover and refrigerate about 30 minutes.

The **LOVE & HONOR**
series comes to
a stunning conclusion
in *Honor's Refuge* . . .

Turn the page for a **sneak peek**
of this exhilarating finale.

Prologue

Missy huddled with three-year-old Lola between the night-stand and the bed, praying her little sister would stay asleep. Her father's fist hit her mother's face with a sickening thud, and Missy's stomach rolled. She really shouldn't have let the macaroni and cheese burn. This was all her fault.

Her mom landed on the floor, clutching her big round belly with the new baby. Her father yelled and kicked her with his boots. Her mom reached forward, and for a moment, Missy was terrified that she was grabbing for her. Instead, she grasped the cord of the telephone. It landed next to Missy as her father stomped on her mom's arm.

She stared at the phone. Nine-one-one. She'd learned that on *Sesame Street* yesterday. In case of a fire, call nine-one-one. Even though this wasn't a fire, maybe a fireman would help her mom. She reached out, pressing the buttons very carefully.

"Nine-one-one, what's your emergency?" a woman said.

Missy trembled, afraid her father would hear her speak, so she said nothing. Pulling Lola closer, she kissed her curly black hair. Her sister started to struggle against her, and Missy worried she would start crying. Just as Lola broke free, her father stormed away and slammed the bedroom door.

Eyes closed, Missy waited for him to come back. Her mom gave a long cry, and Missy cracked open one eye to make sure the door was still shut. She shifted out from her hiding place. Her mom lay with her arms around her stomach, panting. Lola walked over to her and knelt down, patting her on the head. Her mom let out another long moan.

With a loud bang, the door slammed open. Missy's whole body froze in fear. Her hands tingled and her breath wouldn't move past her chest. Her father filled the doorway. He looked at Missy, then at Lola, and walked toward the bed. Missy ducked out of the way, grabbed Lola's hand, and ran to the door.

Her father picked the phone up and stared at it. "What did you do?" he shouted at her mom. He bent and grabbed her by her hair, putting his face close to hers. "What did you do?"

Her breath ended on a hiccup, and she panted, "You better run. They're coming, and they'll find it all."

Missy clung to Lola's hand and crouched in the hall, trying to decide what to do, while her father hung up the phone and then dialed a number. He turned his back on them and spoke in Spanish. "Cops are coming." After a pause he said, "Whatever you think is best." He looked over his shoulder at Missy and narrowed his eyes at her. "Yes, sir."

Missy's heart leapt into her throat. She kept a firm grip on Lola's hand and ran down the hall and through the living room. In the kitchen, she could still smell the burned macaroni and cheese.

"Come on, Lola," she whispered, pushing open the dog door.

Lola hesitated, giant tears sliding down her face. "Mommy said no," she said, pushing her hand against the door.

"You have to go!" Missy looked over her shoulder. Her father must still be on the phone. Thinking that Lola would follow her if she went first, she pushed her hands and head through the small door. Little pebbles on the patio dug into her palms, and the front of her leg scraped against the metal frame, but she didn't cry.

Outside, she lifted the flap and motioned for Lola to follow her. Her sister's lip trembled, but she crawled through.

On the back porch, Missy looked around. Where to hide? He'd look in the fort by the swing set. She took Lola's hand and ran around to the front of the house, to the big bush by the mailbox. If they sat on the curb, he probably couldn't see them. The bush would hide them.

Lola covered her ears with her hands and closed her eyes. "Mommy," she said.

Missy put her arm around her. Her leg stung where she'd hit the dog door. She poked at the bloody scrape as tears fell down her face. "Be quiet, Lola. Let's wait for the firemen."

Instead of a fire truck, though, a police car came. Missy didn't know what she'd done to make the police come instead of the firemen, but she was so happy to see two officers get out of the car that she couldn't even speak.

The woman spotted them and knelt next to them by the mailbox. She had nice eyes and smelled like peppermint. "It's not safe out here by the road," she said, putting a hand on Lola's head. "Where are your parents?"

"Mommy," Lola cried, then looked over her shoulder toward the house.

Missy's lower lip trembled. "Mommy's hurt."

"Is your dad here?" the policewoman asked.

"Daddy's bad," Lola said. She covered her ears again.

As the policewoman stood up, she talked into the radio on her shoulder, using words and numbers that Missy didn't understand.

"It's okay, Lola," Missy said as the officers walked toward the house. "We'll be okay now."

CHAPTER

★

ONE

OCTOBER 20

When Melissa Braxton eyed Phil Osbourne's black truck turning into the parking lot, she snatched up her book and opened it. She settled back into the booth to give a false appearance of relaxation. She didn't want him to think she'd sat here just anticipating his arrival, watching every car that drove by. He didn't need or want that kind of attention.

She didn't put the book down until she felt him slide into the booth across from her. She intentionally looked startled at his arrival. "Oh, hi," she said with a grin. "Glad you made it."

Phil had dark blond hair, gray-green eyes set on a square face, and a mouth that didn't smile often enough. Normally, he wore his EMT uniform to their Thursday morning breakfasts, but today he had on a light-blue T-shirt that stretched across his broad chest and emphasized his healthy tan.

"You ever going to finish that book?" he asked as he settled into the booth.

She found the gumption to blink in innocence. "I beg your pardon?"

"You've been reading that same book for a couple of weeks now."

She should have given his observation skills a little more credit. She kept the book in her car just for the "reading, not waiting" ruse. She shrugged, then said, "I only read it here."

The diner owner, Delilah Pérez, arrived with a pot of coffee. She was Phil's mom's best friend, and Phil had grown up around her. She usually waited on them instead of one of the waitresses.

"Morning, Phil," she said as she set a container of cinnamon next to his coffee cup.

He smiled up at her. "Delilah. Good to see you."

"Regular?"

"Yes, ma'am."

Delilah looked at Melissa. "What about you, hon? What's this morning's story?"

The Cuban diner had all the flavors she remembered from her grandparents' kitchen. "Hmm, how about plantain and corned beef hash?" she asked.

"You want spice?"

"Oh, yes, ma'am." Melissa pulled her braid over her shoulder and toyed with the end of it while she redirected her attention to Phil. "I don't see how you can eat oatmeal day after day. This place could bring so much flavor to your life."

"I like flavor. Just not at eight in the morning." He rested his forearms on the table, linking his fingers. "How are you?"

How was she? She didn't think "desperately in love with you and wishing you'd notice me" was the answer he sought. So she went to where he would follow. "Rough night. A woman with three kids called at two. The police took her husband, but she was afraid he'd come back before morning, so she wanted to get out of there as fast as possible."

Melissa operated a domestic abuse shelter. Everyone kept the location mostly a secret. She and her partner had spread the contact information to doctors' offices, hospitals, therapists, schools, and emergency services. She gave the victims a safe home, provided family and individual counseling, and helped them start new lives—usually away from Miami. Phil provided medical care whenever she couldn't convince someone to go to the hospital.

"How old?" He sprinkled some cinnamon into his coffee.

"Four, five, and seven."

He shook his head as he stirred the rich brew. "Poor kids."

"I know. They're shell-shocked right now."

He held up the cinnamon as if asking if she wanted some, but she shook her head.

"I didn't get a lot of time to speak with her," she said. "I have a meeting with her during lunch to start the initial counseling."

As Phil took a sip of his coffee, she studied his face. Normally at breakfast, he had a hint of a beard and tired eyes from working the night shift. This morning, he looked rested and groomed, and she could smell the hint of his aftershave. "Big plans today?"

He put his cup down and smiled. "Actually, I have a couple of friends coming to town."

"Friends?" She knew his parents and brother from church,

but she had never met any of his friends from the Army. "Where are they coming from?"

"Alaska and Virginia."

"From the service?"

He nodded.

"That will be nice. You going to play tour guide?"

Another smile. Wow, two in one morning! "Nah. Drumstick is helping me with a project. Pot Pie is his business partner."

With raised eyebrows, Melissa repeated, "Drumstick and Pot Pie?"

"That's what we call them. Those were their nicknames on our team."

He sounded animated, almost happy. She loved that his friends generated this kind of energy in him. "Let me guess, your nickname was Ozzy Osbourne."

"No. Close, though." He took another sip of coffee. "Doc Oz."

"Right! Of course. Because you're a doctor."

"I was the medic. When they first named me, they didn't know I was actually a doctor. Eventually they did, but I thought Doc Oz fit perfectly. Though, in tight situations, Ozzy took less energy to say, and they often just reverted to that."

She stared at him in awe. Those had to be the most words he'd strung together on one side of a conversation in all the time she'd known him. Before she could reply, Delilah arrived with the food. Melissa smiled as the owner slid her hash onto the table. The spicy smell of the peppers wafted up with the steam. Phil glanced at his oatmeal and thanked Delilah, then looked at Melissa. She bowed her head and listened to his voice soften as he spoke to God.

"Father, we thank You for the way You constantly bless us. Thank You for this meal, and we ask that You bless it to the nourishment of our bodies and bless our bodies to Your service. Amen."

Delilah set a hot sauce bottle on the table before Melissa could ask for it, then winked at her as she walked away. Melissa doused her hash liberally while Phil sprinkled sliced almonds and raisins over his oatmeal.

"So, I'm going to guess Pot Pie's name is probably Swanson," she said, "hearing how it works."

He looked surprised. "Well done."

"I'm stuck on Drumstick, though. Let me think about it some more."

"I have no doubt you'll be able to deduce it."

They ate in silence for several minutes before she asked, "How long are they here for?"

He shrugged one shoulder. "Until they're done."

"What's this project?"

He paused, looking at her for several heartbeats. "Something for a friend."

"Another elusive friend? Well, you're just building a village, aren't you?"

He ignored her like she knew he would. Disappointment tried to cloud her contentment at spending the morning with him. She wanted more. More than that, she wanted him to want more. She'd made the initial step in asking him to breakfast the first time. He'd suggested lunch the next Sunday. That was where it all began and exactly where it all ended.

She'd made up her mind today to just ask him about it. Did he want to see her beyond this? Was he attracted to her? Should she give up?

Not when he had friends coming to town today, though. Seeing how animated he'd become filled her heart. She didn't want to risk infringing on that.

She took a sip of her coffee and washed down a bite of plantain. "My abuelita used to make this," she said to fill the silence. "My uncle has always corned his own beef for his deli, and whenever he had some left over, she'd make big batches of hash. She said potatoes made her sneeze, so she made it the way her mom made it in Cuba, with plantains."

"Oh, right. Your family owns that deli. I still haven't been there. Work seems to keep me on this side of Miami."

"Yep. My great-grandfather opened that deli in the late sixties. It's been handed down from son to son since."

He chewed on a raisin. "What will happen if there's not a son?"

"You take that back," she said with a laugh.

"Did you ever work in the deli?"

Images of customers lined up out the door and meat slicers and giant vats of pickles ran across her mind. "Yes."

"I'd like to see that."

She couldn't stop the little tug on her lips in response to his interest. "I worked there all through high school and college." Her smile faded as memories from her childhood filtered through her mind and her thoughts turned to her sister. Would she ever find her? "So, friends in town today. Will I see you Sunday?"

He ripped a piece of toast in half and spread orange marmalade on it. "I will see you Sunday." He reclined against the bench while he ate. "I may have friends with me, but I'll be there, regardless."

"Good. I'm speaking." She finished the last of her hash

and took a final sip of her coffee. "I have to run. I have a mom who needs a ride to the bus station at ten."

As she slid out of the booth, he reached out and touched her forearm. She immediately stilled. "I'm sorry I was late. It's good to see you."

Unsure of what brought on the intenseness emanating from him, she stared into his eyes for probably a second too long. Finally, she said, "Drumstick is Sanders, right? For Kentucky Fried Chicken?"

A slow grin covered his face. It made her heart flutter. "Impressive," he said.

Heat filled her face, but she couldn't help smiling as she left the diner.

With Melissa gone, the room felt so much emptier. Phil stirred his oatmeal, then dropped his spoon and let it clatter against the bowl. He kicked himself for being late. He'd gone to a Narcotics Anonymous meeting first thing, then hit traffic getting to the diner.

He looked forward to every single moment he could snatch with Melissa. The first time she'd smiled at him, her brown eyes shone with a light that had stripped his ability to speak. When she'd asked him out to breakfast, he couldn't believe she could possibly have an interest in him. The next Sunday he found her in church, where she wore a yellow sundress that glowed against her dark tan skin. Her black hair fell in thick curls down her back, and she smelled like summer peaches. Somehow, the invitation to lunch rolled off his tongue before he could talk himself out of it. And now, for over a year, he'd tortured himself by snatching a couple of meals a week with her. Every time he asked her how she was, he tensed up, waiting to hear that she'd met some really great guy and was desperately happy and couldn't meet him for breakfast or lunch anymore.

Even though she deserved to meet some really great guy who made her desperately happy.

He tossed his napkin over his bowl and pulled his wallet out of his shorts pocket. He'd worn shorts this morning, displaying the prosthetic leg he always kept hidden, but she'd had her nose buried in a book when he got there. It wasn't like she didn't know about his injury, but he wanted to see her reaction anyway because she'd never actually seen it.

Why? Why continue to put himself through this?

Because you're in love, you idiot.

He just needed to stop. If Melissa deserved anything, it was a whole man. Not someone who'd gotten addicted to narcotics in medical school, walked out on a career because he couldn't stand to have all sorts of access to drugs in his office, and joined the Army to run away from everything Miami could offer him. And that was just the beginning of the end of him.

Delilah slid into the booth across from him. "Why do you put yourself through this?"

He stared into the rich brown eyes of his mother's best friend, who had eerily echoed his own thoughts. "She needs someone who is whole."

"You're a whole lotta something, but it ain't smarts." She tapped the table. "She pines for you. I watch her. As soon as she sees you coming, she snatches up her book and pretends to be reading, but she'll watch for you the whole time."

Something inside of him started to bloom with hope, but

he quickly doused it. "No. Look, Dee, I love you, but you need to stay out of this. I'm in as deep as I'm able. End of story." He took a twenty-dollar bill out of his wallet and set it on the table. He had quit trying to make her give him a check for breakfast and just figured what it should be every week.

She ignored the money and pointed at him. "If it's the end of that story, then it's time to start a new page. Brand-new." She slid out of the booth and stood over him. "Just to warn you, there's a mom with three kids behind you."

He let out a deep sigh and steeled himself for the stares. Adults pretended not to see, but children didn't know how to be subtle. As he slid out of the booth, the metal on his prosthetic leg caught the red lights shining behind the counter. Finding his balance and getting to his feet, he turned and made eye contact with the kid in the booth behind him.

The little boy's eyes widened, and he whispered, "Mom!" more loudly than some people shout.

Knowing the attention his leg—well, his lack of leg—received, he kept his head up and his eyes forward as the kids in that booth whisper-screamed among themselves. Relieved to get to the door, he pushed it open and stepped out into the heat of the late October morning.

The farther he walked away from the diner, the lighter he felt. Aunt Dee needed to mind her own business.

His phone chirped. He scanned the incoming call. "Well, if it ain't Drumstick Sanders. How are you, my brother?"

"Finer than a frog hair split three ways," Bill Sanders said. His Alabama twang made Phil grin. "We're on the tarmac headed for the terminal."

Phil glanced at his watch. They'd arrived much earlier than expected.

As if reading his mind, Bill said, "My flight from Alaska changed, so we were able to push up travel all the way across the board."

"With the traffic, I'm about twenty minutes away."

"Ain't no thing. I'm sure by the time we get to the gate and then get to baggage claim, we'll be twenty minutes."

"Sounds good."

Even though he'd never admit it out loud, he was a little nervous about Bill and Daniel coming. In the almost two years since he'd gotten medically released from the Army, he'd had plenty of phone conversations, group messages, video conferences, and the like with the men he'd served with in the military. He'd seen them at an awards ceremony in Washington, DC, but he'd not been in a good mental state. Since then, he'd attended two weddings. However, both times he'd made his travel arrangements super tight so that he'd have an excuse to leave as soon as possible, limiting his exposure.

He'd needed to distance himself from the warriors in his life. Being with them did nothing but remind him of everything he'd lost the day that a bullet from a Chukuwereije soldier in the jungles of Katangela, Africa, had pierced the femoral artery in his left leg.

Still, while he battled nerves, he also felt very anticipatory. These were his brothers-in-arms, closer to him than his actual brother only because they'd served together in a Special Forces A-Team for five years. The things they'd seen, the things they'd done, the way they'd watched each other's backs for years, had burned into his heart and soul in a way that made them family in his mind, despite the close core family he himself had.

As if on cue, his phone rang, and his brother's name appeared across the screen. "Yo, Winston," he said as he unlocked his truck.

"Hey. I have those tickets you wanted." His older brother was an attorney in the state attorney's office. He could always get his hands on Dolphins tickets.

"That's great, man. Thanks."

"I forwarded you the email confirmation."

"You're planning on going to the game with us still, right?"

"I wanted to, but I have a last-minute conflict. I do want to meet your friends. I'll be by in the morning with the keys to my boat if you still want to borrow it."

"I do."

Winston's voice was muffled, then he said, "I have another call. Love you."

"Love you too." Before Phil pulled into traffic, he put a reminder on his phone for next Friday to have dinner with Winston. That would give him a week to take care of the business with Daniel and Bill.

As he pulled up to the loading zone at the airport, Daniel came out the door. The tall Black man carried an air of authority around him that made him stand out in a crowd. Right behind him was Bill. He had a closely trimmed dark beard and a red baseball cap covering his black hair. The last time Phil had seen him, he'd had a dark tan, but clearly, the Alaskan autumn had faded that away.

Phil pulled up right next to them and rolled his window down. "Looking for a ride, soldier?"

Daniel rested his forearm against the truck's frame and leaned into the open window. "Ozzy, my man. Good to see you."

Bill tossed their suitcases into the back. Daniel opened the cab door. "I'm calling shotgun so I don't have to fold myself up to get into the back seat."

"Fair enough," Bill said in a drawl. "No judgment." As he slid into the back seat, he leaned forward and slapped Phil on the shoulder. "Good to see you."

"Thanks for coming."

As Phil pulled out into the airport traffic, contentment he hadn't felt in a long time settled into his soul. He needed these men in his life. He needed to know people who had been there and done that, people who understood without requiring an explanation.

He glanced over at Daniel. "How's civilian life?"

His friend grinned as he pointed to the back seat. "Well, other than starting a company with that jackal, it's perfect. Food's good, mornings are relaxed." He paused. "How are you?"

Phil smiled as he merged onto the interstate. "Better now, man. Better now."

Hallee Bridgeman is the *USA Today* bestselling author of several action-packed romantic suspense books and series. An Army brat turned Floridian, Hallee and her husband finally settled in central Kentucky, where they have raised their three children. When she's not writing, Hallee pursues her passion for cooking, coffee, campy action movies, and regular date nights with her husband. An accomplished speaker and active member of several writing organizations, Hallee can be found online at www.halleebridgeman.com.

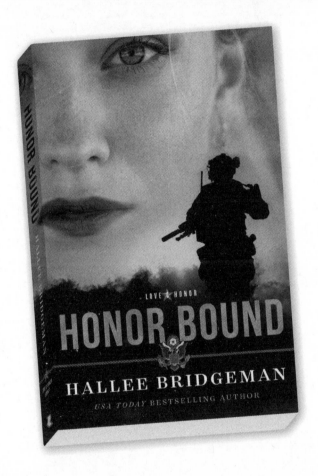